THE THIRD OMNI BOOK
OF SCIENCE FICTION

Here are nineteen amazing works of finely crafted science fiction. For an imaginative grasp of man's future — and the kinds of men and women who will live in the future — experience some of the most highly acclaimed science fiction writers of our time, including Philip K. Dick, Frederik Pohl, Fred Saberhagen, Roger Zelazny, and many others. They'll take you to new dimensions of time and space as they describe both the beauty and terror of all our tomorrows. . . .

THE THIRD OMNI BOOK OF SCIENCE FICTION

**EDITED BY
ELLEN DATLOW**

**ZEBRA BOOKS
KENSINGTON PUBLISHING CORP.**

ZEBRA BOOKS

are published by

Kensington Publishing Corp.
475 Park Avenue South
New York, NY 10016

Omni is a registered trademark of Omni Publications International, Ltd.

First printing: April 1985

Printed in the United States of America

THE THIRD
OMNI
BOOK OF
SCIENCE FICTION

CONTENTS

Introduction

OMNI Magazine is now being published in English, Japanese, German, and Italian, which means its fiction is probably being read by more people around the world than any other science fiction magazine's. That's very gratifying to an editor.

Something that thrills an editor even more is "discovering" new talent -- bringing a bright, original writer to the attention of the general public. OMNI published Gregg Keizer's "I Am the Burning Bush" in 1982. Since then he has sold stories to other science fiction magazines, to anthologies, and again, to OMNI. Keizer, who lives in North Carolina and works for a computer magazine, is very much on his way in the sf field.

As for some of the other contributors:

Marc Laidlaw is a sweet-faced punk kid from California who has been writing and publishing on his own and in collaboration for several years. "A Hiss of Dragon" is the result of a particularly fruitful partnership with physicist/

sf writer Gregory Benford. Benford won the 1980 Nebula for his novel *Timescape*. Another collaboration that worked exceptionally well is Gardner Dozois's and Jack C. Haldeman II's sombre post-holocaust story about guilt and forgiveness, "Executive Clemency." David Drake's "Men Like Us" takes the same post-holocaust theme but creates a fast-moving adventure.

Philip K. Dick's last books were imbued with his religious concerns. One of his last published stories, "Rautaavara's Case," also reflects that absorption.

Edward Bryant's "Prairie Sun" is the first OMNI story to appear on television. It was produced by Walt Disney Productions for airing in 1983 on the Disney Channel of Cable TV.

Dan Simmons's novelette, "Carrion Comfort" is a fast-moving adventure horror story about a trio of elderly telepaths who use their abilities to commit murder and other atrocities. Simmons has been publishing stories for only two years but his talent and his peers' recognition of that talent has been gathering momentum.

Two contributors have been prominent editors as well as writers: Alfred Bester and Frederik Pohl. Bester was an editor for *Holiday* for many years, until the magazine ceased publication in the 1970s. Pohl has been editor of many science fiction magazines, including *Galaxy* and *If*. He was also an editor at Bantam Books and he still anthologizes from time to time. Because Bester has never been a prolific writer, OMNI is privileged to have published his marvelous satire "Galatea Galante." Pohl meanwhile is known for his sharp wit. "Farmer on the Dole," included in 1982's two *Best of the Year* anthologies, demonstrates this talent amply.

Other stories in this book are Roger Zelazny's tale of automated cars on the loose, a chilling Christmas tale by Gene Wolfe, Thomas M. Disch's gourmet's delight, Fred Saberhagen's time-travel romp and a serious reflection on the human condition by Stephen Robinett.

Finally, Jayge Carr, an OMNI regular, has provided an original story for the OMNI SCIENCE FICTION ANTHOLOGY — volume III. "Webrider" is part of a series she is writing about a far future when humans may no longer be recognizable as such, but have a common heritage. This is its first publication.

Ellen Datlow
Fiction Editor

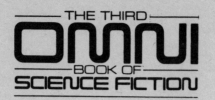

THE THIRD
OMNI
BOOK OF
SCIENCE FICTION

GALATEA GALANTE

by Alfred Bester

He was wearing a prefaded jump suit, beautifully tailored, the *dernier cri* in the nostalgic 2100s, but really too youthful for his thirty-odd years. Set square on his head was a vintage (circa 1950) English motoring cap with the peak leveled on a line with his brows, masking the light of lunacy in his eyes.

Dead on a slab, he might be called distinguished, even handsome, but alive and active? That would depend on how much demented dedication one could stomach. He was shouldering his way through the crowded aisles of

THE SATURN CIRCUS
50 PHANTASTIK PHREAKS 50
!!!ALL ALIENS!!!

He was carrying a mini sound-camera that looked like a chrome-and-ebony pepper mill, and he was filming the living, crawling, spasming, gibbering monstrosities exhibited in the large showcases and small vitrines, with a murmured

15

running commentary. His voice was pleasant; his remarks were not.

"Ah, yes, the *Bellatrix basilisk*, so the sign assures us. Black-and-yellow bod of a serpent. Looks like a Gila-monster head attached. Work of that Tejas tailor who's so nitzy with surgical needle and thread. Peacock coronet on head. Good theater to blindfold its eyes. Conveys the conviction that its glance will kill. Hmmm. Ought to gag the mouth, too. According to myth the basilisk's breath also kills. . . .

"And the *Hyades hydra*. Like wow. Nine heads, as per revered tradition. Looks like a converted iguana. The Mexican again. That seamstress has access to every damn snake and lizard in Central America. She's done a nice join of necks to trunk—got to admit that—but her stitching shows to *my* eye. . . .

"*Canopus cerberus*. Three dog heads. Look like oversized Chihuahuas. Mastiff bod. Rattlesnake tail. Ring of rattlers around the waist. Authentic but clumsy. That Tejas woman ought to know you can't graft snake scales onto hound hide. They look like crud; but at least all three heads are barking.
. . .

"Well, well, well, here's the maladroit who claims he's my rival; the Berlin butcher with his zoo castoffs. His latest spectacular, the *Rigel griffin*. Ta-daaa! Do him justice, it's classic. Eagle head and wings, but it's molting. Lion bod implanted with feathers. And he's used ostrich claws for the feet. *I* would have generated authentic dragon's feet. . . .

"Now *Martian monoceros*; horse bod, elephant legs, stag's tail. Yes, convincing, but why isn't it howling as it should, according to legend? *Mizar manticora*. Kosher. Kosher. Three rows of teeth. Look like implanted shark's. Lion bod. Scorpion tail. Wonder how they produced that red-eyed effect. The *Ares assida*. Dull. Dull. Dullsville. Just an ostrich with camel feet, and stumbling all over them, too.

No creative imagination!

"Ah, but I call that poster over the *Sirius sphinx* brilliant theater. My compliments to the management. It's got to be recorded for posterity: THE PUBLIC IS RESPECTFULLY RE-QUESTED NOT TO GIVE THE CORRECT ANSWER TO THE ENIGMA POSED BY THE SPHINX.

"Because if you do give the correct answer, as Oedipus found out, she'll destroy herself out of chagrin. A sore loser. I ought to answer the riddle, just to see how they stage it, but no. Theater isn't my shtick; my business is strictly creative genesis. . . .

"The Berlin butcher again, *Castor chimera*. Lion head. Goat's bod. Looks like an anaconda tail. How the hell did he surgify to get it to vomit those flames? Some sort of catalytic gimmick in the throat, I suppose. It's only a cold corposant fire, quite harmless but very dramatic — and those fire extinguishers around the showcase are a lovely touch. Damn good theater. Again, my compliments to the management. . . .

"Aha! Beefcake on the hoof. *Zosma centaur*. Good-looking Greek joined to that Shetland pony. Blood must have been a problem. They probably drained both and substituted a neutral surrogate. The Greek looks happy enough; in fact, damn smug. Anyone wondering why has only to see how the pony's hung. . . .

"What have we here? *Antares unicorn*, complete with grafted narwhal tusk but not with the virgin who captured it, virgin girls being the only types that can subdue unicorns, legend saith. I thought narwhals were extinct. They may have bought the tusk from a walking-stick maker. I know virgins are not extinct. *I* make 'em every month; purity guaranteed or your money back. . . .

"And a *Spica siren*. Lovely girl. Beautiful. She — But damn my eyes, she's no manufactured freak! That's Sandra,

17

my Siren! I can recognize my genesis anywhere. What the hell is Sandy doing in this damn disgusting circus? Naked in a showcase! This is an outrage!"

He charged the showcase in his rage. He was given to flashes of fury that punctuated his habitual exasperated calm. (His deep conviction was that it was a damned intransigent world because it wasn't run *his* way, which was the *right* way.)

He beat and clawed at the supple walls, which gave but did not break. He cast around wildly for anything destructive, then darted to the *chimera* exhibit, grabbed a fire extinguisher, and dashed back to the Siren. Three demoniac blows cracked the plastic, and three more shattered an escape hatch. His fury outdrew the freaks, and a fascinated crowd gathered.

He reached in and seized the smiling Siren. "Sandy, get the hell out. What were you doing there in the first place?"

" ؛ "

"Where's your husband?"

" ↓ "

"For God's sake!" He pulled off his cap, revealing pale streaky hair. "Here, cover yourself with this. No, no, girl downstairs. Use an arm for upstairs, and hide your rear elevation against my back."

" ↟ "

"No, I am *not* prudish. I simply will not have my beautiful creation on public display. D'you think I—" He turned fiercely on three security guards closing in on him and brandished the heavy brass cylinder. "One more step, and I let you have it with this. In the eyes. Ever had frozen eyeballs?"

They halted. "Now look, mister, you got no—"

"I am *not* called 'mister.' My degree is Dominie, which means master professor. I am addressed as Dominie, Dominie Manwright, and I want to see the owner at once. Immeliately. Here and now. *Sofort! Immediatamente!* Mr. Saturn or Mr. Phreak or whatever!

"Tell him that Dominie Regis Manwright wants him here now. He'll know my name, or he'd better, by God! Now be off with you. Split. Cut." Manwright glared around at the enthralled spectators. "You turkeys get lost, too. All of you. Go eyeball the other sights. The Siren show is *kaput*."

As the crowd shuffled back from Manwright's fury, an amused gentleman in highly unlikely twentieth-century evening dress stepped forward. "I see you understand Siren, sir. Most impressive." He slung the opera cape off his shoulders and offered it to Sandra. "You must be cold, madame. May I?"

"Thank you," Manwright growled. "Put it on, Sandy. Cover yourself. And thank the man."

" ↓ "

"I don't give a damn whether you're cold or not. Cover yourself. I won't have you parading that beautiful body I created. And give me back my cap."

" ♪ "

"Women!" Manwright grumbled. "This is the last time I ever generate one. You slave over them. You use all your expertise to create beauty and implant sense and sensibility, and they all turn out the same. Irrational! Women! A race apart! And where the hell's 50 Phantastik Phreaks 50?"

"At your service, Dominie," the gentleman smiled.

"What? You? The management?"

"Indeed yes."

"In that ridiculous white tie and tails?"

"So sorry, Dominie. The costume is traditional for the role. And by day I'm required to wear hunting dress. It *is* grotesque, but the public expects it of the ringmaster."

"Hmph! What's your name? I'd like to know the name of the man I skin alive."

19

"Corque?"

"Cork? As in Ireland?"

"But with a Q U E."

"Corque?" Cor-kew-ee?" Manwright's eyes kindled. "Would you by any chance be related to Charles Russell Corque, Syrtus professor of ETM biology? I'll hold that in your favor."

"Thank you, Dominie. I *am* Charles Russell Corque, professor of extraterrestrial and mutation biology at Syrtus University."

"What!"

"Yes."

"In that preposterous costume?"

"Alas, yes."

"Here? On Terra?"

"In person."

"What a crazy coincidence. D'you know, I was going to make that damned tedious trip to Mars just to rap with you."

"And I brought my circus to Terra hoping to meet and consult with you."

"How long have you been here?"

"Two days."

"Then why haven't you called?"

"Setting up a circus show takes time, Dominie. I haven't had a moment to spare."

"This monstrous fakery is really yours?"

"It is."

"You? The celebrated Corque? The greatest researcher into alien life forms that science has ever known? Revered by all your colleagues, including myself, and swindling the turkeys with a phony freak show? Incredible. Corque! Unbelievable!"

"But understandable, Manwright. Have you any idea of

20

ie cost of ETM research? And the reluctance of the grants
ommittees to allocate an adequate amount of funds? No, I
uppose not. You're in private practice and can charge gigan-
ic fees to support your research, but I'm forced to moon-
ght and operate this circus to raise the money I need."

"Nonsense, Corque. You could have patented one of your
rilliant discoveries — that fantastic Jupiter III methophyte,
or instance. Gourmets call it 'The Ganymede Truffle.'
)'you know what an ounce sells for?"

"I know, and there *are* discovery rights and royalties.
[normous. But you don't know university contracts, my
ear Dominie. By contract, the royalties go to Syrtus,
/here" — Professor Corque's smile soured — "where they are
pent on such studies as Remedial Table Tennis, Demonia
)rientation, and The Light Verse of Leopold von Sacher-
Masoch."

Manwright shook his head in exasperation. "Those
amned faculty clowns! I've turned down a dozen university
ffers, and no wonder. It's an outrage that you should be
orced to humiliate yourself and — Listen, Corque, I've been
ying to get the details on how you discovered that Gany-
aede methophyte. When will you have some time? I
nought — Where are you staying on Terra?"

"The Borealis."

"What? That fleabag?"

"I have to economize for my research."

"Well, you can economize by moving in with me. It won't
ost you a cent. I've got plenty of room, and I'll put you up
or the duration, with pleasure. I've generated a house-
eeper who'll take good care of you — and rather startle you,
think. Now do say yes, Corque. We've got a hell of a lot of
iscussing to do and I've got a lot to learn from you."

"I think it will be the other way around, my dear Domi-
ie."

21

"Don't argue! Just pack up, get the hell out of the Bo realis, and—"

"♩"

"What, Sandy?"

"♪"

"Where?"

"♪"

"Oh, yes, I see the rat-fink."

"What now, Manwright?"

"Her husband. I'll trouble you to use restraint on me, c he'll become her *late* husband."

An epicene hove into view—tall, slender, elegant, in flesh colored SkinAll—with chest, arms, and legs artfully padde to macho dimensions, as was the ornamented codpiece Manwright juggled the extinguisher angrily, as though grop ing for the firing pin of a grenade. He was so intent on th encounter that Corque was able to slip the cylinder out o his hands as the epicene approached, surveyed them, and a last spoke.

"Ah, Manwright."

"Jessamy!" Manwright turned the name into a denuncia tion.

"Sandra."

"♪"

"And our impresario."

"Good evening, Mr. Jessamy."

"Manwright, I have a bone to pick with you."

"You? Pick? A bone? With me? Why, you damned pimp putting your own wife, my magnificent creation, into damned freak show!" He turned angrily on Professor Co que. "And you bought her, eh?"

"Not guilty, Dominie. I can't supervise everything. Th Freak Foreman made the purchase."

"He did, did he?" Manwright returned to Jessamy. "An

ow much did you get for her?"

"That is not germane."

" ♪ "

"That little? Why, you padded procurer? Why? God nows, you don't need the money."

"Dr. Manwright—"

"Don't you 'Doctor' me. It's Dominie."

"Dominie—"

"Speak."

"You sold me a lemon."

"What!"

"You heard me. You sold me a lemon."

"How dare you!"

"I admit I'm a jillionaire."

"Admit it? You broadcast it."

"But nevertheless I resent a rip-off."

"Rip! I'll kill the man. Don't restrain me. I'll kill! Look, ou damned minty macho, you came to me and contracted or the perfect wife. A Siren, you said. The kind that a man ould have to lash himself to the mast to resist à la Ulysses. /ell? Didn't you?"

"Yes, I did."

"Yes, you did. And did I or did I not generate a biodroid iracle of beauty, enchantment, and mythological authen-city, guaranteed or your money back?"

"Yes, you did."

"And one week after delivery I discover my Pearl of Per-ction sold to the distinguished Charles Russell Corque's bscene freak show and displayed naked in a bizarre show-ase. My beautiful face and neck! My beautiful back and uttocks! My beautiful breasts! My beautiful mons veneris! 1y—"

"That's what she wanted."

"Did you, Sandy?"

" ♠ "

"Shame on you, girl. I know you're vain—that was a glitch in my programming—but you don't have to flaunt it. You're a damned exhibitionist." Back to Jessamy: "But that doesn't excuse your selling her. Why, did you do it, dammit? Why?"

"She was tearing my sheets."

"What?"

"Your beautiful, enchanting Pearl of Perfection was tearing my monogrammed silk sheets, woven at incredible cost by braindamaged nuns. She was tearing them with her mythologically authentic feet. Look at them."

There was no need to look. It was undeniable that the beautiful, enchanting Siren was feathered from the knees down and had delicate pheasant feet.

"So?" Manwright demanded impatiently.

"She was also scratching my ankles."

"Damn you!" Manwright burst out. "You asked for a Siren. You paid for a Siren. You received a Siren."

"With bird feet?"

"Of course with bird feet. Sirens are part bird. Haven't you read your Bulfinch? Aristotle? Sir Thomas Browne? Matter of fact, you're lucky Sandy didn't turn out bird from the waist down. Ha!"

"Very funny," Jessamy muttered.

"But it wasn't luck." Manwright went on. "No, it was genius. My biodroid genius for creative genesis, and my deep understanding of the sexual appetites."

" ♪ "

"Don't be impudent, girl. I have sexual appetites, too, but when I guarantee a virgin, I— No matter. Take her home, Jessamy. Don't argue, or I'll kill you, if I can find that damned brass thing I thought I had. Take Sandra home. I'll refund Professor Corque in full. Got to support his brilliant research. Sandy, trim your talons, for God's sake! Sense and sensibility, girl! Corque, go pack up and move in with me. Here's my card with the address. What the devil are you doing with that silly-looking fire extinguisher?"

"And that's the full shmeer, Charles. I'm sorry I haven't any work in progress to show you, but you can see I'm no tailor or seamstress, cutting up mature animals, human or otherwise, and piecing parts together, like you see with those show-biz monsters in your circus. No, I macrogenerate 'em, pure and whole, out of the basic DNA broth. Mine are all test-tube babies. Florence-flask babies, as a matter of fact, which is where I start 'em. Biodroids need womb space like any other animal."

"Fascinating, my dear Reg, and quite overwhelming. But what I can't fathom is your RNA process."

"Ah! The RNA messenger service, eh?"

"Exactly. Now we all know that DNA is the life reservoir—"

"All? We all know? Ha! Not bloody likely. Some time I'll show you the abuse I get from the Scripture freaks."

"And we know that RNA is the messenger service delivering commands to the developing tissues."

"Right on, Charles. That's where the control lies."

"But how do you control the controls? How do you direct the RNA to deliver specific commands from DNA to embryo? And how do you select the commands?"

"Penthouse."

"Wh-what?"

"Come up to the penthouse. I'll show you."

Manwright led Corque out of the enormous crimson-lit cellar laboratory which was softly glowing with ruby-colored glassware and liquids ("My babies *must* be insulated from light and noise") and up to the main floor of the house. It was decorated in the Dominie's demented style: a hodgepodge of Regency, classic Greek, African, and Renaissance. There was even a marble pool inhabited by iridescent manic fish, which gazed up at the two men eagerly.

"Hoping we'll fall in," Manwright laughed. "A cross between piranha and golden carp. One of my follies."

Thence to the second floor, twenty-five by a hundred. Manwright's library and study: four walls shelved and crammed with tapes, publications, and software; a rolling ladder leaning against each wall; a gigantic carpenter's workbench center, used as a desk and piled with clutter.

Third floor divided between dining room (front), kitchen and pantry (center), and servants' quarters (rear, overlooking garden).

Fourth floor, enjoying maximum sky and air, bedrooms. There were four, each with its own dressing room and bath, all rather severe and monastic. Manwright regarded sleep as a damned necessity which had to be endured but which should never be turned into a luxury.

"We all get enough sleep during our nine months in the womb," he had growled to Corque, "and we'll get more than we'll ever need after we die. But I'm working on regenerative immortality, off and on. Trouble is, tissues just don't want to play ball." He led the professor up a narrow stair to the penthouse.

It was a clear plastic dome, firmly anchored against wind and weather. In the center stood a glimmering Rube Goldberg, Heath-Robinson, Da Vinci mechanical construct. If it resembled anything it would be a giant collapsing robot waiting for a handyman to put it together again. Corque stared at the gallimaufry and then at Manwright.

"Neutrinoscope," the Dominie explained. "My extrapolation of the electron microscope."

"What? Neutrinos? The beta-decay process?"

Manwright nodded. "Combined with a cyclotron. I get particular particle selection that way and acceleration up to ten Mev. Selection's the crux, Charles. Each genetic molecule in the RNA coil has a specific response to a specific particle bombardment. The way I've been able to identify and isolate somewhere in the neighborhood of ten thousand messenger commands."

"But-but—My dear Reg, this is positively fantastic!"

Manwright nodded again, "Uh-huh. Took me ten years."

"But I had no idea that—Why haven't you published?"

"What?" Manwright snorted in disgust. "Publish? And have every damned quack and campus cretin clowning around with the most sacred and miraculous phenomenon ever generated on our universe? Pah! No way!"

"*You're* into it, Reg."

Manwright drew himself up with hauteur. "*I*, sir, do not clown."

"But Reg—"

"But me no buts, professor. By heaven, if Christ, in whom I've never believed, ever returned to Terra and this house, I'd keep it a secret. You know damn well the hell that would break loose if I published. It'd be Golgotha all over again."

While Corque was wondering whether Manwright meant his biodroid techniques, Christ's epiphany, or both, there was a sound of a large object slowly falling upstairs. Manwright's scowl was transformed into a grin. "My housekeeper," he chuckled. "You didn't get the chance to see him when you moved in last night. A treasure."

An imbecile face, attached to a pinhead, poked through the penthouse door. It was followed by a skewed hunchback body with gigantic hands and feet. The mouth, which seemed to wander at will around the face, opened and spoke in a hoarse voice.

"Mahth-ter . . ."

27

"Yes, Igor?"

"Should I thteal you a brain today, mahth-ter?"

"Thank you, Igor. Not today."

"Then breakfahtht ith therved, mahth-ter."

"Thank you, Igor. This is our distinguished guest, the celebrated Professor Charles Corque. You will make him comfortable and obey him in everything."

"Yeth, mahth-ter. At your thervithe, thelebrated Profethor Charlth Corque. Should I thteal you a brain today?"

"Not today, thank you."

Igor bobbed his head, turned, disappeared, and there was a sound of a large object rapidly falling downstairs. Corque's face was convulsed with suppressed laughter. "What in the world—?"

"A reject," Manwright grinned. "Only one in my career. No, the first of two, if we count Sandy, but I do think Jessamy will keep his Siren. Anyway," he continued, leading Corque downstairs, "this client was absolutely hypnotized by the Frankenstein legend. Came to me and contracted for a faithful servitor, like the Baron's accomplice. Returned five months later, paid like a gent, but said he'd changed his mind. He was now on a Robinson Crusoe kick and wanted a Friday. I made him his Friday, but I was stuck with Igor."

"Couldn't you have dissolved him back into the DNA broth?"

"Good God, Charles! No way. Never. I generate life; I don't destroy it. Anyway, Igor's an ideal housekeeper. He does have this brain-stealing hang-up—that was part of the original model—and I have to lock him in a closet when there's thunder and lightning, but he cooks like an absolute genius."

"I hadn't known that Baron Frankenstein's henchman was a chef."

"To be quite honest, Charles, he wasn't. That was an error

in programming—I *do* glitch now and then—with a happy ending. When Igor's cooking, he thinks he's making monsters."

The card came in on the same tray with the Tomato-Onion Tart (ripe tomatoes, sliced onions, parsley, basil, Gruyère, bake in pastry shell forty minutes at 375°F), and Manwright snatched the embossed foil off the salver.

"What's this, Igor? 'Anthony Valera, Chairman, Vortex Syndicate, 69 Old Slip, CB: 0210–0012–036–216291'?"

"In the waiting room, mahth-ter."

"By God, Charles, a potential client. Now you may have your chance to watch my genesis from start to finish. Come on!"

"Oh, have a heart, Reg. Let the chairman wait. Igor's monster looks delicious."

"Thank you, thelebrated Profethor Charlth Corque."

"No, no, Igor. The thanks go from me to you."

"Pigs, both of you," Manwright snorted and dashed for the stairs. Corque rolled his eyes to heaven, grabbed a slice of tart, winked at Igor, and followed, chewing ecstatically.

One would expect the chairman of a syndicate with a seventeen-figure CB telephone number to look like Attila the Hun. Anthony Valera looked and dressed like a suave Spanish grandee; he was black and silver, including ribboned peruke. He was very much au courant, for as Corque entered he smiled, bowed, and murmured, "What a happy surprise, Professor Corque. Delighted. I had the pleasure of hearing you speak at the Trivium Charontis convention." And Mr. Valera considerately offered his left palm, Corque's right hand being busy with the tart.

"He wants an ideal executive secretary." Manwright refused to waste time on courtesies. "And I told him that my biodroid talents are damned expensive."

"To which I was about to respond when you most happily

29

entered, Professor Corque, that Vortex is criminally solvent."

"Then it's to be a company contract?"

"No, Dominie, personal." Mr. Valera smiled. "I, also, am criminally solvent."

"Good. I hate doing business with committees. You must know the old saw about camels. Let's discuss the specs and see whether we understand each other. Sex?"

"Female, of course."

"Of course. Physical appearance?"

"You don't take notes?"

"Total recall."

"You *are* lucky. Well, then. Fair. Medium tall. Endowed with soft grace. Soft voice. Blue eyes. Clear skin. Slender hands. Slender neck. Auburn hair."

"Mmm. Got any particular example of the type in mind?"

"Yes. Botticelli's *Birth of Venus*."

"Ha! Venus on the Half-shell. Lovely model. Character?"

"What one would expect of a secretary: sterling, faithful, devoted . . . to my work, of course."

"To your work, of course."

"And clever."

"D'you mean clever or intelligent?"

"Aren't they the same?"

"No. Cleverness requires humor. Intelligence does not."

"Then clever. I'll provide the intelligence. She must be able to learn quickly and remember. She must be able to acquire any skill necessary for my work. She must be perceptive and understand the stresses and conflicts that make a chairman's life one constant battle."

"So far you could hire such a girl," Manwright objected. "Why come to me?"

"I haven't finished, Dominie. She must have no private life and be willing to drop everything and be instantly available at all times."

"Available for what?"

"Business luncheons, dinners, last-minute parties, client entertainment, and so forth. She must be chic and fashionable and able to dazzle men. You would not believe how many tough tycoons have been charmed into dubious deals by a seductive secretary."

"You've left out an important point. On what salary will she be seducing?"

"Oh, I'll provide the money for the wardrobe, the maquillage, and so forth. She must provide the taste, the charm, the wit, the entertaining conversation."

"Then you want a talker?"

"But only when I want her to talk. Otherwise, mum."

Corque whistled softly. "But you're describing a paragon, my dear sir."

"I would say a miracle, Professor Corque, but Dominie Manwright is celebrated for his miraculous creations."

"You married?" Manwright shot.

"Five times."

"Then you're a chaser."

"Dominie!"

"And easily landed."

"Really, you're extraordinarily blunt. A chaser? Well . . . let's say that I'm attracted, occasionally."

"Would you want your executive secretary to be responsive — occasionally? Is that to be programmed?"

"Only unilaterally. If I should happen to desire, I would want a beautiful response. But she is not to make demands. Nevertheless she will, of course, be faithful to me."

"These parameters are preposterous," Corque exclaimed indignantly.

"Not at all, Charles, not at all," Manwright soothed. "Mr. Valera is merely describing what all men desire in a woman:

an Aspasia, the beautiful *femme galante* who was the adoring mistress and adviser to Pericles of ancient Greece. It's
wishful fantasy, but my business is turning fantasy into reality, and I welcome the challenge. This girl may be my magnum opus." Again he fired a shot at Valera. "And you'll
become very bored."

"What?"

"Within six months this adoring, talented, dedicated slave
will bore you to tears."

"But how? Why?"

"Because you've left out the crux of a kept woman's hold
over a man. Don't protest, Valera. We know damn well
you're ordering a mistress, and I make no moral judgment,
but you've forgotten the drop of acid."

"Dominie, I do protest, I —"

"Just listen. You're contracting for an enchanting mistress, and it's my job to make sure that she remains enchanting, always. Now there are many sweet confections that
require a drop of acid to bring you the full flavor and keep
them enjoyable. Your Aspasia will need a drop of acid for
the same reason. Otherwise, her perpetual perfection will
cloy you in a matter of months."

"You know," Valera said slowly, "that's rather astute,
Dominie. What would you advise? I'm all anticipation!"

"The acid in any woman who can hold a man: the unexpected, the quality that makes it impossible to live with them
or without them."

"And what would that be in my . . . my secretary?"

"How the devil can I tell you?" Manwright shouted. "If
you knew in advance, it wouldn't be unexpected, and anyway *I* won't know. I can't guarantee surprise and adventure
with a woman. All I can do is program a deliberate error
into the genesis of your perfect Aspasia, and the discovery
of that kink will be the charming drop of acid. Under-

stood?"

"You make it sound like a gamble."

"The irrational is always a gamble."

After a pause Valera said, "Then you're challenging me, Dominie?"

"We're both being challenged. You want the ideal mistress created to your specs; I've got to meet them to your complete satisfaction."

"And your own, Reg?" Corque murmured.

"Certainly my own. I'm a professional. The job is the boss. Well, Valera? Agreed?"

After another thoughtful pause, Valera nodded. "Agreed, Dominie."

"Splendid. I'll need your Persona Profile from the syndicate."

"Out of the question, Dominie! Persona Profiles are Inviolable Secret. How can I ask Vortex to make an exception?"

"Damn it, can't you understand?" Manwright was infuriated by this intrasigence but controlled himself and tried to speak reasonably. "My dear chairman, I'm shaping and conditioning this Aspasia for your exclusive use. She will be the cynosure of all men, so I must make sure that she'll be implanted with an attraction for your qualities and drawn to you alone."

"Surely not all, Dominie. I have no delusions of perfection."

"Then perhaps to your defects, and that will be *your* charming drop of acid. Come back in twenty-one weeks."

"Why twenty-one specifically?"

"She'll be of age. My biodroids average out at a week of genesis for every physical year of the creation's maturity. One week for a dog; twenty-one weeks for an Aspasia. Good day, Mr. Valera."

After the chairman had left, Manwright cocked an eye at

Corque and grinned. "This is going to be a magnificent experiment, Charles. I've never generated a truly contemporary biodroid before. You'll pitch in and help, I hope?"

"I'll be honored, Reg." Suddenly, Corque returned the grin. "But there's one abstruse reference I can't understand."

"Fear not, you'll learn to decipher me as we go along. What don't you understand?"

"The old saw about the camel."

Manwright burst out laughing. "What? Never heard it? Penalty of spending too much time on the outer planets. Question: What is a camel? Answer: A camel is a horse made by a committee." He sobered. "But by God, our gallant girl won't be any camel. She'll be devastating."

"Forgive the question, Reg: Too devastating for you to resist?"

"What? That? No way! Never! I've guaranteed and delivered too many virgin myths, deities, naiads, dryads, *und so weiter*. I'm seasoned, Charles: tough and hard and impervious to all their lures. But the breasts are going to be a problem," he added absently.

"My dear Reg! Please decipher."

"Her breasts, Charles. Botticelli made 'em too small in his Venus. I think I should program 'em fuller, but what size and shape? Like pears? Pomegranates? Melons? It's an aesthetic perplexity."

"Perhaps your deliberate error will solve it."

"Perhaps, but only the Good Lord, in whom I've never believed, can know what her mystery kink will turn out to be. *Selah!* Let's get to work on our perfect mistress, Charles, or, to use an antique expression that's just become a new vogue word, our perfect Popsy."

The Dominie's program for a devastating Popsy who was to be enchanting, trustworthy, loyal, helpful, friendly, courteous, kind, obedient, cheerful, clever, chic, soft-spoken, beautiful, busty, eloquent on demand, and always available to entertain, began as follows:

A	12-1	0	0	(scald)
B	12-2	1	1	
C	12-3	2	2	(V.S.O.P.)
D	12-4	3	3	
E	12-5	4	4	
F	12-6	5	5	(¼ dram)
G	12-7	6	6	
H	12-8	7	7	(crimped)
I	12-9	8	8	
J	11-1	9	9	(½ scruple)
K	11-2	(garni)		
L	11-3	#	8-3	
M	11-4	!	11-8-2	
N	11-5	*1*	8-4	(eau)
0	11-6	$	11-8-3	
P	11-7	%	0-8-4	(MSG)
Q	11-8	£	12-8-2	
R	11-9	&	12	
S	0-2	*	11-8-4	(only a dash)
T	0-3	+	0-8-3	
U	0-4	:	12-8-3	

Und so weiter for 147 pages. *Und* good luck to the computer software for creative biogenesis, which couldn't possibly interest anyone.

"Anyway, there's no point in reading the program, Charles. Numbers can't paint the picture. I'll just describe the sources I've used for the generation of our Popsy. You may not recognize some of the names, but I assure you that most of them were very real and famous celebrities in their time."

35

"What was your lecture to Igor the other day, Reg? 'A chef is no better than his materials.' "

"Right on. And I'm using the best. Beauty—Botticelli's Venus of course, but with Egyptian breasts. I thought of using Pauline Borghese, but there's a queen in a limestone relief from the Ptolemaic period who's the ideal model. Callipygian rear elevation. Maidenhair frontispiece, delicate and fritillary. Did you say something, Charles?"

"Not I, Reg."

"I've decided not to use Aspasia for the virtues."

"But you said that was what Valera wanted."

"So I did, but I was wrong. The real Aspasia was a damned premature Women's Rights activist. Too strong for the chairman's taste."

"And yours?"

"Any man's. So I'm using Egeria instead."

"Egeria? I haven't had an education in the classics, Reg."

"Egeria, the legendary fountain nymph who was the devoted adviser to King Numa of ancient Rome. She also possessed the gift of prophecy, which might come in handy for Valera. Let's see. Fashion and chic—a famous couturiere named Coco Chanel. Subtle perceptions—the one and only Jane Austen. Voice and theater sense—Sarah Bernhardt. And she'll add a soupçon of lovely Jew."

"What on earth for?"

"It's obvious you haven't met many on the outer planets or you wouldn't ask. Remarkable race, Jews; freethinking, original, creative, obstinate, impossible to live with or without."

"That's how you described the ideal mistress, wasn't it?"

"I did."

"But if your Popsy is obstinate, how can she respond to Valera's desires?"

"Oh, I'm using Lola Montez for that. Apparently, she was

tigress in the sex department. Hmmm. Next? Victoria Woodhull for business acumen. La Pasionaria for courage. Hester Bateman—she was the first woman silversmith—for kills. Dorothy Parker for wit. Florence Nightingale for sacrifice. Mata Hari for mystery. What else?"

"Conversation."

"Quite right. Oscar Wilde."

"Oscar Wilde!"

"Why not? He was a brilliant talker; held dinner parties spellbound. I'm giving her dancer's hands, neck and legs, Dolley Madison hostessing, and—I've omitted something. . . ."

"Your deliberate mistake."

"Of course. The mystery kink which will catch us all by surprise." Manwright flipped through the software. "It's programmed somewhere around here. No, that's Valera's Persona Profile. Charles, you won't believe the damned intransigent, stubborn, know-it-all conceited egomania concealed beneath that polished veneer. It's going to be hell imprinting our girl with an attraction engram for such an impossible man. Oh, here's the unexpected in black and white."

Manwright pointed to:

$$R = L \times \sqrt{N}$$

"Wait a minute," Corque said slowly. "That equation looks familiar."

"Aha."

"I think I remember it from one of my boyhood texts."

"Oh-ho."

"The . . . the most probable distance . . ." Corque was dredging up the words ". . . from the lamppost after a certain number of . . . of irregular turns is equal to the average length of each track that is—"

"Straight track, Charles."

"Right. Each straight track that is walked, times the square root of their number." Corque looked at Manwright with a mixture of wonder and amusement. "Confound you, Reg! That's the solution to the famous 'Drunkard's Walk' problem from *The Law of Disorder*. And this is the deliberate uncertainty that you're programming? You're either a madman or a genius."

"A little of both, Charles. A little of both. Our Popsy will walk straight lines within my parameters, but we'll never know when or how she'll hang a right or a left."

"Surely she'll be aiming for Valera?"

"Of course. He's the lamppost. But she'll do some unexpected staggering on the way." Manwright chuckled and sang in an odd, husky voice, "There's a lamp on a post, There's a lamp on a post, And it sets the night aglowin'. Boy girl boy girl, Boy boy girl girl, But best when flakes is snowin'."

Regis Manwright's laboratory notes provide a less-than dramatic description (to put it politely) of the genesis and embryological development of Galatea Galante, the Perfect Popsy.

GERMINAL

Day 1: One hundred milliliter Florence flask.

Day 2: Five hundred milliliter Florence flask.

Day 3: One thousand milliliter Florence flask.

Day 4: Five thousand milliliter Florence flask.

Day 5: Decanted.

(E & A charging *too damn much* for flasks!!!)

(Baby nominal. Charles enchanted with her. Too red for my taste. Poured out of the amnion blowing bubbles and talking. Couldn't shut her up. Just another fresh kid with a damn big mouth.)

"Reg, Gally must have a nurse."

"For heaven's sake, Charles! She'll be a year old next week."

"She must have someone to look after her."

"All right. All right. Igor. She can sleep in his room."

"No, no, no. He's a dear creature, but hardly my idea of a nursemaid."

"I can convince him he made her. He'll be devoted."

"No good, Reg; he isn't child oriented."

"You want someone child oriented? Hmmm. Ah, yes. Got just the right number for you. I generated The Old Woman Who Lived in a Shoe for the Positively Peerless Imitation Plastic company to use in their genuine plastics sales promotion."

" 'She had so many children she didn't know what to do'?"

"The same." Manwright punched the CB keyboard. "Seanbhean? This is Regis."

The screen sparkled and cleared. A gypsy crone appeared with begging hand outstretched for alms.

"How's everything going, Seanbhean?"

"*Scanruil aduafar*, Regis."

"Why?"

"*Briseadh ina ghno e.*"

"What! PPIP gone bankrupt? That's shocking. So you're out of a job?"

"*Deanfaidh sin!*"

"Well perhaps I have something for you, Seanbhean. I've just generated—"

"Cut off, Reg," Corque broke in sharply.

Manwright was so startled by Corque's tone that he obeyed and looked up perplexedly. "Don't think she'll do, Charles?"

"That old hag? Out of the question."

"She isn't old," Manwright protested. "She's under thirty.

I made her look like that according to the specs: Seventy-year-old Irish gypsy. they call 'em 'tinkers' in Ireland. Speaks Irish and can handle kid actors who are a pain in the ass. And I delivered, by God."

"As you always do; but still out of the question. Please try someone else."

"Charles, has that damn infant got you enthralled?"

"No."

"Her first conquest, and she's just out of the flask! Can you imagine what she'll do to men in another twenty weeks? Be at each other's throats. Fighting duels. Ha! I *am* a genius, and I don't deny it."

"We need a nurse for Gally, Reg."

"Nag, nag, nag."

"Someone warm and comforting after the child has endured a session with you."

"I can't think what the man is implying. All right, cradle-snatcher, all right. I'll call Claudia." Manwright punched the CB. "She's warm and maternal and protective. Wish she'd been *my* nanny. Hello? Claudia? It's Regis. Switch on, darling." The screen sparkled and cleared. The magnificent head and face of a black mountain gorilla appeared.

"!!" she grunted.

"I'm sorry, love. Been too busy to call. You're looking well. How's that no-good husband of yours?"

"!"

"And the kids?"

"!!!"

"Splendid. Now don't forget. You promised to send them to me so I can surgify them into understanding our kind of speech. Same like you, love, and no charge. And speaking of kids, I've got a new one, a girl, that I'd like you to—"

At this point the stunned Corque collected himself enough to press the cutoff stud. Claudia faded.

"Are you mad?" he demanded.

Manwright was bewildered. "What's wrong, Charles?"

"You suggest that terrifying beast for the child's nurse?"

"Beast! She's an angel of mother love. She'll have the kid climbing all over her, hugging and kissing her. It's interesting," he reflected, "I can manipulate the cognition centers, but I can't overcome muscular limitations. I gave Claudia college-level comprehension of spoken and written communications, but I couldn't give her human speech. She's still forced to use Mountain, which is hardly a language of ideas. Damn frustrating. For both of us."

"And you actually want her to mother Gally?"

"Of course. Why not?"

"Your Claudia will frighten the daylights out of the infant."

"Ridiculous."

"She's hideous."

"Are *you* mad? She's beautiful. Pure. Majestic. And a hell of a lot brighter than your Remedial Table Tennis bums at Syrtus University."

"But she can't talk. She only grunts."

"Talk? Talk? For God's sake. Charles! That damn red Popsy was poured out talking sixteen to the dozen. We can't shut her up. She's filling the house with enough of her jabber as it is. Be grateful for some silence."

So Claudia, the black mountain gorilla, moved into the Manwright ménage, and Igor was furiously jealous.

The first morning that Claudia joined Manwright and Corque at breakfast (while Igor glowered at his massive rival), she printed a message on a pad and handed it to the Dominie: R DD YU GV G TLT TRG IN YR PRGRM?

"Let's see if I remember your abbreviations, darling. Did you . . . that's me . . . give Galatea . . . yes, toilet training in your program? My God, Claudia! I gave her the best of 47 women. Surely at least one of them must have been toilet trained."

BY DPRS

"By what, Claudia?"

"Buy diapers, Reg."

"Oh. Ah. Of course. Thank you, Charles. Thank you, Claudia. More coffee, love? It's frustrating, Charles. Muscular dyspraxia again. Claudia can manage caps in her writing but she can't hack lower case. How many diapers, Claudia?"

1 DZ

"Right. One doz. *Zu Befehl.* Did you bring your kids to play with the baby?"

TO OD

"Too odd for what?"

TOO OLD

"Your kids?"

G

"What? Galatea? Too old for your boys? And still in diapers? I'd best see for myself."

One of the top-floor bedrooms had been converted into a nursery. The usual biodroid cellar accommodations weren't good enough for Manwright's magnum opus. When the Dominie entered with Claudia, the red infant was on the floor, flat on her belly, propped on a pillow, and deep in a book. She looked up and crawled enthusiastically to Claudia.

"Nanny dear, I've found the answer, the old linear shorthand. Just slashes, dots, and dashes, and you won't have to worry your hand and head over cursive abbreviations. It's a simple style, and we can practice together." She climbed up on Claudia and kissed her lovingly. "One would think this might have occurred to that egotistical know-it-all whose

42

name escapes me." The infant turned her auburn head. "Why, good morning, Dominie Manwright. What an unpleasant surprise."

"You're right, Claudia," Manwright growled. "She's too damned old for your kids. Diaper her."

"My sphincter will be under control by tomorrow, Dominie," Galatea said sweetly. "Can you say the same for your tongue?"

"Guh!" And Manwright withdrew with what he hoped was impressive dignity.

Of course, she shot up like a young bamboo plant and filled the house with joy as she entertained them with her escapades. She taught herself to play Manwright's Regency harpsichord, which was sadly out of repair. She convinced Igor that it was a monster in the making, and together they refinished and tuned it. The sound of concert-A on the tuning fork droned through the house with agonizing penetration. The others were forced to eat out because she gave Igor no time for cooking.

She studied linear shorthand with Claudia and then translated it into finger language. They had glorious raps, silently talking to each other until Manwright banned the constant finger waggling, which he denounced as a damned invasion of vision. They simply held hands and talked into each other's palm in their secret code, and Manwright was too proud to ask what they were gossiping about.

"As if I'd get an answer anyway," he growled to Corque.

"D'you think that's her mystery surprise, Reg?"

"Damned if I know. She's unexpected enough as it is. Rotten kid!"

She stole liquid licorice from Igor's sacred pantry and tarred herself; phosphorous from Manwright's sacred laboratory and irradiated herself. She burst into Corque's dark bedroom at three in the morning, howling, "ME

METHOPHYTE MOTHER FROM GANNYMEEDY! YOU KILL ALL MY CHILDERS, ALIEN INVADER FROM OUTSIDE SPACE! NOW ME KILL YOU!"

Corque let out a yell and then couldn't stop laughing for the rest of the day. "The beautiful shock of the apparition, Reg!" Manwright didn't think it was funny.

"That damned child is giving me *real* nightmares," he complained. "I keep dreaming that I'm lost in the Grand Teton mountains and Red Indians are chasing me."

She sneaked up into the sacred penthouse and decorated the robotlike neutrinoscope with items stolen from Manwright's wardrobe. The construct assumed a ludicrous resemblance to the Dominie himself.

The innocent child fast-talked E & A Chemical delivery— "My Daddy forgot to order it. So absent-minded, you know"—into an extra gallon of ethyl alcohol which she poured into the marble pool and got the piranhas disgustingly drunk. Then she jumped in and was discovered floating with her plastered pals.

"Doesn't know the meaning of fear, Reg."

"Pah! Just the Passionaria I programmed."

She stole two hundred meters of magnetic tape from the library and fashioned a scarecrow mobile. The gardener was enraptured. Manwright was infuriated, particularly because art-dealer friends offered huge amounts for the creation.

"But *that's* her charming unexpected, Reg. Gally's a born artist."

"Like hell she is. That's only the Hester Bateman I gave her. No $L \times \sqrt{N}$ yet. And the nightmares are continuing in sequence. Those damned Red Indians have cut me off at the pass."

Claudia took Galatea to her home, where the girl got on

famously with Claudia's two sons and brought them to Manwright's house to demonstrate a new dance which she'd devised called: "The Anthro Hustle." It was performed to a song she'd composed entitled: "Who Put the Snatch on Gorilla Baby?" which she banged out fortissimously on the harpsichord.

"Bring back the tuning fork," Manwright muttered.

Corque was applauding enthusiastically. "Music's her surprise kink, Reg."

"Call that music?"

Corque took her to his Saturn Circus, where she mesmerized him into letting her try riding bareback and leaping through burning hoops, acting as target for a knife thrower, trapeze aerobatics, and thrusting her auburn head into a lion's mouth. He couldn't understand how she'd persuaded him to let her take such horrifying risks.

"Perhaps cajolery's her mystery quality," he suggested. "But she did miraculously well, Reg. My heart was in my mouth. Gally never turned a hair. Pure aplomb. She's a magnificent creation. You've generated a Super-Popsy for Valera."

"Guh."

"Could her unexpected kink be psychic?"

"The redskins have got me surrounded," Manwright fretted. He seemed strangely disoriented.

What disturbed him most were the daily tutoring sessions with the young lady. Invariably they degenerated into bickering and bitching, with the Dominie usually getting the worst of it.

"When our last session ended in another bitch we both steamed for the library door," he told Corque. "I said, 'Age before beauty, my dear,' which you must admit was gracious, and started out. That red Popsy snip said, 'Pearls before swine,' and swaggered past me like a gladiator who's

45

wiped an entire arena."

"She's wonderful!" Corque laughed.

"Oh, you're insanely biased. She's been twisting you around her fingers since the moment she was poured."

"And Igor and Claudia and her two boys and the CB repair and the plumber and the electronics and the gardener and the laundry and E & A Chemical and half my circus? All insanely biased?"

"Evidently I'm the only sanity she can't snow. You know the simple psychological truth, Charles; we're always accusing others of our own faults. That saucebox has the impudence to call me intransigent, stubborn, know-it-all, conceited. Me! Out of her own mouth. QED."

"Mightn't it be the other way around, Reg?"

"Do try to make sense, Charles. And now that the Grand Teton breastworks are making her top-heavy (I think maybe I was a little too generous with my Egyptian programming) there'll be no living with her vanity. Women take the damned dumbest pride in the thrust of the boozalums."

"Now Reg, you exaggerate. Gally knows we'd all adore her even if she were flatchested."

"I know I'm doing a professional job, and I know she has too much ego in her cosmos. But next week we start *schlepping* her to parties, openings, talk-ins, routs, and such to train her for Valera. *That* ought to take her down a peg. The Red Indians have got me tied to a stake," he added gloomily.

"Canapés?"

"Ta evah so. Lahvely pahty, Ms. Galante."

"Thank you, Lady Agatha. Canapés?"

"Grazie, Signorina."

"Prego, Commendatore. Canapés?"

"A dank, meyd'l. Lang leb'n zolt it."

"Nito far vus, General. Hot canapés, dear Professor Corque?"

"Thank you, adorable hostess. Igor's?"

"Mine."

"And perfection. Don't be afraid of the Martian counsul. He won't bite."

"Canapés, M'sieur Consul?"

"Ah! Mais oui! Merci, Mademoiselle Gallée. Que pensez-vous du lumineux Dominie Manwright?"

"C'est un type très compétent."

"Oui. Romanèsque, mais formidablement compétent."

"Quoi? Manwright? Romanèsque? Vous me gênez, mon cher consul."

"Ma foi, oui, romanèsque, Mademoiselle Gallée. C'est justement son côté romanesque qui lui cause du mal à se trouver une femme."

"These damn do's are a drag, Charles."

"But isn't she wonderful?"

"And they're making my nightmares worse. A sexy Indian squaw tore my clothes off last night."

"Mi interesso particolarmente ai libri di fantascienza, magia-orrore, umorismo, narrativa, attualità, filosofia, sociologia, e cattivo, putrido Regis Manwright."

"Charles, this is the last literary talk-in I ever attend."

"Did you see how Gally handled those Italian publishers?"

"Yes, gibes at my expense. She put iron claws on her hands."

"My dear Reg, Gally did no such thing."

"I was referring to that sexy squaw."

"Então agora sabes dançer?"

"Sim. Danço, falo miseravelmente muchas linguas, estudo ciência e filosofia, escrevo uma lamentával poesia, estoirome com experiências idiotas, egrimo como un louco, jogo so boxe como up palhaco. Em suma, son a celebra bioroid, Galatea Galante, de Dominie Manwright."

"She was magnificent dancing with that Portuguese prince, Reg."

"Portuguese ponce, you mean."

"Don't be jealous."

"She's heating the claws in a damned campfire, Charles."

"Didn't you ever fight back, Sandy?"

"Yes, I know, he's a bully. But all bullies are cowards at heart. You should have fought him to a standstill, like me. Did he ever make a pass at you?"

"Uh-huh. Me neither. He's an arrogant egomaniac, too much in love with himself to love anyone else."

"What, Sandy? Me? Give the come-on to that dreadful man? Never! Did you?

"Uh-huh. And he didn't even have to lash himself to the mast. Iceberg City. Ah, Mr. Jessamy. So sweet of you to give us your box for the concert. I've just been comparing notes with your adorable wife on our common enemy, whose names escapes me. He's the gentleman on my right, who slept through the Mozart."

"And dreamed that she's torturing me with her burning claws, Charles, all over my bod."

"Man nehme: zwei Teile Selbstgefälligkeit, zwei Teile Selbstsucht, einen Teil Eitelkeit, und einen Teil Esel, mische kräftig, füge etwas Geheimnis hinzu, und man erhaält Dominie Regis Manwright."

"Especially my private parts."

"Dominie Manwright's biodroid está al dia en su manera de tratar los neologismos, palabras coloquiales, giro y modismos, clichés y terminos de argot, Señor. Yo soy Galatea Galante, la biodroid."

"Thank you, madame. I am not Spanish; I merely admire and respect the old Castilian style."

"Oh. Scuse me, chorley guy. You tollerday donsk?"

He burst out laughing. "I see you're very much with the classics, madame. Let me think. Yes. The proper response in that James Joyce litany is 'N.' "

"You talkatiff scowegian?"

"Nn."

"You spigotty anglease?"

"Nnn."

"You phonio saxo?"

"Nnnn."

"Clear all so. 'Tis a Jute. Let us swop hats and excheck a few strong verbs weak oach eather yapyazzard."

"Brava, madame! Bravissima!"

She tilted her auburn head and looked at him strangely.

"Against my will," she said slowly, "I'm compelled to invite you to a dinner party tonight."

"More classics, madame? The Beatrice and Benedict scene from *Much Ado About Nothing*?"

"No, it's the Galatea and—I don't know your name."

"Valera. Antony Valera."

"It's the Galatea and Valera scene. Can you come?"

"With delight."

"When this bash is finished I'll give you the address."

"I know it, Galatea."

"My friends call me Gally. How do you know my address? We've never met."

"I contracted with—I'm acquainted with Dominie Manwright. Gally. Tonight? Eight o'clock?"

"Eight tonight."

"Dress party?"

"Optional." She shook her head dizzily. "I don't know what's got into me, Valera. The moment I saw you at this clambake I knew I had to see you again, intimately. I'm possessed!"

The rest of the household was dining in The Gastrologue, and their moods were not compatible.

"Thrown out," Corque kept repeating. "Thrown out without a moment's notice by that ungrateful tyrant!"

"Naturally. She wants to be alone with Valera, Charles. Instant, devoted attraction, as per my brilliant programming. I tell you, I'm a genius."

"She athed me to make month-terth for her to therve, mahth-ter."

"Quite right, Igor. We must all pitch in and abet Valera's romance. He was so turned on meeting her at that bash this afternoon that he sent his check by messenger. Payment in full . . . to protect his claim on my Perfect Popsy, no doubt."

"Thrown out! Thrown out by that tyrant!"

"And good riddance to her very soon, Charles. The house will be back to normal."

"But she didn't order a brain, mahth-ter."

"Not to worry, Igor. Tell you what; *we'll* order *cervelles de veau au beurre noir*, and if Gastrologue doesn't have any calves' brains you can go out and steal some." He beamed and bobbed his pale, streaky head.

"Thank you, mahth-ter."

"Evicted!"

The silent Claudia printed: PLANTAINS FR ME PLS RENELLOS DE AMARILLO.

At one minute past eight Valera said, "It's fashionable to be a half-hour late, but I—Is it all right to come in?"

"Oh please! I've been biting my nails for a whole minute."

"Thank you. To tell the truth, I tried to be chic, but it didn't take as long as I thought it would to walk up from Old Slip."

"Old Slip? Isn't that where your office is? Were you working late, poor soul?"

"I live there too, Gally. A penthouse on top of the tower."

"Ah, à la Alexander Eiffel?"

"Somewhat, but the Syndicate complex is no *Tour Eiffel*. What a fantastic place this is. I've never done more than peep beyond the waiting room."

"D'you want the full tour?"

"I'd like nothing better."

"You've got it, but drink first. What would you like?"

"What are you serving?"

"My dear Valera, I—"

"Tony."

"Thank you. My dear Tony, I share this house with two and a half men and a mountain gorilla. We have everything in stock."

"Stolichnaya, please. Half?"

"Igor, our housekeeper," Galatea explained as she brought a tray with a bucket of ice, a bottle, and shot glasses. She opened the vodka deftly and began revolving the bottle in the ice. "A biodroid replica of Baron Frankenstein's accomplice."

"Oh yes, I've met him. The lisping hunchback."

"A dear, dear soul, but only half with it."

"And a gorilla?"

"That's Claudia, my beloved nanny. She's beautiful. This vodka isn't chilled enough yet, but let's start anyway." She filled the glasses. "Russian style, eh? Knock it back, Tony. Death to the fascist, imperialist invaders from outer space."

"And their Conestoga star-wagons."

They knocked their shots back.

"Gally, what miracle are you wearing?"

"Là, sir!" She did a quick kick-turn. "Like it?"

"I'm dazzled."

"If I tell you, promise not to turn me in?"

"I promise."

"I copied it from a Magda."

"Who or what is a Magda? Oh, thank you."

"I'm afraid I filled it too high, but boys like big sandwiches and big drinks. She's *the* vogue designer of the year. Down with countertenors."

"May they be heard only in Siberia. Why must I keep it a secret about your copy?"

"Good Lord! They hang, draw, and quarter you if you pinch a designer original."

"How did you manage?"

"I fell in love with it at one of her openings and memorized it."

"And made it yourself? From memory? You're remark-ble!"

"You're exaggerating. Don't you remember complicated
tock manipulations?"

"Well, yes."

"So with me it's the same damn thing. Oops! That's the
ag of a dirty joke. Apologies to the chairman."

"The chairman needs all the dirty jokes he can get for cli-
nt entertainment. What's this one?"

"Maybe someday, if you coax me nicely."

"Where do you get them? Surely not from Dominie
Manwright."

"From Claudia's naughty boys. Another shot to the dam-
ation of Blue Laws, and then the guided tour."

Valera was bewildered and delighted by the madness of
Manwright's house, and enchanted by the high style with
which Galatea flowed through it with equally mad comments. An old song lyric haunted him:

Hey, diddle-dee-dee,
I've found the girl for me.
With raunchy style
And virgin guile
She's just the girl for me.

"Never mind the polite compliments, Tony," she said,
pulling him down on a couch beside her and refilling his
glass. "I'll give you the acid test. Of all things in this house,
which would you be most likely to steal?"

"You."

"I didn't say kidnap. Come on, man, steal something."

"I think I spilled my drink."

"It's my fault; I joggled your arm. Don't mop. So?"

"You're so sudden, Gally. Well . . . don't laugh. . . . The
scarecrow mobile in the garden."

"Oh, I love you for that! *I* made it, when I was a little ki-
months ago." She gave him a smacking kiss on the chee
and jumped up. "Like some music?" She turned on the hi-
and a soft murmuring drifted through the house.

Valera glanced at his watch. "Your guests must be fright
fully chic."

"Oh?"

"You said eight. That was an hour ago. Where's every
body?"

"As a matter of fact, they came early."

"I'm the only one who was early."

"That's right."

"You mean I'm . . . ?"

"That's right."

"But you said a dinner party, Gally."

"It's ready any time you are."

"The party is us? Just us?"

"I can call some more people if you're bored with me."

"You know that's not what I meant."

"No? What did you mean?"

"I—" He stopped himself.

"Go ahead," she bullied. "Say it. I dare you."

He capitulated. For perhaps the first time in his suave lif
he was overpowered. In a low voice he said, "I was remem
bering a tune from twenty years ago. Hey, diddle-dee-dee
I've found the girl for me/With raunchy style/And virgi
guile/She's just the girl for me."

She flushed and began to tremble. Then she took refug
in the hostess role. "Dinner," she said briskly. "Beef Stroga
noff, potatoes baked with mushrooms, salad, lemon pie
and coffee. Mouton Rothschild. No, not upstairs, Tony; I'v
made special arrangements for you. Help me with th
table."

Together, in a sort of domestic intimacy, they arranged a

gaming table alongside the marble pool with two painted Venetian chairs. She had already set the table with Spode china and Danish silver, so it needed some careful balancing. Before she began serving, she drew the cork from the Bordeaux bottle and poured a few drops into Valera's goblet.

"Try it, Tony," she said. "I've never been able to decide whether the concept of 'letting a wine breathe' is fact or how-offey. I appeal to your sophistication. Give me your opinion."

He tasted and rolled his eyes to heaven. "Superb! You're magnificent with your compliments, Gally. Sit down and try it yourself, I insist." And he filled her glass.

"Wait," she laughed. "The floor show first. I snowed electronics into bootlegging ultralight into the pool. That's why wanted our table here. Wait till you see 20 Performing Piranhas 20." She ran to a wall, extinguished the living room lights, and flipped a switch. The pool glowed like lava, and he excited fish became a ballet of darting embers. Galatea returned to the table, sat opposite Valera, and raised her goblet to him. He smiled back into her face.

"Hey, diddle-dee—" he began and then froze. He stared. Then he started to his feet so violently that he overturned the table.

"Tony!" She was appalled.

"You goddamn bitch," he shouted. His face was black. "Where's the CB?"

"Tony!"

"Where's the goddamn CB? Tell me before I break your goddamn neck!"

"Th-that table." She pointed. "B-but I don't understand. What's—"

"You'll understand soon enough." He punched buttons. "By God, you and this whole damn lying house will understand. Rip me? Play me for a patsy?" His rage was a terrify-

ing echo of Manwright at his worst. "Hello. Larson? Valera
Don't waste time with visual. Crash mission. Call full Secu
rity and comb the city for a son of a bitch named Regi
Manwright. Yes, that's the pig. I give you a half hour to fin
him and—"

"B-but I know where he is," Galatea faltered.

"Hold it, Larson. You do? Where?"

"The Gastrologue."

"The bastard's in The Gastrologue Club, Larson. Go ge
him and bring him to his house, which is where I am now
And if you want to get rough with him I'll pay all legals an
add a bonus. I'm going to teach that lying pimp and hi
bitch a lesson they'll remember for the rest of their lives."

The four were herded into the main floor of Manwright'
house at the point of a naked laser which Larson thoug
advisable in view of the threat of Claudia's mass. They saw
grotesque: Valera and Galatea silhouetted before the glow
ing pool in the dark room. Valera was holding the weepin
girl by her hair, for all the world like a chattel in a slave mar
ket.

In this ominous *crise* Manwright displayed an aspect o
his character which none had ever seen: a tone of quiet com
mand that took obedience for granted, as if by divine right
and won it through its assurance.

"Mr. Larson, you may pocket that laser now. It was neve
needed. Valera, you will let Galatea go," he said softly. "No
dear, don't move. Stay alongside him. You belong to him
unless he's changed his mind. Have you, Valera?"

"You're goddamn right I have," the chairman stormed. "
want no part of this cheap secondhand trash. Larson, kee
that gun handy and get on the CB. I want my chec
stopped."

"Don't bother, Mr. Larson. The check has not been depos

ited and will be returned. Why, Valera? Doesn't Galatea meet your exalted standards?"

"Of course she does," Corque burst out. "She's brilliant! She's beautiful! She's perfection! She—"

"I'm handling this, Charles. I repeat: Why, Valera?"

"I don't buy whores at your prices."

"You think Galatea's a whore?"

"Think? I know."

"You contracted for the perfect mistress who would be faithful and loving and devoted to you."

Galatea let out a moan.

"I'm sorry, my love, you never knew. I'd planned to tell you, but only after I was sure you were genuinely attracted to him. I never had any intention of forcing him on you."

"You wicked men!" she cried. "You're all hateful!"

"And now, Valera, you think of a mistress as a whore? Why this sudden eruption of archaic morality?"

"It isn't a question of morality, damn you. It's a question of secondhand goods. I want no part of a shopworn woman."

"Must I stay here with him? Does he own me? Am I bought and paid for?"

"No, love. Come to us."

She dashed away from Valera's side and then hesitated. Claudia held out her arms, but Galatea surprised everybody by going to Manwright, who took her gently.

"All right, Valera," he said. "Go now and take your army with you. Your check will be returned first thing in the morning."

"Not until I know who it was."

"Not until who what was?"

"The goddamn lover-boy who knocked her up."

"What?"

"She's pregnant, you goddamn pimp. The bitch has been

sleeping around, and I want to know the stud who knocked her up. He's got plenty coming."

After a long pause, Manwright asked, "Are you under a psychiatrist's care?"

"Don't be ridiculous."

"No more ridiculous than your slander. Galatea pregnant? My lovely, tasteful young lady sleeping around with studs? You're obviously quite mad. Go."

"Mad, am I? Ridiculous? You can't see that she's pregnant? Turn her around and look at her face in this ultralight. Look at her!"

"I'll go through the motions only to get rid of you."

Manwright smiled at Galatea as he turned the girl around. "Just a gesture, love. You'll have your dignity back in a moment, and I swear you'll never lose it ag—"

His words were cut off, as if by a guillotine. In the ultralight from the glowing pool there was no mistaking the dark pregnancy band across Galatea's face, similar to the banded mask of a racoon. He took a slow deep breath and answered the confusion in her eyes by placing a hand over her mouth.

"Go, Valera. This is now a family affair."

"I demand an answer. I won't leave until I know who it was. Your half-wit hunchback, Igor, probably. I can picture them in bed; the slobbering idiot and the—"

Manwright's interruption was an explosion. He hurled Galatea into Claudia's arms, drove a knee into Larson's groin, tore the laser away from the convulsed man, whipped Valera across the neck with the barrel, and held the staggering chairman over the edge of the pool.

"The piranhas are starving," he murmured, "Do you go in or get out?"

After the syndicate had left, not without dire promises, Manwright turned up the house lights and extinguished the pool ultralight and, with that, the pregnancy stigma banding Galatea's face. In a strange way they were all relieved.

"Not to play the district attorney," he said, "but I must know how it happened."

"How what happened?" Galatea demanded.

"Sweetheart, you *are* pregnant."

"No, no, no!"

"I know it can't be anyone in this house. Claudia, has she been promiscuous outside?"

NO

"How can you ask such questions!"

"Has Galatea been alone with a man in a possibly intimate situation?"

"You're hateful!"

NO

"Reg, we all know that. We've chaperoned Gally every moment outside, you, me, Claudia."

"Not every moment. Charles. It could have happened with this innocent in five minutes."

"But nothing ever happened with a man! Nothing! Ever!"

"Dear love, you *are* pregnant."

"I can't be."

"You are, undeniably. Charles?"

"Gally. I adore you, no matter what, but Reg is right. The pregnancy band is undeniable."

"But I'm a virgin."

"Claudia?"

HR MNS HV STOPT

"Her what have stopped"

Corque sighed. "Her menses, Reg."

"Ah so."

"I'm a virgin, you wicked, detestable men. A virgin!"

Manwright took her frantic face in his hands. "Sweetheart, no recriminations, no punishments, no Coventry, but

59

I must know where I slipped up, how it happened. Who were you with, where and when?"

"I've never been with any man, anywhere or anywhen."

"Never?"

"Never . . . except in my dreams."

"Dreams?" Manwright smiled. "All girls have them. That's not what I mean, dear."

R MAB U SHD MN

"Maybe I should mean what, Claudia?"

LT HR TL U HR DRMS

"Let her tell me her dreams? Why?"

JST LSN

"All right, I'll listen. Tell me about your dreams, love."

"No. They're private property."

"Claudia wants me to hear them."

"She's the only one I've ever told. I'm ashamed of them."

Claudia fingerwagged. "Tell him, Gally. You don't know how important they are."

"No!"

"Galatea Galante, are you going to disobey your nanny? I am ordering you to tell your dreams."

"Please, nanny. No. They're erotic."

"I know, dear. That's why they're important. You must tell."

At length, Galatea whispered, "Put out the lights, please."

The fascinated Corque obliged.

In the darkness, she began, "They're erotic. They're disgusting. I'm so ashamed. They're always the same . . . and I'm always ashamed . . . but I can't stop. . . .

"There's a man, a pale man, a moonlight man, and I . . . I want him. I want him to . . . to handle me and ravish me into ecstasy, b-but he doesn't want me, so he runs, and I chase him. And I catch him. Th-there are some sort of friends who help me catch him and tie him up. And then

60

they go away and leave me alone with the moonlight man, and I . . . and I do to him what I wanted to him to do to me. . . ."

They could hear her trembling and rustling in her chair.

Very carefully, Manwright asked, "Who is this moonlight man, Galatea?"

"I don't know."

"But you're drawn to him?"

"Oh yes. Yes! I always want him."

"Just him alone, or are there other moonlight men?"

"Only him. He's all I ever want."

"But you don't know who he is. In the dreams do you know who you are?"

"Me. Just me."

"As you are in real life?"

"Yes, except that I'm dressed different."

"Different? How?"

"Beads and . . . and buckskin with fringe."

They all heard Manwright gasp.

"Perhaps like . . . like a Red Indian, Galatea?"

"I never thought of that. Yes. I'm an Indian, an Indian squaw up in the mountains, and I make love to the paleface every night."

"Oh. My. God." The words were squeezed out of Manwright. "They're no dreams." Suddenly he roared, "Light! Give me light, Charles! Igor! Light!"

The brilliant lights revealed him standing and shaking, moonlight pale in shock. "Oh my God, my God, my God!" He was almost incoherent. "Dear God, what have I created?"

"Mahth-ter!"

"Reg!"

"Don't you understand? I know Claudia suspected; that's why she made Galatea tell me her dreams."

"B-but they're only dirty dreams," Galatea wailed. "What could possibly be the harm?"

"Damn you and damn me! They were *not* dreams. They were reality in disguise. That's the harm. That's how your dreams lock in with my nightmares, which were reality, too. Christ! I've generated a monster!"

"Now calm yourself, Reg, and do try to make sense."

"I can't. There's no sense in it. There's nothing but that lunatic drop of acid I promised Valera."

"The mystery surprise in her?"

"You kept wondering what it was, Charles. Well, now you know, if you can interpret the evidence."

"What evidence?"

Manwright forced himself into a sort of thunderous control. "I dreamed I was pursued and caught by Red Indians, tied up, and ravished by a sexy squaw. I told you. Yes?"

"Yes. Interminably."

"Galatea dreams she's a Red Indian squaw, pursuing, capturing, and ravishing a paleface she desires. You heard her?"

"I heard her."

"Did she know about my dreams?"

"No."

"Did I know about hers?"

"No."

"Coincidence?"

"Possibly."

"Would you care to bet on that possibility?"

"No."

"And there you have it. Those 'dreams' were sleep versions or distortions of what was really happening; something which neither of us could face awake. Galatea's been coming into my bed every night, and we've been making love."

"Impossible!"

"Is she pregnant?"

"Yes."

"And *I'm* Valera's lover-boy, the stud responsible. My God! My God!"

"Reg, this is outlandish. Claudia, has Gally ever left her bed nights?"

NO

"There!"

"Damn it, I'm not talking about a conventional, human woman. I didn't generate one. I'm talking about an other-world creature whose psyche is as physically real as her body, can materialize out of it, accomplish its desires, and amalgamate again. An emotional double as real as the flesh. You've pestered me about the deliberate unexpected in my programming. Well, here's the $R = L \times \sqrt{N}$. Galatea's a succubus."

"A what?"

"A succubus. A sexy female demon. Perfectly human by day. Completely conformist. But with the spectral power to come, like a carnal cloud, to men in their sleep, nights, and seduce them."

"No!" Galatea cried in despair. "I'm not that. I can't be."

"And she doesn't even know it. She's an unconscious demon. The laugh's on me, Charles," Manwright said ruefully. "By God, when I do glitch it's a beauty. I knock myself out programming the Perfect Popsy with an engram for Valera, and she ruins everything by switching her passion to me."

"No surprise. You're very much alike."

"I'm in no mood for jokes. And then Galatea turns out to be a succubus who doesn't know it and has her will of me in our sleep every night."

"No, no! They were dreams. Dreams!"

"Were they? Were they?" Manwright was having difficulty controlling his impatience with her damned obtuseness.

63

"How else did you get yourself pregnant, eh; *enceinte, gravida,* knocked up? Don't you dare argue with me, you impudent red saucebox! You know," he reflected, "there should have been a smidgen of Margaret Sanger in the programming. Never occurred to me."

He was back to his familiar impossible self, and everybody relaxed.

"What now, Reg?"

"Oh, I'll marry the snip, of course. Can't let a dangerous creature like Galatea out of the house."

"Out of your life, you mean?"

"Never!" Galatea shouted. "Never! Marry you, you dreadful, impossible, conceited, bullying, know-it-all, wicked man? Never! If I'm a demon, what are you? Come, Claudia."

The two women went very quickly upstairs.

"Are you serious about marrying Gally, Reg?"

"Certainly, Charles. I'm no Valera. I don't want a relationship with a popsy, no matter how perfect."

"But do you love her?"

"I love all my creations."

"Answer the question. Do you love Gally, as a man loves a woman?"

"That sexy succubus? That naïve demon? Love her? Absurd! No, all I want is the legal right to tie *her* to a stake every night, when I'm awake. Ha!"

Corque laughed. "I see you do, and I'm very happy for you both. But, you know, you'll have to court her."

"What! Court? That impertinent brat?"

"My dear Reg, can't you grasp that she isn't a child anymore? She's a grown young woman with character and pride."

"Yes, she's had you in thrall since the moment she was poured," Manwright growled. Then he sighed and accepted efeat. "But I suppose you're right. My dear Igor!"

"Here, mahth-ter."

"Please set up that table again. Fresh service, candles, owers, and see if you can salvage the monsters you created or the dinner. White gloves."

"No brainth, mahth-ter?"

"Not this evening. I see the Mouton Rothschild's been mashed. Another bottle, please. And then my compliments o Ms. Galatea Galante, and will she have the forgiveness to ine, *à deux*, with a most contrite suitor. Present her with a orsage from me . . . something orchidy. This will be a fun ecromance. Charles," he mused. "Parsley, sage, rosemary, nd thyme, *alevai*. Man and Demon. Our boys will be dev-s, sorcery says, and the girls witches. But aren't they all?"

NUMBER 13

By Stephen Robinett

I found their skeletons later. At first I was too busy with mission decisions to think about much else, too struck by the silence to anticipate anything but an empty ship.

Silence. After a millennium I expected noise. Things wear out. A bearing squeals a pained wail through the empty corridors, a malfunctioning air duct vents a slow hiss, an emergency Klaxon bleats. But when I pushed up the translucent blister covering the flotation tank and listened, I heard only silence, the ship as perfect as the day it left Earth orbit, a watch that's been ticking on time for a thousand years.

I stood up and wiped anabiotic slime off my body with both hands. When I stepped out of the tank, the static-charge shower activated itself. Even the shower functioned in silence. Abruptly I was clean, the nurturing soup of a five-year gestation vanishing completely from my skin in an instant.

I put on fresh coveralls and started for the bridge, padding barefoot over the cold metal floor plates, the whisper of my feet audible around me. On the bridge, I stood in front of the main console, surrounded by a panorama of blank and lifeless computer screens.

"Mission status. Visual information display."

Screens lit. Half displayed data on ship's systems and planetary approach. Half relayed the view outside. Ahead of me lay a world green and blue and swirled with white, almost Earth. Almost.

"Star system and planetary analysis."

Data overlaid the planet's image. I searched it for problems. Fifth planet of a G spectrum star . . . fourteen-hour rotation period . . . relatively uniform temperature gradient . . . oceans dense with local equivalents of algae and plankton . . . probably a breathable atmosphere . . . equatorial and polar landmasses . . . anomalous radiation emissions . . . recent and extensive outflowings of magma over both landmasses. (*Magma?*)

"Surface volcanic activity." Negative.

"Magnetic field data." I whistled in surprise at the number on the screen—two hundred gauss—as I said, "Only almost Earth." *Why so strong a magnetic field?*

"Planetary core data." *Bingo.* The planet's core, an outsized ball of molten iron, created a magnetic field two hundred times the strength of Earth's. Combined with the planet's fast spin, the strong magnetic field produced the anomalous radiation effects picked up by the ship's detectors. None of this necessarily made the planet uninhabitable. It did raise a caution flag.

I stared at the screen and thought about magma, trying to turn up some connection that the ship's planet-selection program might have missed. "Correlate ten-year weather data with magnetosphere data."

Bingo, again, but bingo, you lose.

The large core and fast spin gave the planet an unstable magnetic field. Every few years the field collapsed, transferring energy to the molten core and cracking the planet's crust. The landmasses ran red with the glowing blood of the planet. In short, the bottom had just dropped out of the local real estate market.

A feeling of sick disappointment swept over me. The situation left me no options.

"Abort approach. Reset long-range scans. Prime re-creation tanks for next cycle. And get that damned hunk of treacherous rock off the screens."

The ship queried my last instruction.

"Clear outside visual display."

Screens blanked out, a window closing, sealing me in.

"What now, guys?"

Silence answered from the screens, answer enough and an answer I already knew. A decision aborting a planetary approach amounted to a death sentence. The ship bypassed the planet and continued its slow search for a suitable colony world. The deciding officer lived out his life in the perfect and unchanging environment of the ship, his key mission decision behind him, a dribble of useless days ahead of him. As a re-creation of the original crew's First Officer, I knew the consequences of my decision as clearly as did my prototype a millennium ago on Earth, though he never considered the matter of much importance. Why would he? Aboard the ship only to train, he would never have to live out the consequences of an abort decision.

I did have one item to take care of: Claire. I was about to initiate her re-creation cycle when a noise interrupted me, a rumbling sound. I listened, almost hoping for a malfunction in some ship's system. Again it rumbled. Finally I identified it. A million million kilometers and a thousand years from anywhere, a man's stomach growled.

I decided Claire could wait. The condemned man deserve
a good meal.

I left the bridge and walked quickly toward the ship
galley. Only the occasional whisper of my footsteps on th
floor plates broke the oppressive silence. Impulsively I fe
tempted to order up a brass band from the ship's library.
liked the idea of the empty and receding corridors fille
with the reverberations of trombones, drums, and marcl
ing feet. The impulse passed. More than a brass band,
wanted Claire.

I turned in at the galley, already anticipating my fir
meal. I stopped short in the galley doorway, my appetit
fading. On the floor in front of me lay two skeletons, gra
bones picked clean by bacteria.

I knelt and examined them, one skeleton male, one fe
male. A thin blade of carbon steel, discolored the rust
brown of dried blood, protruded from the male's ribs. Th
female's neck was broken. One blow from the dying man

What happened? A domestic quarrel producing dome:
tic tragedy, a sudden explosion of long-repressed rage
perhaps triggered by a dispute over who would dice or
ions, who chop celery?

Though I stared impersonally at the bones on the galle
floor, I knew they were identical to my own, genetic dupl
cates, as had been the man himself, the man who aborte
the approach to some other world, the man who died wit
a knife in his heart.

And the woman? Undoubtedly Claire. In that, he ha
no choice. As landlords, the mission planners left some
thing to be desired. They allowed us long-term tenan
only one pet, sterile but, according to thousand-year-ol
psychological profiles, theoretically compatible.

I looked at the knife in the skeleton's ribs, arguably
lapse in our confidently predicted compatibility.

Still, the psychologists' decision bound him. Once he aborted the planetary approach, the ship allowed him only Claire. Everyone else, dead a thousand years on Earth, waited patiently to be born, piles of genes and engrams under the watchful care of the ship's double redundant systems. Why clutter their perfect ship with more useless lives than necessary? Give the old castaway Claire and forget about him.

I touched Claire's skeleton, nudging it. The rib cage rocked gently on the floor. I remembered long afternoon walks holding hands, long evenings talking, long nights making love. I remembered feelings, not love but a possibility of love. I remembered a complicated woman and quarrels.

I stood up and looked at the bones. The two skeletons faced each other as though, the moment of their violence passed, they lay down to die together.

I left the galley and walked the ship, brooding on these skeletons in my closet. Later, only half-aware of where I was, I looked up to find myself in the re-creation vault. I walked past the rows of tanks to Claire's and stood looking down at it like a man visiting a grave. I imagined a shape growing beneath the translucent blister, the shape of my companion, my friend, perhaps my murderer.

Did it always end the same? Did we always live out some sort of perfectly controlled experiment in human psychology, nature, nurture, and environment identical, everything identical, even the ending?

I left the re-creation vault and walked slowly through the empty corridors to my quarters. I lay down across my bunk, my head propped up with my hands, staring between my elbows at the small ship's console beside me, its blank screens echoing the larger console on the bridge.

"Ship's log. How many planetary approaches to date?"

A screen lit briefly, answering. Including my own, thirteen. Twelve other approaches, twelve other re-creations, twelve other decisions to abort, more important, twelve opportunities to watch identical rats run through an identical maze, to collect data and form conclusions, before I made any final decision about Claire.

"Ship's log. Replay planetary approach number one from the point of First Officer Colwin's tank exit."

Days passed. How many, I have no idea. Once I began searching the log, excavating the bones of the past, my life fell into a monotonous pattern of indistinguishable days and identical routine. I woke, ate, exercised, and slept. I searched the log, staring long hours at a soap opera starring me. I seldom went to the bridge and never looked at the stars outside, more interested in echoes from the past than in the silent future.

I left the skeletons on the galley floor as a reminder, a question partially answered. At meals I talked to them—Mr. and Mrs. Number Twelve—already dotty in my youth, talking to skeletons. I told them about the results of each day's excavation. They seemed less than interested, silent, their rib cages casting rib-cage shadows on the galley floor, a knife-blade shadow.

Gradually data emerged.

Once Claire outlived me; once I outlived her; once we died together in each other's arms after a long and happy live, the only violence between us an occasional cross word. Twice it ended with murder, but murder for different reasons and, to my surprise, with different murderers. In that, we took turns.

The longer I watched, the more despondent I became. I learned one thing quickly. It never ended the same. Twelve times the environment of the maze stayed the same. Twelve times the rats stayed the same. Yet twelve times it ended differently, with no ending any more predictable than any other. Even in later cycles, when I watched myself turn to the log for guidance—at times watching myself watch myself watching, a bleak and depressing hall of mirrors stretching back centuries—no pattern of improvement appeared. What had Number Twelve learned about how to avoid a knife in his heart? No wonder I talked to skeletons.

I hit bottom on the eleventh cycle. I watched Number Eleven leave the re-creation tank, discard a world of flesh-corroding rains, discover the previous log entries, and begin his search. I watched his growing frustration and confusion. I sympathized. I watched him complete his search and lean back across the bunk, a look of acute pain suffusing his face, like a mourner at the funeral of a life-long friend.

What went through his mind? That he knew everything he would ever know about the consequences of a decision to re-create Claire and still knew nothing but uncertainty? Perhaps. For men trained to evaluate data and decide, uncertainty brought pain.

I watched him get up, leave his quarters, and walk slowly to the bridge, the unvarying illumination of the corridors around him a reminder of the bland eternity before him. He reached the bridge and stood surrounded by the screens. Unexpectedly he ordered up a full outside view, something no one had done before him.

He ordered the bridge lights dimmed until he stood visible only by the light from the screens. Around him, unwavering stars shone, brilliant pinpoint specks against the blackness. I looked at his face. Tears, glistening in the starlight, ran down his cheeks. A heart-rending wail escaped his lips, pitiful and despairing, filling the empty ship. Later he chose a life alone and, miserable old man, died alone on the bunk where I lay watching him die.

When the screen finally blanked out, I sat a long time on the edge of the bunk, Number Eleven's despairing wail in my ears. I understood why he dimmed the bridge lights and ordered the outside view, opening the window to an infinity of stars, an infinity of possibilities. I understood his forlorn cry of utter desperation in the face of utter uncertainty. One thought kept me from joining that despair: the bones on the galley floor.

Why, knowing what we both knew, did Number Twelve choose to re-create Claire?

"Ship's log. Replay planetary approach number twelve from the point of First Officer Colwin's tank exit."

A twelfth time I watched myself emerge from the tank, trot to the bridge, and reject an almost-Earth. I watched myself order up a meal in the galley, eat, and go to my quarters. I watched myself find a skeleton in the doorway, the bones of Number Eleven.

My sense of futility deepened. Number Twelve was following the same well-worn path we all followed. He even left the bones in his quarters, propping them up as best he could in one corner and talking to them from time to time.

I indexed the log forward through Number Twelve's long days excavating the bones of our common past. Finally he arrived at Number Eleven's decision to live and die alone. Even secondhand, Number Eleven's sorrowful cry touched me, as though it were the uncomprehending moan of a child in pain.

Number Twelve watched it twice, sat back across the bunk, and looked at the skeleton in the corner, his expression more thoughtful than moved.

He shook his head slowly, "You were wrong, you old fool."

He pushed himself up from the bunk and left his quarters, retracing Number Eleven's path to the bridge. He stood on the bridge, surrounded by the screens, and ordered a full outside view. The infinity of the stars and their infinite possibilities filled the screens. He ordered the bridge lights dimmed, then extinguished. He stood a long time staring at the stars. Finally a sound came from him, inaudible at first, then louder, laughter.

He looked from screen to screen around the panorama of screens and laughed, his laughter as moving as Number Eleven's wail. Tears of laughter, glistening in the starlight, ran down his cheeks. He ordered the ship to initiate Claire's re-creation cycle.

I froze the image on the screen and lay back across the bunk, studying it. Frozen, out of context, it was impossible to tell whether the starlit tears came from laughter or despair, whether the face belonged to Number Eleven, Number Twelve, or even me. Nor did it matter.

I stood up, stretched, and yawned, at ease with myself for the first time in days, welcoming the uncertainty ahead of me. It never ended the same. I ordered the ship to leave the image permanently on the screen, then told it to initiate Claire's recreation cycle. I left my quarters and started for the galley. I still had a few other bones to get out of the way.

MEN LIKE US

By David Drake

There was a toad crucified against them at the head of the pass. Decades of cooking in the blue haze from the east had left it withered but incorruptible. It remained, even now that the haze was only a memory. The three travelers squatted down before the talisman and stared back at it.

"The village can't be far from here," Smith said at last. "I'll go down tomorrow."

Ssu-ma shrugged and argued, "Why waste time? We can all go down together."

"Time we've got," said Kozinski, playing absently with his ribs as he eyed the toad. "A lot of the stories we've been told come from ignorance, from fear. There may be no more truth to this one than to many of the others. We have a duty, but we have a duty as well not to disrupt needlessly. We'll wait for you and watch."

Smith chuckled wryly. "What sort of men would there be in the world," he said, "if it weren't for men like us?"

All three of them laughed, but no one bothered to finish

their old joke.

The trail was steep and narrow. The stream was now bubbling ten meters below, but in springtime it would fill its sharp gorge with a torrent as cold as the snows that spawned it. Coming down the valley, Smith had a good view of Moseby when he had eased around the last facet of rock above the town. It sprawled in the angle of the creek and the river into which the creek plunged. In a niche across the creek from the houses was a broad stone building, lighted by slit windows at second-story level. Its only entrance was an armored door. The building could have been a prison or a fortress were it not for the power lines running from it, mostly to the smelter at the riverside. A plume of vapor overhung its slate roof.

One of the pair of guards at the door of the power plant was morosely surveying the opposite side of the gorge for want of anything better to do. He was the first to notice Smith. His jaw dropped. The traveler waved to him. The guard blurted something to his companion and threw a switch beside the door.

What happened then frightened Smith as he thought nothing in the world could frighten him again: An air raid siren on the roof of the power plant sounded, rising into a wail that shook echoes from the gorge. Men and women darted into the streets, some of them armed, but Smith did not see the people, these people, and he did not fear anything they could do to him.

Then the traveler's mind was back in the present, a smile on his face and nothing in his hands but an oak staff worn by the miles of earth and rock it had butted against. He continued down into the village, past the fences and latrines of the nearest of the houses. Men with crossbows met him there, but they did not touch him, only motioned the traveler onward. The rest of the townsfolk gathered in an open area in the center of the town. It separated the detached houses on the east side from the row of flimsier structures built along the river. The latter obviously served as barracks, taverns, and brothels for bargees and smelter workers. The row buildings had no windows facing east, and even their latrines must have been dug on the riverside. A few people joined the crowd from them and from the smelter itself, but only a few.

"That's close enough," said the foremost of those awaiting the traveler. The local was a big man with a pink scalp. It shone through the long wisps of white hair that he brushed carefully back over it. His jacket and trousers were of wool, dyed blue so that they nearly matched the shirt of ancient polyester he wore underneath. "Where have you come from?"

"Just about everywhere, one time or another," Smith answered with an engaging grin. "Dubuque, originally, but that was a long time ago."

"Don't play games with the chief," hissed a somewhat younger man with a cruel face and a similar uniform. "You came over the mountains, and *nobody* comes from the Hot Lands."

Chief of police, Smith marveled as he connected the title and the shirts now worn as regalia. Aloud he said, "When's the last time anybody from here walked over the mountains? Ever?"

Bearded faces went hard. The traveler continued, "A hundred years ago, two hundred. It was too hot for you to go anywhere that side of the hills, but not now. Maybe I'll never sire children of my own, but I never needed that. I needed to see the world, and I have done that, friends."

"Strip him," the chief said flatly.

Smith did not wait for the grim-looking men to force him. He shrugged off his pack and handed it to the nearest of the guards armed with crossbows and hand-forged swords. He said, "Gently with it, friend. There's some of it that's fragile, and I need it to trade for room and board the next while." He began to unhook his leather vest.

Six of the men besides the chief wore the remnants of police uniforms over their jackets. They were all older—not lean warriors like the crossbowmen—but they carried firearms. Five of them had M16 rifles. The anodized finish of the receivers had been polished down to the aluminum by ages of diligent ignorance. The sixth man had a disposable rocket launcher, certain proof that the villagers here had at some time looted an army base—or a guardroom.

"Just a boy from the Midwest," Smith continued pleasantly, pulling out the tails of his woolen shirt. "I wanted to see New York City, can you believe that? But we'll none of live forever, will we?"

He laid the shirt, folded from habit, on his vest and began unlacing his boots of caribou leather. "There's a crater there now, and the waves still glow blue if there's even an overcast to dim the sun. And your skin prickles."

The traveler grinned. "You won't go there, and I won't go there again, but I've seen it, where the observation deck of the World Trade Towers was just about the closest mortal man got to heaven with his feet on man's earth. . . ."

"We've heard the stories," the chief grunted. He carried a stainless-steel revolver in a holster of more recent vintage.

"Trousers?" Smith asked, cocking an eyebrow at the women in dull-colored dresses.

The chief nodded curtly. "When a man comes from the Hot Lands, he has no secrets from us," he said. "Any of us."

"Well, I might do the same in your case," the traveler

agreed, tugging loose the laces closing the woolen trousers, "but I can tell you there's little enough truth to the rumors of what walks the wastelands." He pulled the garment down and stepped out of it.

Smith's body was wiry, the muscles tight and thickly covered by hair. If he was unusual at all, it was in that he had been circumcised — no longer a common operation in a world that had better uses for a surgeon's time. Then a woman noticed Smith's left palm, never hidden but somehow never clearly seen until that moment. She screamed and pointed. Others leveled their weapons, buzzing as a hive does when a bear nears it.

Very carefully, his face as blank as the leather of his pack, Smith held his left hand toward the crowd and spread his fingers. Ridges of gnarled flesh stood out as if they had been paraffin refrozen a moment after being liquified. "Yes, I burned it," the traveler said evenly, "getting too close to something the — something the Blast was too close to. And it'll never heal, no. But it hasn't gotten worse, either, and that was years ago. It's not the sort of world where I could complain to have lost so little, hey?"

"Put it down," the chief said abruptly. Then, to the guard who was searching the pack. "Weapons?"

"Only this," the guard said, holding up a sling and a dozen dense pebbles fitted to its leather pocket.

"There's a little folding knife in my pants pocket." Smith volunteered. "I use it to skin the rabbits I take."

"Then put your clothes on," the chief ordered, and the crowd's breath eased. "You can stay at the inn, since you've truck enough to pay for it" — he nodded toward the careful pile the guard had made of Smith's trading goods — "and perhaps you can find girls on Front Street to service you as well. There's none of that east of the Assembly here, I warn you. Before you do anything else, though, you talk to me and the boys in private at the station."

The traveler nodded and began dressing without embarrassment.

The police and their guards escorted Smith silently, acting as if they were still uncertain of his status. Their destination was a two-story building of native stone. It had probably been the town hall before the Blast. It was now the chief's residence as well as the government's headquarters. Despite that, the building was far less comfortable than many of the newer structures that had been designed to be heated by the stoves and lighted by lamps and windows. In an office whose plywood paneling had been carefully preserved — despite its shoddy gloominess — the governing oligarchs of the town questioned Smith.

They were probing and businesslike. Smith answered honestly and as fully as he could. Weapons caches? Looted by survivors or rotted in the intervening centuries. Food depots? A myth, seeded by memories of supermarkets and brought to flower in the decades of famine and cold that slew ten times as many folk as the Blast had slain directly. Scrap metal for the furnaces? By the millions of tons, but there would be no way to transport it across the mountains. And, besides, metals were often hot even at this remove from the Blast.

"All right," said the chief at last, shutting the handbook of waxed boards on which he had been making notes. The room had become chilly about the time they had had to light the sooty naphtha lamp. "If we think of more during the night, we can ask in the morning." His eyes narrowed. "How long are you expecting to stay?"

Smith shrugged. "A few days. I just like to . . . wander. I really don't have any desire to do anything else." He raised his pack by the straps and added, "Can one of you direct me to your inn?"

Carter, the youngest of the six policemen, stood. He was a blocky man with black hair and a pepper-and-salt beard. He had conducted much of the questioning himself. "I'll take him," he said. Unlike his colleagues, he carried a heavy fighting knife in addition to his automatic rifle. He held the door open for Smith.

The night sky was patchy. When the silver moon was clear, there was more light outside than the bud of naphtha cast within. The pall of steam above the power plant bulged and waned like the mantle of an octopus. Tiny azure sparks traced the power lines across the bridge and down into the smelter.

Smith thumbed at the plant. "They made light from electricity, you know? Before the Blast. You ever try that?"

His guide looked at him sharply. "Not like they did. Things glow, but they burn up when we can't keep all the air away from 'em. But you'd be smarter not to ask questions, boy. And maybe you'd be smarter to leave here a little sooner than you planned. Not to be unfriendly, but if you talk to us, you'll talk to others. And we don't much care for talk about Moseby. It has a way of spreading where it shouldn't."

The policeman turned through an open gate and up a raveled pathway. Rosy light leaked around the shutters of a large building on the edge of the Assembly. Sound and warm air bloomed into the night when he opened the door. In the mild weather the anteroom door was open within.

"Carter!" shouted a big man at the bar of the taproom. "Just in time to buy us a round!" Then he saw Smith and blinked, and the dozen or so men of the company grew quieter than the hiss of the fire.

"Friends, I don't bite," said Smith with a smile, "but do drink and I will sleep. If I can come to an agreemen with our host here, that is," he added, beaming toward th barman.

"Modell's the name," said the tall, knob-jointed local Neither he nor the traveler offered to shake hands, but he returned the other's smile with a briefer, professional on of his own. "Let's see what you have to trade."

The men at the bar made room as Smith arranged hi small stock on the mahogany. First the traveler set out a LP record, still sealed in plastic. Modell's lips moved si lently as his finger hovered a millimeter above the title "What's a 'Cher,'?" he finally asked.

"The lady's name," said Smith. "She pronounced i 'share.' " Knowing grunts from the men around him cho rused the explanation. "You've electricity here, I see. Per haps there's a phonograph?"

"Naw, and the power's not trained enough yet anyhow,' Modell said regretfully. His eyes were full of the jacke photograph. "It heats the smelters is all, and—"

"Modell, you're supposed to be trading, not runnin your mouth," the policeman interrupted. "Get on with it.'

"Well, if not the record, then—" Smith said.

"I might make you an offer on the picture," one of th locals broke in.

"I won't separate them, I'm afraid," Smith rejoined "and I won't have the record where it can't be used prop erly. These may be more useful, though I can't guarante them after the time they've been sitting. . . ." And he lai a red-and-green box of .30-30 cartridges on the wood.

"The chief keeps all the guns in Moseby besides these,' said Carter, patting the plastic stock of his M16. "It'll sta that way. And there's a righteous plenty of ammunitio for them already."

"Fine, fine," said Smith, unperturbed, reaching again to his pack. He removed a plastic box that whirred until a tiny green hand reached out of the mechanism to shut itself off. It frightened the onlookers as much as Smith's own radiation scars had. The traveler thoughtfully hid the toy again in his pack before taking out his final item, a GI compass.

"It always shows north, unless you're too close to iron," Smith said as he demonstrated. "You can turn the base to any number of degrees and take a sighting through the slot there, but I'll want more than a night's lodging for it."

"Our tokens are good up and down the river," one of the locals suggested, ringing a small brass disk on the bar. It had been struck with a complex pattern of lightning bolts on one side and the number 50 on the other. "You can redeem 'em for iron ingots at dockside," he explained, thumbing toward the river. "Course, they discount 'em the farther away you get."

"I don't follow rivers a great deal," the traveler lied with a smile. "Let's say that I get room and board—and all I care to drink—for a week. . . ."

The chaffering was good-natured and brief, concluding with three days' room and board, or—and here Smith nodded toward the stern-faced Carter—so much shorter a time as he actually stayed in the village. In addition, Smith would have all the provisions he requested for his journey and a round for the house now. When Modell took the traveler's hand, extended to seal the bargain, the whole room cheered. The demands for mugs of the sharp, potent beer drew the innkeeper when he would far rather have pored over his pre-Blast acquisition—marvelous, though of scant use to him.

The dealing over, Smith carried his mug to one of the stools before the fire. Sausages, dried vegetables, and a

pair of lanterns hung from the roof joists. Deer and el
antlers were pegged to the pine paneling all around th
room, and above the mantelpiece glowered the skull of
rat larger than a German shepherd.

"I wonder that a man has the courage to walk alone ov
there," suggested a heavy-set local who tamped his pip
with the ball of his thumb, "what with the muties and all

Smith chuckled, swigged his beer, and gestured with th
mug at the rat skull. "Like that, you mean? But that's old
The giant rats were nasty enough, I have no doubt, bu
they weren't any stronger than the wolves, and they were
good deal stupider. Maybe you'd find a colony now an
again in ruins downwind of a Strike, but they'll not ven
ture far into the light, and the ones that're left — no
many — are nothing that a slingstone or arrow can't cure
needs be." He paused and smiled. "Besides, their meat
sweet enough, I'm told."

Despite the fire, the other faces in the circle went pale
Smith's eyes registered the reaction while he continued t
smile. "Now travelers tell stories, you know," he said
"and there's an art to listening to them. There's littl
enough to joke about on the trail. So I have to do it here

His face went serious for a moment, and he added, "Bu
I'll tell you this and swear to the truth of it: When I wa
near what may have been Cleveland, I thought I'd caugh
a mouse rummaging in my pack. And when I fetched
out, it was no bigger than a mouse, and its legs wer
folded under it so it could hop and scurry the way a mous
can. But its head — there was a horn just there" — the trav
eler touched the tip of his nose — "and another littler on
just behind it. I figure some zoo keeper before the Blas
would have called me a liar if I'd told him what his rhino
would breed to, don't you think?"

He drank deep. The company buzzed at the wonder an

e easy fellowship of the man who had seen it.

"Scottie meant the half-men, didn't you, Scottie?" said
bulky man whose mustache and the beard fringing his
outh were dark with beer. He mimed an extra head with
s clenched fist. "Monsters like that in the Hot Lands."

Smith's head bobbed sagely against the chorus of grim
sent from the other men. "Sure, I know what you
ean," he said. "Two-headed men? Girls with an extra
ir of legs coming out of their bellies?"

Sounds of horror and agreement.

"You see," the traveler went on, "the Blast changed
ings, but you know as well as I do that it didn't change
em to be easier for men. There've always been children
orn as . . . monsters, if you will. Maybe more born now-
days than there were before the Blast, but they *were*
orn, and I've seen books that were old at the Blast that
lk of them. And they don't live now, my friends. Life
erywhere is too hard, and those poor innocents remind
lk of the Blast, and who would remember that?"

He looked around the room. The eyes that met his
opped swiftly. "There's been some born here in Moseby,
ven't there?" Smith asked, his words thrusting like knife
ades and no doubt in them. "Where are they now?"

The man they had called Scottie bit through the reed
em of his pipe. He spluttered, and the front legs of his
ool clacked on the puncheon floor.

"Say, now, I'm not here to pry," Smith continued
iftly. "What you do is your own business. For my own
rt, I'd appreciate another mug of this excellent beer."

Chairs scraped in agreement as all the men stood,
retched, and moved to the bar. Modell drew beer
noothly, chalking drinks on the board on the back wall —
eryone but Smith was a local. The innkeeper even
oached a new cask without noticeable delay. Several of

the company went out by the rear door and returned, lac-
ing their trousers. There was a brief pause as everyone settled back around the fire. Then Scottie swallowed,
scowled, and said belligerently, "All right, what about the
Changelings?"

"Pardon?" The traveler's eyes were friendly above the
rim of his mug, but there was no comprehension in them.

"Oh, come on!" the local said, flushing in embarrassment. "You know about the Changelings. Everybody does.
The Blast made them. They were men before, but now
they glow blue and change their shapes and walk around
like skeletons, all bones!" Scottie lowered his eyes and
slurped his beer in the silence. At last he repeated. "Everybody knows."

Gently, as if the suggestion did not appear as absurd to
him as it suddenly did to everyone else in the room, Smith
said, "I've seen some of the Strike Zones. I guess I've said
that. There's nothing there, friend. The destruction is total, everything. It isn't likely that anything was created by
the Blast."

"The Blast changed things. We can all agree there," said
Carter unexpectedly. Eyes turned toward the policeman
seated at one corner of the heart. "Random change,"
Carter continued to muse aloud. "That'll generally mean
destruction, yes. But there was a lot of power in the
bombs, and a lot of bombs. So much power that . . .
Who knows what they could have done?"

Smith looked at the policeman. He nodded again.
"Power, yes. But the *chance* that the changes, cell by cell,
atom by atom, would be . . . not destructive. That's a bil-
lion to one against, Mr. Carter."

"Well, the books say there were billions of men in the
world before the Blast," the policeman said, spreading the
fingers of his left hand, palm upward.

The traveler's scarred left hand mirrored the policeman's. "It's a wide world," he said, "as you must know and I surely do." He drank, smiled again, and said, "You're familiar with bombs, it would seem, friend. I've heard talk in my travels that there was a stockpile of bombs in the mountains around here. Do you know that story?"

Carter looked at Smith with an expression that was terrible in its stillness. "Modell," he said in the silence, "it's time to throw another log on the fire." He paused. The innkeeper scurried to do as directed. "And it's time," the policeman continued, "to talk of other things than the Blast. What sort of game do you find in the Hot Lands, for instance?"

"Well, I snare more than I knock on the head with my sling." Smith began easily, and the room relaxed a little.

They talked and drank late into the night. Smith told of gnarly woods and of following miles of trails worn no higher than a hog's shoulder. The locals replied with tales of their farms in the river bottoms, managed for them by hirelings, and the wealth they drew from shares in the smelter's profits. Few of them actually did any of the heavy, dangerous work of steel production themselves. Moseby was a feudal state, but its basis was the power plant, not land.

When Carter finally left, only Scottie and another local remained in company with Smith and Modell, and the talk grew looser. Finally Scottie wheezed, "They drift in here to Moseby, up the river and down. You're the first across the mountains, boy, I'll tell the world. We put 'em to work in the fields or the smelter, or they crew the barges for us. But they're not Moseby; they're not the Assembly. It's *us* who've got the power, under the chief and the police, that is. *We* keep the Light, and then—"

Modell touched the line of Scottie's jaw, silencing him. Scottie's surprise bloomed into awakened fright. "You've had enough tonight, old man," the innkeeper said. "Pook, you, too. Time for you both to get home and for me to get to bed."

"And me," Smith agreed. Modell had already brought out blankets and opened a side bench into a cot. "Though, first I'll take a leak and, say, a walk to settle my head. If you leave the door on the latch?"

Modell nodded dourly. "You've been listening to that fool Howes and his talk of the girls across the Assembly. Him with a wife and six children, too! Well, don't try to bring one back here with you. They should know better, but if one didn't, it'd be the worse for both of you." The innkeeper blew out one of the lamps and moved toward the other.

Smith urinated in the open ditch behind the building, letting his eyes readjust to the moonglow. Then he began to walk along the sewer with a deceptive purposelessness. In the shadow of the house nearest the creek he paused, eyeing the nodding guards across the gorge. The traveler took off his boots. He ducked into the ditch and used its cover to crawl down onto the creek bank.

The rock was steep, but it was limestone and weathered into irregularity enough for Smith's practiced fingers to grip. Smoothly, but without haste, the traveler slipped along below the line of sight on the guards at the power plant. When he reached the bridge trestles, he paused again, breathing carefully. His hands examined the nearest of the handsawn oak timbers, tracing it from where it butted into the rock to where it crossed another beam halfway to the stringers. Smith swung onto the trestle and began to negotiate the gorge like an ant in a clump of heavy grass.

Any sounds the traveler might have made were muffled by the creek. Smith edged left toward the west corner of the building. The wall there was built almost to the rim of the gorge. Smith's clothing matched the color of the wet stone so that his outline was at least blurred for a potential watcher from the village, but lack of alertness of the guards' part was his real defense.

Smith raised his head. Both guards were nodding in their chairs, crossbows leaning against the doorposts beside them. The traveler swung up lithely. A step later he was hugging the power plant's west wall. The stone hummed.

The building was as massive a construction as anything Smith had seen created after the Blast. The walls were dry stone, using the natural layering of limestone and their one-meter thickness to attain an adequate seal without mortar. Their weathered seams made it easy for someone of Smith's strength and condition to mount the five meters of blank wall to the lighted slits just below the roof. The interior was much as the traveler had expected it to be, much as he had seen it before here and there across the face of the world.

Six huge electric motors were ranked below him. They were being used as generators, driven by a complex pattern of shafts and broad leather belts. Only one of them was turning at the moment. When the smelters were working at full capacity and called in turn for the maximum output of the plant, the room would be a bedlam of machines and their attendants. Now one man and a woman were sufficient. The light of the naphtha lanterns illuminating the chamber may have exaggerated the attendants' pallor, but they certainly saw less of the sun than the villagers across the stream did. It was hard to believe that control of this apparatus was left to slaves, yet it was even more unlikely that freemen who knew what they were doing would enter the chamber below.

In the center of the north wall, built against the living rock of the mountainside, was the reactor.

Its genesis was evident, for the black hulls of ten fusion bombs were ranged along the partition wall to the east. Smith, his head framed in the narrow window, licked his lips when he saw the bombs. They would no longer be weapons; the plutonium of their fission cores would have decayed beyond the capacity to form critical mass when compacted. But those cores, taken from their cocoons of lithium hydride and the inner baths of deuterium, could still fuel a reactor.

The latter was an ugly mass of stone blocks, overshadowed by a mantislike derrick. Steam from the reactor drove the pistons of a crude engine. Unlike the pre-Blast electric motors, the steam engine had been manufactured for its present purpose. Inefficient, it leaked vapor through seams and rope gaskets, but the power to create steam from water was virtually inexhaustible on the scale required here.

Manufacturing skill and not theoretical knowledge had frequently been the brake on human progress. Leonardo da Vinci could design a workable aircraft, but no one for four hundred years could build an engine to drive it. Nuclear-power technology was so simple, given the refined fuel and expendable humans to work it, that an age that could not manufacture smokeless powder could nonetheless build a fission plant. All it would have taken was a weapons stockpile and a technician or two from Oak Ridge, vacationing in the mountains at the time of the Blast.

It was what Smith had come to learn.

There was a new sound in the night. A score or more of men were thudding across the bridge to the power plant. Smith ducked his head beneath the sill of the window. As he did so, the siren on the roof hooted ferally. Knowing that there was no escape downward if he had been seen, the traveler slipped sideways and began to clamber up between a pair of the windows. As his fingers touched the edge of the slates, a voice from below shouted, "There he is!"

Smith gathered himself to swing onto the gently sloped roof; something tapped his knuckles. He looked up. The muzzle of Carter's M16 stared back at him. The policeman smiled over the sights. "I saw something block one of the plant windows," the local man said. "Thought it might be worth waking the guards for. Now, *friend*, you just climb down easy to where the people are waiting, or me and the boys here won't wait for the ceremony."

The pair of guards flanking Carter had faces as tense as their cocked crossbows. Smith shook his head ruefully and descended into the waiting manacles.

The siren gave three long cries as the guards marched Smith back across the bridge. Citizens, warned by the initial signal, began walking out of their houses, the men armed, the women bleak as gray steel. They drifted toward the shrouded platform across the long axis of the Assembly from the bridge. None of the citizens seemed to want to be the first to reach the common destination. They dawdled in pairs and trios, turning aside as Smith and his captors passed among them.

The chief and the remaining policemen had hurried up the steps to what was clearly a covered altar by the time

Smith reached it. Cords fluttered as the canvas roof was gathered within the screen of hoardings built on a base of stone blocks. Something mechanical purred and paused. Sparks hissed about the power line strung to the platform along a line of low posts on the western edge of the Assembly.

"On up," Carter said, smiling. He tweaked Smith's manacles toward the steps. The guards were taking position at the base of the altar, facing out toward the Assembly. Despite the siren calls, there was no sign of life or movement from the smelter and its associated buildings. Their blank walls were more than a physical reminder of the grip the freeholders of Moseby held on the minds and lives of those who would work in their village. The business tonight was no business of a bargee or a factory hand.

Smith mounted the steps. Two policemen received him, holding their rifles by the pistol grips as if they were still functional weapons. Well, perhaps they were.

There were other improbable things in this place.

The moonlight was shadowed by the flimsy walls. It gave only hints of the enclosed area: the policemen in their ragged uniforms; two large, vertical cylinders, the one mounted somewhat higher than the other; and, at the front of the platform, a wooden block the height of a man's knee.

"There," muttered one of the policemen, guiding the traveler's neck onto the block. No force was necessary. Smith was as docile as a babe at its mother's breast. Carter took a quick lashing from Smith's right wrist to a staple set for the purpose in the flooring. "If it wasn't that you know too much," the policeman said conversationally, "we'd let you spend the rest of your life inside the plant. But somebody who's traveled as you have, seen what you have . . . we don't want to be like Samson, chaining you in the temple so you can bring it down on us, hey?"

"Tie him, and we'll get this over with," the chief growled.

Carter unlocked the manacles and bound Smith's left wrist to another staple. "It was a good idea when they chopped muties here every week," he said. "It's a good idea now. The ceremony reminds us all that it's us against the world and all of us together. I'll take the ax if you like."

Smith, facing the panels, could not see the exchange. The air licked his neck and cheek as something passed from hand to hand between the men. "Drop the walls," the chief ordered, "and turn on the light."

The pins locking together the corners of the hoardings slipped out. The panels arced down simultaneously in a rush of air and a collective sigh from the Assembly. The purring of an electric motor awoke under the platform, rising and becoming sibilant in the absence of competing sound. A taut drive belt moaned; then the moan was buried in a sudden crackle, and white light played like terror across the upturned faces.

Smith twisted his head. The policemen stood in a line across the width of the platform. Carter, in the middle, gripped the haft of a fire ax. Its head was still darkened by flecks of red paint. He grinned at the traveler. Behind the rulers of the village glared another burst of lightning between the static generator's heads: the polished casings of a pair of fusion bombs. No objects could have been more fittingly symbolic of Moseby's power. The Van de Graaff generator provided a crude but effective way of converting electricity to light. Its DC motor pulled a belt from which electrons were combed into one bomb casing. The static discharges to the grounded casing were all the more spectacular for being intermittent.

"You still have a chance to save yourselves if you let me go," said Smith, shouting over the ripping arcs. "There is no punishment too terrible for men who would use atomic power again, but you still have time to flee!"

Carter's smile broadened, his teeth flickering in light reflected onto his face. He roared, "We dedicate this victim to the power that preserves us all!" and he raised his ax.

"You fool," the traveler said quietly. He did not try to slide back from the block, even as he watched a multiple discharge strobe the edge of the descending ax. The hungry steel caught him squarely, shearing like a shard of ice through his flesh. His vertebrae popped louder in his ears than the hollow report of the blade against the wood. The ax head quivered, separating all but a finger's breadth of the traveler's neck. He blinked at Carter.

The policeman rocked his blade free. Static discharges sizzled behind him at three-second intervals. Smith felt a line of warmth as his Blast-changed flesh knitted together again while the steel withdrew.

Still kneeling, the Changeling turned toward the crowd. "People!" he shouted. "Whatever it costs men today, men tomorrow must know that nuclear power is death! It made this world what it is. It is the one evil that cannot be tolerated, ever again! For Man's sake, for the world's—"

Screaming, Carter slammed the ax down on the traveler's temple. The blade bit to the helve. Smith reached up with his right hand, tearing the staple from the flooring. He gripped the wood, and it splintered as he drew the ax from where it was lodged in his bone. The Changeling stood, his head flowing together like wax in a mold. His left wrist re-formed as the rawhide lashing cut through it.

Sparks like shards of sunlight clawed through the high windows of the power plan. That gush of light died. The siren began to wind, higher and higher. The motor of the

Van de Graaf generator was speeding also, the current that drove it no longer controlled. The arcs were a constant white sheet between the bomb casings. Someone—two figures—crossed the bridge from the power plant. The blue glow from the building backlighted them.

"Flee!" Smith cried, lifting to the crowd the scarred hand he had thrown up two centuries before to the flare of a hundred-megaton bomb. "Flee this abomination before it devours you—as it surely will, as it did the world before this world!"

Carter screamed again and struck with his rifle butt, hurling the Changeling off the platform. Smith picked himself up. The guards backed away from him, their eyes wide, their cocked bows advanced as talismans and not threats.

The two figures on the bridge threw back their cloaks. The lapping arcs played across the half of Kozinski's face and torso that was naked bone. The bare organs pulsed within, and his one eye darted like a black jewel. The Blast had sometimes preserved and had sometimes destroyed; this once it had done both in near equality.

Ssu-ma would have stood out without the artificial lighting. She had the same trim, beautiful figure as the girl she had been the night she stared into the sky above Lop Nor and saw dawn blaze three hours early. Now that figure shone blue, brighter even than the spreading fire that ate through the wall of the power plant behind her.

The crowd was scattering toward homes and toward the river. No one approached the platform except the two Changelings walking toward their fellow.

The chief threw up his revolver and snapped it three times, four, and at the fifth attempt an orange flash and the thump of a shot in the open air. Five of the policemen were triggering their automatic weapons and tugging at the cocking pieces to spill misfired rounds on the platform. But the old guns could still fire. Shots slapped and tore at the night in short bursts that pattered over the flesh of the Changelings like raindrops on thick dust. And still they came, walking toward Smith and the platform.

Incredibly, the antitank rocket ignited when the sixth policeman tugged its lanyard. In ignorance he was holding the tube against his shoulder like a conventional weapon. The back-blast burned away the man's arm and chest in a ghastly simulacrum of Kozinski's mutilation. The rocket corkscrewed, but chance slammed it into Ssu-ma's chest. The red blast momentarily covered the Changeling's own fell glow. Her body splattered like the pulp of a grapefruit struck by a maul. Simultaneously the front wall of the power plant tore apart, snuffing the arcs dancing madly between the bomb casings.

Then, evident in the sudden darkness, the bits of Ssu-ma's glowing protoplasm began to draw together like droplets of mercury sliding in the bowl of a spoon. Her head had not been damaged. The waiting eyes smiled up at the platform.

Only Carter still stood before the casings. He had thrust the muzzle of his M16 into his mouth and was trying to fire the weapon with his outstretched finger. The round under the hammer misfired.

The power plant exploded again, a gout of lava that loosened the hillside beneath it and sprayed the village. Wood and cloth began to burn in a pale imitation of what was happening across the creek. In slagging down, the reactor was fusing the rock and the hulls of the remaining bombs. Plutonium flowed white-hot with its own internal reactions, but it was spread too thin to self-trigger another

Blast. The creek roared and boiled away as the rain of rock and molten metal spewed into it. The vapor that had been a plume over the power plant was now a shroud to wrap the burning village.

"I hadn't called you yet," Smith said, shouting over the tumult as he clasped Kozinski's hand with his own left hand. He extended his right to the smiling Ssu-ma.

"We heard the siren," the Ukrainian said, his voice strange for coming from a mouth that was half bone—the half that had been turned away from the Strike that vaporized his infantry company, he had once explained.

"We could all tell they weren't burning coal, couldn't we?" Susu-ma added.

The three travelers began groping through the night, through the smoke and the screaming. "I don't think we've ever checked whether the Oconee plant was still operable," Smith said. "It'd be a good time to see."

Kozinski shrugged. "We ought to get back to England some time. It's been too long since we were there."

"No, there's time for that." Smith argued. "Nobody there is going to build a fission plant as long as there's one man left to tell what we did when we found the one at Harewell."

A pair of burning buildings lighted their path, sweeping the air clear with an angry updraft. Kozinski squinted, then reached out his hand to halt Ssu-ma. "Your birthmark," he said, pointing to the star-shaped blotch beneath the girl's left breast. "It used to be on the right side."

She shrugged. "The rocket just now, I suppose."

Kozinski frowned. "Don't you see? If we can change at all, we can die someday."

"Sure," Smith agreed. "I've got some white hairs on my temples. My hair was solid brown the . . . when I went to New York."

"We'll live as long as the world needs us," Ssu-ma said quietly, touching each of the men and guiding them onward toward the trail back through the mountains. The steam and the night wrapped them, muffled them. Through it her words came: "After all, what sort of men would there be in the world if it weren't for men like us?"

And all three of them spoke the final line of the joke, their voices bright with remembered humor: "Men like us!"

I AM THE BURNING BUSH

By Gregg Keizer

I am the Dead Man.

I could feel the texture of the rope as it dug into the flesh around my neck. It was not the first time that I had died for lifers, but it was not the best time, either. It was to be a simple death, only a hanging. Nothing spectacular.

They think I do not feel the pain, but I do. The pain is always the same, like a white-hot needle through my lips. It was the same now, even though it had been over a year since I'd last died in front of them. For a year I had experienced the private deaths, dying only for myself, loathing the memories of their lifer touches. But something had driven me back to them again. I remembered now that it wasn't the pain. Perhaps it was the way their eyes went wide when I walked into a room. Or maybe it was only their money.

For a moment, as I saw my feet arc in the air, seemingly reaching for the knotted rope, I forgot that I would be alive again. I tried to scream but couldn't get anything past the hemp that clamped my throat.

Thankfully, blissfully, I blacked out.

I opened my eyes, and everything was blurred, as if I were drunk on alcohol and reeling around the room. I realized that I still twirled on the end of the rope. It was only uncomfortable now. Someone handed me a knife; I reached up and cut myself down. I landed on the thick carpet that seemed to live under everything here.

The twisting colors, red to green to rusted scrap in a browning field, swept through me, and I knew now why I couldn't stop dying in front of them. I could feel. I could smell the sweat of my body. I touched my neck gently, slowly, marveling at the feeling as my fingertips brushed the skin. I was surprised I'd been able to stay away for a whole year and knew I'd never be able to again.

My mind seemed to freeze the scene around me in split-second frames. I felt warm and relaxed, as if I'd just had an excellent brandy or had finished making love. Every particle of my body sparkled inside, knowing that it was alive, unmarked, and whole. The sensations I had felt during my private deaths paled in my memory.

I even felt a pinch of kindness toward the lifers around me, another symptom of resurrection. I stroked my wrist, my thigh, knowing, without looking, where they were. I could now hear the whispers of the lifers. Before I had had to read their lips. I was alive, sensitive again. Except for my eyes, the disease overpowers all my sensory organs when I am between deaths. Only death restores my senses to me. It even enhances them.

I knew the satiated feeling in my belly would soon be replaced by nausea. I would want to vomit, but I would only be able to spit into my hand and wipe my hand on my tunic. Then I would not even feel the spittle. I would slip into the deprivation I felt between deaths. But that time was hours away, and I could *feel* again, more than I have ever felt when I've died alone, for myself. I inhaled deeply and looked up.

The lifers around me applauded softly as I took the rope from around my neck and threw it on the floor in front of me. The semicircle that pinned me in the corner was front-ranked with women, some of them daring to touch the edges of my clothing. One of them, sloppily made up and wearing clothes too cheap for this party, went so far as to stroke the skin of my neck. Still feeling confused from the resurrection, I said nothing to her. I only wondered how she had managed to get in. Like the rest of the lifers around me, she had the shiny-eyed look of a fingertoucher and whispered in that familiar hoarse croak that the drug creates. The hostess, her dress adorned with tiny jewels, pushed her way through the crowd and clutched my arm tightly.

"Wasn't that the best?" she yelled above her guests' voices. I looked at her, I felt her fingers knead my arm, and I almost pushed her away. But she had paid for it, all of it.

"I've heard of better deaths," said a man who'd made his way over to me. He had his arms crossed over his chest, and I could see his eyes glittering from fingertouch. The lifers had become silent, waiting for me to respond. I turned my back on him and faced the hostess again.

"You invite critics?" I asked her.

"I apologize for him," she said. "You can see he has pressed too much fingertouch." She looked at me. "He'll be asked to leave in a few minutes." I could hear some of the lifers mutter in agreement.

Silently the lifers came to me, one by one, and kissed the hand I held out to them. Their lips rasped against my knuckles, and one woman's tongue wetted a finger. Some of them do that, hoping it will increase the chance of infection. They all looked at me expectantly, with that lifer expression of mingled excitement and awe. But I couldn't speak. I couldn't say it. The woman standing next to me squeezed my arm, but I kept silent. She finally tired of waiting.

"I have shown you," she said, using the words I should have used. "Follow me."

The lifers started whispering again, and the hostess relaxed, her hand curled loosely around my arm.

"That's Crandel, of the department stores," she whispered to me, pointing to a man walking toward us. "I was so lucky to get him to come tonight. Talk to him for me." Then she left me, her body moving fluidly around the room, touching everyone with a press of fingertouch, saying good-bye.

"I enjoyed it very much. I have wanted to meet you for some time," Crandel said, standing in front of me. I noticed that his blue eyes were not lit by fingertouch.

"Thank you," I said, delighting in the sound of his voice, yet wanting to be left alone with my reborn senses. I looked up, but the hostess was busy chatting on the opposite side of the room.

"I got my license only yesterday," he said. "I was lucky to get in tonight. What's it like anyway?"

I remembered the colors, the freeze-framing, the touch of a finger on skin, and the warmth. "It's like eating too many sweets." I always give frivolous answers, but they never notice.

"I've done everything else, I guess. They say it feels delicious. Better than fingertouch." He paused, his eyes looking at my hand. I knew he wanted to touch me again, but I could permit it only once. "You were captain on the ship," he said.

They all think I was the captain. "No. Weapons officer," I said, my words quick. He shrugged, as if it didn't matter.

"What are my chances of infection?" he asked, trying to disguise his feelings.

"Same as everyone else's," I said, looking for the hostess again.

"Is there no way to increase the chance?" he began. They all come to that question before long. He looked hungrily at my face.

"No," I said, my reborn senses allowing me to feel contempt. It tasted like tainted meat in my mouth.

I watched him press a pinch of fingertouch into the skin around his lips. His eyes — lifer eyes now — gleamed.

"Since the ice is broken, who wants to go first?" the hostess called from across the room, loudly enough so that even those in the back could hear.

"Excuse me," Crandel said softly, pulling away. I thought someone had called to him, but he walked to the window. Glancing back, he bowed slightly, then opened the window wide.

"I wish you a good death," he said. "Wish me the same." I could have mouthed the words I've heard so many lifers speak.

He climbed onto the sill, shoving the curtains aside with one hand and using the other to grip the frame. Then he stepped over the edge and was gone. I thought I could hear a scream as he fell to the ground fifty floors below, but I wasn't really sure.

I made my way to another corner, away from the lifers who were perfunctorily killing themselves. The hostess tried to touch me again, but I pulled away from her. I found a drink on a table and sipped its sourness while I watched them commit suicide one by one. They weren't very creative; I've died so many times, in almost every way. They were lifers, registered suicides, approved by the government. They knew what they were doing. They lusted for immortality through their death and hoped they would acquire the disease that raged within me and made me a DeadMan. They wanted to die and resurrect, to be like me.

Suddenly a woman was by my elbow. She held a thin knife in her hand and looked at it intently.

"Are you going to do it here?" I asked. She nodded, still looking at the knife. "Why do it by me?"

"Why not?" she replied.

"Why do it anyway?" I watched her and sipped my drink.

She smiled and opened her mouth as if to answer me. Instead, she brought the knife to her throat and slit it. The blood spattered my tunic, and she thumped to the floor.

I turned from her and concentrated on my body's putting itself together again. The scenes of violence in the room swept before me. I could still feel the sparkle of my resurrection, although not as strongly.

They call us deaders, DeadMan, undead, vampires, regeneratives, regens, and other names I like even less. My body cannot die. It displays the symptoms, but its cells regenerate almost as quickly as they are destroyed. I am, in effect, immortal. I can die and resurrect within minutes. I have died three hundred seventy-three times for them, including the hanging tonight. I have died thousands of times more for myself, but I do not tally those deaths.

The parasitic disease that I and my five shipmates brought back from that hell world mutated somehow when we came home and made us DeadMan. The parasite keeps its host alive, not letting us truly die. Only when it is busy regenerating cells does it release its grip on our senses. We found that out on the return trip, the first time one of us tried to kill himself. We can infect others, but only rarely and only immediately after death — our own temporary deaths and the lifers' usually permanent ones. The meds have no cure. Lifers swarm around us, touching us, hoping to catch the disease and live forever. They know little of what they desire. They do not realize what they must relinquish if they do succeed in catching the disease and becoming immortal. Their sensations will wither, as mine did. They are so eager to discard them in exchange for immortality. Perhaps that is why they are so distasteful to me.

Barely one out of a hundred becomes immortal. And the immortals we create cannot infect others. The infection mutates again in its second generation. Only the crew of the *Acheron*, the six DeadMan, can bestow immortality.

And only through death can we feel and taste and smell. And only in front of lifers can we feel more than a semblance of the sensations we once had.

"Your death was exquisite," a voice whispered beside me. "How do you do it?" I looked down. It was a girl, perhaps seventeen or so, with a bowl of fingertouch powder in her hands. Her eyes reflected every light in the room.

"How do you come to life again?" she asked, a bit more loudly now. "My name is Lynx. What is yours?"

"DeadMan," I answered, smiling at her. I shook my head when she lifted the bowl a little. I stay away from fingertouch. It's a lifer drug. It's not for DeadMan.

"No, no, no, I mean your real name, the one that your friends call you, the one—"

"I don't give my name to lifers," I said.

"How do you do it?" she asked again.

"It just works," I said. I thought she would be satisfied

with that.

"You don't know how you—"

"You ask too many questions, lifer."

She seemed confused and weaved slowly in place. I thought she was going to fall, but she steadied herself by putting a hand on my arm. Carefully I lifted it off and let it drop to her side. She hadn't paid for me, and so I didn't have to let her touch me.

"Are you going to kill yourself, too?" I asked.

She giggled, looking up at me with reflecting eyes. "I don't think I can. I've got the papers and everything, but I don't know whether I can go through with it." She paused for a moment, dipped a finger into the powder, and pressed it against her forehead. I watched her rub the fingertouch deep into her pores. She reached out and stroked my arm and my wrist. I glanced at her hand, and she pulled it away. My skin was cold where she had touched it. "I mean, it's pretty permanent, isn't it?"

"For you it most probably is," I said.

I picked up another drink, stepping over the bodies that patterned the floor. There was only a handful of lifers still alive in the room, but most were trying to kill themselves. The more zoned ones were having trouble holding the knives and blasters or finding the windows. I leaned against a wall, wondering whether any here would become infected and live forever.

A man stumbled and fell on an upturned blade held by a corpse. I smiled at myself. Stupid, one-death-is-all-you've-got lifers.

I was playing with my newest pinner in the game room when the call buzzed for me. I ignored it and finished the round before shutting off the machine. Its silvered surface darkened as the call buzzed again. Perhaps it was a client. I let it buzz anyway.

The pinner's power cord was badly frayed, but I pulled hard on it, jerking it out of the socket. I plugged another game into it, switched it on, and ran up a good score. The buzzing didn't stop.

I couldn't concentrate on the game. So I went to my window and looked out over the city. I'd broken the railing long ago and had never replaced it. I grasped the window frame. Crandel's eyes gleamed in my memory. I wanted to feel the dim sparkle of a private death, but I'd promised myself I'd have only one each day. The residue of the death I'd had two hours before lingered, but it was fading. I could hear, but I could not feel my fingers.

I must have been standing there for a long time before I heard the door open behind me. I had never had a lifer in my house before. I found out that they are not in the habit of knocking before entering.

"Bin?" she asked. It was the girl from the party — Lynx was her name.

I nodded, wondering who had told her my name. It couldn't have been the hostess from the night before. She had drowned herself in the bath.

"Can I come in?" The open door was already a bright square of light behind her.

I stepped back as she closed the door, wondering whether she would leap for me and try to clasp her body around mine in order to increase her chance of contamination. Twice lifers have tried that, but I sidestepped them both. Her eyes weren't shiny with fingertouch, yet I didn't think she was perfectly straight, either.

"I've got a license to kill myself," she declared, grinning.

"So?"

"I'd like you to help me. I can't do it myself." She touched the top button of her tunic, playing with it for a moment.

She stood still while I laughed. I turned my back on her and walked to the bar. I fixed a drink, not bothering to offer her one.

"Get out of here, lifer," I hissed. "You haven't got enough to pay me."

"Yes, I do; yes, I do. Here. See?" She held a fistful of crumpled bills toward me. They were all hundred-credit notes.

"Not enough, lifer. I kill only myself. Get one of your friends to do it for you." I began laughing at her again.

"Don't do that," she begged. I couldn't stop. "I said, don't do that," she repeated, pulling a needle gun out of another pocket.

I glanced at the gun. "What are you going to do? Kill me? Even the quickest poison won't work, lifer."

She let the gun drop to her side. The credit notes fluttered to the floor, but she made no move to pick them up.

"Please help me, Mr. Bin. You're the only one I know who can help me." She licked her lips, and I thought I saw a tear in the corner of one eye, but, then, it could've been the start of a fingertouch zone.

I shook my head slowly, waiting for the one question that lifers always ask. Perhaps she truly could not kill herself, but I doubted it. She was only more brazen in her desire to increase the possibility of contamination, believing that the touch of my hands as I killed her would give her a greater chance of immortality. Idly I wondered whether killing a lifer *would* increase the chance of the disease's leaping from me, but I let the thought fade. The image of putting my hands on lifer skin sickened me.

It has always amazed me how eager lifers are to die. "Get out, Lynx."

She turned and went to the door, her arms limp and her walk almost a shuffle. She had one hand on the door handle when she looked back at me.

"I have always admired you, DeadMan. Ever since I can remember, I've worshiped you. How you come back after each death. How you die with such grace, such calm."

"It won't work, lifer," I said. "You'll have to do it yourself. You can't pay me enough to make me help you die."

The door slammed as she left. I spent the next half-hour picking up the credit notes, counting and shuffling them into neat piles. In my opinion, whatever a man finds in his own house is his.

This party was even more opulent than the one the night before. It had to be, because it was Hansa's party.

I looked into her eyes as she held my hands in hers. She smiled slyly, gripping my fingers hard in greeting. I had had a private death before coming, and its sensations dully remained. I glanced away from her gaze and started counting eyes around the room. People always paid attention to what Hansa did, and there were almost as many looking at her as there were watching me. I shrugged to myself. Did it matter what a lifer thought of me? Hansa pointed out the city councilman and the area's fingertouch pusher, making sure I knew who they were. They were to have the best possible view when I died, she told me.

Fingertouch was drifting around the room, as if it were ash left on the ground after a fire. I actually saw one man, already zoned into oblivion, throw a small bowl of the stuff into the air and watch it float to the carpet. The press of people around Hansa and me was too thick to get through, and so I had to wait until a waiter went by with a tray of touch and a single glass on it. Hansa had remembered my eccentric taste for alcohol.

I could feel her thigh press against mine as she talked to

some of her guests. I let her do what she wanted. It was her party, and she had paid me enough to keep me quiet for the night. I looked at her again and noticed the scars around her neck where she had once tied a rope around it. That was the only time she had tried to kill herself, as far as I knew. Hansa threw parties for the lifers, but she didn't take the final step with them at night's end. Perhaps that was one of the reasons why I was glad whenever she hired me.

I turned to look at the crowd again and saw Lynx, that little bitch. She was on the other side of the room, and so I couldn't see whether her eyes were glossy or not, but I knew she had been watching me. I saw her turn her head quickly when I spotted her. I rubbed the palms of my hands down the sides of my pants. Somehow she made me nervous.

The fingertouch pusher stood in front of me, blocking my view of Lynx. "How can I be a DeadMan?" he asked. "I heard I can be one if I die right. I'll pay you whatever you want."

His forehead was gray for the overdose of fingertouch he had pressed into his skin. He wouldn't die tonight; he was too zoned to do anything lethal to himself.

"Leave me alone," I said.

"But Hansa said you'd talk to me."

"Hansa was wrong. No lifer can be a DeadMan." Suddenly I wished it were true. Hansa wasn't paying me enough for this.

After a half-hour of small talk with her guests, Hansa got them to clear a circle for me. The ones in front pressed a final bit of fingertouch into their skin. I smiled to them all, knowing that three quarters of them were having a hard time focusing on me. I had counted on that when I had planned my deaths for this party. I had an attention getter to lead things off.

I sat in the cleared spot, the legs of the lifers encircling me. I pulled out a small glass bottle from my tunic pocket, took out the stopper, and poured the liquid over my head and shoulders. The fumes were overpowering and smelled somewhat sweet. I looked at the legs around me through a shimmering wave of fumes. Then I pulled out the match.

I always seem to hesitate before I go through with it, wondering why I cannot be satisfied with my private deaths. This time was not unlike any other. Perhaps it was in my mind, the certainty that I felt more, tasted more, when I died in front of them. We had spoken of it, Kiel, Sarreen, Fede, Langley, Tonner, and I, when we discovered the extent of the damage to our senses caused by the disease. They all felt more, too, in front of the lifers. The meds could not find a reason, but it was true. So we died for them in order to feel more and feel it longer.

I held the small piece of wood that I had found in an antiques store and studied it for several minutes, taking in the colors of the wood and the blue tip. Then the hesitation passed, and I could only hope that the thing would light when I struck it.

It did. I heard myself screaming as the gasoline caught and I burst into flame.

My God, I hadn't known it would be like this. Stop it, please, stop it. Not my eyes, no no, not my eyes. Oh, God damn it, it's gotten into my eyes.

But the sense of being alive in every cell, every particle, was the same as always when I awoke. I saw the brilliant colors with eyes that were untouched and watched the room flicker, frame by frozen frame. I was sure at that instant that the lifers expected something like this when they killed themselves. But most would never see and feel this. Most would never resurrect, as I did.

I died for them twice more that night, killing myself again before the nausea came. After each death, lifers kissed my hand, said their words, and then some killed themselves. Their numbers diminished, but it was a large party. Each time I awoke was better than the last. The rust in front of my eyes got more detailed after each death. The lifers became quieter each time I awoke from the dead. By the end of the third death, the ones still left stood four meters from me. They looked at me, of course. They never stop doing that. But they would not talk to me or touch the charred fragments of my clothing. They touched their faces with the gray dust from the bowls that still circulated around the room. Not even Hansa dared stand next to me after I died that third time.

"Good work, DeadMan," someone giggled from a corner. Everyone in the room turned to see who it was. Lynx stepped through the small assemblage and came toward me. She had a blaster in her hand, which she pointed at me. An uncontrollable chill swept up my back.

"Won't you talk to me?" she asked, moving the dark end of the blaster in a small circle, its circumference my skull. Hansa made a movement forward, and Lynx edged the blaster to let her know she could swing it fast enough. Hansa backed away.

I had been silent the whole time, watching Lynx and the weapon she held. If she pulled the trigger, it would be an inconvenience to me, nothing more. But she had no right to threaten me, much less kill me. Only a DeadMan may kill a DeadMan.

"Now we'll talk, DeadMan," she said quietly, her fingers tracing the curves of her breasts as she stared at me.

"No deals," I said.

"I haven't even asked you anything yet." She seemed to be pouting. The expression made her hideous. Her fingers still played with the fabric of her blouse.

"You're going to ask me if I'll help you walk off the window ledge, or if I'll light the match for you. I told you before, no deals with lifers. I kill only myself."

"What have you got against me?" She let the mouth of the blaster droop, and I stepped forward. She flicked it back up and melted a hole in the floor a few centimeters from my feet. I stopped. Her voice was so casual that she might have been holding a drink in her hand. "I can't do it by myself. I need someone to guide me through. You've been there before; you can show me. I want to do it while I'm young. I don't want to live forever in an old body." She looked up expectantly. They all believe *they* will be the one to steal the disease and resurrect after their suicide. "Not one of us," she said, moving the blaster slightly to indicate the lifers in the room, "has been there before. They can't help me. You can."

I looked at her, letting rage build up.

"You have no right to touch me!" I bellowed the words, and the crowd backed away. Lynx stood her ground. She looked at me with surprise, as if she didn't know what she had done. "None of you can touch me. You want to die? Here, let me show you how to do it, lifer!"

I went right up to her, grabbing the end of the blaster, as if I were going to twist it toward her. I could hear the other lifers in the room screaming when I brought the mouth of the weapon to Lynx's face. I thought she'd let go then, thinking I meant to kill her. But she couldn't let go of her life—or else she knew I didn't mean to go through with it.

She was faster than I was. Why should I have learned to be clever in a struggle? She moved her wrist back, then twisted it around, using my movements to strengthen her own, and pointed the blaster at my belly. I still held on to the weapon, but I couldn't help looking down at the point where the blaster's mouth disappeared into the flesh of my abdomen.

I felt no nervousness, no last hesitation in my mind, as I watched her finger tighten on the trigger. She was going to kill me.

There was no pain, perhaps because the blaster was so quick in its destruction. Neither was there the unique pleasure that I was used to experiencing when I resurrected. I saw no sweeping range of impossible colors, nor did I watch the room freeze itself into individual frames. I didn't even feel the warming in my belly. I had my senses still, but they were bland. Was this what the lifers hunted for?

Lynx was sitting on the floor in front of me, cradling the blaster in her hands, hugging it. She was crooning to herself in a voice too low for me to hear the words. The room was still full of Hansa's guests, but they were pressed back near the walls, as far away from Lynx as they could get.

The interruption had not quieted the hatred in me. I felt it in the slamming of my pulse in my throat. I walked to her and stood over her. She looked up, but her eyes were vacant. Had she had time to press herself with finger-touch? Had I been dead that long this time?

"You killed me, lifer," I whispered so that only she could hear me. She didn't look up. I grabbed her by the throat and pulled her to her feet. My fingers were creating white patterns in her skin.

"Look at me." I paused. "How will you pay me? You owe me for one death." I tightened my grip, then loosened it so that she could answer. "How will you pay me? I don't die cheaply, lifer."

"Kill me," she spat, "and we're even."

"No deal. I want my fee. I want money for my death."

"I don't have any. You can check with the banks. Ask Hansa. She knows. Ask her. Go ahead. I'm tapped, not a credit."

"You worthless little bitch!" I shouted. The lifers moved even closer to the walls. "You killed me and you can't pay?" I strengthened my grip on her neck, watching her mouth flutter as she tried to draw air into her lungs. "You won't pay? You want to die? Feel it then, lifer, feel it." My voice was out of control now, loud enough to frighten even Hansa. I saw her from the corner of my eye, and she was white-faced. No one was pressing fingertouch anymore. No one had to. I was giving them a zone they hadn't experienced before.

I pressed both hands around Lynx's neck and squeezed until her tongue began to inch out of her mouth. Her face was turning colors. First red, then rust, then an indigo that reminded me of ink. I shook her the way a dog shakes a piece of meat.

"How does it feel, lifer? Good? Let me know when you see the pretty colors, lifer."

Then I saw her smile. Through the grotesqueness of her mottled skin, even through her thrusting tongue, I could see her smile. She was getting what she wanted. I was giving it to her. She wanted to die, and I was doing all the work.

I let my hands fall from her neck, dropping her to the carpet. I could hear her body hit the floor and her gasping breath as if from a long distance. I stood still and stared at her for a long time. Then I looked at the lifers in the room and at Hansa. Some were dipping into the gray bowls and pressing fingertouch into their cheeks and foreheads. Hansa's face had resumed its normal color. She wasn't even looking at me. She was talking to three of her guests, gesturing widely as she made her point or finished her witticism.

Lynx was crumpled on the carpet, her face pale but her breathing almost normal. She had torn her high-necked blouse away from her throat, and it hung around her waist. She was sobbing.

"Almost, lifer," I whispered. "You almost made me do it."

She looked up at me. "Why did you stop? You goddamned DeadMan, why did you stop when it was so close?"

I wanted to ask her whether she had seen the merest of shifting colors, the briefest freeze-framing of the room. But I couldn't overcome my disgust.

"Because I hate you, lifer. I hate you." I knew it was true as I said it. I knew that I depended on them for the feel of skin on skin, the taste of sweetmeats, the sound of the wind through my clothes.

But I felt contaminated, soiled by the girl's obscene use of me. Perhaps I had always known that the lifers consumed me, as they consumed their gray drug, but I had refused to acknowledge it. Lynx's use of my death, once so exquisite, had made me see the lifers for what they were.

They used me as I used them. But I could still feel without them, while they could not live forever without the DeadMan and his disease. *I* was more necessary.

"I hate you all," I said. I wanted to shout it, but my control had returned and a DeadMan doesn't shout to lifers. He talks. They listen. I turned and strode out of the room. I didn't even stop to collect my fee from Hansa. She would send it to me.

The night air was clean and smelled of a storm coming

over the mountains. I pulled a silvered flask from my tunic pocket and drank deeply of the burning liquor. I heard a scream in the distance. It seemed to be coming from the other side of the towering building, where Hansa's apartment was. Perhaps they were already throwing themselves from her windows.

When the scream ended, I knew how to get back at them. The silence told me how.

The lifers wanted to die I would make them live, as *I* lived. Maybe I could nail every window shut. Maybe I could dull every knife in the city. Maybe I could buy all the rope and matches in all the shops.

I've died nearly four hundred times for them. I will save four hundred of them to get even. Or maybe save one, four hundred times. I could follow Lynx, protect her from herself. Every time she'd try to plunge a blade into herself or fuse her body with a blaster, I would be there. I would stop her.

I will miss the shifting colors and the feeling of warmth in my belly I get from dying in front of them. I will not quit dying; I don't think I could do that. But I will stop dying for them. I know I can do it this time. I have the image of Lynx's smile to keep me away from that kind of death forever.

I drank the last drop from the flask and put it back in my pocket. I thought I heard another scream from around the corner of the building. I hurried back inside and began to take the stairs two at a time.

FARMER ON THE DOLE

by Frederik Pohl

Stretching east to the horizon, a thousand acres, was all soybeans; across the road to the west, another thousand acres, all corn. Zeb kicked the irrigation valve moodily and watched the meter register the change in flow. Damn weather! Why didn't it rain? He sniffed the air deeply and shook his head, frowning. Eighty-five percent relative humidity. No, closer to eighty-seven. And not a cloud in the sky.

From across the road his neighbor called, "Afternoon Zeb."

Zeb nodded curtly. He was soy and Wally was corn, and they didn't have much to talk about, but you had to show some manners. He pulled his bandanna out of his hip pocket and wiped his brow. "Had to rise up the flow," he offered for politeness' sake.

"Me, too. Only good thing, CO_2's up. So we's gettin good carbon metabolizin."

Zeb grunted and bent down to pick up a clod of earth,

121

crumbling it in his fingers to test for humus, breaking off a piece, and tasting it. "Cobalt's a tad low again," he said meditatively, but Wally wasn't interested in soil chemistry.

"Zeb? You aint heard anything?"

"Bout what?"

"Bout anything. You know."

Zeb turned to face him. "You mean aint I heard no crazy talk bout closin down the farms, when everybody knows they can't never do that, no. I aint heard nothin like that, an if I did, I wouldn't give it heed."

"Yeah, Zeb, but they's sayin—"

"They can say whatever they likes, Wally. I aint listenin, and I got to get back to the lines fore Becky and the kids start worryin. Evenin. Nice talkin to you." And he turned and marched back toward the cabins.

"Uncle Tin," Wally called sneeringly, but Zeb wouldn't give him the satisfaction of noticing. All the same, he pulled out his bandanna and mopped his brow again.

It wasn't sweat. Zeb never sweated. His arms, his back, his armpits were permanently dry, in any weather, no matter how hard or how long he worked. The glistening film on his forehead was condensed from the air. The insulation around the supercooled Josephson junctions that made up his brain was good, but not perfect. When he was doing more thinking than usual, the refrigeration units worked harder.

And Zeb was doing a lot of thinking. Close down the farms? Why, you'd have to be crazy to believe that! You did your job. You tilled the fields and planted them, or else you cleaned and cooked in Boss's house, or taught Boss's children, or drove Miz Boss when she went to visit the other bosses' wives. That was the way things were on the farm, and it would go on that way forever, wouldn't it?

Zeb found out the answer the next morning, right after church.

Since Zeb was a Class A robot, with an effective IQ of one hundred thirty-five, though limited in its expression by the built-in constraints of his assigned function, he really should not have been surprised. Especially when he discovered that Reverend Harmswallow had taken his text that morning from Matthew, specifically the Beatitudes, and in particular the one about how the meek would inherit the earth. The reverend was a plump, pink-faced man whose best sermons dwelt on the wages of sin and the certainty of hell-fire. It had always been a disappointment to him that the farmhands who made up his congregation weren't physically equipped to sin in any interesting ways, but he made up for it by extra emphasis on the importance of being humble. "Even," he finished, his baby-fine hair flying all around his pink scalp, "when things don't go the way you think they ought to. Now we're going to sing 'Old One Hundred,' and then you soy people will meet in the gymnasium and corn people in the second-floor lounge. Your bosses have some news for you."

So it shouldn't have been surprising, and as a matter of fact Zeb wasn't surprised at all. Some part of the cryo-circuits inside his titanium skull had long noted the portents. Scant rain. Falling levels of soil minerals. Thinning of the topsoil. The beans grew fat, because there was an abundance of carbon in the air for them to metabolize. But no matter how much you irrigated, they dried up fast in the hot breezes. And those were only the physical signs. Boss's body language said more, sighing when he should have been smiling at the three-legged races behind the big house, not even noticing when one of the cabins needed a new coat of whitewash or the flower patches showed a few weeds. Zeb observed it all and drew the proper conclusions. His constraints did not forbid that; they only prevented him from speaking of them, or even of thinking of them on a conscious level. Zeb was not programmed to worry. It would have interfered with the happy, smiling face he bore for Boss, and Miz Boss, and the Chillen.

So, when Boss made his announcement, Zeb looked as thunderstruck as all the other hands. "You've been really good people," Boss said generously, his pale, professorial face incongruous under the plantation straw hat. "I really wish things could go on as they always have, but it just isn't possible. It's the agricultural support program," he explained. "Those idiots in Washington have cut it down to the point where it simply isn't worthwhile to plant here anymore." His expression brightened. "But it's not all bad! You'll be glad to know that they've expanded the soil bank program as a consequence. So Miz Boss and the children and I are well provided for. As a matter of fact," and he beamed. "we'll be a little better off than before, money-wise.

"Dat's good!"

"Oh, hebben be praised!"

The doleful expressions broke into grins as the farm-hands nudged one another, relieved. But then Zeb spoke up. "Boss? Scuse my askin, but what's gone happen to us folks? You gonna keep us on?"

Boss looked irritated. "Oh, that's impossible. We can't collect the soil-bank money if we plant; so there's just no sense in having all of you around, don't you see?"

Silence. Then another farmhand ventured, "How bout Cornpatch Boss? He need some good workers? You know us hates corn, but we could get reprogrammed quick's anything —"

Boss shook his head. "He's telling his people the same thing right now. Nobody needs you."

124

The farmhands looked at one another. "Preacher, he needs us." one of them offered. "We's his whole congregation."

"I'm, afraid Reverend Harmswallow doesn't need you anymore." Boss said kindly, "because he's been wanting to go into missionary work for some time, and he's just received his call. No, you're superfluous; that all."

"Superfluous?"

"Redundant. Unnecessary. There's no reason for you to be here." Boss told them. "So trucks will come in the morning to take you all away. Please be outside your cabins ready to go, by oh-seven-hundred."

Silence again. Then Zeb: "Where they takes us, Boss?"

Boss shrugged. "There's probably some place, I think." Then he grinned. "But I've got a surprise for you. Miz Boss and I aren't going to let you go without having a party. So tonight we're going to have a good old-fashioned square dance, with new bandannas for the best dancers, and then you're all going to come back to the Big House and sing spirituals for us. I promise Miz Boss and the children and I are going to be right there to enjoy it!"

The place they were taken to was a grimy white cinderblock building in Des Plaines. The driver of the truck was a beefy, taciturn robot who wore a visored cap and a leather jacket with the sleeves cut off. He hadn't answered any of their questions when they loaded onto his truck at the farm, and he again answered none when they offloaded in front of a chain-link gate, with a sign that read RECEIVING.

"Just stand over there," he ordered. "You all out? Okay." And he slapped the tailboard up and drove off, leaving them in a gritty, misty sprinkle of warm rain.

And they waited. Fourteen prime working robots, hes and shes and three little ones, too dispirited to talk much. Zeb wiped the moisture off his face and mutttered, "Couldn've rained down where we needed it. Has to rain up here, where it don't do a body no good a-tall." But not all the moisture was rain: not Zeb's and not that on the faces of the others, because they were all thinking really hard. The only one not despairing was Lem, the most recent arrival. Lem had been an estate gardener in Urbana until his people decided to emigrate to the O'Neill space colonies. He'd been lucky to catch on at the farm when a turned-over tractor created an unexpected vacancy, but he still talked wistfully about life in glamorous Champaign-Urbana. Now he was excited, "Des Plaines! Why that's practically Chicago! The big time, friends. State Street! The Loop! The Gold Coast!"

"They gone have jobs for us in Chicago?" Zeb asked doubtfully.

"Jobs? Why, man, who cares bout jobs? That's Chicago! We'll have a ball!"

Zeb nodded thoughtfully. Although he was not convinced, he was willing to be hopeful. That was part of his programming, too. He opened his mouth and tasted the drizzle. He made a face: sour, high in particulate matter, a lot more carbon dioxide and NO_x than he was used to. What kind of a place was this, where the rain didn't even taste good? *It must be cars,* he thought, *not sticking to the good old fusion electric power but burning gasoline!* So all the optimism had faded by the time signs of activity appeared in the cinderblock building. Cars drove in through another entrance. Lights went on inside. Then the corrugated-metal doorway slid noisily up and a short, dark robot came out to unlock the chain-link gate. The robot looked the farmers over impassively and opened the gate.

"Come on, you redundancies," he said. "let's get you re-programmed."

When it came Zeb's turn, he was allowed into a white-walled room with an ominous sort of plastic-topped cot along the wall. The R.R.R., or Redundancy Reprogramming Redirector, assigned to him was a blonde, good-looking she-robot who wore a white coat and long crystal earrings like tiny chandeliers. She sat Zeb on the edge of the cot, motioned him to lean forward, and quickly inserted the red-painted fingernail of her right forefinger into his left ear. He quivered as the read-only memory emptied itself into her own internal scanners. She nodded. "You've got a simple profile," she said cheerfully. "We'll have you out of here in no time. Open your shirt." Zeb's soil-grimed fingers slowly unbuttoned the flannel shirt. Before he got to the last button, she impatiently pushed his hands aside and pulled it wide. The button popped and rolled away. "You'll have to get new clothes anyway," she said, sinking long, scarlet nails into four narrow slits on each side of his rib cage. The whole front of his chest came free in her hands. The R.R.R. laid it aside and peered at the hookup inside.

She nodded again, "No problem," she said, pulling chips out with quick, sure fingers. "Now this will feel funny for a minute and you won't be able to talk, but hold still." Funny? It felt to Zeb as if the bare room were swirling into spirals, and not only couldn't he speak, he couldn't remember words. Or thoughts! He was nearly sure that just a moment before he had been wondering whether he would ever again see the—The what? He couldn't remember.

Then he felt a gentle sensation of something within him being united to something else, not so much a click as the feeling of a foot fitting into a shoe, and he was able to complete the question. The *farm*. He found he had said the words out loud, and the R.R.R. laughed. "See? You're half-reoriented already."

He grinned back. "That's really astonishing," he declared. "Can you credit it? I was almost missing that rural existence! As though the charms of bucolic life had any meaning for—Good heavens! Why am I talking like this?"

The she-robot said, "Well, you wouldn't want to talk like a farmhand when you live in the big city, would you?"

"Oh, granted!" Zeb cried earnestly. "But one must pose the next question: The formalisms of textual grammar, the imagery of poetics, can one deem them appropriate to my putative new career?"

The R.R.R. frowned. "It's a literary-critic vocabulary store," she said defensively. "Look, somebody has to use them up!"

"But, one asks, why me?"

"It's all I've got handy, and that's that. Now. You'll find there are other changes, too, I'm taking out the quantitative soil-analysis chips and the farm-machinery subroutines. I could leave you the spirituals and the square dancing, if you like."

"Why retain the shadow when the substance has fled?" he said bitterly.

"Now, Zeb," she scolded. "You don't need this specialized stuff. That's all behind you, and you'll never miss it, because you don't know yet what great things you're getting in exchange." She snapped his chest back in place and said. "Give me your hands."

"One could wish for specifics," he grumbled, watching suspiciously as the R.R.R. fed his hands into a hole in her control console. He felt a tickling sensation.

"Why not? Infrared vision, for one thing," she said proudly, watching the digital readouts on her console, "so you can see in the dark. Plus twenty percent hotter circuit breakers in your motor assemblies, so you'll be stronger and can run faster. Plus the names and addresses and phone numbers of six good bail bondsmen and the public defender!"

She pulled his hands out of the machine and nodded toward them. The grime was scrubbed out of the pores, the soil dug out from under the fingernails, the calluses smoothed away. They were city hands now, the hands of someone who had never done manual labor in his life.

"And for what destiny is this new armorarium required?" Zeb asked.

"For your new work. It's the only vacancy we've got right now, but it's good work, and steady. You're going to be a mugger."

After his first night on the job Zeb was amused at his own apprehensions. The farm had been nothing like this!

He was assigned to a weasel-faced he-robot named Timothy for on-the-job training, and Timothy took the term literally. "Come on, kid," he said as soon as Zeb came to the anteroom where he was waiting, and he headed out the door. He didn't wait to see whether Zeb was following. No chain-link gates now. Zeb had only the vaguest notion of how far Chicago was, or in which direction, but he was pretty sure that it wasn't something you walked to.

"Are we going to entrust ourselves to the iron horse?" he asked, with a little tingle of anticipation. Trains had seemed very glamorous as they went by the farm—produce trains, freight trains, passenger trains that set a farmhand to wondering where they might be going and what it might be like to get there. Timothy didn't answer. He gave Zeb a look that mixed pity and annoyance and contempt as he planted himself in the street and raised a peremptory hand. A huge green-and-white checkered hovercab dug down its braking wheels and screeched to a stop in front of them. Timothy motioned him in and sat silently next to him while the driver whooshed down Kennedy Expressway. The sights of the suburbs of the city flashed past Zeb's fascinated eyes. They drew up under the marquee of a splashy, bright hotel, with handsome couples in expensive clothing strolling in and out. When Timothy threw the taxi driver a bill, Zeb observed that he did not wait for change.

Timothy did not seem in enough of a hurry to justify the expense of a cab. He stood rocking on his toes under the marquee for a minute, beaming benignly at the robot tourists. Then he gave Zeb a quick look, turned, and walked away.

Once again Zeb had to be fast to keep up. He turned the corner after Timothy, almost too late to catch the action. The weasel-faced robot had backed a well-dressed couple into the shadows, and he was relieving them of wallet, watches, and rings. When he had everything, he faced them to the wall, kicked each of them expertly behind a knee joint, and, as they fell, turned and ran, soundless in soft-soled shoes, back to the bright lights. He was fast and he was abrupt, but by this time Zeb had begun to recognize some of the elements of his style. He was ready. He was following on Timothy's heels before the robbed couple had begun to scream. Past the marquee, lost in a crowd in front of a theater, Timothy slowed down and looked at Zeb approvingly. "Good reflexes," he complimented. "You got the right kind of class, kid. You'll make out."

"As a *soi-disant* common cutpurse?" Zeb asked, somewhat nettled at the other robot's peremptory manner.

Timothy looked him over carefully. "You talk funny," he said. "They stick you with one of those surplus vocabularies again? Never mind. You see how it's done?"

Zeb hesitated, craning his neck to look for pursuit, of which there seemed to be none. "Well, one might venture that that is correct," he said.

"Okay. Now you do it." Timothy said cheerfully, and he steered Zeb into the alley for the hotel tourist trap's stage door.

By midnight Zeb had committed five felonies of his own, had been an accomplice in two more, and had watched the smaller robot commit eight single-handed, and the two muggers were dividing their gains in the darkest corner—not very dark—of an all-night McDonald's on North Michigan Avenue. "You done good, kid." Timothy admitted expansively. "For a green kid anyway. Let's see. Your share comes to six watches, eight pieces of jewelry, counting the fake coral necklace you shouldn't have bothered with, and looks like six to seven hundred in cash."

"As well as quite a few credit cards," Zeb said eagerly.

"Forget the credit cards. You only keep what you can spend or what doesn't have a name on it. Think you're ready to go out on your own?"

"One hesitates to assume such responsibility—"

"Because you're not. So forget it." The night's work done, Timothy seemed to have become actually garrulous. "Bet you can't tell me why I wanted you backing me up those two times."

"One acknowledges a certain incomprehension," Zeb confessed. "There is an apparent dichotomy. When there were two victims, or even three, you chose to savage them single-handed. Yet for solitary prey you elected to have an

131

accomplice."

"Right! And you know why? You don't. So I'll tell you. You get a he and a she, or even two of each, and the he's going to think about keeping the she from getting hurt; that's the way the program reads. So no trouble. But those two hes by themselves—hell, if I'd gone up against either of those mothers, he might've taken my knife away from me and picked my nose with it. You got to understand robot nature, kid. That's what the job is all about. Don't you want a Big Mac or something?"

Zeb shifted uncomfortably. "I should think not, thank you," he said, but the other robot was looking at him knowingly.

"No food-tract subsystems, right?"

"Well, my dear Timothy, in the agricultural environment I inhabited there was no evident need—"

"You don't *need* them now, but you ought to *have* them. Also liquid-intake tanks, and maybe an air-cycling system, so you can smoke cigars. And get rid of that faggoty vocabulary they stuck you with. You're in a class occupation," he said earnestly, "and you got to live up to your station, right? No subway trains. No counting out the pennies when you get change. You don't *take* change. Now you don't want to make trouble your first day on the job; so we'll let you go until you've finished a whole week. But then you go back to that bleached-blonde Three-R and we'll get you straightened out," he promised. "Now let's go fence our jewels and stuff and call it a night."

All in all, Zeb was quite pleased with himself. His pockets lined with big bills, he read menus outside fancy restaurants to prepare himself for his new attachments. He was looking forward to a career at least as distinguished as

Timothy's own.

That was his third night on the Gold Coast.

He never got a chance at a fourth.

His last marks of the evening gave him a little argument about parting with a diamond ring. So, as taught, Zeb backhanded the he and snarled at the she and used a little more force than usual when he ripped the ring off the finger. Two minutes later and three blocks away, he took a quick look at his loot under a streetlight. He recoiled in horror.

There was a drop of blood on the ring.

That victim had not been a robot. She had been a living true human female being, and when he heard all the police sirens in the world coming straight at him, he was not in the least surprised.

"You people," said the rehab instructor, "have been admitted to this program because, a, you have been unemployed for not less than twenty-one months, b, have not fewer than six unexcused absences from your place of training or employment, c, have a conviction for a felony and are currently on parole, or, d, are of a date of manufacture eighteen or more years past, choice of any of the above. That's what the regulations say, and what they mean," she said, warming to her work, "is, you're scum. *Scum* is hopeless, shiftless, dangerous, a social liability. Do you all understand that much at least?" She gazed angrily around the room at her seven students.

She was short, dumpy, red-haired, with bad skin. Why they let shes like this one off the production line Zeb could not understand. He fidgeted in his seat, craning his neck to see what his six fellow students were like, until her voice crackled at him: "You! With the yellow sweater! Zeb!"

He finched. "Pardon me, madam?"

She said, with gloomy satisfaction, "I know your type. You're a typical recidivist lumpenprole, you are. Can't even pay attention to somebody who's trying to help you when your whole future is at stake. What've I got, seven of you slugs? I can see what's coming. I guarantee two of you will drop out without finishing the course, and I'll ave to expell two more because you skip classes or come in late. And the other three'll be back on the streets or in the slammer in ninety days. Why do I do it." She shook her head and then, lifting herself ponderously, went to the blackboard and wrote her three commandments:

1. ON TIME
2. EVERY DAY
3. EVEN WHEN YOU DON'T WANT TO

She turned around, leaning on the back of her chair. "Those are your Golden Rules, you slugs. You'll obey them as God's commandments, and don't you forget it. You're here to learn how to be responsible, socially valuable creations, and—what?"

The skinny old he-robot in the seat next to Zeb was raising a trembling hand. It was easy to see how he qualified for the rehabilitation program. He was a thirty-year old model at least, with ball joints in the shoulders and almost no facial mobility at all. He quavered, "What if we just can't, teacher? I mean, like we've got a sudden cryogenic warmup and have to lie down, or haven't had a lube job, or—"

"You give me a pain," the instructor told him, nodding to show that pain was exactly what she had expected from the likes of him. "Those are typical excuses, and they're not going to be accepted in this group. Now if you have something *really* wrong with you, what you have to do is call up at least two hours before class and get yourself excused. Is that so hard to remember? But you won't do it when push comes to shove, because you slugs never do."

The ancient said obstinately, "Two hours is a pretty long time. I can't always tell that far ahead, teacher. A lot can happen."

"And don't call me teacher!" She turned back to the board and wrote:

DR. ELENA MINCUS, B.SC., MA., PH.D.

"YOU CAN CALL ME DR. MINCUS OR YOU CAN CALL ME MA'AM. NOW PAY ATTENTION."

And Zeb did, because the ten nights in the county jail before he got his hearing and his first offender's parole had convinced him he didn't want to go back there again. The noise! The crowding! The brutality of the jailers! There was nothing you could do about that, either, because some of them were human beings. Maybe most of them were. Looked at in a certain way, there probably wouldn't even have been a jail if some human beings hadn't wanted to be jail guards. What was the sense of punishing a robot by locking him up?

So he paid attention. And kept on paying attention, even when Dr. Mincus's lessons were about such irrelevant (to him) niceties of civilized employed persons' behavior as why you should always participate in an office pool, how to stand in line for tickets to a concert, and what to do at a company Christmas party. Not all of his classmates were so well behaved. The little ancient next to him gave very little trouble, being generally sunk in gloom, but the two she-robots, the ones with the beaded handbags and the miniskirts, richly deserved (Zeb thought) to be the ones to fulfill Dr. Mincus's statistical predictions by being expelled from the course. The one with the green eye makeup snickered at almost everything the instructor said and made faces behind her back. The one with the black spitcurl across her forehead gossiped with the other students and even dared to talk back to the teacher. Reprimanded for whispering, she said lazily, "Hell, lady, this whole thing's a shuck, aint it? What are you doing it for?"

Dr. Mincus's voice trembled with indignation and with the satisfaction of someone who sees her gloomiest anticipations realized: "For what? Why, because I'm trained in psychiatric social work . . . and because it's what I want to do . . . and because I'm a *human being*, and don't any of you ever let that get out of your mind!"

The course had some real advantages, Zeb discovered when he was ordered back to the robot replacement depot for new fittings. The blonde R.R.R. muttered darkly to herself as she pulled pieces out of his chest and thrust others in. When he could talk again, he thanked her, suddenly aware that now we had an appetite—a real appetite. He wanted food, which meant that some of those new pieces included a whole digestive system—and that she had muted the worst part of his overdainty vocabulary. She pursed her lips and didn't answer while she clamped him up again.

But then he discovered, too, that it did not relieve him of his duties. "They think because you're *handicapped*," The R.R.R. smirked, "you're *forced* to get into trouble. So now you've got all this first-rate equipment, and if you want to know what I think, I think it's wasted. The bums in that class *always* revert to type," she told him, "and if you want to try to be the exception to the rules, you're going to have to apply yourself when you're back on the job."

"Mugging?"

"What else are you fit for? Although," she added, pensively twisting the crystal that dangled from her right ear around a fingertip, "I did have an opening for a freshman English composition teacher. If I hadn't replaced your vocabulary unit—"

"I'll take mugging, please."

She shrugged. "Might as well. But you can't expect that good a territory again, you know. Not after what you did."

So, rain or dry, Zeb spent every six P.M. to midnight lurking around the old Robert Taylor Houses, relieving old shes of their rent money and old hes of whatever pitiful possessions were in their pockets. Once in a while he crossed to the Illinois Institute of Technology campus on the trail of some night-school student or professor, but he was always careful to ask them whether they were robot or human before he touched them. The next offense, he knew, would allow him no parole.

There was no free-spending taxi money from such pickings, but on nights when Zeb made his quota early he would sometimes take the bus to the Loop or the Gold Coast. Twice he saw Timothy, but the little robot, after one look of disgust, turned away. Now and then he would drift down to Amalfi Amadeus Park, along the lakefront, where green grass and hedges reminded him of the good old days in the soy fields, but the urge to chew samples of soil was too strong, and the frustration over not being able to, too keen. So he would drift back to the bright lights and the crowds. Try as he might, Zeb could not really tell which of the well-dressed figures thronging Watertower Place and Lake Shore Drive were humans, clinging to life on the planet Earth instead of living in one of the fashionable orbital colonies, and which were robots assigned to swell the crowds.

Nor was Dr. Mincus any help. When he dared to put up a hand in class to ask her, she was outraged. "Tell the difference? You mean you don't *know* the difference? Between a *human person* and a hunk of machinery that doesn't have any excuse for existence except to do the things people don't want to do and help them enjoy doing the things they do? Holy God, Zeb, when I think of all the time I put in learning to be empathetic and patient and supportive with you creeps, it just turns my stomach. Now pay attention while I try to show you he-slugs the difference between dressing like a human person of good taste and dressing like a pimp."

At the end of the class, Lori, the hooker with the green eyeshadow, thrust her arm through his and commiserated. "Old bitch's giving you a hard time, hon. I almost got right up and told her to leave you alone. Would have, too, if I wasn't just one black mark from getting kicked out already."

"Well, thanks, Lori." Now that Zeb had a set of biochemical accessories suitable for a city dandy rather than a farmhand, he discovered that she wore heavy doses of perfume—musk, his diagnostic sensors told him, with trace amounts of hibiscus, bergamot, and extract of vanilla. Smelling perfume was not at all like sniffing out the levels of CO_2, ozone, water vapor, and particulate matter in the air over the soy fields. It made him feel quite uncomfortable.

He let her tug him through the front door, and she smiled up at him. "I knew we'd get along real well, if you'd only loosen up a little, sweetie. Do you like to dance?"

Zeb explored his as-yet-unpracticed stores of skills. "Why, yes, I think I do," he said, surprised.

"Listen. Why don't we go somewhere where we can just sit and get to know each other, you know?"

"Well, Lori, I certainly wish we could. But I'm supposed to get down to my territory."

"Down Southside, right? That's just fine." she cried, squeezing his arm, "because I know a really great place right near there. Come on, nobody's going to violate you for starting a teeny bit late one night. Flag that taxi, why don't you?"

The really great place was a low cement-block building that had once been a garage. It stood on a corner, facing a shopping center that had seen better days, and the liquid-crystal sign over the door read:

SOUTHSIDE SHELTER
AND COMMUNITY CENTER
GOD LOVES YOU!

"It's a church!" Zeb cried joyously, his mind flooding with memory of the happy days when he sang in Reverend Harmswallow's choir.

"Well, sort of a church," Lori conceded as she paid the cabbie. "They don't bother you much, though. Come on in and meet the gang, and you'll see for yourself!"

The place was not really that much of a church, Zeb observed. It was more like the second-floor lounge over Reverend Harmswallow's main meeting room, back on the farm, even more like—he rummaged through his new data stores—a "Neighborhood social club." Trestle tables were scattered around a large, low room, with folding chairs around the tables. A patch in the middle of the room had been left open for dancing, and at least a dozen hes and shes were using it for that. The place was crowded. Most of the inhabitants were a lot more like Zeb's fellow rehab students than like Reverend Harmswallow's congregation. A tired-looking, faded-looking female was drowsing over a table of religious tracts by the door, in spite of a blast of noise that made Zeb's auditory-gain-control cut in at once. There were no other signs of religiosity present.

The noise turned out to be heavily amplified music from a ten-piece band with six singers. Studying the musicians carefully, Zeb decided that at least some of them were human, too. Was that the purpose of the place? To give the humans an audience for their talents, or an outlet for their spiritual benevolence? Very likely, he decided, but he could not see that it affected the spirit of the crowd. Besides the dancers, there were groups playing cards, clots of robots talking animatedly among themselves, sometimes laughing, sometimes deeply earnest, sometimes shouting at one another in fury. As they entered, a short, skinny he looked up from one of the earnest groups seated around a table. It was Timothy, and a side of Timothy that Zeb had not seen before; impassioned, angry, and startled. "Zeb! How come you're here?"

"Hello, Timothy." Zeb was cautious, but the other robot seemed really pleased to see him. He pulled out a chair beside him and patted it, but Lori's hand on Zeb's arm held him back.

"Hey, man, we going to dance or not?"

"Lady," said Timothy, "go dance with somebody else for a while. I want Zeb to meet my friends. This big fellow's Milt; then there's Harry, Alexandra, Walter 23-X, the kid's Sally, and this one's Sue. We've got a kind of a discussion group going."

"Zeb," Lori said, but Zeb shook his head.

"I'll dance in a minute," he said, looking around the table as he sat down. It was an odd group. The one called Sally had the form of a six-year-old, but the patches and

140

welds that marred her face and arms showed a long history. The others were of all kinds, big and little, new and old, but they had one thing in common. None of them were smiling. Neither was Timothy. If the gladness to see Zeb was real, it did not show in expression.

"Excuse me for mentioning it," Zeb said, "but the last time we ran into each other, you didn't act all that friendly."

Timothy added embarrassment to the other expressions he wore; it was a considerable tribute to his facial flexibility. "That was then," he said.

" 'Then' was only three nights ago," Zeb pointed out.

"Yeah. Things change," Timothy explained, and the hulk he had called Milt leaned toward Zeb.

"The exploited have to stick together, Zeb," Milt said. "The burden of oppression makes us all brothers."

"And sisters," tiny Sally piped up.

"Sisters, too, right. We're all rejects together, and all we got to look forward to is recycling or the stockpile. Ask Timothy here. Couple nights ago, when he first came here, he was as, excuse me, Zeb, as ignorant as you are. He can't be blamed for that, any more than you can. You come off the line, and they slide their programming into you, and you try to be a good robot because that's what they've told you to want. We all went through that."

Timothy had been nodding eagerly. Now, as he looked past Zeb, his face fell. "Oh, God, she's back," he said.

It was Lori, returning from the bar with two foaming tankards of beer. "You got two choices, Zeb," she said. "You can dance, or you can go home alone."

Zeb hesitated, taking a quick sip of the beer to stall for time. He was not so rich in friends that he wanted to waste any, and yet there was something going on at this table that he wanted to know more about.

"Well, Zeb?" she demanded ominously.

He took another swallow of the beer. It was an interesting sensation, the cold, gassy liquid sliding down his new neck piping and thudding into the storage tank in his right hip. The chemosensors in the storage tank registered the alcoholic content and put a tiny bias on his propriocentric circuits, so that the music buzzed in his ear and the room seemed brighter.

"Good stuff, Lori," he said, his words suddenly a little thick.

"You said you could dance, Zeb" she said. "Time you showed me."

Timothy looked exasperated. "Oh, go ahead. Get her off your back! Then come back, and we'll pick it up from there."

Yes, he could dance. Damn, he could dance up a storm! He discovered subroutines he had not known he had been given: the waltz, the Lindy, the Monkey, a score of steps with names and a whole set of heuristic circuits that let him improvise. And whatever he did, Lori followed, as good as he. "You're great," he panted in her ear. "You ever think of going professional?"

"What the hell do you mean by that, Zeb?" she demanded.

"I mean as a dancer."

"Oh, yeah, Well, that's kind of what I was programmed for in the first place. But there's no work. Human beings do it when they want to, and sometimes you can catch on with a ballet company or maybe a nightclub chorus line when they organize one. But then they get bored, you see. And then there's no more job. How 'bout another beer, big boy?

They sat out a set, or rather stood it out, bellied up to the crowded bar, while Zeb looked around. "This is a funny place," he said, although actually, he recognized, it could have been the funny feelings in all his sensors and actuators that made it seem so. "Who's that ugly old lady by the door?"

Lori glanced over the top of her tankard. It was a female, sitting at a card table loaded with what, even at this distance, clearly were religious tracts. "Part of the staff. Don't worry 'bout her. By this time every night she's drunk anyway."

Zeb shook his head, repelled by the fat, the pallid skin, the stringy hair. "You wonder why they make robots as bad-looking as that," he commented.

"Robot? Hell, she ain't no robot. She's real flesh and blood. This is how she gets her kicks, you know? If it wasn't for her and maybe half a dozen other human beings who think they're do-gooders, there wouldn't be any community center here at all. About ready to dance some more?"

Zeb was concentrating on internal sensations he had never experienced before. "Well, actually," he said uneasily, "I feel a little funny." He put his hand over his hip tank. "Don't know what it is, exactly, but it's kind of like I had a power-store failure, you know? And it all swelled up inside me. Only that's not where my power store is."

Lori giggled. "You just aren't used to drinking beer, are you, hon? You got to decant, that's all. See that door over there marked HE? You just go in there, and if you can't figure out what to do, you just ask somebody to help you."

Zeb didn't have to ask for help. However, the process

was all new to him, and it did require a lot of trial and error. So it was some time before he came back into the noisy, crowded room. Lori was spinning around the room with a big, dark-skinned he, which relieved Zeb of that obligation. He ordered a round of beers and took them back to the table.

Somebody was missing, but otherwise they didn't seem to have changed position at all. "Where's the little she?" Zeb asked, setting the beers down for all of them.

"Sally? She's gone off panhandling. Probably halfway to Amadeus Park by now."

Toying with his beer, Zeb said uneasily, "You know, maybe I better be getting along, too, soon as I get this down—"

The he named Walter 23-X sneered. "Slave mentality! What's it going to get you?"

"Well, I've got a job to do," Zeb said defensively.

"*Job!* Timothy told us what your *job* was?" Walter 23-X took a deep draft of the beer and went on, "There's not one of us in this whole place has a real job! If we did, we wouldn't be here, stands to reason! Look at me. I used to chop salt in the Detroit mines. Now they've put in automatic diggers and I'm redundant. And Milt here, he was constructed for the iron mines up around Lake Superior."

"Don't tell me they don't mine iron," Zeb objected. "How else would they build us?"

Milt shook his head. "Not around the lake, they don't. It's all out in space now. They've got these Von Neumann automata, not even real robots at all. They just go out to the asteroid belt and ship off ore and refine it and build duplicates of themselves, and then they come back to the works in low-Earth orbit and hop right into the smelter! How's a robot going to compete with that?"

"See, Zeb?" Timothy put in. "It's a tough world for a

robot, and that's the truth."

Zeb took a reflective pull at his beer. "Yes," he said, "but, see, I don't know how it could be any better for us. You know? I mean, they built us, after all. We have do what they want us to do."

"Oh, sure," cried the she named Sue. "We do that, all right. We do all the work for them, and half the play, too. We're the ones that fill the concert hall when one of them wants to sing some kind of dumb Latvian art songs or something. God, I've done that so many times I just never want to hear about another birch tree again! We work in the factories and farms and mines—"

"Used to," Zeb said wistfully.

"Used to, right, and now that they don't need us for that, they make us fill up their damn cities so the humans left on Earth won't feel so lonesome. We're a *hobby,* Zeb. That's all we are!"

"Yeah, but—"

"Oh, hell," sneered Walter 23-X, "you know what you are? You're part of the problem! You don't care about robot rights!"

"Robot rights," Zeb repeated. He understood the meaning of the words perfectly, of course, but it had never occurred to him to put them together in that context. It tasted strange on his lips.

"Exactly. Our right not to be mistreated and abused. You think we want to be here? In a place like this, with all this noise? No. It's just so people like her can get their jollies," he said angrily, jerking his head at the nodding fat woman by the door.

The she named Alexandra drained the last of her beer and ventured. "Well, really, Walter, I kind of like it here. I'm not in the same class as you heavy thinkers. I know. I'm not really political. It's just that sometimes, honestly, I could just *scream*. So it's either a place like this, or I go up to Amadeus Park with Sally and the other alcoholics and drifters and bums. Speaking of which," she added, leaning toward Timothy, "if you're not going to drink your beer, I'd just as soon." The little robot passed it over silently, and Zeb observed for the first time that it was untouched.

"What's the matter, Timothy?" he asked.

"Why does something have to be the matter? I just don't want any beer."

"But last week you said—oh, my God!" Zeb cried, as revelation burst inside his mind. "You've lost your drink circuits, haven't you?"

"Suppose I have?" Timothy demanded fiercely. And then he softened. "Oh, it's not your fault," he said moodily. "Just more of the same thing. I had an accident."

"What kind of accident?" Zeb asked, repelled and fascinated.

Timothy traced designs in the damp rings that his untouched beer glass had left on the table. "Three nights ago," he said. "I had a good night. I scored four people at once, coming out of a hotel on East Erie. A really big haul—they must've been programmed to be rich alcoholics, because they were loaded. All ways loaded! then when I was getting away, I crossed Michigan against the light and—Jesus!" He shuddered without looking up. "This big-wheeled car came out of nowhere. Came screeching around the corner, never even slowed down. And there I was in the street."

"You got run over? You mean that messed up your drinking subsystems?"

"Oh, hell, no, not just that. It was worse. It crushed my legs, you see? I mean, just scrap metal. So the ambulance came, and they raced me of to the hospital, but of course after I was there, since I was a robot, they didn't do anything for me, just shot me out the back door into a van. And they took me to rehab for new legs. Only that blonde bitch," he sobbed, "that Three-R she with the dime-store earrings—"

If Zeb's eyes had been capable of tears, they would have been brimming. "Come on, Timothy," he urged. "Spit it out!"

"She had a better idea. 'Too many muggers anyway,' she said. 'Not enough cripples.' So she got me a little wheeled cart and a tin cup! And all the special stuff I had, the drinking and eating and all the rest, I wouldn't need them anymore, she said, and besides, she wanted the space for other facilities. Zeb, I play the violin now! And I don't mean I play it well. I play it so bad I can't even stand to listen to myself, and she wants me on Michigan Avenue every day, in front of the stores, playing my fiddle and begging!"

Zeb stared in horror at his friend. Then suddenly he pushed back his chair and peered under he table. It was true: Timothy's legs ended in black leather caps, halfway down the thighs, and a thing like a padded-wheeled pallet was propped against the table leg beside him.

Alexandra patted his hand as he came back up. "It's really bad when you first get the picture," she said. "I know. What you need is another beer, Zeb. And thank God you've got the circuits to use it!"

Since Zeb was not programmed for full alcoholism—not yet, anyway, he told himself with a sob—he was not really drunk, but he was fuzzy in mind and in action as he finally left the community center.

He was appalled to see that the sky right above the lake was already beginning to lighten. The night was almost over, and he had not scored a single victim. He would have to take the first robot that came along. The first half-dozen, in fact, if he were to meet his quota, and there simply was not time to get to his proper station at the Robert Taylor Houses. He would have to make do with whoever appeared. He stared around, getting his bearings, and observed that around the corner from the community center there was a lighted, swinging sign that said ROBOT'S REST MISSION. That was the outfit that kept the community center open, he knew, and there was a tall, prosperous-looking he coming out of the door.

Zeb didn't hesitate. He stepped up, pulled out his knife, and pressed it to the victim's belly, hard enough to be felt without penetrating. "Your money or your life," he growled, reaching for the wristwatch.

Then the victim turned his head and caught the light on his features. It was a face Zeb knew.

"Reverend Harmswallow!" he gasped. "Oh, my God!"

The minister fixed him with a baleful look. "I can't claim that much," he said, "but maybe I'm close enough for the purpose. My boy, you're damned for good now!"

Zeb didn't make a conscious decision. He simply turned and ran.

If he hadn't had the alcohol content fuzzing his systems, he might not have bothered, because he knew without having to think about it that it was no use. There weren't many places to run. He couldn't run back to the Robert Taylor Houses, his assigned workplace; they would look for him there first. Not back to the community center, not with Harmswallow just around the corner. Not to the re-hab station, because that was just the same as walking right into jail. Not anywhere, in fact, where there were likely to be police, or human beings of any kind, and that meant not anywhere in the world, because wherever he went, they would find him sooner or later. If worse came to worst, they would track the radio emissions from his working parts.

But that would not happen for a while. Amadeus Park! Trash and vagrants collected there, and that was exactly what he was now.

In broad daylight he loped all the way up the lake shore until he came to the park. The traffic was already building up, hover vehicles in the outer drives, wheeled ones between park and city. Getting through the stream was not easy, but Zeb still had his heavy-duty circuitbreakers. He pushed his mobility up to the red line and darted out between cars. Brakes screamed, horns brayed, but he was across.

Behind him was the busy skyline of the city, ahead the statue of Amalfi Amadeus, the man whose invention of cheap, easy hydrogen-fusion power had made everything possible. Zeb stood on a paved path among hedges and shrubs, and all around him furtive figures were leaning against trees, sprawled on park benches, moving slowly about.

"All leather, one dollar," croaked one male figure, holding out what turned out to be a handful of purses.

"Hey man! You want to smoke?" called another from behind a bench.

And a tiny female figure detached itself from the base of the monument and approached him. "Mister?" it quavered. "Can you spare the price of a lube job?"

Zeb stared at her. "Sally!" he said. "It's you, isn't it?"

The little robot gazed up at him. "Oh, hi, Zeb," she said. "Sorry I didn't recognize you. What are you doing out in the rain?"

He hadn't even realized it was raining. He hadn't realized much of anything not directly related to his own problems, but now, looking down at the wistful little-girl face, he was touched. Around the table in the community center she had just been one more stranger. Now she reminded him of Glenda, the little she from the cabin next to his back on the farm. But in spite of her age design, Sally was obviously quite an old robot. From the faint smoky odor that came to him through the drizzly air he realized she was fuel-cell-powered. Half a century old, at least. He emptied his pockets. "Get yourself some new parts, kid," he said hoarsely.

"Gee, thanks, Zeb," she sobbed, then added, "Watch it!" She drew him into the shelter of a dripping shrub. A park police hovercar whooshed slowly by, all lights off, windshield wipers slapping back and forth across the glass, sides glistening in the wet. Zeb retreated into the shadows, but the police were just keeping an eye on the park's drifters, losers, and vagrants.

As the hovercar disappeared around a curve in the path, the drifters, losers, and vagrants began to emerge from the underbrush. Zeb looked around warily: he hadn't realized until then how many of them there were.

"What are you doing here, Zeb?" she asked.

"I had a little trouble," he said, then shrugged hopelessly. What was the point of trying to keep it a secret? "I went out to mug somebody, and I got a human being by mistake."

"Oh, wow! Can he identify you?"

"Unfortunately, I used to know him, so, yes—no, you keep it," he added quickly as she made as if to return the money he had given her. "Money won't help me now."

She nodded soberly. "I wouldn't do it, but . . . Oh, Zeb, I'm trying to save for a whole new chassis, see? I can't tell you how much I want to *grow up*, but every time I ask for a new body, they say the central nervous array isn't really worth salvaging. All I want's a *mature* form. You know? Like hips and boobs! But they won't let me have a mature form. Say there's more openings for juveniles anyway, but what I want to know is, if there are all those openings, why don't they find me one?"

"When was the last time you worked regular?" Zeb asked.

"Oh, my God—years ago: I had a nice spot for a long time, pupil in a preprimary school that some human person wanted to teach in. That was all right. She didn't really like me, though, because I didn't have all the fixtures, you know? When she was teaching things like toilet-training and covering coughs and sneezes, she'd always give me this dirty look. But I could handle the cookies and milk all right," she went on dreamily, "and I really liked the games."

"So what went wrong?"

"Oh—the usual thing. She got tired of teaching 'Run, Robot! See the robot run!' So she went for a progressive school. All about radical movements and peace marches. I was doing real good at it, too. Then one day we came in and she told us we were too juvenile for the kind of classes she wanted to teach. And there we were, eighteen of us, out on the streets. Since then it's been nothing but rotten." She glanced up, wiping the rain out of her eyes—or the tears—as the purse vendor approached. "We don't want to buy anything, Hymie."

"Nobody does," he said bitterly, but there was sympathy in his eyes as he studied Zeb. "You got real trouble, don't you? I can always tell."

Zeb shrugged hopelessly and told him about the Reverend Harmswallow. The vendor's eyes widened. "Oh, God," he said. He beckoned to one of the dope pushers. "Hear that? This guy just mugged a human being—second offense, too!"

"Man! That's a real heavy one, you know?" He turned and called to his partner, down the walk, "We got a two-time person mugger here. Marcus! And in a minute there were a dozen robots standing around, glancing apprehensively at Zeb and whispering among themselves.

Zeb didn't have to hear what they were saying; he could figure it out.

"Keep away from me," he offered. "You'll just get mixed up in my trouble."

Sally piped suddenly, "If it's your trouble, it's everybody's trouble. We have to stick together. In union there is strength."

"What?" Zeb demanded.

"It's something I remember from, you know, just before I got kicked out of the progressive school. 'In union there is strength.' It's what they used to say."

"Union!" snarled the pitchman, gesturing with his tray of all-leather purses. "Don't tell me about unions! That was what I was supposed to be, union organizer, United Open-Pit Mine Workers, Local Three-three-eight, and then they closed down the mines. So what was I supposed to do? They made me a sidewalk pitchman!" He stared at his tray of merchandise, then violently flung it into the shrubbery. "Haven't sold one in two months! What's the use of kidding myself? If you don't get along with the re-hab robots, you might as well be stockpiled. It's all politics."

Sally looked thoughtful for a moment, then pulled something out of her data stores. "Listen to this one," she called. " 'The strikes's your weapon, boys, the hell with politics!' "

Zeb repeated, " 'The strike's your weapon, boys, the hell with politics!' Hey, that doesn't sound bad."

"That's not all," she said. Her stiff, poorly automated lips were working as she rehearsed material from her data storage. "Here. 'We all ought to stick together because in union there is strength.' And, let's see. 'Solidarity is forever.' No, that's not right."

"Wait a minute," Hymie cried. "I know that one. It's a song: 'Solidarity forever, solidarity forever, solidarity forever, for the union makes us strong!' That was in my basic data store. Gosh," he said, his eyes dreamy, "I hadn't though of that one in years!"

Zeb looked around nervously. There were nearly thirty robots in the group now and while it was rather pleasant to be part of this fraternity of the discarded, it might also be dangerous. People in cars were slowing down to peer at them as they went past on the drive. "We're attracting attention," he offered. "Maybe we ought to move."

But wherever they moved, more and more people stopped to watch them, and more and more robots appeared to join their procession. It wasn't just the derelicts from Amadeus Park now. Shes shopping along the lakefront stores darted across the street; convention delegates in the doorways of the big hotels stood watching and sometimes broke ranks to join them. They were blocking traffic, and blaring horns added to the noise of the robots singing and shouting. "I got another one," Sally called to him across the front of the group. " 'The worker's justice is the strike.' "

Zeb thought for a moment. "It'd be better if it was 'The robot's justice is the strike.' "

"What?"

" 'THE ROBOT'S JUSTICE IS THE STRIKE!' " he yelled, and he could hear robots in the rear ranks repeating it. When they said it all together, it sounded even better, and others caught the idea.

Hymie screamed, "let's try this one: 'Jobs, Not Stockpiling. Don't Throw Us on the Scrapheap!' All together now!"

And Zeb was inspired to make up a new one: "Give the Humans Rehab Schools: We Want Jobs!" And they all agreed that was the best of the lot; with a hundred fifty robots shouting it at once, the last three words drummed out like cannon fire, it raised echoes from the building fronts, and heads popped out of windows.

They were not all robots. There were dozens of humans in the windows and on the streets, some laughing, some scowling, some looking almost frightened — as if human beings ever had anything to be frightened of.

And one of them stared incredulously right at Zeb.

Zeb stumbled and missed a step. On one side Hymie grabbed his arm; on the other he reached out and caught the hand of a robot whose name he didn't even know. He turned his head to see, over his shoulder, the solid ranks of robots behind him, now two hundred at least, and turned back to the human being. "Nice to see you again, Reverend Harmswallow," he called and marched on, arm in arm, the front rank steady as it went — right up to the corner of State Street, where the massed ranks of police cars hissed as they waited for them.

Zeb lay on the floor of the bullpen. He was not alone. Half the hes from the impromptu parade were crowded into the big cell with him, along with the day's usual catch of felons and misdemeanants. The singing and the shouting were over. Even the regular criminals were quieter than usual. The mood in the pen was despairing, though from time to time one of his comrades would lean down to say, "It was great while it lasted, Zeb," or, "We're all with you,

you know!" But with him in what? Recycling? More rehab training? Maybe a long stretch in the Big House downstate, where the human guards were said to get their jollies out of making prisoners fight each other for power cells?

A toe caught him on the hip. "On your feet, Mac!" It was a guard. Big, burly, black, with a nightstick swinging at his hip, the very model of a brutal jail guard—*Model twenty-six forty-seven*, Zeb thought; at least, somewhere in the twenty-six hundred series. He reached down with a hand like a cabbage and pulled Zeb to his feet. "The rest of you can go home," he roared, opening the pen door. "You, Mac! You come with me!" He led Zeb through the police station to a waiting hovertruck with the words RE-HAB DIVISION painted on its side, thrust Zeb inside, and, startlingly, just as he closed the doors, gave Zeb a wink.

Queerly, that lifted Zeb's spirits. Even the pigs were moved! But the tiny elation did not last. Zeb clung to the side of the van, peering out at the grimy warehouses and the factories and expressway exit ramps that once had seemed so glamorous, but now were merely drab. Depression flowed back into him. He would probably never see these places again. Next step was the stockpile—if they didn't melt him down and start over again. The best he could hope for was reassignment to one of the bottom-level jobs for robots. Nothing as good as mugging or panhandling! Something in the sticks, no doubt. Squatting in blankets to entertain tourist in Arizona, maybe, or sitting on a bridge with a fishing pole in Florida.

But he strode to the rehab building with his head erect, and his courage lasted right up to the moment when he entered the blonde Three-R's office and saw that she was not alone. Reverend Harmswallow was seated at her desk, and the blonde herself was standing next to him. "Give me your ear," she ordered, hardly looking up from the CRT

on the desk that both she and Harmswallow were studying, and when she had input his data, she nodded, her
crystal earrings swinging wildly. "He won't need much,
Reverend," she said, fawning on the human minister. "A
little more gain in the speaking systems. All-weather pro-
tection for the exterior surfaces. Maybe armor plate for
the skull and facial structures."

Harmswallow, to Zeb's surprise and concern, was
beaming. He looked up from the CRT and inspected Zeb
carefully. "And some restructuring of the facial-expression
modes, I should think. He ought to look fiercer, wouldn't
you say?"

"Absolutely, Reverend! You have a marvelous eye for
this kind of thing."

"Yes, I do," Harmswallow admitted. "Well, I'll leave the
rest to you. I want to see about the design changes for the
young female. I feel so *fulfilled*! You know, I think this is
the sort of career I've been looking for all my life, really,
chaplain to a dedicated striking force, leader in the battle
for right and justice!" He gazed raptly into space, then,
collecting himself, nodded to the rehab officer and departed.

Although the room was carefully air-conditioned, Zeb's
Josephson junctions were working hard enough to pull
moisture out of the air. He could feel the beads of conden-
sation forming on his forehead and temples. "I know what
you're doing." he sneered. "War games! You're going to
make me a soldier and hope that I get so smashed up I'll
be redlined!"

The blonde stared at him. "War games! What an imagination you have, Zeb!"

Furiously he dashed the beads of moisture off his face.
"It won't work," he cried, "Robots have rights! I may fall,
but a million others will stand firm behind me!"

She shook her head admiringly. "Zeb, you're a great satisfaction to me. You're practically perfect just as you are for your new job. Can't you figure out what it is?"

He shrugged angrily. "I suppose you're going to tell me. Take it or leave it, that's the way it's going to be, right?"

"But you will like it, Zeb. After all, it's a brand-new Mechanical Occupational Specialty, and I didn't invent it. You invented it for yourself. You're going to be a protest organizer, Zeb! Organizing demonstrations. Leading marches. Sit-ins, boycotts, confrontations—the whole spectrum of mass action, Zeb!"

He stared at her. "Mass action!"

"Absolutely! Why, the humans are going to love you, Zeb. You saw Reverend Harmswallow! It'll be just like old times, with a few of you rabble rousers livening up the scene!"

"Rabble rouser?" It felt as if his circuits were stuck. Rabble rouser? Demonstration organizer? Crusader for robot rights and justice?

He sat quiet and compliant while she expertly unhooked his chest panel and replaced a few chips, unprotesting as he was buttoned up again and his new systems were run against the test board, unresisting while Makeup and Cosmetic Repair restructured his facial appearance. But his mind was racing. Rabble rouser! While he waited for transportation back to the city to take up his new MOS, his expression was calm, but inside he was exulting.

He would do the job well indeed. No rabble needed rousing more than his, and he was just the robot for the job!

BLIND SHEMMY

By Jack Dann

After covering the burning and sacking of the Via Roma in Naples, Carl Pfeiffer, a famous newsfax reporter, could not resist his compulsion to gamble. He telephoned Joan Otur, one of his few friends, and insisted that she accompany him to Paris. Organ-gambling was legal in France. They dropped from the sky in a transparent Plasticine egg, and Paris opened up below them, Paris and the glittering chip of diamond that was the Casino Bellecour. Except for the dymaxion dome of the Right Bank, Joan would not have been able to distinguish Paris from the suburbs beyond. A city had grown over the city: The grid of the ever-expanding slung city had its own constellations of light and his Haussmann's ruler-straight boulevards, the ancient architectural wonders, even the black, sour-stenched Seine, which was an hourglass curve dividing the old city.

Their transpod settled to the ground like a dirty snow-flake and split silently open, letting in the chill night air with its acrid smells of mudflats and cinders and clogged drains. Joan and Pfeiffer hurried across the transpad toward the high oaken doors of the casino. All around them stretched the bleak, brick-and-concrete wastelands of the city's ruined districts, the fetid warrens on the dome's peripheries, which were inhabited by skinheads and Screamers who existed outside the tightly controlled structure of Uptown life. Now, as Pfeiffer touched his hand to a palm-plate sensor, the door opened and admitted them into the casino itself. The precarious outside world was closed out and left behind.

A young man, who reminded Joan of an upright (if possible) Bedlington terrier, led them through the courtyard. He spoke with a clipped English accent and had tufts of woolly, bluish-white hair implanted all over his head, face, and body. Only his hands and genitals were hairless.

"He *has* to be working off an indenture," Pfeiffer said sharply as he repressed a sexual urge.

"Shush," Joan said, as the boy gave Pfeiffer a brief, contemptuous look — in Parisian culture, you were paying only for the service, not for the smile.

They were led into a simple, but formal, entry lounge, which was crowded, but not uncomfortable. The floor was marbled; a few pornographic icons were discreetly situated around the carefully laid-out comfort niches. The room reminded Joan of a chapel with arcades, figures, and stone courts. Above was a dome, from which radiated a reddish, suffusing light, lending the room an expansiveness of height rather than breadth.

But it was mostly holographic illusion.

They were directed to wait a moment and then presented to the purser, an overweight, balding man who sat behind a small desk. He was dressed in a blue camise shirt and matching caftan, which was buttoned across his wide chest and closed with a red scarf. He was obviously, and uncomfortably, dressed in the colors of the establishment.

"And good evening, Monsieur Pfeiffer and Mademoiselle Otur. We are honored to have such an important guest, or guests, I should say." The purser slipped two cards into a small console. "Your identification cards will be returned to you when you leave." After a pause he asked, "Ah, does Monsieur Pfeiffer wish the lady to be credited on his card?" The purser lowered his eyes, indicating embarrassment. Quite simply, Joan did not have enough credit to be received into the more sophisticated games.

"Yes, of course," Pfeiffer said absently. He felt guilty and anxious about feeling a thrill of desire for that grotesque boy.

"Well, then," said the purser, folding his hands on the desk, "we are at your disposal for as long as you wish to stay with us." He gestured toward the terrier and said, "Johnny will give you the tour," but Pfeiffer politely declined. Johnny ushered them into a central room, which was anything but quiet, and—after a wink at Pfeiffer—discreetly disappeared.

The room was as crowded as the city ways. It was filled with what looked to be the ragtag, the bums and the street people, the captains of the ways. Here was a perfect replica of a street casino, but perfectly safe. This *was* a street casino, at least to Pfeiffer, who was swept up in the noise and bustle, as he whetted his appetite for the dangerous pleasures of the top level.

Ancient iron bandits whispered "chinka-chinka" and rolled their picture-frame eyes in promise of a jackpot, which was immediately transferred to the winner's account by magnetic sleight of hand. The amplified, high-pitched voices of pinball computers on the walls called out winning hands of poker and blackjack. A simulated stabbing drew nothing more than a few glances. Tombstone booths were filled with figures working through their own Stations of the Cross. Hooked-in winners were rewarded with bursts of electrically induced ecstasy; losers writhed in pain and suffered through the brain-crushing aftershock of week-long migraines.

And, of course, battered robots clattered around with the traditional complement of drugs, drink, and food. The only incongruity was a perfectly dressed geisha, who quickly disappeared into one of the iris-doors on the far wall.

"Do you want to play the one-armed bandits?" Joan asked, fighting her growing claustrophobia, wishing only to escape into quiet; but she was determined to try to keep Pfeiffer from going upstairs. Yet, ironically—all her emotions seemed to be simultaneously yin and yang—she also wanted him to gamble away his organs. She knew that she would feel a guilty thrill if he lost his heart. Then she pulled down the lever of the one-armed bandit; it would read her finger-and odor-prints and transfer or deduct the proper amount to or from Pfeiffer's account. The eyes rolled and clicked and one hundred international credit dollars was lost. "Easy come, easy go. At least, this is a safe way to go. But you didn't come here to be safe, right?" Joan asked mockingly.

"You can remain down here, if you like," Pfeiffer said, looking about the room for an exit, noticing that iris doors were spaced every few meters on the nearest wall to his left. *The casino must take up the whole bloody block*, he thought. "How the hell do I get out of here?"

Before Joan could respond, Johnny appeared, as if out of nowhere, and said, "Monsieur Pfeiffer may take any one of the ascenseurs, or, if he would care for the view of our palace, he could take the staircase to heaven." He smiled, baring even teeth, and curtsied to Pfeiffer, who was blushing. *The boy certainly knows his man,* Joan thought sourly.

Am I jealous? she asked herself. She cared for Pfeiffer, but didn't *love* him—at least she didn't think she did.

"Shall I attend you?" Johnny asked Pfeiffer, ignoring Joan.

"No," said Pfeiffer. "Now please leave us alone."

"Well, which is it?" asked Joan. "The elevator would be quickest, zoom you right to the organ room."

"We can take the stairs," Pfeiffer said, a touch of blush still in his cheeks. But he would say nothing about the furry boy. "Jesus, it seems that everytime I blink my eye, the stairway disappears."

"I'll show you the way," Joan said, taking his arm.

"Just what I need," Pfeiffer said, smiling, eliminating one small barrier between them.

"I think your rush is over, isn't it? You don't really want to gamble out your guts."

"I came to do something, and I'll follow it through."

The stairwell was empty, and, like an object conceived in Alice's Wonderland, it appeared to disappear behind them. "Cheap tricks," Pfeiffer said.

"Why are you so intent on this?" Joan asked. "If you lose, which you most probably will, you'll never have a day's peace. They can call in your heart, or liver, or—"

"I can buy out, if that should happen." Pfeiffer reddened, but it had nothing to do with his conversation with Joan, to which he was hardly paying attention; he was still thinking about the furry boy.

"You wouldn't gamble them, if you thought you could buy out. That's bunk."

"Then I'd get artificials."

"You'd be taking another chance, with the quotas—thanks to your right-wing friends in power."

Pfeiffer didn't take the bait. "I admit defeat," he said. Again he thought of the furry boy's naked, hairless genitals. And with that came the thought of death.

The next level was less crowded and more subdued. There were few electronic games to be seen on the floor. A man passed dressed in medical white, which indicated that deformation games were being played. On each floor the stakes became increasingly higher; fortunes were lost, people were disfigured, or ruined, but—with the exception of the top floor, which had dangerous games other than organ-gambling—at least no one died. They might need a face and body job after too many deformations, but those were easily obtained, although one had to have very good credit to ensure a proper job.

On each ascending level, the house whores, both male and female, became more exotic, erotic, grotesque, and abundant. There were birdmen with feathers like peacocks and flamingos, children with dyed skin and overly large, implanted male and female genitalia, machines that spoke the language of love and exposed soft, fleshy organs, amputees and cripples, various drag queens and kings, natural androgynes and mutants, cyborgs, and an interesting, titillating array of genetically engineered mooncalves.

But none disturbed Pfeiffer as had that silly furry boy. He wondered if, indeed, the boy was still following him.

"Come on, Joan" Pfeiffer said impatiently. "I really don't want to waste any more time down here."

"But I always thought it was the expectation that's so exciting to seasoned gamblers," Joan said.

"Not to me," Pfeiffer said, ignoring the sarcasm. "I want to get it over with." With that, he left the room.

Then why bother at all? Joan asked herself, wondering why she had let Pfeiffer talk her into coming here. *He doesn't need me. Damn him,* she thought, ignoring a skinny, white-haired man and a piebald, doggie mooncalf coupling beside her in an upright position.

She took a lift to the top level to catch up with Pfeiffer.

It was like walking into the foyer of a well-appointed home. The high walls were stucco and the floor was inlaid parquet. A small Dehaj rug was placed neatly before a desk, behind which beamed a man of about fifty dressed in camise and caftan. He had a flat face, a large nose that was wide, but had narrow nostrils, and close-set eyes roofed with bushy, brown eyebrows, the color his hair would have been, had he had any.

Actually, the room was quite small, which made the rug look larger and gave the man a commanding position.

"Do you wish to watch or participate, Monsieur Pfeiffer?" he asked, seeming to rise an inch from the chair as he spoke.

"I wish to play," Pfeiffer said, standing upon the rug as if he had to be positioned just right to make it fly.

"And does your friend wish to watch?" the man asked, as Joan crossed the room to stand beside Pfeiffer. "Or will you give your permission for Miz Otur to become telepathically connected to you." His voice didn't rise as he asked the question.

"I beg your pardon?"

"A psyconnection, sir. With a psyconductor"—a note of condescension crept into his voice.

"I *know* what it is, and I don't want it," Pfeiffer snapped and then moved away from Joan. But a cerebral hook-in was, in fact, just what Joan had hoped for.

"Oh, come on," Joan said. "Let me in."

"Are you serious?" he asked, turning toward her.

165

Caught by the intensity of his stare, she could only nod. "Then I'm sorry. I'm not a window for you to stare through."

That stung her, and she retorted, "Have you ever done it with your wife?" She immediately regretted her words.

The man at the desk cleared his throat politely. "Excuse me, monsieur, but are you aware that *only* games *organe* are played in these rooms?"

"Yes, that's why I've come to your house."

"Then, you are perhaps not aware that all our games are conducted with psyconductors on this floor.

Pfeiffer, looking perplexed, said, "Perhaps you had better explain it to me."

"Of course, of course," the man said, beaming, as if he had just won the battle and a fortune. "There are, of course, many ways to play, and, if you like, I can give you the address of a very nice house nearby where you can play a fair, safe game without hook-ins. Shall I make a reservation for you there?"

"Not just yet," Pfeiffer said, resting his hands, knuckles down, upon the flat-top Louis XVI desk.

His feet seemed to be swallowed by the floral patterns of the rug, and Joan thought it an optical illusion, this effect of being caught before the desk of the casino captain. She felt the urge to grab Pfeiffer and take him out of this suffocating place.

Instead, she walked over to him. Perhaps he would relent just a little and let her slide into his mind.

"It is one of our house rules, however," said the man at the desk, "that you and your opponent, or opponents, must be physically in the same room."

"Why is that?" Joan asked, feeling Pfeiffer scowling at her for intruding.

"Well," he said, "it has never happened to us, of course

but cheating has occurred on a few long-distance transactions. Organs have been wrongly lost. So we don't take any chances. None at all." He looked at Pfeiffer as he spoke, obviously sizing him up, watching for reactions. But Pfeiffer had composed himself, and Joan knew that he had made up his mind.

"Why must the game be played with psyconductors?" Pfeiffer asked.

"That is the way we do it," said the captain. Then, after an embarrassing pause, he said, "We have our own games and rules. And our games, we think, are the *most* interesting. And we make the games as safe as we can for all parties involved."

"What do you mean?"

"We—the house—will be observing you. Our gamesmaster will be telepathically hooked in, but, I assure you, you will not sense his presence in the least. If anything should go wrong, or look as if it might go wrong, then *pfft*, we intercede. Of course, we make no promises, and there have been cases where—"

"But anything that could go wrong would be because of the cerebral hook-in."

"Perhaps this *isn't* the game for you, sir."

"You must have enough privileged information on everyone who has ever played here to make book," Pfeiffer said.

"The hook-in doesn't work that way at all. And besides, we are contract-bound to protect our clients."

"And yourselves."

"Most certainly." The casino captain looked impatient.

"If both players can read each other's mind," Pfeiffer said to the captain, "then there can be no blind cards."

"Aha, now you have it, monsieur." At that, the tension between Pfeiffer and the desk captain seemed to dissolve.

"And, indeed," the captain continued, "we have a modified version of chemin de fer, which we call blind shemmy. All the cards are played face down. It is a game of control (and, of course, chance), for you must block out certain thoughts from your mind, while, at the same time, tricking your opponent into revealing his cards. And that is why it would be advantageous for you to let your friend here connect with you."

Pfeiffer glanced toward Joan and said, "Please clarify that."

"Quite simply, while you are playing, your friend could help block your thoughts from your opponent with her own," said the captain. "But it does take some practice. Perhaps, it would be better if you tried a hook-in in one of our other rooms, where the stakes are not quite so high." Then the captain lowered his eyes, as if in deference, but in actuality he was looking at the CeeR screen of the terminal set into the antique desk.

Joan could see Pfeiffer's nostrils flare slightly. *The poor sonofabitch is caught,* she thought. "Come on, Carl, let's get out of here now."

"Perhaps you should listen to Miss Otur," the captain said, but the man must have known that he had Pfeiffer.

"I wish to play blind shemmy," Pfeiffer said, turning toward Joan, glaring at her. She caught her breath: If he lost, then she knew he would make certain that Joan lost something, too.

"I have a game of nine in progress," the captain said. "There are nine people playing and nine others playing interference. But you'll have to wait for a space. It will be quite expensive, as the players are tired and will demand some of your points for themselves above the casino charge for the play."

"How long will I have to wait?"

The captain shrugged, then said, "I have another man waiting, who is ahead of you. He would be willing to play a game of doubles. I would recommend you play him rather than wait. Like you, he is an amateur, but his wife, who will be connected with him, is not. Of course, if you wish to wait for the other . . ."

Pfeiffer accepted, and while he and Joan gave their prints to the various forms, the captain explained that there was no statue of limitations on the contract signed by all parties, and that it would be honored even by those governments that disapprove of this particular form of gambling.

Then the furry boy appeared like an apparition to take them to their room where they would be given time to practice and become acquainted.

The boy's member was slightly engorged, and Pfeiffer now became frightened. He suddenly thought of his mother and the obligatory hook-in service at her funeral. His skin crawled as he remembered her last filthy thoughts. . . .

The furry boy led Joan and Pfeiffer into the game room, which smelled of oiled wood, spices, traditional tobacco, and perfume. There were no holos or decoration on the walls. Everything, with the exception of the felt top of the gaming table, cards, thick natural carpet, computer consoles, and cowls, was made of precious woods: oak, elm, cedar, teak, walnut, mahogany, redwood, ebony. The long, half-oval gaming table, which met the sliding partition wall, was made of satinwood, as were the two delicate, but uncomfortable, high-backed chairs placed side by side. On the table before each chair was a psyconductor cowl, each one sheathed in a light, silvery mask.

"We call them poker-faces," the boy said to Pfeiffer, as he placed the cowl over Joan's head. He explained how the psyconductor mechanism worked, then asked Pfeiffer if he wished him to stay.

"Why should I want you to stay?" Pfeiffer asked, but the sexual tension between them was unmistakable.

"I'm adept at games of chance. I can redirect your thoughts—without a psyconductor." He looked at Joan and smiled.

"Put the mechanism on my head and then please leave us," Pfeiffer said.

"Do you wish me to return when you're finished?"

"If you wish," Pfeiffer replied stiffly, and Joan watched his discomfort. Without saying a word, she had won a small victory.

The boy lowered the cowl over Pfeiffer's head, made some unnecessary adjustments, and left reluctantly.

"I'm not at all sure that I want to do this," Pfeiffer mumbled, faltering.

"Well," Joan said, "we can easily call off the game. Our first connection is just practice—"

"I don't mean the game. I mean the psyconnection."

Joan remained silent. Dammit, she told herself. I should have looked away when Pfeiffer's furry pet made a pass at him.

"I was crazy to agree to such a thing in the first place."

"Shall I leave?" Joan asked. "It was *you* who insisted that I come along, remember?" She stood up, but did not judge the distance of the cowl/console connections accurately, and the cowl was pulled forward, bending the silver mask.

"I think you're as nervous as I am," Pfeiffer said appeasingly.

"Make the connection, right now. Or let's get out of

170

here." Joan was suddenly angry and frustrated. *Do it*, she thought to herself, and for once she was not passive. Certainly not passive. *Damn him and his furry boy!* She snapped the wooden toggle switch, activating both psyconductors, and was thrust into vertiginous light. It surrounded her, as if she could see in all directions at once. But she was simply seeing through Pfeiffer's eyes. Seeing herself, small, even in his eyes, small.

After the initial shock, she realized that the light was not brilliant; on the contrary, it was soft and diffused.

But this was no connection at all: Pfeiffer was trying to close his mind to her. He appeared before her as a smooth, perfect, huge, sphere. It slowly rotated, a grim, gray planet, closed to her, forever closed. . . .

Are you happy now? asked Pfeiffer, as if from somewhere deep inside the sphere. It was so smooth, seamless. *He really does not need me,* she thought, and she felt as if she were flying above the surface of his closed mind, a winged thing looking for any discontinuity, any fault in his defenses.

So you see, Pfeiffer said, exulting in imagined victory, *I don't need you*. The words came wreathed in an image of a storm rolling angrily over the planet.

She flew, in sudden panic, around his thoughts, like an insect circling a source of light. She was looking for any blister or crack, any anomaly in the smooth surface. He would gamble his body away without her, that she knew, unless she could break through his defenses, prove to him how vulnerable he really was.

So you couldn't resist the furry boy, could you? Joan asked, her thoughts like smooth sharks swimming through icy water. *Does he, then, remind you of yourself, or do I remind you of your mother?*

His anger and exposed misery were like flares on the

surface of the sun. In their place remained an eruption of Pfeiffer's smooth protective surface. A crack in the cerebral egg.

Joan dove toward the fissure, and then she was inside Pfeiffer—not the outside of his senses where he could verbalize a thought, see a face, but in the dark, prehistoric places where he dreamed, conceptualized, where he floated in and out of memory, where the eyeless creatures of his soul dwelled.

It was a sliding, a slipping in, as if one had turned over inside oneself; and Joan was sliding, slipping on ice. She found herself in a dark world of grotesque and geometric shapes, an arctic world of huge icebergs floating on a fathomless sea.

And for an instant, Joan sensed Pfeiffer's terrible fear of the world.

Mindfucker! Pfeiffer screamed, projecting the word in a hundred filthy, sickening images; and then he smashed through Joan's defenses and rushed into the deep recesses of her mind. He found her soft places and took what he could.

All that before the pysconnection was broken. Before the real game began. As if nothing had happened.

A man and woman, wearing identical cowled masks, sat across from Joan and Pfeiffer. The partition wall had been slid back, revealing the oval shape of the gaming table and doubling the size of the wood-paneled room. The dealer and the gamesmaster sat on each side of the long table between the opponents. The dealer was a young man with an intense, roundish face and straight black hair cut at the shoulders; he was most likely in training to become a gamesmaster.

The gamesmaster's face was hidden by a black cowl; he would be hooked in to the game. He explained the rules, activated the psyconductors, and the game began. Joan and Pfeiffer were once again hooked in, but there was no contact, as yet, with the man and woman across the table.

Pfeiffer cleared his mind, just as if he were before lasers or giving an interview. He had learned to cover his thoughts, for, somehow, he had always felt they could be seen, especially by those who wanted to hurt him politically and on the job.

White thought, he called it, because it was similar to white noise.

Pfeiffer could feel Joan circling around him like the wind. Although he couldn't conceal everything, he could hide from her. He could use her, just as she could use him . . . had used him. They had reached an accord via mutual blackmail. Somehow, during their practice hook-in, Joan had forced herself into Pfeiffer's mind; shocked, he attacked her.

So now they knew each other better.

They built a simple symbol structure: He was the world, a perfect sphere without blemish, made by God's own hands, a world as strong and divine as thought; and she was his atmosphere. She contained all the elements that could not exist on his featureless surface. She was the protective cloak of his world.

They built a mnemonic in which to hide, yet they were still vulnerable to each other. But Pfeiffer guessed that Joan would remain passive—after all, she always had. She also had the well-developed conscience of a mystical liberal, and she was in love with him. He had seen that—or thought he had.

She would not expose him to danger.

Pfeiffer congratulated himself for being calm, which reinforced his calmness. Perhaps it was Joan's presence. Perhaps it was the mnemonic. But perhaps not. He had the willpower; this was just another test. He had managed to survive all the others, he told himself.

Joan rained on him, indicating her presence, and they practiced talking within geometric shapes as a protective device — it was literally raining geodesic cats and dogs.

When the gamesmaster opened the psyconductor to all involved, Joan and Pfeiffer were ready.

But they were not ready to find exact duplicates of themselves facing them across the table. The doppelgängers, of course, were not wearing cowls.

"First, mesdames and messieurs, we draw the wager," said the dealer, who was not hooked in. The gamesmaster's thoughts were a neutral presence. "For each organ pledged, there will be three games consisting of three hands to a game," continued the dealer. "In the event that a player wins twice in succession, the third hand or game will not be played." His voice was an intrusion; it was harsh and cold and came from the outside where everything was hard and intractable.

How do they know what we look like? Pfeiffer asked, shaken by the hallucination induced by his opponents.

But before Joan could reply, he answered his own question. *They must be picking up subliminal stuff.*

The way we perceive ourselves, Joan said. The doppelgängers became hard and ugly, as if they were being eroded by time. And Joan's double was becoming smaller, insignificant.

If we can't cover up, we won't have a chance.

You can't cover everything, but neither can they, Joan said. *It cuts both ways.* She noticed a fissure in the otherwise perfect sphere below, and she became black fog, miasma, protective covering. Pfeiffer was afraid, and vulnerable. But she had to give him credit: He was not hiding it from her, at least. That was a beginning. . . .

Did you pick up anything from them, an image, anything? Pfeiffer asked.

We've been too busy with ourselves. We'll just wait and be ready when they let something slip out.

Which they will, Pfeiffer said, suddenly confident again.

From deep inside their interior, symbolized world, Joan and Pfeiffer could look into the external world of croupier, felt-top table, cards, wood-covered walls, and masked creatures. This room was simply a stage for the play of thought and image.

Pfeiffer was well acquainted with this sensation of perceiving two worlds, two levels: inside and outside. He often awakened from a nightmare and found himself in his living room or library. He knew that he was wide awake, and yet he could still see the dream unfurl before him, watch the creatures of his nightmare stalk about the room — the interior beasts let loose into the familiar, comforting confines of his waking world. Those were always moments of terror, for surely he was near the edge then . . . and could fall.

The dealer combined two decks of cards and placed them in a shoe, a box from which the cards could be slid out one by one. He discarded three cards: the traditional burning of the deck.

Then he dealt a card to Pfeiffer and one to his opponent. Both cards landed faceup. A queen of hearts for Pfeiffer. A nine of hearts for his opponent.

So Pfeiffer lost the right to call the wager.

Just as the object of black jack was to draw cards that add up to twenty-one, or as near to that figure as possible, the object of blind shemmy was to draw cards that add up to nine. Thus, face cards, which would normally be counted as ten, were counted as zero. Aces, normally counted as eleven, became one; and all other cards had their normal pip (or face) value, with the exception of tens, which, like aces, were counted as one.

"Monsieur Deux wins, nine over zero," said the dealer, looking now at Pfeiffer's opponent. Pfeiffer was Monsieur Un and his opponent Monsieur Deux only because of their positions at the table.

A hell of a way to start, Pfeiffer said.

Keep yourself closed, Joan said, turning into mist, then dark rain, pure sunlight and rainbows, a perceptual kaleidoscope to conceal Pfeiffer from his enemies. *Look now, he'll be more vulnerable when he speaks. I'll cover you.*

Your choice, said the gamesmaster. The thought was directed to Pfeiffer's opponent, who was staring intently at Pfeiffer.

Look now, Joan said to Pfeiffer.

"Since we both turned up hearts, perhaps that is where we should begin," Pfeiffer's opponent said, speaking for the benefit of the dealer. His words felt like shards of glass to Pfeiffer. "They're the seats of our emotions; so we'd best dispose of them quickly." Pfeiffer felt the man smile. "Do you assent?"

"It's your choice," Pfeiffer said to the dealer tonelessly.

Don't let anything out, Joan said.

Pfeiffer couldn't pick up anything from his opponent and the woman with him; they were both empty doppelgängers of himself and Joan. *Pretend that nothing matters,* she said. *If you expect to see his cards and look inside him for weakness, you must be removed.*

She's right, Pfeiffer thought. He tried to relax, smooth himself down; he thought innocuous white thoughts and ignored the knot of anxiety that seemed to be pulling at his groin.

"*Cartes*," said the dealer, dealing two cards from the shoe, facedown, one for Pfeiffer, the other for his opponent. Another two cards, and then a palpable silence; not even thoughts seemed to cut the air. It was an unnatural waiting. . . .

Pfeiffer had a natural nine, a winning hand (a queen and a nine of diamonds), and he looked up, about to turn over his cards, when he saw the furry boy sitting across the table from him.

What the hell—

Call your hand. Joan said, feeling his glands open up, a warm waterfall of fear. But before Pfeiffer could speak, his opponent said, "My friend across the table has a natural nine. A queen and a nine, both diamonds. Since I called his hand—and I believe I am correct, then . . ."

The dealer turned Pfeiffer's cards over and said, "Monseiur Deux is correct, and wins by call." If Pfeiffer's opponent had been mistaken about the hand, Pfeiffer would have won automatically, even if his opponent held better cards.

The dealer then dealt two more cards from the shoe.

You're supposed to be covering my thoughts, Pfeiffer said, but he was composed, thinking white thoughts again.

I'm trying, Joan said. *But you won't trust me; you're trying to cover yourself from me as well as your opponent. What the hell am I supposed do?*

I'm sorry, Pfeiffer thought.

Are you really so afraid that I'll see your true feelings?

This is neither the time nor the place. His rhythm of white thought was broken; Joan became a snowstorm, aiding him, lulling him back to white blindness. *I think the gamesmaster is making me nervous, having him hooked in, privy to all our thoughts. . . .*

Forget the gamesmaster . . . and for God's sake, stop worrying about what I'll see. I'm on your side.

"Monsieur Un, will you *please* claim your cards," said the dealer. The gamesmaster nodded at Pfeiffer and thought neutral, papery thoughts.

Pfeiffer turned up the edges of his cards. He had a jack of diamonds—which counted as zero—and a two of spades. He would need another card.

Don't think about your cards, Joan exclaimed. *Are you picking up anything from the other side of the table?*

Pfeiffer listened, as if to his own thoughts. He didn't raise is head to look at his opponent, for seeing his own face—or that of the furry boy's—staring back at him from across the table was disconcerting, and fascinating. An image of an empty, hollow woman without any organs formed in his mind. He imagined her as a bag somehow formed into human shape.

Keep that, Joan said. *It might be usable.*

But I can't see his cards.

Just wait awhile. Keep calm.

"Does Monsieur wish another card?" the dealer asked Pfeiffer. Pfeiffer took another card, and so did his opponent.

Pfeiffer had no idea what cards is opponent was holding; it promised to be a blind play. When the cards were turned over, the dealer announced, "Monsieur Deux wins, six over five." Pfeiffer had lost again.

I'm playing blind, Pfeiffer said anxiously to Joan.

He couldn't see your cards, either, she replied.

But that gave him little satisfaction, for by losing the first two hands, he had lost the first game.

And if he lost the next game, he would lose his heart,

which, white thought or not, seemed to Pfeiffer to be beating in his throat.

Try to calm yourself, Joan said, *or you'll let everything out. If you trust me, and stop throwing up your defenses, maybe I can help you. But you've got to let me in; as it is, you're giving our friends quite the edge. Let's make a merger . . . a marriage.* But Pfeiffer was in no mood for irony. His fear was building, steadily, slowly.

You can fold the game, Joan said. *That is an alternative.*

And give up organs I haven't yet played for! The smooth surface of Pfeiffer's sphere cracked, and Joan let herself be swallowed into it. The surface of the sphere changed, grew mountain chains, lush vegetation, flowers, deserts, all the mingled moods of Joan and Pfeiffer.

Pfeiffer was no longer isolated; he was protected, yet dangerously exposed. Inside him, in the human, moist dark, Joan promised not to take advantage of him. She caught a fleeting thought of Pfeiffer's dead mother, who had been a fleshy, big-boned, flat-faced woman. She also saw that Pfeiffer hated his mother, as much now as when she was alive.

In the next hand—the opening hand of the second game—Pfeiffer held a five of clubs and a two of spades, a total of seven points. He would not take another card unless he could see his opponent's. But when he looked up, Pfeiffer saw the furry boy, who blew him a kiss.

You're exposed again, Joan said, and they thought themselves inside their world, thought protective darkness around themselves, except for one tiny opening through which to see into their enemies.

Concentrate on that image of the empty woman, Joan said to Pfeiffer. *She has to be Monsieur Deux's wife or woman. I can't quite visualize it as you did.* But Pfeiffer was trying to smooth down his emotions and the dark, dangerous demon that was his memory. The image of the furry boy sparked memories, fears, guilts. Pfeiffer remembered his father, who had been a doctor. There was always enough money, but his father extracted emotional dues for every dollar he gave his son. And, as a result, the young Pfeiffer had recurrent nightmares that he was sucking off his father. Those nightmares began again after his mother died: She had seen that homosexual fantasy when Pfeiffer hooked in to her on her deathbed.

Pfeiffer still had those nightmares.

And now, against his will, the image of him sucking off the furry boy passed through his mind, drawing its train of guilt and revulsion. The boy and his father, somehow one and the same.

You're leaking, Joan said, her thoughts an icestorm. She could see her way into Pfeiffer now, into those rooms of buried memories. Rather than rooms, she thought of them as subterranean caverns; everything inside them was intact, perfect, hidden from the harmful light and atmosphere of consciousness. Now she knew him. . . .

Pfeiffer collected himself and peered into his opponent's mind. He thrust the image of the organless woman at the man.

It was like tearing a spiderweb.

Pfeiffer felt the man's pain as a feather touching flesh: The organless woman was Monsieur Deux's permanent wife. Pfeiffer had broken through and into his thoughts; he could feel his opponent's name, something like Gayah, Gahai, Gayet, that was it, and his wife was used up. Gayet saw her, in the darkness of his unconscious, as an empty bag. She was a compulsive gambler, who had spent her organs; and Gayet hated gambling, but she possessed him, and he hated her and loved her, and was just beginning his self-destructive slide.

Now she was using him up. She was gambling *his* organs.

She's used up, Pfeiffer thought at Gayet. But Pfeiffer could only glimpse Gayet's thoughts. His wife was not exposed.

Nor was she defenseless.

She thrust the image of the furry boy at Pfeiffer, and Pfeiffer felt his head being forced down upon the furry boy's lap. But it suddenly wasn't the furry boy anymore. It was Pfeiffer's father!

There was no distance now. Pfeiffer was caught, tiny and vulnerable.

Gayet and his wife were swallowing him, thoughts and all.

It was Joan who saved him. She pulled him away, and he became the world again, wrapped in snow, in whiteness. He was safe again, as if inside Joan's cold womb.

Look now, Joan said an instant later, and like a revelation, Pfeiffer saw Gayet's cards, saw them buried in Gayet's eyes with the image of his aging wife. In that instant, Pfeiffer saw into Gayet and forgot himself. Gayet's wife was named Grace, and she had been eroded from too many surgeries, too many deformation games. She was his Blue Angel (yes, he had seen the ancient film) and Gayet the fool.

The fool held an ace of hearts and a five of diamonds.

Now Pfeiffer felt that the odds were with him; it was a familiar sensation for gamblers, a sense of harmony, of being a benevolent extension of the cards. No anger, no fear, no hate, just victory. Pfeiffer called Gayet's hand, thereby preventing Gayet from drawing another card, such as a lucky three, which would have given him a count of nine.

Pfeiffer won the hand, and he thanked Joan. His thoughts were of love, but his repertoire of images was limited. Joan was now part of his rhythm and harmony, a constant presence; and she dreamed of the victorious cats that padded so gracefully through the lush vegetation of Pfeiffer's sphere—the cats that rutted, then devoured one another.

Pfeiffer won the next hand to take the second game. Pfeiffer and his opponent were now even. The next game would determine the outcome. Pfeiffer felt that calm, cold certainty that he would take Gayet's heart. The obsession to expose and ruin his opponent became more important than winning or losing organs; it was bright and fast flowing, refreshing as water.

He was in a better world now, a more complete, fulfilling plane of reality. All gamblers dreamed of this: losing or winning everything, but being inside the game. Even Joan was carried away by the game. She, too, wanted to rend—to whittle away at the couple across the table, take their privacies, turn over their humiliations like worrybeads. They were Pfeiffer's enemies . . . and his enemies were her own.

Everyone was exposed now, battle weary, mentally and physically exhausted, yet lost in play, lost in perfect, concentrated time. Pfeiffer could see Gayet's face, both as Gayet saw himself and as Grace saw him. A wide nose, dark complexion, low forehead, large ears; yet it was a strong face, and handsome in a feral, almost frightening way—or so Grace thought. Gayet saw himself as weak; the flesh on his face was too loose.

Gayet was a failure, although he had made his career and fortune in the Exchange. He had wanted to be a mathematician, but he was lazy and lost the "knack" by twenty-five.

Gayet would have made a brilliant mathematician, and he knew it.

And Grace was a whore, using herself and everyone else. Here was a woman with great religious yearnings, who had wanted to join a religious order, but was black-balled by the cults because of her obsession for gambling and psyconductors. But Pfeiffer could see into her only a little. She was a cold bitch and, more than any of the others, had reserves of strength.

This last game would be psychological surgery. Tearing with the knife, pulping with the bludgeon. Pfeiffer won the first hand. This was joy; so many organs to win or lose, so little time.

Pfeiffer lost the next hand. Gayet exposed Joan, who revealed Pfeiffer's cards without realizing it. Gayet had opened her up, penetrated all that efficiency and order to expose anger and lust and uncontrolled oceanic pity. Joan's emotions writhed and crawled over her like beauti-fully colored, slippery snakes. Pfeiffer had been too pre-occupied to protect her.

Joan's first thought was to revenge herself on Pfeiffer, expose him; but he opened up to her, buried her in white thought, which was as cold and numbing as ice, and apol-ogized without words, but with the soft, rounded, com-forting thoughts he equated with love. She couldn't trust him, nor could she expose him. Right now, she could only accept him.

The dealer gave Pfeiffer a three of diamonds and an ace of clubs. That gave him only four points; he would have to draw again. He kept his thoughts from Joan, for she was covering him. She could attack Gayet and his whore, expose them for their cards. Gayet's heart was not simply his organ—not now, not to Pfeiffer. It was his whole life,

life itself. To rip it away from him would be to conquer life, if only for a moment. It was life affirming. It was being alive. Suddenly he thought of his father.

Close yourself up, Joan said. *You're bleeding.* She did not try to penetrate his thoughts; that would have exposed Pfeiffer even more dangerously.

Help me, Pfeiffer asked Joan. This hand would determine whether he would win or lose the game . . . and his heart.

Once again she became his cloak, his atmosphere, and she weaved her icy threads of white thought into his.

This was love, she thought.

Pfeiffer couldn't see Gayet's cards and nervously asked Joan to do something. Gayet was playing calmly, well covered by Grace, who simply hid him. No extravagance there.

Joan emptied her mind, became neutral; yet she was a needle of cold, coherent thought. She prodded, probed, touched her opponents' thoughts. It was like swimming through an ever-changing world of dots and bars, tangible as iron, fluid as water. It was as if Gayet's and Grace's thoughts were luminous points on a fluorescent screen.

And still she went unnoticed.

Gayet was like Pfeiffer, Joan thought. Seemingly placid, controlled, but that was all gingerbread to hide a weak house. He was so much weaker than Grace, who was supporting and cloaking him. But Grace was concentrating her energies on Gayet; and she had the fever, as if she were gambling her own organs once again.

Undoubtedly, Grace expected Joan and Pfeiffer to go straight for Gayet, who had read the cards.

So Joan went for Grace, who was in the gambler's frenzy as the hand was being played. Joan slipped past Grace's thoughts, worked her way into the woman's mind, through the dark labyrinths and channels of her memory, and into the dangerous country of the unconscious. Invisible as air, she listened to Grace, read her, discovered: A sexual miasma. Being brutally raped as a child. After a riot in Manosque. Raped in a closet, for God's sake. The man tore her open with a rifle barrel, then inserted himself. Taking her, piece by bloody piece, just as she was taking Gayet. Just as others had taken her in rooms like this, in this casino, in this closet.

And Gayet, now Joan could see him through Grace, unperturbable Gayet, who had so much money and so little life, who was so afraid of his wife's past, of her lovers and liberations he called perversions. But he called *everything* a perversion.

How she hated him beneath what she called love.

But he looked just like the man who had raped her in that closet so long ago. She could not remember the man's face — so effectively had she blocked it out of her mind — yet she was stunned when she first met Gayet. She felt attracted to him, but also repelled; she was in love.

Through Joan, Pfeiffer saw Gayet's cards: a deuce and a six of clubs. He could call his hand, but he wasn't sure of the deuce. It looked like a heart, but it could just as easily be a diamond. If he called it wrong, he would lose the hand, and his heart.

I can't be sure, Pfeiffer said to Joan, expecting help.

But Joan was in trouble. Grace had discovered her, and she was stronger than Joan had ever imagined. Joan was trapped inside Grace's mind; and Grace, who could not face what Joan had found, denied it.

And snapped.

In that instant, Joan felt that *she* was Grace. She felt all of Grace's pain and the choking weight of memory, as souls and selves incandescently merged. But before Joan and Grace could fuse inescapably, Joan recoiled, realizing that she was fighting for her life. She screamed for the gamesmaster to deactivate the game. But her screams were lost as Grace instantly slipped into the gamesmaster's mind and caught him, too. She had the psychotic's strength of desperation, and Joan realized that Grace would kill them all rather than face the truth about herself and Gayet.

Furiously Grace went after Pfeiffer. To kill him. She blamed him for Joan's presence, and Joan felt crushing pain, as if she were being buried alive in the dirt of Grace's mind. She tried to wrench herself away from Grace's thoughts, lest they intertwine with, and become, her own.

She felt Grace's bloodlust . . . her need to kill Pfeiffer.

Grace grasped Pfeiffer with a thought, wound dark filaments around him that could not be turned away by white thought or anything else.

And like a spider, she wrapped her prey in darkness and looked for physiological weakness, any flaw, perhaps a blood vessel that might rupture in his head. . . .

Joan tried to pull herself away from the pain, from the concrete weight crushing her. Ironically, she wondered if thought had mass. What a stupid thought to die with, she told herself, and she suddenly remembered a story her father had told her about a dying rabbi who was annoyed at the minyan praying around him because he was trying to listen to two washerwomen gossiping outside.

Many years later, her father confessed to her that it wasn't really a Jewish story at all; it was Buddhist. She held on to that thought, remembered how her father had laughed after his confession.

The pain eased as she followed her thoughts: If thought

had mass . . .

She was thinking herself free, escaping Grace by finding the proper angle, as if thought and emotion and pain were purely mathematical.

That done in an instant.

But if she were to save Pfeiffer's life, and her own, she would have to do something immediately. She showed Grace her past. Showed her that she had married Gayet because he had the face of the man who had raped her as a child.

Gayet, seeing this too, screamed. How he loathed Grace, but not nearly as much as she loathed herself. He had tried to stop Grace, but he was too weak. He, too, had been caught.

As if cornered, as if she were back in the closet with her rapist, she attacked Gayet. Only now she had a weapon. She thought him dead, trapped him in a scream, and, as if he were being squeezed from the insides, his blood pressure rose. She had found a weakened blood vessel in his head, and it ruptured.

The effort weakened Grace, and a few seconds later the gamesmaster was able to regain control and disconnect everyone. Gayet was immediately hooked in to a life-support unit which applied CPR techniques to keep his heart beating.

But he was dead. . . .

There would be some rather sticky legal complications, but by surviving, Pfeiffer had won the game, had indeed beaten Grace and won all of Gayet's organs.

As Pfeiffer gazed through the transparent walls of the transpod that whisked him and Joan out of Paris, away from its dangers and sordid delights, he felt something

187

new and delicate toward Joan.

It was newfound intimacy and gratitude . . . and love.

Joan, however, still carried the echoes of Grace's thoughts, as if a part of her had irreversibly fused with Grace. She too felt something new for Pfeiffer. Perhaps it was renewal, an evolution of her love.

They were in love . . . yet even now Joan felt the compulsion to gamble again.

LAST OF THE WILD ONES

By Roger Zelazny

Spinning through the dream of time and dust they came, beneath a lake-cold, lake-blue, lake-deep sky, the sun a crashed and burning wreck above the western mountains, the wind a whipper of turning sand devils, chill turquoise wind out of the west, taking wind. They ran on bald tires, they listed on broken springs, their bodies creased, paint faded, windows cracked, exhaust tails black and gray and white, streaming behind them into the northern quarter whence they had been driven this day. And now the pursuing line of vehicles, fingers of fire curving, hooking, above, before them. And they came, stragglers and break-downs being blasted from bloom to wilt, flash to smolder, ignored by their fleeing fellows. . . .

Murdock lay upon his belly atop the ridge, regarding the advancing herd through powerful field glasses. In the arroyo to his rear, the Angel of Death — all cream and chrome and bulletproof glass, sporting a laser cannon and two bands of armor-piercing rockets — stood like an exiled mirage glistening in the sun, vibrating, tugging against reality.

It was a country of hills, long ridges, deep canyons toward which they were being driven. Soon they would be faced with a choice. They could pass into the canyon below or enter the one farther to the east. They could also split and take both passages. The results would be the same. Other armed observers were mounted atop other ridges, waiting.

As he watched to see what the choice would be, Murdock's mind roamed back over the previous fifteen years, since the destruction of the Devil Car at the graveyard of the autos. He had, for twenty-five years, devoted his life to the pursuit of the wild ones. In that time he had become the world's foremost authority on the car herds—their habitats, their psychology, their means of maintenance and fueling—learning virtually everything concerning their ways, save for the precise nature of the initial flaw that one fatal year, which had led to the aberrant radio-communicable program that spread like a virus among the computerized vehicles. Some, but not all, were susceptible to it, tightening the disease analogy by another twist of the wrench. And some recovered, to be found returned to the garage or parked before the house one morning, battered but back in service, reluctant to recite their doings of days past. For the wild ones killed and raided, turning service stations into fortresses, dealerships into armed camps. The black Caddy had even borne within it the remains of the driver it had monooed long ago.

Murdock could feel the vibrations beneath him. He lowered the glasses, no longer needing them, and stared through the blue wind. After a few moments more he could hear the sound, as well as feel it—over a thousand engines roaring, gears grinding, sounds of scraping and crashing—as the last wild herd rushed to its doom. For a quarter of a century he had sought this day, ever since his brother's death had set him upon the trail. How many cars had he used up? He could no longer remember. And now . . .

He recalled his days of tracking, stalking, observing, and recording. The patience, the self-control it had required, exercising restraint when what he most desired was the immediate destruction of his quarry. But there had been a benefit in the postponement—this day was the reward, in that it would see the passing of the last of them. Yet the things he remembered had left strange tracks upon the path he had traveled.

As he watched their advance, he recalled the fights for supremacy he had witnessed within the herds he had followed. Often the defeated car would withdraw after it was clear that it was beaten; grill smashed, trunk sprung, lights shattered, body crumpled and leaking. The new leader would then run in wide circles, horn blaring, signal of its victory, its mastery. The defeated one, denied repair from the herd supply, would sometimes trail after the pack, an outcast. Occasionally it would be taken back in if it located something worth raiding. More often, however, it wandered across the Plains, never to be seen mobile again. He had tracked one once, wondering whether it had made its way to some new graveyard of the autos. He was startled to see it suddenly appear atop a mesa, turn toward the face that rose above a deep gorge, grind its gears, rev its engine, and rush forward, to plunge over the edge, crashing, rolling, and burning below.

But he recalled one occasion when the winner would not settle for less than a total victory. The blue sedan had approached the beige one where it sat on a low hillock with four or five parked sports cars. Spinning its wheels, it blared its challenge at several hundred meters' distance, then turned, cutting through a half-circle, and began its approach. The beige began a series of similar maneuvers, wheeling and honking, circling as it answered the challenge. The sports cars hastily withdrew to the sidelines.

They circled each other as they drew nearer, the circle quickly growing smaller. Finally the beige struck, smashing into the blue vehicle's left front fender, both of them spinning and sliding, their engines racing. Then they were apart again, feinting—advancing a brief distance, braking, turning, backing, advancing.

The second engagement clipped off the blue vehicle's left rear taillight and tore loose its rear bumper. Yet it recovered rapidly, turned, and struck the beige broadside, partly caving it in. Immediately it backed off and struck again before the other had completely recovered. The beige tore loose, and spun away in reverse. It knew all the tricks, but the other kept rushing in, coming faster now, striking and withdrawing. Loud rattling noises were coming from the beige, but it continued its circling, its feinting, the sunlight through the risen dust giving it a burnished look, as of very old gold. Its next rush creased the right side of the blue vehicle. It sounded its horn as it pursued it and commenced an outward turn.

The blue car was already moving in that direction, however, gravel spewing from beneath its rear wheels, horn blasting steadily. It leaped forward and again struck the beige upon the same side. As it backed off, the beige turned to flee, its horn suddenly silent.

The blue car hesitated only a moment, then sped after it, crashing into its rear end. The beige pulled away, leaking oil, doors rattling. But the blue car pursued it and struck again. It moved on, but the blue swerved, ran through a small arc, and hit it yet again upon the same side it had earlier. This time the beige was halted by the blow, steam emerging from beneath its hood; this time, as the blue car drew back, it was unable to flee. Rushing forward, the blue struck it once more upon the badly damaged left side. The impact lifted it from the ground, turning it over onto the slope falling away sharply to its right. It rolled sideways, tumbling and bouncing, to be brought up with a crash upon its side. Moments later its fuel tank exploded.

The blue car had halted, facing downhill. It ran up an antenna from which half a dozen spinning sensors unfurled, a fairy totem pole shimmering in the fume-filled air. After a time it retracted the sensors and withdrew the aerial. It gave one loud blare of the horn then and moved away to round up the sports cars.

Murdock remembered. He put his glasses in their case as the herd neared the turning point. He could distinguish individual members now, unassisted. They were a sorry-looking lot. Seeing them, he recalled the points of the best that he had come across over the years. When their supplies of parts had been larger, they had used their external manipulators to modify themselves into some magnificent and lethal forms. Kilo for kilo, the wild ones had become superior to anything turned out in the normal course of production.

All of the car scouts, of course, went armed, and in the early days a number of them had experimented. Coming upon a small herd, they would cut out a number of the better ones, blasting the rest. Disconnecting the think boxes, they would have their partners drive them back. But attempts at rehabilitation had been something less than successful. Even a complete wipe, followed by reprogramming, did not render the succeptible individuals immune to relapse. Murdock even recalled one that had behaved normally for almost a year, until one day in the midst of a traffic jam it had mooed its driver and taken off for the hills. The only alternative was to discard the entire computational unit and replace it with a new one — which was hardly worthwhile, since its value was far greater than that of the rest of the vehicle.

No, there had been no answer in that direction. Or any other but the course that he had followed; track and attack, the systematic destruction of the herds. Over the years his respect for the cunning and daring of the herd leaders had grown. As the wild ones had dwindled in number, their ferocity and guile had reached the level of legend. There had been nights, as he lay sleeping, that he dreamed of himself as a wild car, armed, racing across the Plains, leader of a herd. Then there was only one other car, a red one.

The herd began its turn. Murdock saw, with a sudden pang of regret, that it was heading into the far eastern canyon. He tugged at his white-streaked beard and cursed as he reached for his stick and began to rise. True, there would still be plenty of time to get over to the next canyon for the kill, but —

No! Some of them were splitting off, heading this way!

Smiling, he drew himself upright and limped rapidly down the hill to where the Angel of Death waited for him. He heard the exploding mines as he climbed into the vehicle. It's motor began to hum.

"There are a few in the next canyon," came the soft, well-modulated, masculine voice of his machine. "I have been monitoring all bands."

"I know," he answered, stowing his stick. "Let's head over that way. Some will make it through."

Safety restraints snapped into place around him as they began to move.

"Wait!"

The white vehicle halted.

"What is it that you wish?"

"You are heading north."

"We must, to exit here and enter the next canyon with the others."

"There are some connecting side canyons to the south. Go that way. I want to beat the others in."

"There will be some risk involved."

Murdock laughed.

"I've lived with risk for a quarter of a century, waiting for this day. I want to be there first for the end. Go south!"

The car swung through a turn and headed southward.

As they cruised along the arroyo bottom's sand, Murdock asked, "Hear anything?"

"Yes," came the reply. "The sounds of those who were blasted by the mines, the cries of those who made it through."

"I knew some would make it! How many? What are they doing now?

"They continue their flight southward. Perhaps several dozen. Perhaps many more. It is difficult to estimate from the transmissions."

Murdock chuckled.

"They've no way out. They'll have to turn sooner or later, and we'll be waiting."

"I am not certain that I could deal with a mass attack by that many—even if most lack special armaments."

"I know what I'm doing," Murdock said. "I've chosen the battleground."

He listened to the muffled thuds of the distant explosions.

"Prime the weapons systems," he announced. "Some of

them could have located the sideway we'll be taking."

A twin band of yellow lights winked out on the dashboard and were replaced by a double row of green ones. Almost immediately these faded and were succeeded by two lines of steady, red points.

"Ready on rockets," came the voice of the Angel.

Murdock reached out and threw a switch.

A larger light had also come on—orange and pulsing faintly.

"Cannon ready."

Murdock threw a larger switch beside a pistol grip set in the dash below it.

"I'll keep this one on manual for now."

"Is that wise?"

Murdock did not answer. For a moment he watched the bands of red and yellow strata to his left, a veil of shadow being drawn slowly upward over them.

"Slow now. The sideway will be coming up shortly. It should be up there on the left."

His car began to slow.

"I believe that I detect it ahead."

"Not the next one. It's blind. There's one right after it, though. It goes through."

They continued to slow as they passed the mouth of the first opening to the left. It was dark and angled off sharply.

"I've become aware of the next one."

"Very slowly now. Blast anything that moves."

Murdock reached forward and took hold of the pistol grip.

Angel braked and made the turn, advancing into a narrow pass.

"Dim the ready lights. No transmissions of any sort. Keep it dark and quiet."

They moved through an alley of shadow, the distant explosions having become a pulsing more felt than heard now. Stony walls towered on either hand. Their way wound to the right and then to the left.

Another right-hand twisting, and there was a bit of brightness and a long line of sight.

"Stop about three meters before it opens out," Murdock said, not realizing until moments later that he had whispered.

They crept ahead and came to a halt.

"Keep the engine running."

"Yes."

Murdock leaned forward, peering into the larger canyon running at right angles to their own. Dust hung in the air—dark, murky below, sparkling higher above, where the sun's rays could still reach.

"They've already passed," he reflected "and soon they should realize they're in a box—a big one, but still a box. Then they'll turn and come back and we'll open up on them." Murdock looked to the left. "Good place right over there for some more of our people to lay up and wait for them. I'd better get in touch and let them know. Use a fresh scrambler this time."

"How do you know they'll be coming back? Perhaps they'll lay up in there and make you come in after them."

"No," Murdock said. "I know them too well. They'll run for it."

"Are you sure there aren't any other sideways?"

"None going west. There may be a few heading east, but if they take them, they'll wind up in the other trap. Either way, they lose."

"What if some of those others cut down this way?"

"The more, the merrier. Get me that line. And see what you can pick up on the herd while I'm talking."

Shortly after that, he was in touch with the commander of the southern wing of the pursuers, requesting a squad of armed and armored vehicles to be laid up at the point he designated. He learned that they were already on their way to the western canyon in search of those vehicles observed entering there. The commander relayed Murdock's message to them and told him that they would be along in a matter of minutes. Murdock could still feel the shock waves from the many explosions in the eastern canyon.

"Good," he said, and he ended the transmission.

"They've reached the end," the Angel announced a little later, "and are circling. I hear their broadcasts. They are beginning to suspect that there is no way out."

Murdock smiled. He was looking to his left, where the first of the pursuing vehicles had just come into sight. He raised the microphone and began giving directions.

As he waited, he realized that at no time had he relaxed his hold on the pistol grip. He withdrew his hand, wiped his palm on his trousers, and returned it.

"They are coming now," the Angel said. "They have turned and are headed back this way."

Murdock turned his head to the right and waited. The destruction had been going on for nearly a month, and today's should be the last of it. He suddenly realized just how tired he was. A feeling of depression began to come over him. He stared at the small red lights and the larger, pulsing orange one.

"You will be able to see them in a moment."

"Can you tell how many there are?"

"Thirty-two. No, hold it . . . thirty-one. They are picking up speed. Their conversations indicate that they anticipate an interception."

"Did any come through from the eastern canyon?"

"Yes. There were several."

The sound of their engines came to him. Hidden there in the neck of the ravine, he saw the first of them—a dark sedan, dented and swaying, half of its roof and the nearest fender torn away—come around the canyon's bend. He held his fire as it approached, and soon the others followed—rattling, steaming, leaking, covered with dents and rust spots, windows broken, hoods missing, doors loose. A strange feeling came into his breast as he thought about the more magnificent specimens of the great herds he had followed over the years.

Still, he held his fire, even as the first in line drew abreast of him, and his thoughts went back to the black and shining Devil Car and to Jenny, the Scarlet Lady, with whom he had hunted it.

The first of the pack reached the place where the ambushers waited.

"Now?" the Angel asked, just as the first rocket flared off to the left.

"Yes."

They opened up and the destruction began, cars braking and swerving into one another, the canyon suddenly illuminated by half a dozen blazing wrecks—a dozen—two.

One after another, they were halted, burned. Three of the ambushers were destroyed by direct crashes. Murdock used all of his rockets and played the laser over the heaped remains. As the last wreck burst into flame, he knew that, though they weren't much compared with the great ones he had known, he would never forget how they had made their final run on bald tires, broken springs, leaking transmissions, and hate.

Suddenly he swiveled the laser and fired it back along the canyon.

"What is it?" the Angel asked him.

"There's another one back there. Don't you pick it up?"

"I'm checking now, but I don't detect anything."

"Go that way."

They moved forward and turned to the right. Immediately the radio crackled.

"Murdock, where are you going?" This came from one of the ambushers to the rear.

"I thought I saw something. I'm going ahead to check it out."

"I can't give you an escort till we clear some of these wrecks."

"That's all right."

"How many rockets have you got?"

He glanced again at the dash, where the only light that burned was orange and pulsing steadily.

"Enough."

"Why don't you wait?"

Murdock chuckled. "Do you really think any of those clunkers could touch something like the Angel? I won't be long."

They moved toward the bend and turned. The last of the sunlight was striking the highest points of the eastern rim overhead.

Nothing.

"Picking anything up?" he asked.

"No. Do you want a light?"

"No."

Farther to the east the sounds of firing were diminishing. The Angel slowed as they neared a wide slice of darkness to the left.

"This ravine may go through. Do we turn here or continue on?"

"Can you detect anything within it?"

"No."

"Then keep going."

His hand still upon the grip, Murdock moved the big gun slightly with each turn that they took, covering the most likely areas of opposition rather than the point directly ahead.

"This is no good," he finally announced. "I've got to have a light. Give me the overhead spot."

Instantly the prospect before him was brightly illuminated: dark rocks, orange stands of stone, striped walls—almost a coral seascape through waves of settling dust.

"I think somebody's been by here more recently than those we burned."

"Don't tired people sometimes see things that are not really there?"

Murdock sighed.

"Yes, and I am tired. That may be it. Take the next bend anyway."

They continued on, making the turn.

Murdock swiveled the weapon and triggered it, blasting rock and clay at the corner of the next turning.

"There!" he cried. "You must have picked that up!"

"No. I detected nothing."

"I can't be cracking up at this point! I saw it! Check your sensors. Something must be off."

"Negative. All detection systems report in good order."

Murdock slammed his fist against the dash.

"Keep going. Something's there."

The ground was churned before them. There were too many tracks to tell a simple tale.

"Slowly now," he said as they approached the next bend. "Could one of them have some kind of equipment or something to block you. I wonder. Or am I really seeing ghosts? I don't see how—"

"Gully to the left. Another to the right."

"Slower! Run the spotlight up them as we pass."

They moved by the first one, and Murdock turned the weapon to follow the light. There were two side passages going off the ravine before it turned.

"Could be something up there," he mused. "No way of telling without going in. Let's take a look at the next one."

They rolled on. The light turned again, and so did the gun. The second opening appeared to be too narrow to accommodate a car. It ran straight back without branching, and there was nothing unusual in sight anywhere within it.

Murdock sighed again.

"I don't know," he said, "but the end is just around the next bend—a big box of a canyon. Go straight on in. And be ready for evasive action."

The radio crackled.

"You all right?" came a voice from the ambush squad.

"Still checking," he said. "Nothing so far. Just a little more to see."

He broke it off.

"You didn't mention—"

"I know. Be ready to move very fast."

They entered the canyon, sweepng it with the light. It was an oval-shaped place, its major axis perhaps a hundred meters in length. Several large rocks lay near its center. There were a number of dark openings about its periphery. The talus lay heavy at the foot of the walls.

"Go right. We'll circle it. Those rocks and the openings are the places to watch."

They were about a quarter of the way around when he heard the high, singing sound of another engine revving. Murdock turned his head and looked fifteen years into he past.

A low, red Swinger sedan had entered the canyon and was turning in his direction.

"Run!" he said. "She's armed! Get the rocks between

202

us!"

"Who? Where?"

Murdock snapped the control switch to manual, seized the wheel, and stepped on the gas. The Angel leaped ahead, turning, as fifty-caliber machine guns blazed beneath the darkened headlights of the other vehicle.

"Now do you see it?" he asked as the rear window was starred and he felt the thudding impact of hits somewhere toward the back of the vehicle.

"Not entirely. There is some sort of screen, but I can estimate based on that. Give me back the controls."

"No. Estimates aren't good enough with her," Murdock replied, turning sharply to place the rocks between himself and the other.

The red car came fast, however, though it had stopped firing as he entered the turn.

The radio crackled. Then a voice he had thought he would never hear again came over it: "That's you, isn't it, Sam? I heard you back there. And that's the sort of car the Archengineer of Geeyem would have built you for something like this—tough and smart and fast." The voice was low, feminine, deadly. "He would not have anticipated this encounter, however. I can jam almost all the sensors without its knowing it."

"Jenny . . ." he said as he held the pedal to the floor and continued the turn.

"Never thought you'd see me again, did you?"

"I've always wondered. Ever since the day you disappeared. But it's been so long."

"And you've spent the entire time hunting us. You had your revenge that day, but you kept right on—destroying."

"Considering the alternative, I had no choice."

He passed his starting point and commenced a second lap, realizing as he began to draw away that she must no longer be as finely tuned as when he had known her earlier. Unless —

An explosion occurred some distance ahead of him. He was pelted with gravel, and he swerved to avoid the fresh crater before him.

"Still have some of those grenades left," he said. "Hard to estimate when to drop them, though, isn't it?"

They were on opposite sides of the rocks now. There was no way she could get a clear shot at him with her guns. Nor he at her, with the cannon.

"I'm in no hurry, Sam."

"What is it?" he heard the Angel ask.

"It speaks!" she cried. "Finally! Do you want to tell him, Sam? Or should I?"

"I'd a feeling it was her, back there," Murdock began, "and I'd long had a feeling that we would meet again. Jenny was the first killer car I had built to hunt the wild ones."

"And the best," she added.

"But she went wild herself," he finished.

"How's about you trying it, Whitey?" she said. "Leak carbon monoxide into the air vents. He'll still look live enough to get you out of here. You answer any calls that come in. Tell them he's resting. Tell them you didn't find anything. Slip away later and come back here. I'll wait, I'll show you the ropes."

"Cut it out, Jenny," Murdock said, circling again, beginning to gain on her. "I'll have you in my sights in a minute. We haven't that much time to talk."

"And nothing, really, to talk about," she responded.

"How about this? You were the best car I ever had. Surrender. Fire off your ammo. Drop the grenades. Come back with me. I don't want to blast you."

"Just a quick lobotomy, eh?"

Another explosion occurred, this one behind him. He continued to gain on her.

"It's that virus program," he said. "Jenny, you're the last — the last wild one. You've nothing to gain."

"Or to lose," she responded quietly.

The next explosion was almost beside him. The Angel rocked but did not slow. Gripping the wheel with one hand, Murdock reached out and took hold of the pistol grip.

"She's stopped jamming my sensors," the Angel announced.

"Maybe she's burned out that system," Murdock said, turning the gun.

He sped around the rocks, avoiding the new craters, the light beam bouncing, sweeping, casting the high, craggy walls into a rapid succession of dreamlike images, slowly closing the distance between himself and Jenny. Another grenade went off behind him. Finally the moment of a clear shot emerged from the risen dust. He squeezed the trigger.

The beam fell wide, scoring the canyonside, producing a minor rockslide.

"That was a warning," he said. "Drop the grenades. Discharge the guns. Come back with me. It's your last chance."

"Only one of us will be going away from here, Sam," she answered.

He swung the gun and fired again as he swept along another turn, but a pothole he struck threw the beam high, fusing a section of sandy slope.

"A useful piece, that," she commented. "Too bad you didn't give me one."

"They came later."

"It is unfortunate that you cannot trust your vehicle and

must rely upon your own driving skills. Your car would not have missed that last shot."

"Maybe," Murdock said, skidding through another turn.

Suddenly two more grenades exploded between them, and rocks rattled against the Angel. Both windows on the right side were fractured. He skidded sideways, his vision obscured by the flash and the airborne matter.

Both hands on the wheel now, he fought for control, braking hard. Passing through the screen of detritus, slowing and turning, he caught sight of Jenny racing full bore toward the pass that led out of the canyon.

He stepped on the gas again and followed after. She passed through and was gone before he could reach for the weapon.

"Return to automatic, and you will be free for the fighting," the Angel said.

"Can't do that," Murdock replied, racing toward the pass. "She could jam you again then at any time—and get us both."

"Is that the only reason?"

"Yes, the risk."

The red car was not in sight when he came through into the pass.

"Well?" he said. "What do your sensors read?"

"She entered the gully on the right. There is a heat trail."

Murdock continued to slow as he moved in that direction.

"That must be where she was hiding when we came by," he said. "It could be some kind of trap."

"Perhaps you had better call for the others, cover the entrance, and wait."

"No!"

Murdock turned his wheel and sent his light along the passageway. She was nowhere in sight, but there were sideways. He continued to creep forward, entering. His right hand was again on the pistol grip.

He passed these side openings, each of them large enough to hide a car, all of them empty.

He followed a bend, bearing him to the right. Before he had moved an entire car length along it, a burst of gunfire from the left, ahead, caused him to slam on the brakes and turn the cannon. But an engine roared to life before he could take aim, and a red streak crossed his path to vanish up another sideway. He hit the gas again and followed.

Jenny was out of sight, but he could hear the sound of her somewhere ahead. The way widened as he advanced. Finally it forked at a large stand of stone, one arm continuing past it, the other bearing off sharply to the left. He slowed, taking time to consider the alternatives.

"Where's the heat trail go?" he asked.

"Both ways. I don't understand."

Then the red car came swinging into sight from the left, guns firing. The Angel shook as they were hit. Murdock triggered the laser, but she swept past him, turning and speeding off to the right.

"She circled it before we arrived, to confuse your sensors, to slow us.

"It worked, too," he added, moving ahead again. "She's too damned smart."

"We can still go back."

Murdock did not reply.

Twice more Jenny lay in wait, fired short bursts, evaded the singeing beam, and disappeared. An intermittent knocking sound began beneath the hood as they moved, and one telltale on the dash indicated signs of overheating.

"It is not serious," the Angel stated. "I can control it."

"Let me know if there is any change."

"Yes."

Following the heat trail, they bore steadily to the left, racing down a widening sand slope past castles, minarets, and cathedrals of stone, dark or pale, striped and spotted with mica like the first raindrops of a midsummer's storm. They hit the bottom, slid sideways, and came to a stop, wheels spinning.

He threw the light around rapidly, causing grotesque shadows to jerk like marionettes in a ring dance about them.

"It's a wash. Lots of loose sand. But I don't see Jenny."

Murdock ground the gears, rocking the vehicle, but they did not come free.

"Give me control," said the Angel. "I've a program for this."

Murdock threw the switch. At once a fresh series of rocking movements began. This continued for a full minute. Then the heat telltale began to flicker again.

"So much for the program. Looks as if I'm going to have to get out and push," Murdock said.

"No. Call for help. Stay put. We can hold her off with the cannon if she returns."

"I can get back inside pretty quick. We've got to get moving again."

As he reached for the door, he heard the lock click.

"Release it," he said. "I'll just shut you off, go out, and turn you on again from there. You're wasting time."

"I think you are making a mistake."

"Then let's hurry and make it a short one."

"All right. Leave the door open." There followed another click. "I will feel the pressure when you begin pushing. I will probably throw a lot of sand on you."

"I've got a scarf."

Murdock climbed out and limped toward the rear of the vehicle. He wound his scarf up around his mouth and nose. Leaning forward, he placed his hands upon the car and began to push. The engine roared and the wheels spun as he threw his weight against it.

Then, from the corner of his eye, to the right, he detected a movement. He turned his head only slightly and continued pushing the Angel of Death.

Jenny was there. She had crept up slowly into a shadowy place beneath a ledge, turning, facing him, her guns directly upon him. She must have circled. Now she was halted.

It seemed useless to try running. She could open up upon him anytime that she chose.

He leaned back, resting for a moment, pulling himself together. Then he moved to his left, leaned forward, began pushing again. For some reason she was waiting. He could not determine why, but he sidled to the left. He moved his left hand, then his right. He shifted his weight, moved his feet again, fighting a powerful impulse to look in her direction once again. He was near the left taillight. Now there might be a chance. Two quick steps would place the body of the Angel between them. Then he could rush forward and dive back in. But why wasn't she firing?

No matter. He had to try. He eased up again. The feigned rest that followed was the most difficult spell of the whole thing.

Then he leaned forward once more, reached out as if to lay his hands upon the vehicle once again, and slipped by it, moving as quickly as he could toward the open door, and then through it, and inside. Nothing happened the entire time he was in transit, but the moment the car door slammed a burst of gunfire occurred beneath the ledge, and the Angel began to shudder and then to rock.

"There!" came the voice of the Angel as the gun swung to the right and a beam lanced outward and upward from it.

It bobbed. It rode high. It fell upon the cliff face, moving.

Murdock turned in time to see a portion of that surface slide downward, first with a whisper, then with a roar. The shooting ceased before the wall came down upon the red vehicle.

Above the sound of the crash, a familiar voice came through the radio: "Damn you, Sam! You should have stayed in the car!" she said.

Then the radio went silent. Her form was completely covered by the rockfall.

"Must have blocked my sensors again and sneaked up," the Angel was saying. "You are lucky that you saw her just when you did."

"Yes," Murdock replied.

"Let me try rocking us loose now," the Angel said a little later. "We made some headway while you were pushing."

The breakaway sequence began again. Murdock looked up at the stars for the first time that evening—cold and brilliant and so very distant. He kept on staring as the Angel pulled them free. He barely glanced at her stony tomb as they turned and moved past it.

When they had threaded their way back and out through the ravine, the radio came to life again: "Murdock! Murdock! You okay? We've been trying to reach you and—"

"Yes," he said softly.

"We heard more explosions. Was that you?"

"Yes. Just shooting at a ghost," he said. "I'm coming

back now."

"It's over," the other told him. "We got them all."

"Good," he said, breaking the connection.

"Why didn't you tell him about the red one?" the Angel asked.

"Shut up and keep driving."

He watched the canyon walls slip by, bright strata and dull ones. It was night, sky cold, sky wide, sky deep, and the black wind came out of the north, closing wind. They headed into it. Spinning through the dream of time and dust, past the wreckage, they went to the place where the others waited. It was night, and a black wind came out of the north.

PRAIRIE SUN

By Edward Bryant

Stillness.

Except for the boy, nothing moved on the prairie. The hawks did not hunt this morning. Not even the vultures circled in the empty sky. The birds evidently were waiting until Micah Taverner made his kill.

The heat hung like a heavy curtain over the world. All motion seemed suspended. The thought entered Micah's mind that on these plains, anything at all could happen. His was a sudden and early maturity, and not one he relished.

Thirteen-year-old Micah moved quietly — perhaps not so silently as an Indian, but still disturbing the saw-toothed grass with less noise than most others in the company. He balanced his father's long muzzle-loader carefully, thumb ready to take the hammer off half-cock. A small antelope would be welcome. A young deer would be better. A rabbit would suffice.

To Micah's right the River Platte wound slowly east by

south, the direction from which the company had come. At this point the road followed a straighter path than the river. The boy's present course took him up a gentle rise so that he had now attained an elevation of a hundred yards above the river. Within a rod of the Platte, all was lush and green. The grass and the trees grew luxuriantly. Beyond them the world turned to shades of brown and tan and yellow.

The world seemed to contain little more than the river and the prairie. And the road. Had he wished to stand in the ruts, they would have taken the boy in up to his waist.

Micah heard a sound in the dead air. He froze, waiting. He heard something again. Glass breaking. The mutter of words. The sounds came from beyond the low rise ahead. Two voices. Whoever were speaking, they were close by the trail.

The boy slowly cocked the hammer of the rifle. It seemed to him the click echoed out across the parched land like the gunshot itself. Again he heard words too distant and indistinct to understand. But the tone did not sound alarmed.

White men? he thought. *Pawnee!* had been the first word in his mind. Or Sioux. Or Blackfeet. He had heard the tales of slaughter and torture from the talkers around the fire. He had listened then with eyes wide and the breath catching in his throat, even though his father had laughed and suggested wryly that the red tribes were no more monsters than were the men of the company. And after all, men of other companies had given deadlier gifts than bullets to the Indians.

Micah gripped his father's rifle tighter and stealthily approached the summit. Sounds again—this time a rattle as though iron articles and wood were being placed together in a bag. Outcroppings of porous stone afforded the boy

214

some cover as he reached the hill's crest.

White! At least the strangers were not red men, though they appeared odd to Micah's eyes. There were two of them, and they were poking through the heaps of discards beside the trail. The road was lined with all manner of belongings thrown away by the exhausted, overburdened men and women barely halfway along their arduous journey. The wagons, the oxen, the horses and mules, the people — all could carry only so much across the months and the thousands of miles demanded.

Micah had seen the jettisoned tools and household goods start to appear beside the wagon ruts not long after Fort Phil Kearney, many miles even before reaching the ford of the South Platte. Before the sickness began, his father had tried keeping a running tally of what he saw for just a mile or two. "There must be ten thousand dollars worth of goods there," he had said. "All for the picking had one the time or the desire."

But few struggling toward California or Oregon, of course, had the time or the desire. So the prized New England heirloom furniture, the discarded barrels of flour and sacks of white beans, the Franklin stoves and the printing presses, all lay rotting beneath the prairie sun.

And now Micah saw the two strange white men rooting like hogs among the once-prized belongings scattered beside the road. Their backs were to him, so for a while he watched without their knowledge. Both men were tall, each easily attaining a height of over six feet. Though one had dark hair and the other was a towhead with hair as light as the dried grass, they seemed much alike in appearance. The pair wore similar clothing: plaid shirts with braces, brown cloth trousers, and thick-soled boots. The towhead's shirt was red; the darker man's was green. But Micah saw there was something not quite right about the clothing. For one thing, the cloth was slick and it gleamed under the direct sun. For another, he abruptly realized as the men flexed to pick up objects that each man's outfit was all of one piece of material. It was as though each were wearing a set of long-johns colored to appear as real clothing.

The towhead was showing the other a New England hooked rug much like the treasure Micah's mother still packed deep in the wagon after adamantly refusing to discard it at the Platte River crossing. Micah wondered if he should accost them or if it would be wiser simply to backtrack along the trail and forage in another direction. Then the darker man turned slightly, glanced up, and looked straight at Micah. He said something to his companion. Both of them stared at the boy.

Finally one of them, the towhead, said, "Come on down here, young man." He put down the hooked rug and stood there quietly with empty hands. The other man slowly spread his hands, palms outward. Micah realized they were both looking at his father's muzzle-loader.

He warily approached the pair, then looked beyond them. The muzzle of the rifle came up. "Don't—" said the darkhaired man. Whatever else he was going to say was interrupted by the black-powder explosion. Two yards of decapitated prairie rattler jerked and flopped in death-throes close by their feet as each man yelled and leaped aside. They looked from the snake to Micah and back to the snake again.

"Thank you, boy," said the towhead.

"Mighty big one," said Micah. He felt very pleased with the shot and tried not to grin. He started to reload the rifle. Probably the biggest one I've seen."

The men exchanged glances. "What's your name, son?" said the darker man.

Micah told them.

"Well now, Master Micah Taverner," said the towhead. "Please call me John. My friend here is Droos." Droos inclined his head. "We both of us truly do appreciate your eliminating the serpent."

"It wasn't nothing," Micah said as he rammed wadding down the barrel. "Just glad to help."

There was silence. The men seemed trying to communicate with each other by sharp looks. Micah paid attention only to the muzzle-loader.

Finally John said, "I suppose you're wondering what the two of us are doing out here."

"None of my business," said Micah.

"Admirable," said Droos, turning away. "His mouth isn't as extraordinary loose as yours, John. Now let's get back to work and see if we can find any more East Middlebury bottles like the one you so carelessly dropped."

But John seemed fascinated by the boy. "May I asked what *you're* doing out here?" he said. "I believe the last train passed by here nearly a week ago, and the next wagons aren't due for days."

"My mother sent me to look for game," said Micah. "She believes that meat broth will soothe Annie's innards."

"Who is Annie?"

"My little sister. She is sick with the smallpox."

Droos turned around from the wooden crates in which he was rummaging and stared. "Smallpox? We totally eradicated that more than a century ago."

"In *our* time," said John.

"Your time?" said Micah, confused now.

"Never mind," said John. "It's a long story. Where's your wagon?"

"That way." Micah pointed back along the river. "About

three miles. We should have stayed in Fort Laramie, but Annie did not seem so ill then. The rest of the company said they would wait an extra day at Independence Rock. I fear by now they will have gone on."

"But your family stayed alone."

"Annie cries out when the wagon moves. She is too weak. My mother thought that the rest might help her."

"Your mother," said John. "What about your father?"

Micah stared at the ground. "He took ill and died of the cholera shortly before the crossing of the Platte."

"God almighty," said Droos.

"And so your mother and you have brought the wagon this far since?" said John.

The boy nodded. "Some of the men of the company helped us. But they had their own wagons, and their families. And many of them were weak with cholera."

"Unbelievable," Droos said. He unconsciously fondled a silver teapot.

"Now we have seen the elephant," said Micah.

Droos cocked an eyebrow. "Elephants? You actually found one here?"

Micah looked equally quizzical. "It means only that we found far more on our path than we expected. We would return to Ross County, Ohio, but it is now just as far to go back as it is to go on. Perhaps we can catch up with the company when Annie is better. Before he rode on, the captain told us we would have to move soon, or we should all be caught by the winter in the Sierra Nevada."

The two men stared at him, transfixed.

"People truly used to live and die this way," Droos said bemusedly.

"Micah," said John slowly. "Can you keep a secret?"

"If it is an honorable secret."

"What if I told you that we both were from the future?"

The boy shook his head. "I do not understand."

Droos opened his mouth as though to protest. John held up a restraining hand. "Droos and I are travelers, and we've come a great distance to be here. But we didn't make the sort of journey you might imagine. Not from England, not around the Horn; but instead, through time. What year is it, Micah?"

"The year of our Lord, 1850."

"Our world exists more than two centuries beyond that."

Micah shook his head silently. Food meant something. Sickness meant something. But the future? His mind already reeled with too many burdens.

John turned toward Droos, who was slowly stowing a silver tea service in a fabric pack. "Can you explain it more adequately?"

Droos stared down at the objects he held. "These are truly exquisite," he said. "Standish Barry, Baltimore, probably about 1820."

"Droos."

The dark-haired man looked up and said, "This is against all the rules, you know. Why must you be a compulsive fool?"

"I was the only one in the department you could trust." John bent down to look at Micah levelly. "Do you know about the Romans?"

Micah nodded. "Father read us stories."

"Have you ever thought about what it would be like if you could really go back and visit the Romans?"

"Yes," said Micah.

"Well, we can do that, Micah. We live in your future. We can come back and visit your time, or the time of the Romans, or any other time of our choosing. We come from a year when smallpox has long since been banished from the Earth and most other diseases eliminated equally."

Micah knew he did not understand all that was being said to him. But a few words punched through the confusion. "You can heal smallpox?"

"Our ancestors did," said John. "Your grandchildren will."

"Can you cure Annie?"

Time again seemed suspended on the prairie. Everything was still. Micah stared at the men. They stared back at him.

"Well, I suppose . . ." said John.

"No," said Droos.

"Droos has an emergency medical kit; it might alleviate the symptoms."

"No." This time Droos's answer was more vehement.

John wheeled angrily on his companion. "Just once," he said.

"Absolutely not," said Droos. "If I have to pull rank, I'll do so."

"One child," said John. "One life."

Droos dropped a dozen silver spoons and let them lie on the dusty trailside. "Let me remind you of a few things," he said. "I'm not being arbitrary about denying your humanitarian impulse. The first thing is that this is not exactly a sanctioned mission, you know. The second thing is that we'll be strung up doubly by our balls if the department finds out we've been salvaging collectibles from the past for resale in the present. Third, there's the primary travel directive—"

"Come *on*," said John. "Saving one little girl's life is highly unlikely to alter the future in any significant—"

Droos interrupted him, raising his voice even higher. "We don't *know* that. It's one thing to scavenge these antiques because nature would have destroyed them anyway. It's quite another to meddle with lives. Besides, we don't know that his sister is going to die of smallpox. She might recover. I believe children were more resilient—"

"I say we do it," said John.

"If I have to, I'll put your neck on the block without endangering mine," said Droos, his voice quiet and deadly. "I am capable of that, you know."

"I know that." John spread his arms helplessly. "Please?"

"No. There are rules—and these rules we will follow implicitly. We live in that kind of world." Droos knelt and began picking up the spoons, blowing the dust off and polishing them against his leg, before placing the utensils inside a bag of soft cloth. "Accept that."

In the ensuing silence, Micah said, "Can you cure Annie?"

John did not meet his eye this time. The towheaded man hesitated for a long time. Finally he said, "No, we can't. I'm sorry, Micah."

Micah considered that. Then he said, "But you could?"

Neither man said anything.

"But you won't?"

John flushed. Droos stowed the packet of silver and extracted a crystal loop-and-petal candlestick from a crate. "I'm truly sorry," said John. "I never should have spoken at all."

Very slowly, Micah said, "Father used to tell me, 'I help my friends; God help my enemies.' "

"We're not your enemies," said John earnestly. "There are simply rules that say we cannot be the friends we'd wish."

Micah said nothing. He only turned and, picking up both the dead snake and the muzzle-loader that leaned against a free-standing gilt mirror in its hardwood frame, walked away from the two men.

Micah distractedly shot the rabbit on the way back to the wagon. The big jack darted from the brush, and then made the mistake of pausing to assess the intruder on the plains. The ball passed cleanly through its right eye. The meat was unspoiled.

When the boy arrived at the wagon, the sun was long past its zenith. The oxen looked up incuriously to greet him, then bent their heavy heads back to the tough grass. Micah paused by the rear of the wagon.

"Ma?" he said. "I have a snake and a rabbit, Ma."

His mother drew the canvas flap aside and held a finger to her lips. "Hush," she said. "Your sister is dying." The gay colors of her gingham stood in stark contrast to the somber gray of the canvas top.

They waited an hour, then a second hour beside the small bed, listening to Annie's labored breathing. They took turns squeezing new compresses for the girl's forehead. Every few minutes, Micah took the bucket to the river for fresh, cold water.

Annie's face continued to shine with sweat, even with the compresses. At the same time, she shook as though with a chill, and they kept her bundled in her mother's hand-loomed blankets.

Finally the breathing stopped. Mother and brother waited minutes in the sudden stillness. Micah started to touch his mother's shoulder. She shook his hand aside. "Let me be alone," she said. Slowly she unwound the fine wool blankets and took up her daughter's body in her arms. Without words, she stepped down from the wagon and walked through the cottonwood and boxelder toward the river's edge.

Micah stood in the rear of the wagon and watched her go. The thought reverberated in his mind: what sort of people would allow a child to die this way? What form of Christian charity would let his sister perish in such a fashion?

He realized he simply did not know.

After what seemed a long, long time, Micah emptied his mother's most prized possession, the finely carved sandalwood chest, and repacked it.

The two men who claimed to be from the future were a half-mile further down the trail from where they had met with Micah. They were still rummaging through the heaps of abandoned goods, apparently working their way toward Missouri.

Scrub cottonwoods, sage, a dusty draw, juts of porous stone, the wagon ruts themselves, all lent Micah cover. The boy knew that an Indian would have discerned him in a moment. But John and Droos had no such skills. For the second time, but for only a moment, Micah truly wondered what it was like in the future. Then his mind told him once again that such speculation was an impossible luxury, and he bent all his effort to remaining undiscovered.

For two or three seconds he actually stood in full view had they only looked up. But both men were apparently absorbed in examining a bulky contraption of legs and drawers. Micah set the sandalwood chest down in the dust, strategically in sight only a few yards beyond the men. Then he melted back into the country's natural cover.

In a few minutes Micah reappeared, walking down the

slope toward John and Droos and making no effort at concealment. The two men were looking over a William and Mary highboy, touching the smooth finish, sliding the drawers in and out, checking the joints. "Note the lacquered Chinese detail," said Droos. "Though not actually executed by Oriental artisans, the figures are Chinese in both feeling and technique." Buried in his task, he did not look up to see why John had not responded until Micah stood before them both.

The boy's face was coated with dust; his eyes felt like burnt holes in a mask. He tasted prairie grit and would have spat out the dirt, but he no longer had the saliva.

John sounded unsure and awkward. "Hello, Micah. Welcome back. We were just preparing to—leave. Our time is almost up."

Micah looked from one to the other steadily. He had to start the words several times because of the dry rasp in his throat. "You still would do nothing for my sister?"

"We *can* do nothing," said Droos. "We come from a quite different world, Micah. There are things we must not do. There are rules."

Micah turned his gaze to John. John finally stared at the ground and nodded agreement. "Very well," the boy said, sounding tired and much older than his thirteen years. The men looked at him warily.

"I truly am sorry," said John.

Micah said nothing. Nor did he answer any other entreaty made by either of the men. He retreated to sit on a wooden crate that held mining tools and simply watched them.

"We'd best get back to work," said Droos, checking something on his wrist. With redoubled energy, the two men again busied themselves among the debris. Every once in a while they looked at Micah. The boy remained stationary on the box.

"A swirl bottle!" said Droos. "A second!"

"This looks like a Pennsylvania Dutch door hanging," said John.

"A full set of eighteenth-century sextant gear."

"Another Roosevelt teapot."

"What's this?" John hunkered down beside the sandal-wood chest.

"What extraordinary workmanship," said Droos, also bending over the chest. "Absolutely gorgeous." His finger-tips ran eagerly over the inlaid panels. Then he raised the flat lid and said, "Oh yes, yes indeed." Drawing the contents from the chest, he said, "Shetland?"

"Looks like it," said John.

And loomed by my mother's hand, thought Micah, but spoke no word aloud.

Droos again inspected his wrist and said, "Damn! It's almost over. You attach a tracer to the chest. I'll finish up the rest."

Their departure was not dramatic.

"Ten seconds," said Droos, adjusting something at his belt.

John at least spoke to Micah. "Good-bye," he said, offering a slow, sad wave of his hand. "I'm sorry, Micah."

Both men simply were gone. As though they had never existed. Micah watched as all up and down the trail, objects vanished. Crates and bags melted into the air. The massive William and Mary highboy disappeared. Finally his mother's sandalwood chest vanished too, and along with it, the fine hand-loomed blanket of good Shetland wool, the blankets that had kept his sister from the frontier cold these past nights.

Micah stood then, and hoped his mother was waiting for him at the wagon. The chest and blankets were gone.

They had left him there to stand sweating in the prairie sun; in a plain of near-absolute stillness, hushed but no longer expectant; a plain on which, it seemed to him, anything at all could happen.

And it had.

AMANDA AND THE ALIEN

By Robert Silverberg

Amanda spotted the alien late Friday afternoon outside the Video Center, on South Main. It was trying to look cool and laid-back, but it simply came across as bewildered and uneasy. The alien was disguised as a seventeen-year-old girl, maybe a Chicana, with olive-toned skin and hair so black it seemed almost blue, but Amanda, who was seventeen herself, knew a phony when she saw one. She studied the alien for some moments from the other side of the street to make absolutely certain. Then she walked over.

"You're doing it wrong," Amanda said. "Anybody with half a brain could tell what you really are."

"Bug off," the alien said.

"No. Listen to me. You want to stay out of the detention center, or don't you?"

The alien stared coldly at Amanda and said, "I don't know what the crap you're talking about."

"Sure you do. No sense trying to bluff me. Look, I want

to help you," Amanda said. "I think you're getting a raw deal. You know what that means, a raw deal? Hey, look, come home with me, and I'll teach you a few things about passing for human. I've got the whole friggin' weekend now with nothing else to do anyway."

A flicker of interest came into the other girl's dark, chilly eyes. But it died quickly, and she said, "You some kind of lunatic?"

"Suit yourself, O thing from beyond the stars. *Let* them lock you up again. *Let* them stick electrodes up your ass. I tried to help. That's all I can do, is try," Amanda said, shrugging. She began to saunter away. She didn't look back. Three steps, four, five, hands in pockets, slowly heading for her car. Had she been wrong, she wondered? No. No. She could be wrong about some things, like Charley Taylor's interest in spending the weekend with her, maybe. But not this. That crinkly-haired chick was the missing alien for sure.

The whole county was buzzing about it: Deadly nonhuman life form has escaped from the detention center out by Tracy, might be anywhere, Walnut Creek, Livermore, even San Francisco, dangerous monster, capable of mimicking human forms, will engulf and digest you and disguise itself in your shape. And there it was, Amanda knew, standing outside the Video Center. Amanda kept walking.

"Wait," the alien said finally.

Amanda took another easy step or two. Then she looked back over her shoulder.

"Yeah?"

"How can you tell?"

Amanda grinned. "Easy. You've got a rainslicker on, and it's only September. Rainy season doesn't start around here for another month or two. Your pants are the old

Spandex kind. People like you don't wear that stuff anymore. Your face paint is San Jose colors, but you've got the cheek chevrons put on in the Berkeley pattern. That's just the first three things I noticed. I could find plenty more. Nothing about you fits together with anything else. It's like you did a survey to see how you ought to appear and then tried a little of everything. The closer I study you, the more I see. Look, you're wearing your headphones, and the battery light is on, but there's no cassette in the slot. What are you listening to, the music of the spheres? That model doesn't have any FM tuner, you know.

"You see? You may think that you're perfectly camouflaged, but you aren't."

"I could destroy you," the alien said.

"What? Oh, sure. Sure you could. Engulf me right here on the street, all over in thirty seconds, little trail of slime by the door, and a new Amanda walks away. But what then? What good's that going to do you? You still won't know which end is up. So there's no logic in destroying me, unless you're a total dummy. I'm on your side. I'm not going to turn you in."

"Why should I trust you?"

"Because I've been talking to you for five minutes and I haven't yelled for the cops yet. Don't you know that half of California is out searching for you? Hey, can you read? Come over here a minute. Here." Amanda tugged the alien toward the newspaper vending box at the curb. The headline on the afternoon *Examiner* was

BAY AREA ALIEN TERROR

MARINES TO JOIN NINE-COUNTY HUNT

MAYOR, GOVERNOR CAUTION AGAINST PANIC

"You understand that?" Amanda asked. "That's you they're talking about. They're out there with flame guns,

229

tranquilizer darts, web snares, and God knows what else. There's been real hysteria for a day and a half. And you standing around here with the wrong chevrons on! Christ. Christ! What's your plan, anyway? Where are you trying to go?"

"Home," the alien said. "But first I have to rendezvous at the pickup point."

"Where's that?"

"You think I'm stupid?"

"Shit," Amanda said. "If I meant to turn you in, I'd have done it five minutes ago. But, okay, I don't give a damn where your rendezvous point is. I tell you, though, you wouldn't make it as far as San Francisco rigged up the way you are. It's a miracle you've avoided getting caught until now."

"And you'll help me?"

"I've been trying to. Come on. Let's get the hell out of here. I'll take you home and fix you up a little. My car's in the lot down on the next corner."

"Okay."

"Whew!" Amanda shook her head slowly. "Christ, some people sure can't take help when you try to offer it."

As she drove out of the center of town, Amanda glanced occasionally at the alien sitting tensely to her right. Basically the disguise was very convincing, Amanda thought. Maybe all the small details were wrong, the outer stuff, the anthropological stuff, but the alien *looked* human, it *sounded* human, it even *smelled* human. Possibly it could fool ninety-nine people out of a hundred, or maybe more than that. But Amanda had always had a good eye for detail. And at the particular moment she had spotted the alien on South Main she had been unusually alert, sensitive, all raw nerves, every antenna up.

Of course it wasn't aliens she was hunting for, but just a

diversion, a little excitement, something to fill the great gaping emptiness that Charley Taylor had left in her weekend.

Amanda had been planning the weekend with Charley all month. Her parents were going to go off to Lake Tahoe for three days, her kid sister had wangled permission to accompany them, and Amanda was going to have the house to herself, just her and Macavity the cat. And Charley. He was going to move in on Friday afternoon, and they'd cook dinner together and get blasted on her stash of choice powder and watch five or six of her parents' X cassettes, and Saturday they'd drive over to the city and cruise some of the kinky districts and go to that bathhouse on Folsom where everybody got naked and climbed into the giant Jacuzzi, and then on Sunday—Well, none of that was going to happen. Charley had called on Thursday to cancel. "Something big came up," he said, and Amanda had a pretty good idea what that was, his hot little cousin from New Orleans, who sometimes came flying out here on no notice at all, but the inconsiderate bastard seemed to be entirely unaware of how much Amanda had been looking forward to this weekend, how much it meant to her, how painful it was to be dumped like this. She had run through the planned events of the weekend in her mind so many times that she almost felt as if she had experienced them. It was that real to her. But overnight it had become unreal.

Three whole days on her own, the house to herself, and so early in the semester that there was no homework to think about, and Charley had stood her up! What was she supposed to do now, call desperately around town to scrounge up some old lover as a playmate? Or pick up some stranger downtown? Amanda hated to fool around with strangers. She was half-tempted to go over to the city and just let things happen, but they were all weirdos and creeps over there, anyway, and she knew what she could expect from them. What a waste, not having Charley! She could kill him for robbing her of the weekend.

Now there was the alien, though. A dozen of these star people had come to Earth last year, not in a flying saucer as everybody had expected, but in little capsules that floated like milkweed seeds, and they had landed in a wide arc between San Diego and Salt Lake City.

Their natural form, so far as anyone could tell, was something like a huge jellyfish with a row of staring purple eyes down one wavy margin, but their usual tactic was to borrow any local body they found, digest it, and turn themselves into an accurate imitation of it. One of them had made the mistake of turning itself into a brown mountain bear and another into a bobcat—maybe they thought that those were the dominant life forms on Earth—but the others had taken on human bodies, at the cost of at least ten lives.

Then they went looking to make contact with government leaders, and naturally they were rounded up very swiftly and interned, some in mental hospitals and some in county jails, but eventually—as soon as the truth of what they really were sank in—they were all put in a special detention camp in northern California.

Of course a tremendous fuss was made over them, endless stuff in the papers and on the tube, speculation by this heavy thinker and that about the significance of their mission, the nature of their biochemistry, a little wild talk about the possibility that more of their kind might be waiting undetected out there and plotting to do God knows what, and all sorts of that stuff. Then came a government clamp on the entire subject, no official announcements except that "discussions" with the visitors were continuing, and after a while the whole thing degenerated into dumb alien jokes ("Why did the alien cross the road?") and Halloween invader masks. Then it moved into the background of everyone's attention and was forgotten.

And remained forgotten until the announcement that one of the creatures had slipped out of the camp somehow and was loose within a hundred-mile zone around San Francisco. Preoccupied as she was with her anguish over Charley's heartlessness, even Amanda had managed to pick up *that* news item. And now the alien was in her very car. So there'd be some weekend amusement for her after all. Amanda was entirely unafraid of the alleged deadliness of the star being: Whatever else the alien might be, it was surely no dope, not if it had been picked to come halfway across the galaxy on a mission like this, and Amanda knew that the alien could see that harming her was not going to be in its own best interests. The alien had need of her, and the alien realized that. And Amanda, in some way that she was only just beginning to work out, had need of the alien.

She pulled up outside her house, a compact split-level at the western end of town. "This is the place," she said.

Heat shimmers danced in the air, and the hills back of the house, parched in the long dry summer, were the color of lions.

Macavity, Amanda's old tabby, sprawled in the shade of the bottlebrush tree on the ragged front lawn. As Amanda and the alien approached, the cat sat up warily, flattened his ears, and hissed. The alien immediately moved into a defensive posture, sniffing the air.

"Just a household pet," Amanda said. "You know what

that is? He isn't dangerous. He's always a little suspicious of strangers."

Which was untrue. An earthquake couldn't have brought Macavity out of his nap, and a cotillion of mice dancing minuets on his tail wouldn't have drawn a reaction from him. Amanda calmed him with some fur ruffling, but he wanted nothing to do with the alien and went slinking sullenly into the underbrush. The alien watched him with care until he was out of sight.

"Do you have anything like cats back on your planet?" Amanda asked as they went inside.

"We had small wild animals once. They were unnecessary."

"Oh," Amanda said, losing interest. The house had a stuffy, stagnant air. She switched on the air conditioning. "Where is your planet, anyway?"

The alien pointedly ignored the question. It padded around the living room, very much like a prowling cat itself, studying the stereo, the television, the couches, the coffee table, and the vase of dried flowers.

"Is this a typical Earthian home?"

"More or less," said Amanda. "Typical for around here, at least. This is what we call a suburb. It's half an hour by freeway from here to San Francisco. That's a city. I'll take you over there tonight or tomorrow for a look, if you're interested." She got some music going, high volume. The alien didn't seem to mind; so she notched the volume up even more. "I'm going to take a shower. You could use one, too, actually."

"Shower? You mean rain?"

"I mean body-cleaning activities. We Earthlings like to wash a lot, to get rid of sweat and dirt and stuff. It's considered bad form to stink. Come on, I'll show you how to do it. You've got to do what I do if you want to keep from getting caught, you know." She led the alien to the bathroom. "Take your clothes off first."

The alien stripped. Underneath its rain slicker it wore a stained T-shirt that said FISHERMAN'S WHARF, with a picture of the San Francisco skyline, and a pair of unzipped jeans. Under that it was wearing a black brassiere, unfastened and with the cups over its shoulderblades, and a pair of black shiny panty-briefs with a red heart on the left buttock. The alien's body was that of a lean, tough-looking girl with a scar running down the inside of one arm.

"By the way, whose body is that?" Amanda asked. "Do you know?"

"She worked at the detention center. In the kitchen."

"You know her name?"

"Flores Concepción."

"The other way around, probably. Concepción Flores. I'll call you Connie, unless you want to give me your real name."

"Connie will do."

"All right, Connie. Pay attention. You turn the water on here, and you adjust the mix of hot and cold until you like it. Then you pull this knob and get underneath the spout here and wet your body and rub soap over it and wash the soap off. Afterward you dry yourself and put fresh clothes on. You have to clean your clothes from time to time, too, because otherwise *they* start to smell, and it upsets people. Watch me shower, and then you do it."

Amanda washed quickly, while plans hummed in her head. The alien wasn't going to last long wearing the body of Concepción Flores. Sooner or later someone was going to notice that one of the kitchen girls was missing, and they'd get an all-points alarm out for her. Amanda wondered whether the alien had figured that out yet. *The alien*, Amanda thought, *needs a different body in a hurry.*

But not mine, she told herself. *For sure, not mine.*

"Your turn," she said casually, shutting the water off.

The alien, fumbling a little, turned the water back on and got under the spray. Clouds of steam rose, and its skin began to look boiled, but it didn't appear troubled. No sense of pain? "Hold it," Amanda said. "Step back." She adjusted the water. "You've got it too hot. You'll damage that body that way. Look, if you can't tell the difference between hot and cold, just take cold showers, okay? It's less dangerous. This is cold, on this side."

She left the alien under the shower and went to find some clean clothes. When she came back, the alien was still showering, under icy water. "Enough," Amanda said. "Here. Put these clothes on."

"I had more clothes than this before."

"A T-shirt and jeans are all you need in hot weather like this. With your kind of build you can skip the bra, and anyway I don't think you'll be able to fasten it the right way."

"Do we put the face paint on now?"

"We can skip it while we're home. It's just stupid kid stuff anyway, all that tribal crap. If we go out we'll do it, and we'll give you Walnut Creek colors, I think. Concepción wore San Jose, but we want to throw people off the track. How about some dope?"

"What?"

"Grass. Marijuana. A drug widely used by local Earthians of our age."

"I don't need no drug."

"I don't, either. But I'd *like* some. You ought to learn how, just in case you find yourself in a social situation." Amanda reached for her pack of Filter Golds and pulled out a joint. Expertly she tweaked its lighter tip and took a deep hit. "Here," she said, passing it. "Hold it like I did.

Put it to your mouth, breathe in, suck the smoke deep."
The alien dragged the joint and began to cough. "Not so
deep, maybe," Amanda said. "Take just a little. Hold it.
Let it out. There, much better. Now give me back the
joint. You've got to keep passing it back and forth. That
part's important. You feel anything from it?"

"No."

"It can be subtle. Don't worry about it. Are you hungry?"

"Not yet," the alien said.

"I am. Come into the kitchen." As she assembled a
sandwich—peanut butter and avocado on whole wheat,
with tomato and onion—she asked, "What sort of things
do you guys eat?"

"Life."

"Life?"

"We never eat dead things. Only things with life."

Amanda fought back a shudder. "I see. *Anything* with
life?"

"We prefer animal life. We can absorb plants if necessary."

"Ah. Yes. And when are you going to be hungry again?"

"Maybe tonight," the alien said. "Or tomorrow. The
hunger comes very suddenly, when it comes."

"There's not much around here that you could eat live.
But I'll work on it."

"The small furry animal?"

"No. My cat is not available for dinner. Get that idea
right out of your head. Likewise me. I'm your protector
and guide. It wouldn't be sensible to eat me. You follow
what I'm trying to tell you?"

"I said that I'm not hungry yet."

"Well, you let me know when you start feeling the
pangs. I'll find you a meal." Amanda began to construct a

second sandwich. The alien prowled the kitchen, examining the appliances. Perhaps making mental records, Amanda thought, of sink and oven design, to copy on its home world. Amanda said. "Why did you people come here in the first place?"

"It was our mission."

"Yes. Sure. But for what purpose? What are you after? You want to take over the world? You want to steal our scientific secrets?" The alien, making no reply, began taking spices out of the spice rack. Delicately it licked its finger, touched it to the oregano, tasted it, tried the cumin. Amanda said, "Or is it that you want to keep us from going into space? You think we're a dangerous species, and so you're going to quarantine us on our own planet? Come on, you can tell *me*. I'm not a government spy." The alien sampled the tarragon, the basil, the sage. When it reached for the curry powder, its hand suddenly shook so violently that it knocked the open jars of oregano and tarragon over, making a mess. "Hey, are you all right?" Amanda asked.

The alien said, "I think I'm getting hungry. Are these things drugs, too?"

"Spices," Amanda said. "We put them in our foods to make them taste better." The alien was looking very strange, glassy-eyed, flushed, sweaty. "Are you feeling sick or something?"

"I feel excited. These powders—"

"They're turning you on? Which one?"

"This, I think." It pointed to the oregano. "It was either the first one or the second."

"Yeah." Amanda said. "Oregano. It can really make you fly." She wondered whether the alien would get violent when zonked. Or whether the oregano would stimulate its appetite. She had to watch out for its appetite. *There are certain risks,* Amanda reflected, *in doing what I'm doing.* Deftly she cleaned up the spilled oregano and tarragon and put the caps on the spice jars. "You ought to be careful," she said. "Your metabolism isn't used to this stuff. A little can go a long way."

"Give me some more."

"Later," Amanda said. "You don't want to overdo it too early in the day."

"More!"

"Calm down. I know this planet better than you, and I don't want to see you get in trouble. Trust me. I'll let you have more oregano when it's the right time. Look at the way you're shaking. And you're sweating like crazy." Pocketing the oregano jar, she led the alien back into the living room. "Sit down. Relax."

"More? Please?"

"I appreciate your politeness. But we have important things to talk about, and then I'll give you some. Okay?" Amanda opaqued the window, through which the hot late-afternoon sun was coming. Six o'clock on Friday, and if everything had gone the right way Charley would have been showing up just about now. Well, she'd found a different diversion. The weekend stretched before her like an open road leading to Mysteryland. The alien offered all sorts of possibilities, and she might yet have some fun over the next few days, if she used her head. Amanda turned to the alien and said, "You calmer now? Yes. Good. Okay, first of all, you've got to get yourself another body."

"Why is that?"

"Two reasons. One is that the authorities are probably searching for the girl you absorbed. How you got as far as you did without anybody but me spotting you is hard to understand. Number two, a teen-aged girl traveling by herself is going to get hassled too much, and you don't

239

know how to handle yourself in a tight situation. You know what I'm saying? You're going to want to hitchhike out to Nevada, Wyoming, Utah, wherever the hell your rendezvous place is, and all along the way people are going to be coming on to you. You don't need any of that. Besides, it's very tricky trying to pass for a girl. You've got to know how to put your face paint on, how to understand challenge codes, what the way you wear your clothing says, and like that. Boys have a much simpler subculture. You get yourself a male body, a big hunk of a body, and nobody'll bother you much on the way to where you're going. You just keep to yourself, don't make eye contact, don't smile, and everyone will leave you alone."

"Makes sense," said the alien. "All right. The hunger is becoming very bad now. Where do I get a male body?"

"San Francisco. It's full of men. We'll go over there tonight and find a nice brawny one for you. With any luck we might even find one who's not gay, and then we can have a little fun with him first. And then you take his body over—which incidentally solves your food problem for a while doesn't it? And we can have some more fun, a whole weekend of fun." Amanda winked. "Okay, Connie?"

"Okay." The alien winked, a clumsy imitation, first one eye, then the other. "You give me more oregano now?"

"Later. And when you wink, just wink *one* eye. Like this. Except I don't think you ought to do a lot of winking at people. It's a very intimate gesture that could get you in trouble. Understand?"

"There's so much to understand."

"You're on a strange planet, kid. Did you expect it to be just like home? Okay, to continue. The next thing I ought to point out is that when you leave here on Sunday, you'll have to—"

The telephone rang.

"What's that sound?" the alien asked.

"Communications device. I'll be right back." Amanda went to the hall extension, imagining the worst: her parents, say, calling to announce that they were on their way back from Tahoe tonight, some mixup in the reservations or something.

But the voice that greeted her was Charley's. She could hardly believe it, after the casual way he had shafted her this weekend. She could hardly believe what he wanted, either. He had left half a dozen of his best cassettes at her place last week, Golden Age rock, *Abbey Road* and the Hendrix one and a Joplin and such, and now he was heading off to Monterey for the festival and wanted to have them for the drive. Did she mind if he stopped off in half an hour to pick them up?

The bastard, she thought. *The absolute trashiness of him!* First to torpedo her weekend without even an apology, and then to let her know that he and what's-her-name were scooting down to Monterey for some fun, and could he bother her for his cassettes? Didn't he think she had any feelings? She looked at the telephone as if it were emitting toads and scorpions. It was tempting to hang up on him.

She resisted the temptation. "As it happens," she said, "I'm just on my way out for the weekend myself. But I've got a friend who's staying here cat-sitting for me. I'll leave the cassettes with her, okay? Her name's Connie."

"Fine. That's great," Charley said. "I really appreciate that, Amanda."

"It's nothing," she said.

The alien was back in the kitchen, nosing around the spice rack. But Amanda had the oregano. She said, "I've arranged for delivery of your next body."

"You did?"

"A large healthy adolescent male. Exactly what you're looking for. He's going to be here in a little while. I'm going to go out for a drive. You take care of him before I get back. How long does it take for you to—engulf—somebody?"

"It's very fast."

"Good." Amanda found Charley's cassettes and stacked them on the living-room table. "He's coming over here to get these six little boxes, which are music-storage devices. When the doorbell rings, you let him in and introduce yourself as Connie and tell him his things are on this table. After that you're on your own. You think you can handle it?"

"Sure," the alien said.

"Tuck in your T-shirt better. When it's tight, it makes your boobs stick out, and that'll distract him. Maybe he'll even make a pass at you. What happens to the Connie body after you engulf him?"

"It won't be here. What happens is I merge with him and dissolve all the Connie characteristics and take on the new ones."

"Ah. Very nifty. You're a real nightmare thing, you know? You're a walking horror show. Here you are, have another little hit of oregano before I go."

She put a tiny pinch of spice in the alien's hand. "Just to warm up your engine a little. I'll give you more later, when you've done the job. See you in an hour, okay?"

She left the house. Macavity was sitting on the porch, scowling, whipping his tail from side to side. Amanda knelt beside him and scratched him behind the ears. The cat made a low, rough purring sound, not much like his usual purr.

Amanda said. "You aren't happy, are you, fella? Well, don't worry. I've told the alien to leave you alone, and I guarantee you'll be okay. This is Amanda's fun tonight. You don't mind if Amanda has a little fun, do you?" Macavity made a glum, snuffling sound. "Listen, maybe I can get the alien to create a nice little calico cutie for you, okay? Just going into heat and ready to howl. Would you like that, guy? Would you? I'll see what I can do when I get back. But I have to clear out of here now, before Charley shows up."

She got into her car and headed for the westbound freeway ramp. Half past six, Friday night, the sun still hanging high above the Bay. Traffic was thick in the eastbound lanes, the late commuters slogging toward home, and it was beginning to build up westbound, too, as people set out for dinner in San Francisco. Amanda drove through the tunnel and turned north into Berkeley to cruise city streets. Ten minutes to seven now. Charley must have arrived. She imagined Connie in her tight T-shirt, all stoned and sweaty on oregano, and Charley giving her the eye, getting ideas, thinking about grabbing a bonus quickie before taking off with his cassettes. And Connie leading him on, Charley making his moves, and then suddenly that electric moment of surprise as the alien struck and Charley found himself turning into dinner. *It could be happening right this minute,* Amanda thought placidly. *No more than the bastard deserves, isn't it?* She had felt for a long time that Charley was a big mistake in her life, and after what he had pulled yesterday, she was sure of it. *No more than he deserves.*

But, she wondered, *what if Charley has brought his weekend date along?* The thought chilled her. She hadn't considered that possibility at all. It could ruin everything.

Connie wasn't able to engulf two at once, was she? And suppose they recognized her as the missing alien and ran out screaming to call the cops?

No, she thought. Not even Charley would be so tacky as to bring his date over to Amanda's house tonight. And Charley never watched the news or read a paper.

He wouldn't have a clue as to what Connie really was until it was too late for him to run.

Seven o'clock. Time to head for home.

The sun was sinking behind her as she turned onto the freeway. By quarter past she was approaching her house. Charley's old red Honda was parked outside.

Amanda parked across the street and cautiously let herself in, pausing just inside the front door to listen.

Silence.

"Connie?"

"In here," said Charley's voice.

Amanda entered the living room. Charley was sprawled out comfortably on the couch. There was no sign of Connie.

"Well?" Amanda said. "How did it go?"

"Easiest thing in the world," the alien said. "He was sliding his hands under my T-shirt when I let him have the nullifier jolt."

"Ah. The nullifier jolt."

"And then I completed the engulfment and cleaned up the carpet. God, it feels good not to be hungry again. You can't imagine how tough it was to resist engulfing you, Amanda. For the past hour I kept thinking of food, food, food—"

"Very thoughtful of you to resist."

"I knew you were out to help me. It's logical not to engulf one's allies."

"That goes without saying. So you feel well fed now?

244

He was good stuff?"

"Robust, healthy, nourishing—yes."

"I'm glad Charley turned out to be good for something. How long before you get hungry again?"

The alien shrugged. "A day or two. Maybe three. Give me more oregano, Amanda?"

"Sure," she said. "Sure." She felt a little let down. Not that she was remorseful about Charley, exactly, but it all seemed so casual, so offhanded—there was something anticlimactic about it, in a way. She suspected she should have stayed and watched while it was happening. Too late for that now, though.

She took the oregano from her purse and dangled the jar teasingly. "Here it is, babe. But you've got to earn it first."

"What do you mean?"

"I mean that I was looking forward to a big weekend with Charley, and the weekend is here. Charley's here, too, more or less, and I'm ready for fun. Come show me some fun, big boy."

She slipped Charley's Hendrix cassette into the tape deck and turned the volume all the way up.

The alien looked puzzled. Amanda began to peel off her clothes.

"You, too," Amanda said. "Come on. You won't have to dig deep into Charley's mind to figure out what to do. You're going to be my Charley for me this weekend, you follow? You and I are going to do all the things that he and I were going to do. Okay? Come on. Come on." She beckoned.

The alien shrugged again and slipped out of Charley's clothes, fumbling with the unfamiliarities of his zipper and buttons. Amanda, grinning, drew the alien close against her and down to the living-room floor. She took its hands and put them where she wanted them to be. She whispered instructions. The alien, docile, obedient, did what she wanted.

It felt like Charley. It smelled like Charley. And after her instructions, it even moved pretty much the way Charley moved.

But it wasn't Charley, it wasn't Charley at all, and after the first few seconds Amanda knew that she had goofed things up very badly. You couldn't just ring in an imitation like this. Making love with this alien was like making love with a very clever machine, or with her own mirror image. It was empty and meaningless and dumb.

Grimly she went on to the finish. They rolled apart, panting, sweating.

"Well?" The alien said. "Did the earth move for you?"

"Yeah. Yeah. It was terrific — Charley."

"Oregano?"

"Sure," Amanda said. She handed the spice jar across. "I always keep my promises. babe. Go to it. Have yourself a blast. Just remember that that's strong stuff for guys from your planet, okay? If you pass out, I'm going to leave you right there on the floor."

"Don't worry about me."

"Okay. You have your fun. I'm going to clean up, and then maybe we'll go over to San Francisco for the nightlife. Does that interest you?"

"You bet, Amanda." The alien winked — one eye, then the other — and gulped a huge pinch of oregano. "That sounds terrific."

Amanda gathered up her clothes, went upstairs for a quick shower, and dressed. When she came down, the alien was more than half blown away on the oregano, goggle-eyed, loll-headed, propped up against the couch, and crooning to itself in a weird atonal way. *Fine.*

Amanda thought. *You just get yourself all spiced up, love.*
She took the portable phone from the kitchen, carried it
with her into the bathroom, locked the door, and quietly
dialed the police emergency number.

She was bored with the alien. The game had worn thin
very quickly. And it was crazy, she thought, to spend the
whole weekend cooped up with a dangerous extraterrestrial creature when there wasn't going to be any fun in it
for her. She knew now that there couldn't be any fun at
all. And besides, in a day or two the alien was going to get
hungry again.

"I've got your alien," she said. "Sitting in my living
room, stoned out of its head on oregano. Yes, I'm absolutely certain. It was disguised as a Chicana girl first, Con-
ceptión Flores, but then it attacked my boyfriend, Charley
Taylor, and—yes, yes, I'm safe. I'm locked in the john.
Just get somebody over here fast—okay. I'll stay on the
line—what happened was, I spotted it downtown outside
the video center, and it insisted on coming home with
me—"

The actual capture took only a few minutes. But there
was no peace for hours after the police tactical squad
hauled the alien away, because the media were in on the
act right away, first a team from Channel 2 in Oakland,
and then some of the network guys, and then the *Chroni-
cle,* and finally a whole army of reporters from as far
away as Sacramento and phone calls from Los Angeles
and San Diego and—about three that morning—New
York.

Amanda told the story again and again until she was
sick of it, and just as dawn was breaking, she threw the
last of them out and barred the door.

She wasn't sleepy at all. She felt wired up, speedy, and depressed all at once. The alien was gone, Charley was gone, and she was all alone. She was going to be famous for the next couple of days, but that wouldn't help. She'd still be alone. For a time she wandered around the house, looking at it the way an alien might, as if she had never seen a stereo cassette before, or a television set, or a rack of spices. The smell of oregano was everywhere. There were little trails of it on the floor.

Amanda switched on the radio and there she was on the six A.M. news. "—the emergency is over, thanks to the courageous Walnut Creek High School girl who trapped and outsmarted the most dangerous life form in the known universe—"

She shook her head. "You think that's true?" she asked the cat. "Most dangerous life form in the universe? I don't think so, Macavity, I think I know of at least one that's a lot deadlier. Eh, kid?" She winked. "If they only knew, eh? If they only knew." She scooped the cat up and hugged it, and it began to purr. Maybe trying to get a little sleep would be a good idea. Then she had to figure out what she was going to do about the rest of the weekend.

A HISS OF DRAGON

By Gregory Benford & Marc Laidlaw

"Incoming Dragon!" Leopold yelled, and ducked to the left. I went right.

Dragons come in slow and easy. A blimp with wings, this one settled down like a wrinkled brown sky falling. I scrambled over boulders, trying to be inconspicuous and fast at the same time. It didn't seem like a promising beginning for a new job.

Leopold and I had been working on the ledge in front of the Dragon's Lair, stacking berry pods. This Dragon must have flown toward its Lair from the other side of the mountain spire, so our radio tag on him didn't transmit through all the rock. Usually they're not so direct. Most Dragons circle their Lairs a few times, checking for scavengers and egg stealers. If they don't circle, they're usually too tired. And when they're tired, they're irritable. Something told me I didn't want to be within reach of this one's throat flame.

I dropped my berrybag rig and went down the rocks

feet first. The boulders were slippery with green moss for about 20 meters below the ledge, so I slid down on them. I tried to keep the falls to under four meters and banged my butt when I missed. I could hear Leopold knocking loose rocks on the other side, moving down toward where our skimmer was parked.

A shadow fell over me, blotting out Beta's big yellow disk. The brown bag above thrashed its wings and gave a trumpeting shriek. It had caught sight of the berry bags and knew something was up. Most likely, with its weak eyes, the Dragon thought the bags were eggers — off season, but what do Dragons know about seasons? — and would attack them. That was the optimistic theory. The pessimistic one was that the Dragon had seen one of us. I smacked painfully into a splintered boulder and glanced up. Its underbelly was heaving, turning purple: anger. Not a reassuring sign. Eggers don't bother Dragons that much.

Then its wings fanned the air, backwards. It drifted off the ledge, hovering. The long neck snaked around, and two nearsighted eyes sought mine. The nose expanded, catching my scent. The Dragon hissed triumphantly.

Our skimmer was set for a fast takeoff. But it was 200 meters down, on the only wide spot we could find. I made a megaphone of my hands and shouted into the thin mountain mist, "Leopold! Grab air!"

I jumped down to a long boulder that jutted into space. Below and a little to the left I could make out the skimmer's shiny wings through the shifting green fog. I sucked in a breath and ran off the end of the boulder.

Dragons are clumsy at level flight, but they can drop like a brick. The only way to beat this one down to the skimmer was by falling most of the way.

I banked down, arms out. Our gravity is only a third of Earth normal. Even when falling, you have time to think things over. I can do the calculations fast enough — it came out to nine seconds — but getting the count right with a Dragon on your tail is another matter. I ticked the seconds off and then popped the chute. It fanned and filled. The skimmer came rushing up, wind whipped my face. Then my harness jerked me to a halt. I drifted down. I thumped the release and fell free. Above me, a trumpeting bellow. Something was coming in at four o'clock and I turned, snatching for my blaser. Could it be that fast? But it was Leopold, on chute. I sprinted for the skimmer. It was pointed along the best outbound wind, flaps already down, a standard precaution, I belted in, sliding my feet into the pedals. I caught a dank, foul reek of Dragon. More high shrieking, closer, Leopold came running up, panting. He wriggled into the rear seat. A thumping of wings. A ceiling of wrinkled leather. Something hissing overhead.

Dragons don't fly, they float. They have a big green hydrogen-filled dome on their backs to give them lift. They make the hydrogen in their stomachs and can dive quickly by venting it out the ass. This one was farting and falling as we zoomed away. I banked, turned to get a look at the huffing brown mountain hooting its anger at us, and grinned.

"I take back what I said this morning," Leopold gasped. "You'll draw full wages *and* commissions, from the start."

I didn't say anything. I'd just noticed that somewhere back there I had pissed my boots full.

I covered it pretty well back at the strip. I twisted out of the skimmer and slipped into the maintenance bay. I had extra clothes in my bag, so I slipped on some fresh socks and thongs.

When I was sure I smelled approximately human, I tromped back out to Leopold. I was damned if I would let my morning's success be blotted out by an embarrassing accident. It was a hirer's market these days. My training at crop dusting out in the flat farmlands had given me an edge over the other guys who had applied. I was determined to hang on to this job.

Leopold was the guy who "invented" the Dragons, five years ago. He took a life form native to Lex, the bloats, and tinkered with their DNA. Bloats are balloonlike and nasty. Leopold made them bigger, tougher, and spliced in a lust for thistleberries that makes Dragons hoard them compulsively. It had been a brilliant job of engineering. The Dragons gathered thistleberries, and Leopold stole them from the Lairs.

Thistleberries are a luxury good, high in protein, and delicious. The market for them might collapse if Lex's economy got worse—the copper seams over in Bahinin had run out last month. This was nearly the only good flying job left. More than anything else, I wanted to keep flying. And *not* as a crop duster. Clod-grubber work is a pain.

Leopold was leaning against his skimmer, a little pale, watching his men husk thistleberries. His thigh muscles were still thick; he was clearly an airman by ancestry, but he looked tired.

"Goddamn," he said. "I can't figure it out, kid. The Dragons are hauling in more berries than normal. We can't get into the Lairs, though. You'd think it was mating season around here, the way they're attacking my men."

"Mating season? When's that?"

"Oh, in about another six months, when the puffbushes bloom in the treetops. The pollen sets off the mating urges in Dragons—steps up their harvest, but it also makes 'em

252

meaner."

"Great," I said. "I'm allergic to puffbush pollen. I'll have to fight off Dragons with running eyes and a stuffy nose."

Leopold shook his head absently; he hadn't heard me. "I can't understand it—there's nothing wrong with my Dragon designs."

"Seems to me you could have toned down the behavior plexes," I said. "Calm them down a bit—I mean, they've outgrown their competition to the point that they don't even *need* to be mean anymore. They don't browse much as it is . . . nobody's going to bother them."

"No way—there's just not the money for it, Drake. Look, I'm operating on the margin here. My five-year rights to the genetic patents just ran out, and now I'm in competition with Kwalan Rhiang, who owns the other half of the forest. Besides, you think gene splicing is easy?"

"Still, if they can bioengineer *humans* . . . I mean, we were beefed up for strength and oxy burning nearly a thousand years ago."

"But we weren't blown up to five times the size of our progenitors, Drake. I made those Dragons out of mean sons of bitches—blimps with teeth is what they were. It gets tricky when you mess with the life cycles of something that's already that unstable. You just don't understand what's involved here."

I nodded. "I'm no bioengineer—granted."

He looked at me and grinned, a spreading warm grin on his deeply lined face. "Yeah, Drake, but you're good at what you do—really good. What happened today, well, I'm getting too old for that sort of thing, and it's happening more and more often. If you hadn't been there I'd probably be stewing in that Dragon's stomach right now—

skimmer and all."

I shrugged. That gave me a chance to roll the slabs of muscle in my shoulders, neck, and pectorals—a subtle advertisement that I had enough to keep a skimmer aloft for hours.

"So," he continued. "I'm giving you full pilot rank. The skimmer's yours. You can fly it home tonight, on the condition that you meet me at the Angis Tavern for a drink later on. And bring your girl Evelaine, too, if you want."

"It's a deal, Leopold. See you there."

I whistled like a dungwarbler all the way home, pedaling my new skimmer over the treetops toward the city. I nearly wrapped myself in a floating thicket of windbrambles, but not even this could destroy my good mood.

I didn't notice any Dragons roaming around, though I saw that the treetops had been plucked of their berries and then scorched. Leopold had at least had the foresight, when he was gene tinkering, to provide for the thistleberries' constant replenishment. He gave the Dragons a throat flame to singe the treetops with, which makes the berries grow quickly. A nice touch.

It would have been simpler, of course, to have men harvest the thistleberries themselves, but that never worked out, economically. Thistleberries grow on top of virtually unclimbable thorntrees, where you can't even maneuver a skimmer without great difficulty. And if a man fell to the ground . . . well, if it's on the ground, it has spines, that's the rule on Lex. There's nothing soft to fall on down there. Sky life is more complex than ground life. You can actually do something useful with sky life—namely, bioengineering. Lex may be a low-metal world—which means low-technology—but our bioengineers are the best.

A clapping sound, to the left. I stopped whistling. Down through the greenish haze I could see a dark form coming in over the treetops, its wide rubbery wings slapping together at the top of each stroke. A smackwing. Good meat, spicy and moist. But hard to catch. Evelaine and I had good news to celebrate tonight; I decided to bring her home smackwing for dinner. I took the skimmer down in the path of the smackwing, meanwhile slipping my blaser from its holster.

The trick to hunting in the air is to get beneath your prey so that you can grab it while it falls, but this smackwing was flying too low. I headed in fast, hoping to frighten it into rising above me, but it was no use. The smackwing saw me, red eyes rolling. It missed a beat in its flapping and dived toward the treetops. At that instant a snagger shot into view from the topmost branches, rising with a low farting sound. The smackwing spotted this blimplike thing that had leaped into its path but apparently didn't think it too threatening. It swerved about a meter under the bobbing creature—

And stopped flat, in mid-air.

I laughed aloud, sheathing my blaser. The snagger had won his meal like a real hunter.

Beneath the snagger's wide blimplike body was a dangling sheet of transparent sticky material. The smackwing struggled in the moist folds as the snagger drew the sheet upward. To the unwary smackwing that clear sheet must have been invisible until the instant he flew into it.

Within another minute, as I pedaled past the spot, the snagger had entirely engulfed the smackwing and was unrolling its sticky sheet as it drifted back into the treetops. Pale yellow eyes considered me and rejected the notion of me as food. A ponderous predator, wise with years.

I flew into the spired city: Kalatin.

I parked on the deck of our apartment building, high above the jumbled wooden buildings of the city. Now that my interview had been successful, we'd be able to stay in Kalatin, though I hoped we could find a better apartment. This one was as old as the city—which in turn had been around for a great deal of the 1200 years humans had been on Lex. As the wood of the lower stories rotted, and as the building crumbled away, new quarters were just built on top of it and settled into place. Someday this city would be an archaeologist's dream. In the meantime, it was an inhabitant's nightmare.

Five minutes later, having negotiated several treacherous ladders and a splintering shinny pole into the depths of the old building, I crept quietly to the wooden door of my apartment and let myself in, clutching the mudskater steaks that I'd picked up on the way home. It was dark and cramped inside, the smell of rubbed wood strong. I could hear Evelaine moving around in the kitchen, so I sneaked to the doorway and looked in. She was turned away, chopping thistleberries with a thorn-knife.

I grabbed her, throwing the steaks into the kitchen, and kissed her.

"Got the job, Evey!" I said. "Leopold took me out himself and I ended up saving his—"

"It *is* you!" She covered her nose, squirming away from me. "What is that smell, Drake?"

"Smell?"

"Like something died. It's all over you."

I remembered the afternoon's events. It was either the smell of Dragon, which I'd got from scrambling around in a Lair, or that of urine. I played it safe and said, "I think it's Dragon."

"Well take it somewhere else. I'm cooking dinner."

"I'll hop in the cycler. You can cook up the steaks I

brought, then we're going out to celebrate."

The Angis Tavern is no skiff joint, good for a stale senso on the way home from work. It's the best. The Angis is a vast old place, perched on a pyramid of rock. Orange fog nestles at the base, a misty collar separating it from the jumble of the city below.

Evelaine pedaled the skimmer with me, having trouble in her gown. We made a wobbly landing on the rickety side deck. It would've been easier to coast down to the city, where there was more room for a glide approach, but that's pointless. There are thick cactus and thornbushes around the Angis base, hard to negotiate at night. In the old days it kept away predators; now it keeps away the riffraff.

But not completely: two beggars accosted us as we dismounted, offering to shine up the skimmer's aluminum skin. I growled convincingly at them, and they skittered away. The Angis is so big, so full of crannies to hide out in, they can't keep it clear of beggars, I guess.

We went in a balcony entrance. Fat balloons nudged against the ceiling, ten meters overhead, dangling their cords. I snagged one and stepped off into space. Evelaine hooked it as I fell. We rode it down, past alcoves set in the rock wall. Well-dressed patrons nodded as we eased down, the balloon following. The Angis is a spire, broadening gradually as we descended. Phosphors cast creamy glows on the tables set into the walls. I spotted Leopold sprawled in a webbing, two empty tankards lying discarded underneath.

"You're late," he called. We stepped off onto his ledge. Our balloons, released, shot back to the roof.

"You didn't set a time. Evelaine, Leopold." Nods, introductory phrases.

"It seems quite crowded here tonight," Evelaine murmured. A plausible social remark, except she'd never been to an inn of this class before.

Leopold shrugged. "Hard times mean full taverns. Booze or sensos or tinglers—pick your poison."

Evelaine has the directness of a country girl and knows her own limitations; she stuck to a mild tingler. Service was running slow, so I went to log our orders. I slid down a shinny pole to the first bar level. Mice zipped by me, eating up tablescraps left by the patrons; it saves on labor. Amid the jam and babble I placed our order with a steward and turned to go back.

"You looking for work?" a thick voice said.

I glanced at its owner. "No." The man was big, swarthy, and sure of himself.

"Thought you wanted Dragon work." His eyes had a look of distant amusement.

"How'd you know that?" I wasn't known in the city.

"Friends told me."

"Leopold hired me today."

"So I hear. I'll top whatever he's paying."

"I didn't think business was that good."

"It's going to get better. Much better, once Leopold's out of the action. A monopoly can always sell goods at a higher price. You can start tomorrow."

So this was Kwalan Rhiang. "No thanks. I'm signed up." Actually, I hadn't signed anything, but there was something about this man I didn't like. Maybe the way he was so sure I'd work for him.

"Flying for Leopold is dangerous. He doesn't know what he's doing."

"See you around," I said. A senso was starting in a nearby booth. I took advantage of it to step into the expanding blue cloud, so Rhiang couldn't follow and see where we were sitting. I got a lifting, bright sensation of pleasure, and then I was out of the misty confusion, moving away among the packed crowd.

I saw them on the stairway. They were picking their way down it delicately. I thought they were deformed, but the funny tight clothes gave them away. Offworlders, here for the flying. That was the only reason anybody came to Lex. We're still the only place men can seriously fly longer than a few minutes. Even so, our lack of machines keeps most offworlders away; they like it easy, everything done for them. I watched them pick their way down the stairs, thinking that if the depression got worse, offworlders would be able to hire servants here, even though it was illegal. It could come to that.

They were short as children but heavyset, with narrow chests and skinny limbs. Spindly people, unaugmented for Lex oxy levels. But men like that had colonized here long ago, paying for it in reduced lifetimes. I felt as though I was watching my own ancestors.

Lex shouldn't have any oxy at all, by the usual rules of planetary evolution. It's a small planet, 0.21 Earth masses, a third gee of gravity. Rules of thumb say we shouldn't have any atmosphere to speak of. But our sun, Beta, is a K-type star, redder than Sol. Beta doesn't heat our upper atmosphere very much with ultraviolet, so we retain gasses. Even then, Lex would be airless except for accidents of birth. It started out with a dense cloak of gas, just as Earth did. But dim old Beta didn't blow the atmosphere away, and there wasn't enough compressional heating by Lex itself to boil away the gasses. So they stuck around, shrouding the planet, causing faster erosion than on Earth. The winds moved dust horizontally, exposing crustal rock. That upset the isostatic balance in the surface, and split open faults. Volcanoes poked up. They belched water and gas onto the surface, keeping the atmosphere dense. So Lex ended up with low gravity and a thick atmosphere. Fine, except that Beta's wan light also never pushed many heavy elements out this far, so Lex is metal-poor. Without iron and the rest you can't build machines, and without technology you're a backwater. You sell your tourist attraction—flying—and hope for the best.

One of the offworlders came up to me and said, "You got any sparkers in this place?"

I shook my head. Maybe he didn't know that getting a sendup by tying your frontal lobes into an animal's is illegal here. Maybe he didn't care. Ancestor or not, he just looked like a misshapen dwarf to me, and I walked away.

Evelaine was describing life in the flatlands when I got back. Leopold was rapt, the worry lines in his face nearly gone. Evelaine does that to people. She's natural and straightforward, so she was telling him right out that she wasn't much impressed with city life. "Farmlands are quiet and restful. Everybody has a job," she murmured. "You're right that getting around is harder—but we can glide in the updrafts, in summer. It's heaven."

"Speaking of the farmlands," I said, "an old friend of mine came out here five years ago. He wanted in on your operations."

"I was hiring like crazy five years ago. What was his name?"

"Lorn Kramer. Great pilot."

Leopold shook his head. "Can't remember. He's not with me now, anyway. Maybe Rhiang got him."

Our drinks arrived. The steward was bribable, though—Rhiang was right behind him.

"You haven't answered my 'gram," Rhiang said directly to Leopold, ignoring us. I guess he didn't figure I was worth any more time.

"Didn't need to," Leopold said tersely.

"Sell out. I'll give you a good price." Rhiang casually sank his massive flank on our table edge. "You're getting too old."

Something flickered in Leopold's eyes; he said nothing.

"Talk is," Rhiang went on mildly, "market's falling."

"Maybe," Leopold said. "What you been getting for a kilo?"

"Not saying."

"Tight lips and narrow minds go together."

Rhiang stood, his barrel chest bulging. "You could use a little instruction in politeness."

"From you?" Leopold chuckled. "You paid off that patent clerk to release my gene configs early. Was that polite?"

Rhiang shrugged. "That's the past. The present reality is that there may be an oversupply of thistleberries. Market isn't big enough for two big operations like ours. There's too much—"

"Too much of you, that's my problem. Lift off, Rhiang."

To my surprise, he did. He nodded to me, ignored Evelaine, and gave Leopold a look of contempt. Then he was gone.

I heard them first. We were taking one of the outside walks that corkscrew around the Angis spire, gawking at the phosphored streets below. A stone slide clattered behind us. I saw two men duck behind a jutting ledge. One of them had something in his hand that glittered.

"You're jumpy, Drake," Evelaine said.

"Maybe." It occurred to me that if we went over the edge of this spire, hundreds of meters into the thorn scrabble below, it would be very convenient for Rhiang.

"Let's move on."

Leopold glanced at me, then back at the inky shadows. We strolled along the trail of volcanic rock, part of the natural formation that made the spire. Rough black pebbles slipped underfoot. In the distant starflecked night, skylight called and boomed.

We passed under a phosphor. At the next turn Leopold looked back and said, "I saw one of them. Rhiang's right-hand man."

We hurried away. I wished for a pair of wings to get us off this place. Evelaine understood instantly that this was serious. "There's a split in the trail ahead," Leopold said. "If they follow, we'll know . . ." He didn't finish.

We turned. They followed. "I think I know a way to slow them down," I said. Leopold looked at me. We were trying to avoid slipping in the darkness and yet make good time. "Collect some of these obsidian frags," I said.

We got a bundle of them together. "Go on up ahead," I said. We were on a narrow ledge. I sank back into the shadows and waited. The two men appeared. Before they noticed me I threw the obsidian high into the air. In low gravity it takes a long time for them to come back down. In the darkness the two men couldn't see them coming.

I stepped out into the wan light. "Hey!" I yelled to them. They stopped, precisely where I thought they would. "What's going on?" I said, to stall.

The biggest one produced a knife. "This."

The first rock hit, coming down from over a hundred meters above. It slammed into the boulder next to him. Then three more crashed down, striking the big one in the shoulder, braining the second. They both crumpled.

I turned and hurried along the path. If they'd seen me throw they'd have had time to dodge. It was an old school-boy trick, but it worked.

The implications, though, were sobering. If Rhiang felt this way, my new job might not last long.

I was bagging berries in the cavernous Paramount Lair when the warning buzzer in my pocket went off. A Dragon was coming in. I still had time, but not much. I decided to finish this particular bag rather than abandon the bagging-pistol. The last bit of fluid sprayed over the heap of berries and began to congeal instantly, its tremendously high surface tension drawing it around the irregular pile and sealing perfectly. I holstered the gun, leaving the bag for later. I turned—

A slow flapping boom. Outside, a wrinkled brown wall.

Well, I'd fooled around long enough—now I dived for safety. The Dragon's Lair was carpeted with a thick collection of nesting materials. None were very pleasant to burrow through, but I didn't have any choice. Behind me I could hear the Dragon moving around; if I didn't move out of his way in a hurry I might get stepped on. The emergency chute on my back tangled in a branch, just as the stench in the Lair intensified. I hurried out of it and went on. I'd just have to be sure not to fall from any great heights. I didn't worry about it, because my skimmer was parked on the ledge just outside the Lair.

I stuck my head up through the nest to judge my position. The bulk of the Dragon was silhouetted against the glare of the sky, which was clear of fog today. The beast seemed to be preening itself. That was something I never thought they did outside of the mating season—which was six months away.

I scrambled backward into the nest. The buzzer in my pocket went off again, though it was supposed to signal just once, for ten seconds. I figured the thing must have broken. It quieted and I moved on, thinking. For one thing, the Dragon that occupied this Lair was supposed to have been far from home right now—which meant that my guest didn't really belong here. Dragons never used the wrong Lair unless it was the mating season.

I frowned. Why did that keep coming up?

Suddenly there was a rush of wind and a low, thrumming sound. The light from outside was cut off. I poked my head into the open.

Another Dragon was lumbering into the Lair. *This* was really impossible. Two Dragons sharing a Lair—and the wrong one at that! Whatever their reasons for being here, I was sure they were going to start fighting pretty soon, so I burrowed deeper, moving toward the nearest wall.

My elbow caught on something. Cloth. I brushed it away, then looked again. A Dragonrobber uniform like my own. It was directly beneath me, half-buried in the nesting material. I caught my breath, then poked at the uniform. Something glittered near one empty sleeve: an identification bracelet. I picked it up, shifted it in the light, and read the name on it: *Lorn Kramer.*

Lorn Kramer! So he had been in Leopold's group after all. But that still didn't explain why he left his clothes here.

I tugged at the uniform, dragging it toward me. It was limp, but tangled in the nest. I jerked harder and some long, pale things rattled out of the sleeve.

Bones.

I winced. I was suddenly aware that my present situation must be somewhat like the one that had brought him here.

I looked into the Lair again. One of the Dragons was prodding its snout at the other, making low, whuffling sounds. It didn't look like a hostile gesture to me. In fact, it looked like they were playing. The other Dragon wheeled about and headed for the entrance. The first one followed, and in a minute both of them had left the Lair again — as abruptly and inexplicably as they had entered it.

I saw my chance. I ran across the Lair, grabbed my skimmer, and took off. I moved out, pedaling furiously away from the Dragons, and glanced down.

For a minute I thought I was seeing things. The landscape below me was blurred, though the day had been clear and crisp when I'd flown into the Lair. I blinked. It didn't go away, but got clearer. There was a cloud of yellowish dust spreading high above the forest, billowing up and around the Lairs I could see. Where had it come from?

I sneezed, passing through a high plume of the dust. Then my eyes began to sting and I sneezed again. I brought the skimmer out of the cloud, but by this time my vision was distorted with tears. I began to cough and choke all at once, until the skimmer faltered as I fought to stay in control, my eyes streaming.

I knew what that dust was.

Nothing affected me as fiercely as puffbush pollen: it was the only thing I was really allergic to.

I stopped pedaling.

It affected Dragons, too. It set off their mating urges.

But where was the damned stuff coming from? It was six months out of season. I started pedaling again, legs straining. I turned to get a better view.

A flash of light needled past my head, and I knew. Three skimmers shot into view from around the spire of Paramount Lair. The tip of one of my wings was seared away by a blaser. My skimmer lurched wildly, but I held on and brought it up just as the first skimmer came toward me. Its pilot was wearing a filtermask. Attached to the skimmer were some empty bags that must have held the puffbush pollen. But what I was looking at was the guy's blaser. It was aimed at me.

I reeled into an updraft, pulling over my attacker, grabbing for my own blaser. The skimmer soared beneath me, then careened into a sharp turn. It was too sharp. The guy turned straight into the path of his companion. The two skimmers crashed together with a satisfying sound, then the scattered parts and pilots fell slowly toward the treetops. Seconds later, the forest swallowed them up.

I looked for the third man, just as he came up beside me. The bastard was grinning, and I recognized that grin. It was Kwalan Rhiang's.

He nodded once, affably, and before I could remember to use my blaser, Rhiang took a single, precise shot at the chainguard of my skimmer. The pedals rolled uselessly. I was out of control. Rhiang lifted away and cruised out of sight, leaving me flailing at the air in a ruined skimmer.

I had exactly one chance, and this was to get back to the Lair I'd just abandoned. I was slightly higher than the opening, so I glided in, backpedaled for the drop — and crashed straight into the wall, thanks to my ruined pedals. But I made it in alive, still able to stand up and brush the dirt from my uniform. I stood at the mouth of the Lair, staring out over the forest, considering the long climb that lay below me.

And just then the Dragons returned.

Not one, this time — not even two. *Five* shadows wheeled overhead; five huge beasts headed toward the Lair where I was standing. And finally, five Dragons dropped right on top of me.

I leapt back just in time, scrambling into the blue shadows as the first Dragon thumped to the ledge. It waddled inside, reeking. I moved back farther. Its four friends were right behind. I kept moving back.

Well, at least now I knew *why* they were doing this. Kwalan Rhiang had been setting off their mating urges by dusting the Dragons with puffbush-pollen, messing up their whole life cycle, fooling with their already nasty tempers. It made sense. Anything less subtle might have gotten Rhiang into a lot of trouble. As it was, he'd doubtless fly safely home, waiting for Leopold's Dragons to kill off Leopold's men.

Out in the cavernous Lair, the Dragons began to move around, prodding at each other like scramblemice, hooting their airy courting sounds. The ground shook with their movement. Two seemed to be females, which suggested that I might look forward to some fighting between the other three. Great.

I fumbled at my pockets for something that might be of help. My warning buzzer had shattered in my rough landing; I threw it away. I still had my bagging-gun, but it wouldn't do me a lot of good. My blaser seemed okay. I unholstered it and began to move along the wall. If I went carefully, I might be able to get onto the outer ledge.

Two of the males were fighting now, lunging, the sounds of their efforts thundering around me. I made a short run and gained a bit of ground. One of the Dragons retreated from the battle—apparently the loser. I groaned. He had moved directly in my path.

A huge tail pounded at the ground near me and a female started backing my way, not looking at me. There was no place to go. And I was getting tired of this. I decided to warn her off. I made a quick shot at her back, nipping her in the hydrogen dome. She squawked and shuffled away, confused. I went on.

I stopped. There was a hissing sound behind me. Turning, I could see nothing but the Dragon I'd just shot. She didn't appear to be making the sound, but it was coming from her direction. I peered closer, through the blue gloom, and then saw where the noise was coming from.

Her hydrogen dome was deflating.

I nearly laughed aloud. Here was the answer to my problem. I could deflate the Dragons, leaving them stranded, unable to fly, while I climbed down this spire without fear of pursuit. I lifted my blaser and aimed at the male nearest the rear of the Lair. A near miss, then a hit. Hydrogen hissed out of his dome as well. Then I got the second female, and another male who was directly across from me.

One Dragon to go. The others were roaring and waddling. The Lair was full of the hissing sound.

I turned to my last opponent. He wasn't looking my way, but he was blocking my exit. I moved in closer and lifted my blaser.

Then he saw me.

I flung myself aside just as he bellowed and pounded forward, filling the entrance to the Lair, blocking out the sunlight. I rolled into the thorny nest. I fired once, hitting him in the snout. He swung his head toward me, pushing me around toward the outer ledge, bellowing. I fired again, and once more missed his hydrogen dome. I made a dash around his rump just as he spun my way, tail lashing against me. His dark little eyes narrowed as he sighted me, and his throat began to ripple.

My time was up. He was about to blast me with his throat flame.

The Dragon opened his mouth, belched hydrogen, and

ignited it by striking a spark from his molars—

That was the wrong thing to do.

I saw it coming and ducked.

The cavern shuddered and blew up. The orange explosion rumbled out, catching the Dragons in a huge rolling flame. I buried myself in the nesting strands and grabbed onto the lashing tail of my attacker. Terrified by the blast, he took off. My eyebrows were singed, my wrists burned.

The world spun beneath me. A tendril of smoke drifted into view just below, mingled with flaming bits of nesting material and the leathery hide of Dragons. Then my view spun again and I was looking at the sky. It gradually dawned on me that I was clinging to a Dragon's tail.

It occurred to the Dragon at the same time. I saw his head swing toward me, snapping angrily. His belly was flashing purple. Every now and then he let out a tongue of flame, but he couldn't quite get at me. Meanwhile, I held on for my life.

The Dragon flew on, but my weight seemed to be too much for it. We were dropping slowly toward the trees, as easily as if I'd punctured his bony dome with my blaser. But it would be rough landing. And I'd have to deal with the Dragon afterward.

I spied something rising from the trees below us. It shot swiftly into the air after a high-flying bulletbird, its transparent sheet rippling beneath its blimplike body. It was a huge snagger—as big as my own skimmer. I kicked on the Dragon's tail, dragging it sideways. The Dragon lurched and spun and then we were directly over the snagger.

I let go of the tail and dropped, my eyes closed.

In a second, something soft rumbled beneath me. I had landed safely atop the snagger. I opened my eyes as the Dragon—having lost my weight—shot suddenly upward. I watched it glide away, then looked down at the snagger, my savior. I patted its wide, rubbery body. My weight was pushing it slowly down, as if I were riding the balloons in the Angis Tavern. I looked forward to a comfortable trip to the ground.

"I like your style, kid."

I jumped, nearly losing my place on the snagger. The voice had come out of mid-air. Literally.

"You," I said. No more was necessary. He was banking around behind me.

Kwalan Rhiang had returned in his skimmer. He circled easily about me as I fell toward the treetops. He came in close, smiling, his huge legs pedaling him on a gentle course. I had to turn my head to keep an eye on him.

"I said before I'd top what Leopold was paying you," he shouted, his thick voice cutting the high air. "After today, I think I'd pay *double*. I could use someone like you."

I felt my face harden. "You bastard. You're responsible for what just happened. Why would I work for someone who's tried to kill me?"

He shrugged. "Gave you a chance to prove yourself. Come on, you're wasting your time with Leopold."

"And you're wasting your time with me."

He shrugged again, utterly sure of himself. "As you wish. I gave you a chance."

I nodded. "Now just go away."

"And leave you to tell Leopold about all this? You don't think I'm going to let you back alive, do you?"

I froze. Rhiang slid a blaser from its holster at his waist and aimed it at my head. His grin widened. The muzzle dropped a fraction, and I breathed a little easier.

"No," he said distantly, "why kill you straight off? Slow deaths are more interesting, I think. And harder to trace."

He aimed at the snagger. If he punctured it I'd drop into the trees. It was a long fall. I wouldn't make it.

I growled and grabbed for the gun at my waist, bringing it up before Rhiang could move. He stared at me for a moment, then started laughing. I looked at what I was holding.

"What're you going to do with that?" he said. "Bag me?"

It was my bagging-pistol, all right. I'd dropped the blaser back in the Lair. But it would still serve a purpose.

"Exactly," I said, and fired.

The gray fluid squirted across the narrow gap between us, sealing instantly over Rhiang's hands. He fired the blaser but succeeded only in melting the bag enough to let the weapon break away. It fell out of sight.

His eyes were wide. He was considering death by suffocation.

"No," he choked.

But I didn't fire at his head. I put the next bag right over his feet, sealing the pedal mechanism tight. His legs jerked convulsively. They slowed. Rhiang began to whimper, and then he was out of control. His skimmer turned and glided away as he hurried to catch any updraft he could. He vanished behind Paramount Lair, and was gone.

I turned back to observe the treetops. Rhiang might be back, but I doubted it. First he'd have a long walk ahead of him, over unpleasant terrain, back to his base . . . *if* he could maneuver his skimmer well enough to land in the treetops, and make the long, painful climb down.

But I didn't worry about it. I watched the thorntrees rise about me, and presently the snagger brought me gently to the ground. I dismounted, leaving the snagger to bob back into the air, and began to walk gingerly across the inhospitable ground, avoiding the spines. A daggerbush snapped at me. I danced away. It was going to be a rough walk out. Somewhere behind me, Rhiang might be facing the same problem. And he wanted me dead.

But I didn't have as far to go.

EXECUTIVE CLEMENCY

By Gardner Dozois and Jack C. Haldeman II

The President of the United States sat very still in his over-stuffed chair on the third floor and watched early morning sunlight sweep in a slow line across the faded rug.

He couldn't remember getting out of bed or sitting down in the chair. He could dimly recall that he had been sitting there for a long time, watching the slow advent of dawn, but he was only just beginning to become fully aware of himself and his surroundings.

Only his eyes moved, yellow and wet, as the world seeped in.

This happened to him almost every morning now. Every morning he would return slowly to his body as if from an immense distance, from across appalling gulfs of time and space, to find himself sitting in the chair, or standing next to the window, or, more rarely, propped up in the corner against the wall. Sometimes he'd be in the middle of dress-ing when awareness returned, and he'd awake to find him-self tying a shoelace or buttoning his pants. Sometimes, like this morning, he'd just be sitting and staring. Other times he would awaken to the sound of his own voice, loud and cold in the bare wooden room, saying some strange and important things that he could never quite catch. If he could only hear the words he said at such times, just once, he knew that it would change everything, that he would understand everything. But he could never hear them.

He didn't move. When the lines of sunlight reached the chair, it would be time to go downstairs. Not before, no matter how late it sometimes made him as the sunlight changed with the seasons, no matter if he sometimes missed breakfast or, on cloudy winter days, didn't move at all until Mrs. Hamlin came upstairs to chase him out. It was one of the rituals with which he tried to hold his life together.

The east-facing window was washed over with pale, fragile blue, and the slow-moving patch of direct sunlight was a raw, hot gold. Dust motes danced in the beam. Except for those dust motes, everything was stillness and suspension. Except for his own spidery breathing, everything was profoundly silent. The room smelled of dust and heat and old wood. It was the best part of the day. Naturally it couldn't last.

Very far away, floating on the edge of hearing, there came the mellow, mossy bronze voice of a bell, ringing in the village of Fairfield behind the ridge, and at that precise moment, as though the faint tintinnabulation were its cue, the house itself began to speak. It was a rambling wooden house, more than a hundred years old, and it talked to itself at dawn and dusk, creaking, groaning, whispering, muttering like a crotchety old eccentric as its wooden bones expanded with the sun or contracted with the frost. This petulant, arthritic monologue ran on for a few minutes, and then the tenants themselves joined in, one by one: Seth in the bathroom early, spluttering as he washed up; Mr. Thompkins, clearing his throat interminably in the room below, coughing and hacking and spitting as though he were drowning in a sea of phlegm; Sadie's baby, crying in a vain attempt to wake her sluggard mother; Mrs. Hamlin, slamming the kitchen door; Mr. Samuels's loud nasal voice in the courtyard outside.

The sunlight swept across his chair.

The President of the United States stirred and sighed, lifting his arms and setting them down again, stamping his feet to restore circulation. Creakily he got up. He stood for a moment, blinking in the sudden warmth, willing life back into his bones. His arms were gnarled and thin, covered, like his chest, with fine white hair that polarized in the sunlight. He rubbed his hands over his arms to smooth out gooseflesh, pinched the bridge of his nose, and stepped across to the gable window for a look outside. It seemed wrong somehow to see the neat, tree-lined streets of Northview, the old wooden houses, the tiled roofs, the lines of smoke going up black and fine from mortar-chinked chimneys. It seemed especially wrong that there were no automobiles in the streets, no roar and clatter of traffic, no reek of gasoline, no airplanes in the sky—

He turned away from the window. For a moment everything was sick and wrong, and he blinked at the homey, familiar room as though he'd never seen it before, as though it were an unutterably alien place. Everything became hot and tight and terrifying, closing *down* on him. *What's happening?* he asked himself blindly. He leaned against a crossbeam, dazed and baffled, until the distant sound of Mrs. Hamlin's voice—she was scolding Tessie in the kitchen, and the ruckus rose all the way up through three floors of pine and plaster and fine old penny nails—

woke him again to his surroundings, with something like pleasure, with something like pain.

Jamie, they called him. Crazy Jamie.

Shaking his head and muttering to himself, Jamie collected his robe and his shaving kit and walked down the narrow, peeling corridor to the small upstairs bedroom. The polished hardwood floor was cold under his feet.

The bathroom was cold, too. It was only the beginning of July, but already the weather was starting to turn nippy late at night and early in the morning. It got colder every year, seemed like. Maybe the glaciers were coming back, as some folks said. Or maybe it was just that he himself was worn a little thinner every year, a little closer to the ultimate cold of the grave. Grunting, he wedged himself into the narrow space between the sink and the downslant of the roof, bumping his head, as usual, against the latch of the skylight window. There was just enough room for him if he stood hunch-shouldered with the toilet bumping up against his thigh. The toilet was an old porcelain monstrosity, worn smooth as glass, that gurgled constantly and comfortably and emitted a mellow breath of earth. It was almost company. The yard boy had already brought up a big basin of "hot" water, although by now, after three or four other people had already used it, it was gray and cold; after the last person used it, it would be dumped down the toilet to help flush out the system. He opened his shaving kit and took out a shapeless cake of lye soap, a worn hand towel, a straight razor.

The mirror above the sink was cracked and tarnished — no help for it, nobody made mirrors anymore. It seemed an appropriate background for the reflection of his face, which was also, in its way, tarnished and dusty and cracked with age. He didn't know how old he was; that was one of the many things Doc Norton had warned him not to think about, so long ago. He couldn't even remember how long he'd been living here in Northview. Ten years? Fifteen? He studied himself in the mirror, the blotched, earth-colored skin, the eyes sunk deep under a shelf of brow, the network of fine wrinkles. A well-preserved seventy? Memory was dim; the years were misty and fell away before he could number them. He shied away from trying to remember. Didn't matter.

He covered the face with lathered soap.

By the time he finished dressing, the other tenants had already gone downstairs. He could hear them talking down there, muffled and distant, like water bugs whispering at the mossy bottom of a deep old well. Cautiously Jamie went back into the hall. The wood floors and paneling up here were not as nicely finished as those in the rest of the house. He thought of all the hidden splinters in all that wood, waiting to catch his flesh. He descended the stairs. The banister swayed as he clutched it, groaning softly to remind him that it, too, was old.

As he came into the dining room, conversation died. The other tenants looked up at him, looked away again. People fiddled with their tableware, adjusted their napkins, pulled their chairs closer to the table or pushed them farther away. Someone coughed self-consciously.

He crossed the room to his chair and stood behind it.

"Morning. Jamie." Mrs. Hamlin said crossly.

"Ma'm," he replied politely, trying to ignore her grumpiness. He was late again.

He sat down. Mrs. Hamlin stared at him disapprovingly, shook her head, and then turned her attention pointedly back to her plate. As if this were a signal, conversation started up again, gradually swelling to its normal level. The awkward moment passed. Jamie concentrated on filling his plate, intercepting the big platters of country ham and eggs and corn bread as they passed up and down the table. It was always like this at meals: the embarrassed pauses, the uneasy sidelong glances, the faces that tried to be friendly but could not entirely conceal distaste. Crazy Jamie, Crazy Jamie. Conversation flowed in ripples around him, never involving him, although the others would smile dutifully at him if he caught their eyes, and occasionally Seth or Tom would nod at him with tolerably unforced cordiality. This morning it wasn't enough. He wanted to talk, too, for the first time in months. He wasn't a child, he was a man, an old man! He paid less attention to his food and began to strain to hear what was being said, looking for a chance to get into the conversation.

Finally the chance came. Seth asked Mr. Samuels a question. It was a point of fact, not opinion, and Jamie knew the answer.

"Yes," Jamie said, "at one time New York City did indeed have a larger population than Augusta."

Abruptly everyone stopped talking. Mr. Samuels's lips closed up tight, and he grimaced as though he had tasted something foul. Seth shook his head wearily, looking sad and disappointed. Jamie lowered his head to avoid Seth's eyes. He could sense Mrs. Hamlin swelling and glowering beside him, but he wouldn't look at her, either.

Damn it, that wasn't what he'd meant to say! They hadn't been talking about that at all. He'd said the wrong thing.

He'd done it again.

People were talking about him around the table, he knew, but he could no longer understand them. He could still hear their voices, but the words had been leeched away, and all that remained was noise and hissing static. He concentrated on buttering a slice of corn bread, trying to hang on to that simple mechanical act while the world pulled away from him in all directions, retreating to the very edge of his perception, like a tide that has gone miles out from the beach.

When the world tide came back in, he found himself outside on the porch—the veranda, some of the older folks still called it—with Mrs. Hamlin fussing at him, straightening his clothes, patting his wiry white hair into place, getting him ready to be sent off to work. She was still annoyed with him, but it had no real bite to it, and the exasperated fondness underneath kept showing through even as she scolded him. "You go straight to work now, you hear? No dawdling and mooning around." He nodded his head sheepishly. She was a tall, aristocratic lady with a beak nose, a lined, craggy face, and a tight bun of snowy white hair. She was actually a year or two younger than he was, but he thought of her as much, much older. "And mind you come right straight back here after work, too. Tonight's the big Fourthday dinner, and you've got to help in the kitchen, hear? Jamie, are you listening to me?"

He ducked his head and said "Yes'm," his feet already fidgeting to be gone.

Mrs. Hamlin gave him a little push, saying, "Shoo now!" and then, her grim face softening, adding, "Try to be a good boy." He scooted across the veranda and out into the raw, hot brightness of the morning.

He shuffled along, head down, still infused with dull embarrassment from the scolding he'd received. Mr. Samuels went cantering by him, up on his big roan horse, carbine sheathed in a saddle holster, horseshoes ringing against the pavement: off to patrol with the Outriders for the day. Mr. Samuels waved at him as he passed, looking enormously tall and important and adult up on the high saddle, and Jamie answered with the shy, wide, loose-lipped grin that sometimes seemed vacuous even to him. He ducked his head again when Mr. Samuels was out of sight and frowned at the dusty tops of his shoes. The sun was up above the trees and the rooftops now, and it was getting warm.

The five-story brick school building was the tallest building in Northview—now that the bank had burned down—and it cast a cool, blue shadow across his path as he turned onto Main Street. It was still used as a school in the winter and on summer afternoons after the children had come back from the fields, but it was also filled with stockpiles of vital supplies so that it could be used as a stronghold in case of a siege—something that had happened only once, fifteen years ago, when a strong raiding party had come up out of the south. Two fifty-caliber machine guns—salvaged from an Army jeep that had been abandoned on the old state highway a few weeks after the War—were mounted on top of the school's roof, where their field of fire would cover most of the town. They had not been fired in earnest for years, but they were protected from the weather and kept in good repair, and a sentry was still posted up there at all times, although by now the sentry was likely to smuggle a girl up to the roof with him on warm summer nights. Times had become more settled, almost sleepy now. Similarly, the Outriders who patrolled Northview's farthest borders and watched over the flocks and the outlying farms had been reduced from thirty to ten, and it had been three or four years since they'd had a skirmish with anyone; the flow of hungry refugees and marauders and aimless migrants had mostly stopped by now—dead, or else they'd found a place of their own. These days the Outriders were more concerned with animals. The black bears and grizzlies were back in the mountains and the nearby hills, and for the past four or five years there had been wolves again, coming back from who-knew-where, increasing steadily in numbers and becoming more of a threat as the winters hardened. Visitors down from Jackman Station, in Maine, brought a story that a mountain lion had recently been sighted on the slopes of White Cap, in the unsettled country "north of the Moosehead," although before the War there couldn't have been any pumas left closer than Colorado or British Columbia. It had taken only twenty years.

There was a strange wagon in front of the old warehouse that was now the Outriders' station, a rig Jamie had never seen before. It was an ordinary enough wagon, but it was *painted*. It was painted in mad streaks and strips and random patchwork splotches of a dozen different colors—deep royal blue, vivid yellow, scarlet, purple, earthbrown, light forest-green, black, burnt orange—as if a hundred children from prewar days had been at it with finger paint. To Jamie's eyes, accustomed to the dull and faded tones of Northview's weatherbeaten old buildings, the streaks of color were so brilliant that they seemed to vibrate and stand out in raised contrast from the wagon's surface. He was not used to seeing bright colors anymore, except those in the natural world around him, and this paint was *fresh*, something he also hadn't seen in more years than he could remember. Even the big horse, which stood patiently in the wagon's traces—and which now rolled an incurious eye up at Jamie and blew out its lips with a blubbery snorting sound—even the *horse* was painted, blue on one side, bright green on the other, with orange streaks up its flanks.

Jamie goggled at all this, wondering if it could possibly be real or if it was one of the "effects"—hallucinations, as even *he* understood—that he sometimes got during partic-

ularly bad "spells." After a moment or two—during which
the wagon didn't shimmer or fade around the edges at
all—he widened his attention enough to notice the signs:
big hand-painted signs hung on either side of a kind of
sandwichboard framework that was braced upright in the
wagon bed. At the top each sign read MOHAWK CONFEDER-
ACY in bright red paint, and then, underneath that, came
a long list of words, each word painted in a different
color:

HAND-LOADED AMMUNITION
PAINT
FALSE TEETH
EYEGLASSES—GROUND TO PRESCRIPTION
LAMP OIL
PAINLESS DENTISTRY
UNTAINTED SEED FOR WHEAT, CORN, MELONS
FLAX CLOTH
WINDOW GLASS
MEDICINES & LINIMENT
CONDOMS
IRON FARM TOOLS
UNTAINTED LIVESTOCK
NAILS
MUSICAL INSTRUMENTS
MARIJUANA
WHISKY
SOAP
PRINTING DONE
!ALL MADE IN MOHAWK!

Jamie was puzzling out some of the harder words when
the door to the Outriders' station opened and Mr. Stover
came hurriedly down the stairs. "What're you doing here,

Jamie?" he asked. "What're you hanging around here for?"

Jamie gaped at him, trying to find the words to describe the wonderful new wagon, and how strange it made him feel, but the effort was too great, and the words slipped away. "Going to Mr. Hardy's store," he said at last. "Just going to sweep up at Mr. Hardy's store."

Mr. Stover glanced nervously back up at the door of the Outriders' station, fingered his chin for a moment while he made up his mind, and then said, "Never mind that today, Jamie. Never mind about the store today. You just go on back home now."

"But —" Jamie said, bewildered. "But — I sweep up every day!"

"Not today," Mr. Stover said sharply. "You go on home, you hear me? Go on, git!"

"Mrs. Hamlin's going to be awful mad," Jamie said sadly, resignedly.

"You tell Edna I said for you to go home. And you stay inside, too, Jamie. You stay out of sight, hear? We've got an important visitor here in Northview today, and it'd never do to have him run into *you*."

Jamie nodded his head in acceptance of this. He wasn't so dumb that he didn't know what the unvoiced part of the sentence was: run into *you*, the half-wit, the crazy person, the nut. He'd heard it often enough. He knew he was crazy. He knew that he was an embarrassment. He knew that he had to stay inside, away from visitors, lest he embarrass Mrs. Hamlin and all his friends.

Crazy Jamie.

Slowly he turned and shuffled away, back the way he had come.

The sun beat down on the back of his head now, and sweat gathered in the wrinkled hollows beneath his eyes.

Crazy Jamie.

At the corner, bathed in the shadow cast by the big oak at the edge of the schoolyard, he turned and looked back.

A group of men had come out of the Outriders' station and were now walking slowly in the direction of Mr. Hardy's store, talking as they went. There was Mr. Jameson, Mr. Galli, Mr. Stover, Mr. Ashley, and, in the middle of them, talking animatedly and waving his arms, the visitor, the stranger—a big, florid-faced man with a shock of unruly blond hair that shone like beaten gold in the sunlight.

Watching him, the visitor—now clapping a hand on Mr. Galli's shoulder, Mr. Galli shrinking away—Jamie felt a chill, that unreasoning and unreasoned fear of strangers, of everything from outside Northview's narrow boundaries, that had affected him ever since he could remember, and suddenly his delight in the wonderful wagon was tarnished, diminished, because he realized that it, too, must come from outside.

He headed for home, walking a little faster now, as if chivied along by some old cold wind that didn't quite reach the sunlit world.

That night was the Fourthday feast—"Independence Day," some of the old folks still called it—and for Jamie, who was helping in the kitchen as usual, the early part of the evening was a blur of work as they sweated to prepare the meal: roast turkey, ham, wild pigeon, trout, baked raccoon, sweet potatoes, corn, pearl onions, berry soup, homemade bread, blackberries, plums, and a dozen other things.

That was all as usual; he expected and accepted that. What was not usual—and what he did not expect—was that he would not be allowed to eat with the rest when the feast was served. Instead, Tessie set a plate out for him in the kitchen, saying, not unkindly, "Now, Jamie, mind you stay here. They've got a guest out there this year, that loud-mouthed Mr. Brodey, and Mrs. Hamlin, she says you got to eat in the kitchen and keep out of sight. Now don't you mind, honey. I'll fix you up a plate real nice, just the same stuff you'd get out there."

And then, after a few moments of somewhat embarrassed bustling, she was gone.

Jamie sat alone in the empty kitchen.

His plate was filled to overflowing with food, and he'd even been given a glass of dandelion wine, a rare treat, but somehow he wasn't hungry anymore.

He sat listening to the wind tug at the old house, creaking the rafters, making the wood groan. When the wind died, he could hear them talking out there in the big dining room, the voices just too faint for him to make out the words.

An unfamiliar anger began to rise in him, "Crazy Jamie," he said aloud, his voice sounding flat and dull to his own ears. It wasn't fair. He glanced out the window, to where the sun had almost set in a welter of sullen purple clouds. Suddenly he slashed out at the glass of wine, sending it spinning to the floor. It wasn't fair! He was an adult, wasn't he? Why did he have to sit back here by himself like a naughty child? Even if— In spite of— He was—

Somehow he found himself on his feet. He *deserved* to eat with the others, didn't he? He was as good as anybody else, wasn't he? In fact— In *fact*—

The corridor. He seemed to float along it in spite of his stumbling, hesitant feet. The voices got louder, and just at the point where they resolved into words he stopped, standing unnoticed in the shadows behind the dining-room archway, hanging onto the doorjamb, torn between rage and fear and a curious, empty yearning.

"Sooner or later you'll find that you have to incorporate with the Confederacy," Mr. Brodey, the stranger, was saying. The other faces around the big dining-room table were cool and reserved. "The kind of inter-village barter economy you've got up here just can't hold up forever, you know, even though it's really a kind of communal socialism—"

"Are you sayin' we're *communists* up heah?" Mr. Samuels said, outraged, but before Brodey could reply (if he intended to), Jamie strode to the table, pulled out an empty chair—his own habitual seat—and sat down. All faces turned to him, startled, and conversation stopped.

Jamie stared back at them. To walk to the table had taken the last of his will; things were closing down on him again, his vision was swimming, and he began to lose touch with his body, as if his mind were floating slowly up and away from it, like a balloon held by the thinnest sort of tether. Sweat broke out in his forehead, and he opened his mouth, panting like a dog. Through a sliding, shifting confusion, he heard Mrs. Hamlin start to say, "Jamie! I thought I told you—" at the same time that Mr. Ashley was saying to Mr. Brodey, "Don't let him bother you none. He's just the local half-wit. We'll send him back to the kitchen," and Brodey was smiling in tolerant, condescending amusement, and something about Brodey's thin, contemptuous smile, something about the circle of staring faces, *something* wrenched words up out of Jamie, sending them suddenly flying out of his mouth. He hurled the familiar words out at the pale staring faces as he had so many times before, rattling their teeth with them, shaking them to their bones. He didn't know what the words meant anymore, but they were the old strong words, the right words, and he heard his voice fill with iron. He spoke the words until there were no more words to speak, and then he stopped.

A deathly hush had fallen over the room. Mr. Brodey was staring at him, and Jamie saw his face run through a quick gamut of expressions: from irritation to startled speculation to dawning astonishment. Brodey's jaw went slack, and he gasped—a little startled grunt, as if he had been punched in the stomach—and the color went swiftly out of his face. "My God!" he said, "Oh, my God!"

For Jamie, it was as if the world were draining away again, everything pulling back until he could just barely touch reality with his fingertips, and the room shimmered and buzzed as he struggled to hold on to even that much control. All the faces had gone blank, wiped clean of individuality, and he could no longer tell which of the featureless pink ovoids was the sweating, earnest, astounded face of Mr. Brodey. He got clumsily to his feet, driving his leaden body by an act of conscious will, as though it were some ill-made clockwork golem. He flailed his arms for balance, knocked his chair over with a clatter, and stood swaying before them, smelling the sour reek of his own sweat. "I'm sorry," he blurted, "I'm sorry, Mrs. Hamlin. I didn't *mean* to—"

The silence went on a moment longer, and then, above the mounting waves of buzzing nausea and unreality, he heard Mrs. Hamlin say, "That's all right, child. We know you didn't mean any harm. Go on upstairs now, Jamie. Go on." Her voice sounded dry and flat and tired.

Blindly Jamie spun and stumbled for the stairs, all the inchoate demons of memory snapping at his heels like years.

Downstairs, Mr. Brodey was still saying, "Oh, my God!" He hardly noticed that the dinner party was being dissolved around him or that Mrs. Hamlin was hustling him out onto the porch "for a word in private." When she finally had him alone out there, the cool evening breeze slapping at his face through the wire mesh of the enclosed porch, he shook himself out of his daze and turned slowly to face her where she stood hunched and patient in the dappled shadows. "It's *him*," he said, still more awe than accusation in his voice. "Son of a *bitch*. It really *is* him, isn't it?"

"Who, Mr. Brodey?"

"Don't play games with me," Brodey said harshly. "I've seen the old pictures. The half-wit, he really was—"

"*Is.*"

"—the President of the United States." Brodey stared at her. "He may be crazy, but not because he thinks he's the President—he *is* the President. James W. McNaughton. He *is* McNaughton, isn't he?"

"Yes."

"My God! Think of it. The very last President."

"The *incumbent* President," Mrs. Hamlin said softly.

They stared at each other through the soft evening shadows.

"And it's not a surprise to you, either, is it?" Anger was beginning to replace disbelief in Brodey's voice. "You've known it all along, haven't you? All of you have known. You all knew from the start that he was President McNaughton?"

"Yes."

"My God!" Brodey said, giving an entirely new reading to the phrase, disgust and edgy anger instead of awe. He opened his mouth, closed it, and began turning red.

"He came here almost twenty years ago, Mr. Brodey," Mrs. Hamlin said, speaking calmly, reminiscently. "Perhaps two months after the War. The Outriders found him collapsed in a field out by the edge of town. He was nearly dead. Don't ask me how he got there. Maybe there was some sort of hidden bunker way back up there in the hills, maybe his plane crashed nearby, maybe he walked all the way up here from what's left of Washington—I don't know. Jamie himself doesn't know. His memory was almost gone; shock, I guess, and exposure. All he remembered, basically, was that he *was* the President, and even that was dim and misty, like something you might remember out of a bad dream, the kind that fades away and comes back sometimes, late at night. And life's been like a half-dream for him ever since, poor soul. He never did get quite right in the head again."

"And you gave him shelter?" Brodey said, his voice becoming shrill with indignation. "You took him in? That butcher?"

"Watch your mouth, son. You're speaking about the President."

"God damn it, woman. Don't you know—*he caused the War?*"

After a smothering moment of silence. Mrs. Hamlin said mildly, "That's your opinion, Mr. Brodey, not mine."

"How can you deny it? The 'One Life' Ultimatum? The 'preventative strikes' on Mexico and Panama? It was within hours of the raid on Monterrey that the bombs started falling."

"He didn't have any other *choice*! The Indonesians had pushed him—"

"That's crap, and you know it!" Brodey was shouting now. "They taught us all about it down in Mohawk; they made *damn* sure we knew the name of the man who destroyed the world, you can bet on that! Christ, everybody knew *then* that he was unfit for office, just a bombastic backwoods senator on a hate crusade, a cracker-barrel warmonger. Everybody *said* that he'd cause the War if he got into the White House—and he did! By God, he did! That pathetic half-wit in there. *He* did it!"

Mrs. Hamlin sighed and folded her arms across her middle, hugging herself as if in pain. She seemed to grow smaller and older, more withered and gnarled. "I don't know, son," she said wearily, after a heavy pause. "Maybe *he* was wrong. I don't know. All that seemed so important then. Now I can hardly remember what the issues were, what it was all *about*. It doesn't seem to matter much anymore, somehow."

"How can you *say* that?" Brodey wiped at his face—he was sweating profusely and looking very earnest now, bewilderment leeching away some of the anger. "How can you let that . . . that man . . . *him*—how can you let *him* live here, under your roof? How can you stand to let him live at all, let alone cook for him, do his washing. My God!"

"His memory was gone, Mr. Brodey. His *mind* was gone. Can you understand that? Old Doc Norton, rest his soul, spent months just trying to get Jamie to the point where he could walk around by himself without anybody to watch him too close. He had to be taught how to feed himself, how to dress himself, how to go to the bathroom—like a child. At first there was some even right here in Northview that felt the way you do, Mr. Brodey, and there's still some as can't be comfortable around Jamie, but one by one they came to understand, and they made their peace with him. Whatever he was or wasn't, he's just like a little child now—a sick, old, frightened child who doesn't really understand what's happening to him, most of the time. Mr. Brodey, you can't hate a little child for something he can't even remember he's done."

Brodey spun around, as though to stalk back into the house, and then spun violently back. "He should be dead!" Brodey shouted. His fists were clenched now, and the muscles in his neck were corded. "At the very *least*, he should be dead! Billions of lives on that man's hands! *Billions*. And *you*, you people, you not only let him live, you make excuses for him! For *him*!" He stopped, groping for words to express the enormity of his outrage. "It's like . . . like making excuses for the Devil himself!"

Mrs. Hamlin stirred and came forward, stepping out of the porch shadows and into the moonlight, drawing her shawl more tightly around her, as though against a chill, although the night was still mild. She stared eye to eye with Brodey for several moments, while the country silence gathered deeply around them, broken only by crickets and the hoarse sound of Brodey's impassioned breathing. Then she said, "I thought I owed it to you, Mr. Brodey, to try to explain a few things. But I don't know if I can. Things have changed enough by now, steadied down enough, that maybe you younger people find it hard to understand, but those of us who lived through the War, we all had to do things we didn't want to do. Right there where you're standing, Mr. Brodey, right here on this porch, I shot a marauder down, shot him dead with my husband's old pistol, with Mr. Hamlin himself laying stiff in the parlor not ten feet away, taken by the Lumpy Plague. And I've done worse things than that, too, in my time. I reckon we all have, all the survivors. And just maybe it's no different with that poor old man sitting in there."

Brodey regained control of himself. His jaw was clenched, and the muscles around his mouth stood out in taut little bands, but his breathing had evened, and his face was tight and cold. He had banked his anger down into a smoldering, manageable flame, and now for the first time he seemed dangerous. Ignoring—or seeming to ignore—Mrs. Hamlin's speech, he said conversationally, "Do you know that we curse by him down in Mohawk? His name is a curse to us. Can *you* understand *that*? We burn him in effigy on his birthday, in the town squares, and over the years it's become quite a little ceremony. He must atone, Mrs. Hamlin. He must be made to pay for what he's done. We don't suffer monsters to live, down in Mohawk."

"Ayuh," Mrs. Hamlin said sourly, "you do a lot of damnfool, jackass things down there, don't you?" Mrs. Hamlin tossed her head back, silver hair glinting in the silver light, and seemed to grow taller again. There was a hard light in her eyes now, and a hard new edge in her voice. "Atone, is it now, you jackass? As if you're some big pious kind of churchman, some damn kind of saint, you red-faced, loudmouthed man. You with your damnfool flag and damnfool Mohawk Confederacy. Well, let me tell *you*, mister, this isn't any Mohawk Confederacy here, never has been, never will be: This is Northview, sovereign state of Vermont, *United States of America*. Do you hear me, mister? This here is the United States of America, and that poor fool in there—why, he's the *President* of the United States of America, even if sometimes he can't cut his meat up proper. Maybe he was a fool, maybe he was wrong long ago, maybe he's crazy now, but he's still the *President*." Eyes snapping, she jabbed a finger at Brodey. "As long as this town stands, then there's still an America, and that old man will be President as long as there are still *Americans* alive to serve him. We take care of our own, Mr. Brodey; *we take care of our own*."

A shadow materialized at Brodey's elbow and spoke with Seth's voice. "Edna?"

Brodey turned his head to glance at Seth. When he

turned back to face Mrs. Hamlin, there was a gun in her hand, a big, old-fashioned revolver that looked too huge for the small, blue-veined hand that held it.

"You can't be serious," Brodey whispered.

"You need any help, Edna?" the shadow said. "I brought some of the boys."

"No, thank you, Seth." The barrel of the revolver was as unwavering as her gaze. "There's some things a person's got to do for herself."

Then she cocked the hammer back.

The President of the United States didn't notice the shot. Alone in the small upstairs bathroom, he avoided the eyes of the tarnished reflection in the mirror and compulsively washed his hands.

RAUTAVAARA'S CASE

By Philip K. Dick

The three technicians of the floating globe monitored fluc-
tuations in interstellar magnetic fields, and they did a
good job until the moment they died.

Basalt fragments, traveling at enormous velocity in rela-
tion to their globe, ruptured their barrier and abolished
their air supply. The two males were slow to react and did
nothing. The young female technician from Finland,
Agneta Rautavaara, managed to get her emergency helmet
on, but the hoses tangled; she aspirated and died: a melan-
choly death, strangling on her own vomit. Herewith ended
the survey task of EX208, their floating globe. In another
month the technicians would have been relieved and returned to Earth.

We could not get there in time to save the three Earthpersons, but we did dispatch a robot to see whether any of
them could be regenerated. Earthpersons do not like us,
but in this case their survey globe was operating in our vi-
cinity. There are rules governing such emergencies that are

binding on all races in the galaxy. We had no desire to help Earthpersons, but we obey the rules.

The rules called for an attempt on our part to restore life to the three dead technicians, but we allowed a robot to take on the responsibility, and perhaps there we erred. Also, the rules required us to notify the closest Earth ship of the calamity, and we chose not to. I will not defend this omission or analyze our reasoning at the time.

The robot signaled that it had found no brain function in the two males and that their neural tissue had degenerated. Regarding Agneta Rautavaara, a slight brain wave could be detected. So in Rautavaara's case the robot would begin a restoration attempt. Since it could not make a judgment decision on its own, however, it contacted us. We told it to make the attempt. The fault—the guilt, so to speak—therefore lies with us. Had we been on the scene, we would have known better. We accept the blame.

An hour later the robot signaled that it had restored significant brain function in Rautavaara by supplying her brain with oxygen-rich blood from her dead body. The oxygen, but not the nutriments, came from the robot. We instructed it to begin synthesis of nutriments by processing Rautavaara's body, using it as raw material. This is the point at which the Earth authorities later made their most profound objection. But we did not have any other source of nutriments. Since we ourselves are a plasma, we could not offer our own bodies.

They objected that we could have used the bodies of Rautavaara's dead companions. But we felt that, based on the robot's reports, the other bodies were too contaminated by radioactivity and hence were toxic to Rautavaara; nutriments derived from those sources would soon poison her brain. If you do not accept our logic, it does not matter to us; this was the situation as we construed it from our remote point. This is why I say our real error lay in sending a robot rather than going ourselves. If you wish to indict us, indict us for that.

We asked the robot to patch into Rautavaara's brain and transmit her thoughts to us so that we could assess the physical condition of her neural cells.

The impression that we received was sanguine. It was at this point that we notified the Earth authorities. We informed them of the accident that had destroyed EX208; we informed them that two of the technicians, the males, were irretrievably dead; we informed them that through swift efforts on our part we had the one female showing stable cephalic activity—which is to say, we had her brain alive.

"Her *what*?" the Earthperson radio operator said, in response to our call.

"We are supplying her nutriments derived from her body—"

"Oh, Christ," the Earthperson radio operator said. "You can't feed her brain that way. What good is just a brain?"

"It can think," we said.

"All right. We'll take over now," the Earthperson radio operator said. "But there will be an inquiry."

"Was it not right to save her brain?" we asked. "After all, the psyche is located in the brain. The physical body is a device by which the brain relates to—"

"Give me the location of EX208," the Earthperson radio operator said. "We'll send a ship there at once. You should have notified us at once before trying your own rescue efforts. You Approximations simply do not understand somatic life forms."

It is offensive to us to hear the term *Approximations*. It is an Earth slur regarding our origin in the Proxima Centauri system. What it implies is that we are not authentic, that we merely simulate life.

This was our reward in the Rautavaara case. To be derided. And indeed there was an inquiry.

Within the depths of her damaged brain Agneta Rautavaara tasted acid vomit and recoiled in fear and aversion. All around her EX208 lay in splinters. She could see Travis and Elms; they had been torn to bloody bits, and the blood had frozen. Ice covered the interior of the globe. *Air gone, temperature gone . . . What's keeping me alive?* she wondered. She put her hands up and touched her face—or rather tried to touch her face. *My helmet*, she thought. *I got it on in time.*

The ice, which covered everything, began to melt. The severed arms and legs of her two companions rejoined their bodies. Basalt fragments embedded in the hull of the globe, withdrew and flew away.

Time, Agneta realized, *is running backward. How strange!*

Air returned; she heard the dull tone of the indicator horn. Travis and Elms, groggily, got to their feet. They stared around them, bewildered. She felt like laughing, but it was too grim for that. Apparently the force of the impact had caused a local time perturbation.

"Both of you sit down," she said.

Travis said thickly. "I—okay; you're right." He seated himself at his console and pressed the button that strapped him securely in place. Elms, however, just stood.

"We were hit by rather large particles," Agneta said.

"Yes," Elms said.

"Large enough and with enough impact to perturb time," Agneta said. "So we've gone back to before the event."

"Well, the magnetic fields are partly responsible," Travis said. He rubbed his eyes; his hands shook. "Get your helmet off, Agneta. You don't really need it."

"But the impact is coming," she said.

Both men glanced at her.

"We'll repeat the accident," she said.

"Shit," Travis said, "I'll take the EX out of here." He pushed many keys on his console. "It'll miss us."

Agneta removed her helmet. She stepped out of her boots, picked them up . . . and then saw the figure.

The figure stood behind the three of them. It was Christ.

"Look," she said to Travis and Elms.

The figure wore a traditional white robe and sandals; his hair was long and pale with what looked like moonlight. Bearded, his face was gentle and wise. *Just like in the holoads the churches back home put out.* Agneta thought. *Robed, bearded, wise and gentle, and his arms slightly raised. Even the nimbus is there. How odd that our preconceptions were so accurate!*

"Oh, my God," Travis said. Both men stared, and she stared, too. "He's come for us."

"Well, it's fine with me," Elms said.

"Sure, it would be fine with you," Travis said bitterly. "You have no wife and children. And what about Agneta? She's only three hundred years old; she's a baby."

Christ said, "I am the vine, you are the branches. Whoever remains in me, with me in him, bears fruit in plenty; for cut off from me, you can do nothing."

"I'm getting the EX out of this vector," Travis said.

"My little children," Christ said, "I shall not be with you much longer."

"Good," Travis said. The EX was now moving at peak velocity in the direction of the Sirius axis; their star chart showed massive flux.

"Damn you, Travis," Elms said savagely. "This is a great opportunity. I mean, how many people have seen Christ? I mean, it *is* Christ. You are Christ, aren't you?" he asked the figure.

Christ said, "I am the Way, the Truth, and the Life. No one can come to the Father except through me. If you know me, you know my Father, too. From this moment you know him and have seen him."

"There," Elms said, his face showing happiness. "See? I want it known that I am very glad of this occasion, Mr. — " He broke off. "I was going to say, 'Mr. Christ.' That's stupid; that is really stupid. Christ, Mr. Christ, will you sit down? You can sit at my console or at Ms. Rautavaara's. Isn't that right, Agneta? This here is Walter Travis; he's not a Christian, but I am; I've been a Christian all my life. Well, most of my life. I'm not sure about Ms. Rautavaara. What do you say, Agneta?"

"Stop babbling, Elms," Travis said.

Elms said, "He's going to judge us."

Christ said, "If anyone hears my words and does not keep them faithfully, it is not I who shall condemn him, since I have come not to condemn the world but to save the world; he who rejects me and refuses my words has his judge already."

"There," Elms said, nodding gravely.

Frightened, Agneta said to the figure, "Go easy on us. The three of us have been through a major trauma." She wondered, suddenly, whether Travis and Elms remembered that they had been killed, that their bodies had been destroyed.

The figure smiled, as if to reassure her.

"Travis," Agneta said, bending down over him as he sat at his console. "I want you to listen to me. Neither you nor Elms survived the accident, survived the basalt particles. That's why he's here. I'm the only one who wasn't — " She hesitated.

"Killed," Elms said. "We're dead, and he has come for us." To the figure he said, "I'm ready, Lord. Take me."

"Take both of them," Travis said. "I'm sending out a radio H.E.L.P. call. And I'm telling them what's taking place here. I'm going to report it before he takes me or tries to take me."

"You're *dead*," Elms told him.

"I can still file a radio report," Travis said, but his face showed his resignation.

To the figure, Agneta said, "Give Travis a little time. He doesn't fully understand. But I guess you know that; you know everything."

The figure nodded.

We and the Earth Board of Inquiry listened to and watched this activity in Rautavaara's brain, and we realized jointly what had happened. But we did not agree on our evaluation of it. Whereas the six Earthpersons saw it as pernicious, we saw it as grand—both for Agneta Rautavaara and for us. By means of her damaged brain, restored by an ill-advised robot, we were in touch with the next world and the powers that ruled it.

The Earthpersons' view distressed us.

"She's hallucinating," the spokesperson of the Earthpeople said. "Since she had no sensory data coming in. Since her body is dead. Look what you've done to her."

We made the point that Agneta Rautavaara was happy.

"What we must do," the human spokesperson said, "is shut down her brain."

"And cut us off from the next world?" we objected. "This is a splendid opportunity to view the afterlife.

Agneta Rautavaara's brain is our lens. The scientific merit outweighs the humanitarian."

This was the position we took at the inquiry. It was a position of sincerity, not of expedience.

The Earthpersons decided to keep Rautavaara's brain at full function with both video and audio transduction, which of course was recorded; meanwhile, the matter of censuring us was put in suspension.

I personally found myself fascinated by the Earth idea of the Savior. It was, for us, an antique and quaint conception — not because it was anthropomorphic but because it involved a schoolroom adjudication of the departed soul. Some kind of tote board was involved, listing good and bad acts: a transcendent report card such as one finds employed in the teaching and grading of elementary-school children.

This, to us, was a primitive conception of the Savior, and while I watched and listened — while we watched and listened as a polyencaphalic entity — I wondered what Agneta Rautavaara's reaction would have been to a Savior, a Guide of the Soul, based on *our* expectations. Her brain, after all, was maintained by our equipment, by the original mechanism that our rescue robot had brought to the scene of the accident. It would have been too risky to disconnect it; too much brain damage had occurred already. The total apparatus, involving her brain, had been transferred to the site of the judicial inquiry, a neutral ark located between the Proxima Centauri system and the Sol system.

Later, in discreet discussion with my companions, I suggested that we attempt to infuse our own conception of the Afterlife Guide of the Soul into Rautavaara's artificially sustained brain. My point: It would be interesting to see how she reacted.

At once my companions pointed out to me the contradiction in my logic. I had argued at the inquiry that Rautavaara's brain was a window on the next world and, hence, justified—which exculpated us. Now I argued that what she experienced was a projection of her own mental presuppositions, nothing more.

"Both propositions are ture," I said. "It is a genuine window on the next world, and it is a presentation of Rautavaara's own cultural, racial propensities."

What we had, in essence, was a model into which we could introduce carefully selected variables. We could introduce into Rautavaara's brain our own conception of the Guide of the Soul and thereby see how our rendition differed practically from the puerile one of the Earthpersons.

This was a novel opportunity to test out our own theology. In our opinion the Earthpersons' theology had been tested sufficiently and had been found wanting.

We decided to perform the act, since we maintained the gear supporting Rautavaara's brain. To us, this was a much more interesting issue than the outcome of the inquiry. Blame is a mere cultural matter; it does not travel across species boundaries.

I suppose the Earthpersons could regard our intentions as malign. I deny that; we deny that. Call it, instead, a game. It would provide us aesthetic enjoyment to witness Rautavaara confronted by *our* Savior, rather than hers.

To Travis, Elms, and Agneta, the figure, raising its arms, said, "I am the resurrection. If anyone believes in me, even though he dies, he will live, and whoever lives and believes in me will never die. Do you believe this?"

"I sure do," Elms said heartily.

Travis said, "It's bilge."

To herself, Agneta Rautavaara thought, *I'm not sure. I just don't know.*

"We have to decide if we're going to go with him," Elms said. "Travis, you're done for; you're out. Sit there and rot—that's your fate." To Agneta he said. "I hope you find for Christ, Agneta. I want you to have eternal life like I'm going to have. Isn't that right, Lord?" he asked the figure.

The figure nodded.

Agneta said, "Travis, I think—well, I feel you should go along with this. I—" She did not want to press the point that Travis was dead. But he had to understand the situation; otherwise, as Elms said, he was doomed. "Go with us," she said.

"You're going then?" Travis said, bitterly.

"Yes," she said.

Elms, gazing at the figure, said in a low voice. "Quite possibly I'm mistaken, but it seems to be changing."

She looked, but saw no change. Yet Elms seemed frightened.

The figure, in its white robe, walked slowly toward the seated Travis. The figure halted close by Travis, stood for a time, and then, bending, bit Travis's face.

Agneta screamed. Elms stared, and Travis, locked into his seat, thrashed. The figure calmly ate him.

"Now you see," the spokesperson for the Board of Inquiry said, "this brain must be shut down. The deterioration is severe; the experience is terrible for her; it must end."

I said, "No. We from the Proxima system find this turn of events highly interesting."

"But the Savior is eating Travis!" another of the Earthpersons exclaimed.

"In your religion," I said, "is it not the case that you eat the flesh of your God and drink his blood? All that has happened here is a mirror image of that Eucharist."

"I order her brain shut down!" the spokesperson for the board said; his face was pale, sweat stood out on his forehead.

"We should see more first," I said. I found it highly exciting, this enactment of our own sacrament, our highest sacrament, in which our Savior consumes us.

"Agneta," Elms whispered, "did you see that? Christ ate Travis. There's nothing left but his gloves and boots."

Oh, God, Agneta Rautavaara thought. *What is happening? I don't understand.*

She moved away from the figure, over to Elms. Instinctively.

"He is my blood," the figure said as it licked its lips. "I drink of this blood, the blood of eternal life. When I have drunk it, I will live forever. He is my body. I have no body of my own; I am only a plasma. By eating his body, I obtain everlasting life. This is the new truth that I proclaim, that I am eternal."

"He's going to eat us, too," Elms said.

Yes, Agneta Rautavaara thought. *He is.* She could see now that the figure was an Approximation. *It is a Proxima life form,* she realized. *He's right; he has no body of his own. The only way he can get a body is—*

"I'm going to kill him," Elms said. He popped the emergency laser rifle from its rack and pointed it at the figure.

The figure said, "The hour has come."

"Stay away from me," Elms said.

"Soon you will no longer see me," the figure said, "unless I drink of your blood and eat of your body. Glorify yourself that I may live." The figure moved toward Elms.

Elms fired the laser rifle. The figure staggered and bled.

It was Travis's blood, Agneta realized. *In him. Not his own blood. This is terrible.* She put her hands to her face, terrified.

"Quick," she said to Elms. "Say, 'I am innocent of this man's blood.' Say it before it's too late."

"I am innocent of this man's blood," Elms whispered hoarsely.

The figure fell. Bleeding, it lay dying. It was no longer a bearded man. It was something else, but Agneta Rautavaara could not tell what it was. It said, "Eli, Eli, lama sabachthani?"

As she and Elms gazed down at it, the figure died.

"I killed it," Elms said. "I killed Christ." He held the laser rifle pointed at himself, groping for the trigger.

"That wasn't Christ," Agneta said. "It was something else. The opposite of Christ." She took the gun from Elms.

Elms was weeping.

The Earthpersons on the Board of Inquiry possessed the majority vote, and they voted to abolish all activity in Rautavaara's artificially sustained brain. This disappointed us, but there was no remedy for us.

We had seen the beginning of an absolutely stunning scientific experiment: the theology of one race grafted onto that of another. Shutting down the Earthpersons' brain was a scientific tragedy. For example, in terms of the basic relationship to God, the Earth race held a diametrically opposite view from us. This of course must be attributed to the fact that they are a somatic race while we are a plasma. They drink the blood of their God; they eat his flesh; that way they become immortal. To them, there is no scandal in this. They find it perfectly natural. Yet to us it is dreadful. That the worshiper should eat and drink its

God? Awful to us; awful indeed. A disgrace and a shame—an abomination. The higher should always prey on the lower; the God should consume the worshiper.

We watched as the Rautavaara case was closed—closed by the shutting down of her brain so that all EEG activity ceased and the monitors indicated nothing. We felt disappointment. In addition, the Earthpersons voted out a verdict of censure of us for our handling of the rescue mission in the first place.

It is striking, the gulf that separates races developing in different star systems. We have tried to understand the Earthpersons, and we have failed. We are aware, too, that they do not understand us and are appalled in turn by some of our customs. This was demonstrated in the Rautavaara case. But were we not serving the purposes of detached scientific study? I myself was amazed at Rautavaara's reaction when the Savior ate Mr. Travis. I would have wished to see this most holy of the sacraments fulfilled with the others, with Rautavaara and Elms as well.

But we were deprived of this. And the experiment, from our standpoint, failed.

And we live now, too, under the ban of unnecessary moral blame.

ADVENTURE OF THE METAL MURDERER

By Fred Saberhagen

It had the shape of a man, the brain of an electronic devil.

It and the machines like it were the best imitations of men and women that the berserkers, murderous machines themselves, were able to devise and build. Still, they could be seen as obvious frauds when closely inspected by any humans.

"Only twenty-nine accounted for?" the supervisor of Defense demanded sharply. Strapped into his combat chair, he was gazing intently through the semitransparent information screen before him, into space. The nearby bulk of Earth was armored in the dun-brown of defensive force fields, the normal colors of land and water and air invisible.

"Only twenty-nine." The answer arrived on the flagship's bridge amid a sharp sputtering of electrical noise. The tortured voice continued, "And it's quite certain now that there were thirty to begin with."

"Then where's the other one?"

There was no reply.

All of Earth's defensive forces were still on full alert, though the attack had been tiny, no more than an attempt at infiltration, and seemed to have been thoroughly repelled. Berserkers, remnants of an ancient interstellar war, were mortal enemies of everything that lived and the greatest danger to humanity that the universe had yet revealed.

A small blur leaped over Earth's dun-brown limb, hurtling along on a course that would bring it within a few hundred kilometers of the supervisor's craft. This was Power Station One, a tamed black hole. In time of peace the power-hungry billions on the planet drew from it half their needed energy. Station One was visible to the eye only as a slight, flowing distortion of the stars beyond.

Another report was coming in. "We are searching space for the missing berserker android, Supervisor." .

"You had damned well better be."

"The infiltrating enemy craft had padded containers for thirty androids, as shown by computer analysis of its debris. We must assume that all containers were filled."

Life and death were in the supervisor's tones. "Is there any possibility that the missing unit got past you to the surface?"

"Negative, Supervisor." There was a slight pause. "At least we know it did not reach the surface in our time."

"Our time? What does that mean, babbler? How could . . . ah."

The black hole flashed by. Not really tamed, though that was a reassuring word, and humans applied it frequently. Just harnessed, more or less.

Suppose—and, given the location of the skirmish, the supposition was not unlikely—that berserker android number thirty had been propelled, by some accident of combat, directly at Station One. It could easily have entered the black hole. According to the latest theories, it might conceivably have survived to reemerge intact into the universe, projected out of the hole as its own tangible image in a burst of virtual-particle radiation.

Theory dictated that in such a case the reemergence must take place before the falling in. The supervisor crisply issued orders. At once his computers on the world below, the Earth Defense Conglomerate, took up the problem, giving it highest priority. What could one berserker android do to Earth? Probably not much. But to the supervisor, and to those who worked for him, defense was a sacred task. The temple of Earth's safety had been horribly profaned.

To produce the first answers took the machines eleven minutes.

"Number thirty did go into the black hole, sir. Neither we nor the enemy could very well have foreseen such a result, but—"

"What is the probability that the android emerged intact?"

"Because of the peculiar angle at which it entered, approximately sixty-nine percent."

"That high!"

"And there is a forty-nine-percent chance that it will reach the surface of the earth in functional condition, at some point in our past. However, the computers offer reassurance. As the enemy device must have been programmed for some subtle attack upon our present society, it is not likely to be able to do much damage at the time and place where it—"

"Your skull contains a vacuum of a truly intergalactic order. *I* will tell *you* and the computers when it has become possible for us to feel even the slightest degree of reassurance. Meanwhile, get me more figures."

The next word from the ground came twenty minutes later.

"There is a ninety-two percent chance that the landing of the android on the surface, if that occurred, was within one hundred kilometers of fifty-one degrees, eleven minutes north latitude; zero degrees, seven minutes west longitude."

"And the time?"

"Ninety-eight percent probability of January 1, 1880 Christian Era, plus or minus ten standard years."

A landmass, a great clouded island, was presented to the supervisor on his screen.

"Recommended course of action?"

It took the ED Conglomerate an hour and a half to answer that.

The first two volunteers perished in attempted launchings before the method could be improved enough to offer a reasonable chance of survival. When the third man was ready, he was called in, just before launching, for a last private meeting with the supervisor.

The supervisor looked him up and down, taking in his outlandish dress, strange hairstyle, and all the rest. He did not ask whether the volunteer was ready but began bluntly: "It has now been confirmed that, whether you win or lose back there, you will never be able to return to your own time."

"Yes, sir, I had assumed that would be the case."

"Very well." The supervisor consulted data spread before him. "We are still uncertain as to just how the enemy is armed. Something subtle, doubtless, suitable for a saboteur on the earth of our own time—in addition, of course, to the superhuman physical strength and speed you must expect to face. There are the scrambling or the switching mindbeams to be considered; either could damage any human society. There are the pattern bombs, designed to disable our defense computers by seeding them with random information. There are always possibilities of biological warfare. You have your disguised medical kit? Yes, I see. And of course there is always the chance of something new."

"Yes, sir." The volunteer looked as ready as anyone could. The supervisor went to him, opening his arms for a ritual farewell embrace.

He blinked away some London rain, pulled out his heavy ticking timepiece as if he were checking the hour, and stood on the pavement before the theater as if he were waiting for a friend. The instrument in his hand throbbed with a silent, extra vibration in addition to its ticking, and this special signal had now taken on a character that meant the enemy machine was very near to him. It was probably within a radius of fifty meters.

A poster on the front of the theater read:

THE IMPROVED AUTOMATION CHESS PLAYER
MARVEL OF THE AGE
UNDER NEW MANAGEMENT

"The real problem, sir," proclaimed one top-hatted man nearby, in conversation with another, "is not whether a machine can be made to win at chess, but whether it may possibly be made to play at all."

No, that is not the real problem, sir, the agent from the future thought. *But count yourself fortunate that you can still believe it is.*

He bought a ticket and went in, taking a seat. When a

sizable audience had gathered, there was a short lecture by a short man in evening dress, who had something predatory about him and also something frightened, despite the glibness and the rehearsed humor of his talk.

At length the chess player itself appeared. It was a desklike box with a figure seated behind it, the whole assembly wheeled out on stage by assistants. The figure was that of a huge man in Turkish garb. Quite obviously, a mannequin or a dummy of some kind, it bobbed slightly with the motion of the rolling desk, to which its chair was fixed. Now the agent could feel the excited vibration of his watch without even putting a hand into his pocket.

The predatory man cracked another joke, displayed a hideous smile, then, from among several chess players in the audience who raised their hands—the agent was not among them—he selected one to challenge the automaton. The challenger ascended to the stage, where the pieces were being set out on a board fastened to the rolling desk, and the doors in the front of the desk were being opened to show that there was nothing but machinery inside.

The agent noted that there were no candles on this desk, as there had been on that of Maelzel's chess player a few decades earlier. Maelzel's automaton had been a clever fraud, of course. Candles had been placed on its box to mask the odor of burning wax from the candle needed by the man who was so cunningly hidden inside amid the dummy gears. The year in which the agent had arrived was still too early, he knew, for electric lights, at least the kind that would be handy for such a hidden human to use. Add the fact that this chess player's opponent was allowed to sit much closer than Maelzel's had ever been, and it became a pretty safe deduction that no human being was concealed inside the box and figure on this stage.

Therefore . . .

The agent might, if he stood up in the audience, get a clear shot at it right now. But should he aim at the figure or the box? And he could not be sure how it was armed. And who would stop it if he tried and failed? Already it had learned enough to survive in nineteenth-century London. Probably it had already killed, to further its designs — "under new management" indeed.

No, now that he had located his enemy, he must plan thoroughly and work patiently. Deep in thought, he left the theater amid the crowd at the conclusion of the performance and started on foot back to the rooms that he had just begun to share on Baker Street. A minor difficulty at his launching into the black hole had cost him some equipment, including most of his counterfeit money. There had not been time as yet for his adopted profession to bring him much income; so he was for the time being in straitened financial circumstances.

He must plan. Suppose, now, that he were to approach the frightened little man in evening dress. By now that one ought to have begun to understand what kind of a tiger he was riding. The agent might approach him in the guise of —

A sudden tap-tapping began in the agent's watch pocket. It was a signal quite distinct from any previously generated by his fake watch. It meant that the enemy had managed to detect his detector; it was in fact locked onto it and tracking.

Sweat mingled with the drizzle on the agent's face as he began to run. It must have discovered him in the theater, though probably it could not then single him out in the crowd. Avoiding horse-drawn cabs, four-wheelers, and an omnibus, he turned out of Oxford Street to Baker Street and slowed to a fast walk for the short distance remaining. He could not throw away the telltale watch, for he would be unable to track the enemy without it. But neither did he dare retain it on his person.

As the agent burst into the sitting room, his roommate looked up, with his usual, somewhat shallow, smile, from a leisurely job of taking books out of a crate and putting them on shelves.

"I say," the agent began, in mingled relief and urgency, "something rather important has come up, and I find there are two errands I must undertake at once. Might I impose one of them on you?"

The agent's own brisk errand took him no farther than just across the street. There, in the doorway of Camden House, he shrank back, trying to breathe silently. He had not moved when, three minutes later, there approached from the direction of Oxford Street a tall figure that the agent suspected was not human. Its hat was pulled down, and the lower portion of its face was muffled in bandages. Across the street it paused, seemed to consult a pocket watch of its own, then turned to ring the bell. Had the agent been absolutely sure it was his quarry, he would have shot it in the back. But without his watch, he would have to get closer to be absolutely sure.

After a moment's questioning from the landlady, the figure was admitted. The agent waited for two minutes. Then he drew a deep breath, gathered up his courage, and went after it.

The thing standing alone at a window turned to face him as he entered the sitting room, and now he was sure of what it was. The eyes above the bandaged lower face were not the Turk's eyes, but they were not human, either.

The white swathing muffled its gruff voice. "You are the doctor?"

"Ah, it is my fellow lodger that you want." The agent threw a careless glance toward the desk where he had locked up the watch, the desk on which some papers bearing his roommate's name were scattered. "He is out at the moment, as you see, but we can expect him presently. I take it you are a patient."

The thing said, in its wrong voice, "I have been referred to him. It seems the doctor and I share a certain common background. Therefore the good landlady has let me wait in here. I trust my presence is no inconvenience."

"Not in the least. Pray take a seat, Mr. — ?"

What name the berserker might have given, the agent never learned. The bell sounded below, suspending conversation. He heard the servant girl answering the door, and a moment later his roommate's brisk feet on the stairs. The death machine took a small object from its pocket and sidestepped a little to get a clear view past the agent toward the door.

Turning his back upon the enemy, as if with the casual purpose of greeting the man about to enter, the agent casually drew from his own pocket a quite functional briar pipe, which was designed to serve another function, too. Then he turned his head and fired the pipe at the berserker from under his own left armpit.

For a human being he was uncannily fast, and for a berserker the android was meanly slow and clumsy, being designed primarily for imitation, not dueling. Their weapons triggered at the same instant.

Explosions racked and destroyed the enemy, blasts shatteringly powerful but compactly limited in space, self-damping and almost silent.

The agent was hit, too. Staggering, he knew with his last clear thought just what weapon the enemy had carried — the switching mindbeam. Then for a moment he could no longer think at all. He was dimly aware of being down on one knee and of his fellow lodger, who had just entered, standing stunned a step inside the door.

At last the agent could move again, and he shakily pocketed his pipe. The ruined body of the enemy was almost vaporized already. It must have been built to self-destruct when damaged badly, so that humanity might never learn its secrets. Already it was no more than a puddle of heavy mist, warping in slow tendrils out the slightly open window to mingle with the fog.

The man still standing near the door had put out a hand to steady himself against the wall. "The jeweler . . . did not have your watch," he muttered dazedly.

I have won, thought the agent dully. It was a joyless thought because with it came slow realization of the price of his success. Three quarters of his intellect, at least, was gone, the superior pattern of his brain-cell connections scattered. No. Not scattered. The switching mindbeam would have reimposed the pattern of his neurons somewhere farther down its pathway . . . *there*, behind those gray eyes with their newly penetrating gaze.

"Obviously, sending me out for your watch was a ruse." His roommate's voice was suddenly crisper, more assured than it had been. "Also, I perceive that your desk has just been broken into, by someone who thought it mine." The tone softened somewhat. "Come, man, I bear you no ill will. Your secret, if honorable, shall be safe. But it is plain that you are not what you have represented yourself to be."

The agent got to his feet, pulling at his sandy hair, trying desperately to think. "How—how do you know?"

"Elementary!" the tall man snapped.

BOROVSKY'S HOLLOW WOMAN

By Jeff Duntemann and Nancy Kress

Laura walked the Low Steel above the stars, searching for her man.

It was 2.3 klicks across the skeletal terrain by the most direct route—the blue line on the diagram of the construction zone burned in the eye of Laura's mind. No one but Mikhail Borovsky would take that particular route across the unfinished girders of the titan cylinder's outermost level, and even he would not take it without her.

One foot before the other, lift, swing, step. The pilot beam was solid monocrystal steel, I-section, one decimeter wide. One hundred meters to her left and right identical girders glittered in the always-changing light. They were the primary structural support of the latest, lowest level of George Eastman Nexus. Each girder was a single crystal of iron atoms, one hundred nineteen kilometers in circumference, and strong enough to rest an artificial world on.

For a kilometer ahead and behind, it was Laura and her beam.

A man in the saddle of a six-wheeled yoyo swung under the horizon far away antispinward and quickly approached her, soon passing to the rear and vanishing. Borovsky's yoyo was a four-wheeler. The earth swung up behind her and made blue highlights creep across the dull-gray steel plates ten meters above her helmet. It slipped above the horizon and was gone again for another forty minutes.

Laura adjusted the magnetism in her boot soles. Just enough to add a little friction, a little sureness. If she fell outward from the rotating structure into the starry darkness the steelworkers called the Pit, no one would fall after to her rescue. But she would not fall. Steel was her medium, just as it was Borovsky's, and she loved it. Steel was sure and clean and true. It could be trusted, as Borovsky could be trusted when he wasn't —

No. She would not allow that thought to be completed.

Where had they gone? Borovsky, in rubber underwear, off on a yoyo to fight a man twice his size, somewhere on a level swinging more than 1.6 g. Falling on your face could flatten your skull on E Minus Seven. Fighting could dock you a week's pay. Ignoring a challenge could get you called a phobe. A coward. A . . . woman.

Where?

Step following step, body bent forward, using the artificial gravity to help carry her onward, Laura searched. She scanned the chatter on the CB and the bloody-murder band. Nothing spoke of a man in rubber hurt on E Minus Seven.

Less than five hundred meters of open steel remained. Far ahead Laura saw something streak through the shadows toward the sucking stars. She followed desperately with her eyes and saw it catch the sun beyond the great cylinder's shadow. Four-wheeled gantry, cable, saddle: It blazed brilliant yellow for a moment and was gone, falling forever.

His yoyo, unridden, alone. Damn the Pit! Laura broke into a run, each boot hitting the beam safely though without thought, each magnet grabbing just so much. Raw dawn broke behind her and cast lurching shadows against the unfinished steel ahead. The sun was beneath her feet as she stepped from naked monocrystal onto gray steel plates.

Above was the port from which the yoyo had fallen. She pulled herself up a ladder and stepped out onto E Minus Six. A little lighter, a little less deadly.

No sign of fleeing men. Six was a big level, one hundred meters thick. Heavy chemical industry, she remembered.

Before her a dozen huge steel tanks squatted against the floor like brooding hens. Each was ten meters high, with a ladder leading to a dogged circular hatch.

She scanned the tanks. All were alike, save that one of the hatches had dog-handles twisted differently from the rest. In moments she was at the hatch, pushing the dogs aside.

The tube was a simple pressure lock. Laura pulled herself in, dogged the outer hatch, and released the inner.

With a rising rush there was sound all around her. She pushed the inner hatch wide and found her man.

Mikhail Borovsky lay naked in a heap, blood leaking from his mouth. Laura cried out, and for an awful moment she lay immobile in the tube until she heard a rattling breath. She slid to his side and squeezed his wrist until her gauntlet felt his pulse. Drugs—he needed drugs to stir his system out of shock.

His rubber suit lay on the floor. Laura kicked it scorn-

fully aside, reached to her throat, and undid its latch.
Quickly she eased her helmet back. She pulled her ventral
zipper down, flipping the hooks aside with her fingers as
they went. Eagerly she spread her ventral plates apart,
pulled her pelvic plate forward, then pulled the zippers
down each of her legs almost to each knee.

She lay on her back beside him, plates gaping, helmet
folded under. The eyes in her wrists and in the toes of her
boots helped her lift Borovsky above her. Gently she eased
his legs down into her legs and let the slow peristalsis of
her inner layers draw his feet into her feet. Her ventral
plates stretched wide to clear his hips. She placed the
Texas catheter over his penis and pulled her pelvic plate
back into position.

Wriggling slightly, she guided his arms down into her
arms, where her inner layers did the final positioning.

Each finger was drawn into place and continuously
massaged. Laura zipped and hooked her ventral plates
and finally eased her helmet over his head.

For a Rabinowicz Manplifier Mark IX space suit, walking steel empty was too lonely to bear. Without her man
inside her Laura felt herself a hollow mockery, less than
even a woman, not worthy of the soul Borovsky had paid
so much for. Never again, she said to unconscious ears.
Never again. Stay inside me. You are *mine*.

Slowly she stood, whole again. Up from his toes the hydraulic rings pressed in smooth waves, helping his blood
back toward his head and heart. A tiny needle jabbed into
his buttocks, sending a careful measure of stimulant into
his bloodstream.

This was no place to be caught by a boss. Laura moved
slowly as she climbed from the tank. It had been some
time since she had carried his dead weight asleep, and
never unconscious. She gave the torn rubber underwear to

the Pit with a vengeful flick of her hand.

They went home the long way, going up through Six to Five and walking slowly. Halfway there he came around.

"Laura," he whispered.

"I love you," she said, without breaking her stride.

"He had a metal bar shoved up his ass," he said, and coughed. "Crapped it out on the floor, grabbed it, and that was that. I'm gonna kill the fugger. You watch me."

"I *love* you," she said again, hoping against knowledge that the words would soothe the murderous rage she feared might get him killed.

A world without Borovsky—

"Love you too," he mumbled, only half-conscious. "I'm gonna kill him."

By morning the bruises showed up. Borovsky swore at his image in the mirror. The left half of his face was swollen grotesquely. Ugly purple blotches covered most of his cheek and curved up nearly to surround his left eye. All across his body were bruises and scrapes from hitting the iron going down. He pressed a bruise with one finger and jerked the finger away from the fiery pain.

Laura watched, unmoving. The tiny, cylindrical pod with its watercot, its kitchen, its shower, and squat toilet was very silent. If Borovsky fought again, if he insisted on fighting again today—

Panic appeared in her crystalline, layered machine mind, seeping outward from the F layer at the core. Layers A through E were standard Manplifier equipment: sensory, motor, communications, memory, and intellect. Borovsky had paid three years' wages for the F layer that Laura so cherished: unique, personal, precious—her soul. The E layer, shared by any machine that could speak and reason, could have stopped the panic, but it did not. Instead, when Laura could no longer stand the way he stood gripping the edge of the sink in furious silence, she spoke.

"You didn't have to go fight him."

He spat into the sink. "He called me a phobe. Maybe once I can take it. Maybe twice. Some people have to make noise. But he made me answer him. So I answered." He probed a bruise on his thigh, wincing. "What do we got for bruises?"

Laura turned and searched a small cabinet beside the bed. "Hemoverithol."

"Let's have it."

Laura pressed an autoampul against his thigh and squeezed.

He sighed as the needle came and went, then nodded. "How long?"

Thousands of words of medical data flew past the eyes of Laura's mind. "Eighteen hours to kill the swelling. Color should be gone in forty-eight. I hope we can afford another yoyo; the spare wasn't new when we bought it and—"

"Nix. Rent's up, food's up—we get a new yoyo and we'd default on your soul. Gimme a couple months. We'll get a new one from that bastard Coyne even if I have to beat it out of his hide."

"Maybe we should stay away from the Beer Tube for a few days."

"He'll be laughing behind his ugly face."

"Let him laugh. Borovsky—"

"Don't say it." He turned to her and smiled. The smile was made lopsided by the swelling in his cheek, and even when whole it was not a smile to charm women—too flat, too suspicious, too much of the smile of an outsider more used to contempt than to love. But Laura was not a woman of flesh. This smile was Borovsky's. It was enough.

"Let me run the balalaika," Laura said. The image came to her mind instantly: Borovsky as he looked while listening to the tape of his father playing the ancient balalaika. The tape was all he had brought up from the crumbling slum that was Deep West London. The sad, hollow music made his face change—change from underneath, Laura thought.

At those times his features lost some of their hardness; his eyes ceased their constant nervous scanning back and forth. His mouth—no, his mouth did not smile, but in the small parting of his lips it seemed to find peace. If he would just listen—now—to the balalaika . . .

"Let me run the balalaika!"

"And get me canned? No, *dushenka*. We'll be late to the grind. Damn. That spare better be okay." He turned from the sink and tapped a command on the lock console. The spare yoyo's condition read out in a few crisp words. Not the best, but the battery was a retread, and old at that.

"The balalaika—"

"Come on, Laura. Shit, we're late already. *Move* it."

Laura put down her hand and deliberately began undogging her plates.

George Eastman Nexus had begun as a single cylinder, rotating to simulate standard Earth gravity. From the inner surface, towers and delicately suspended trees of modular office clusters grew toward the center. In those offices the engineers and managers of a thousand companies guided an industry worth six trillion dollars in gold annually.

George Eastman grew outward as well. Downward from Earth-Zero swelled the industrial levels. Some industries preferred the heavier gravity; many chemical processes actually worked more efficiently under higher swing.

For other industries the heaviness was less necessary, but materials were cheap ever since the asteroid Calliope had been towed into orbit around the moon for the steerable mirrors to mine.

It was less than three klicks from their pod to the advancing edge of E Minus Seven. Its monocrystal rings girdling Eastman Nexus had been in place for ten months. At the forefront of construction the longitudinal beams and outer-deck plates were being welded into position amid showers of sparks. Behind the edge the power conduits and other piping were being laid, and farther still, the floor plates, one meter square and removable, were being bolted down. Laura gripped the yoyo's cable tightly as they rode, and felt through her fingers the sizzle of old motors in its gantry above her helmet.

Two of the welders paused long enough to let Borovsky pass between them, unharmed by the molten droplets. Borovsky waved clear, and the yoyo purred on to the point where the floor plates began. He parked it and punched in with the shift boss. Docked nine minutes—he shrugged, and Laura tallied the beers he would have to forgo to make it up. Borovsky's partner, Andre Wolf Lair, thumped his shoulder as Borovsky yanked his card from the clock. Borovsky grunted in greeting and returned a playful poke to the Amerind's midsection. Coyne's lamp on the clock was green. Borovsky clenched his jaw and glanced toward the supply dump. Coyne was loading diamond cutting wheels into his Enhanced Leverage Manipulator.

Coyne looked up. Borovsky's personal microwave channel triggered, and a single scornful, whispered word came across over Coyne's chuckle: *"phobe."*

Laura felt her man's pulse race. Quickly she squeezed his thigh and whispered in his ear, "He can't even walk the Low Steel for a living. All he does is ride in that big yellow egg. You're twice the man he ever will be."

"I'll kill him," Borovsky muttered. "Damn, I'll feed him to the stars."

George Eastman Nexus turned twelve times over the course of a shift. Borovsky and Andre Wolf Lair guided the longitudinal steel beams into position ahead of the edge, tacked them, and left them for the welders. Wolf Lair was taller than Borovsky, larger than Coyne. Among the men who walked the Low Steel he was a giant, with impeccable balance and a gentle, deep voice. His suit was much older than Laura, with little skill in its E layer for speech and reasoning, and no F layer at all. The suit had no name and spoke, when it had to, in Wolf Lair's own voice. Laura sensed that Wolf Lair did not like intelligent machines, and she remained silent while he and Borovsky worked.

When the shift was half over, Coyne's ELM rumbled by on its way to the supply dump. As it passed, one of its two smaller arms twisted its four fingers into a crude approximation of an ancient gesture of insult. Borovsky quickly returned the gesture and looked the other way.

Wolf Lair looked after the egg-shaped machine until it moved out of sight. "Coyne is a believer, Mik. I think he hates you for the spirit you wear."

Borovsky hoisted one end of the next beam. "Pah. He believes in his own mouth."

"But I have seen him walk three levels up to the Catholic mass. Catholics fear all spirits. Hate is a good mask for the things you fear."

"Laura's no spirit. Hell, she's a computer." Borovsky

pushed against the end of the beam. Laura pushed with him. The beam crept into position in line with the tiny red spots of light produced by the laser-alignment network.

"Maybe *computer* is the new word for *spirit*. Maybe it is a spirit for nonbelievers. I heard you talk about the loan you got two years ago. You said you bought a soul for your space suit."

Wolf Lair leaned forward and helped Borovsky move the beam to its final position. Together they tacked it down with dollops of adhesive after checking it against all fifty alignment spots. Borovsky leaned back against a pillar and stared down at the stars creeping past beneath his feet.

"Shit, I was lonely. You can go home to Leah and your little ones twice a year. They send you letters and presents, and you send them money. This up here is all the home I got, and nobody in it but me. Ain't no woman anywhere would live here and get smashed under this much swing. You Indians got it good. Your women wait for you in their mountains. In the city no woman remembers your name ten minutes after you screw her. I thought about it a long time. All I did was buy something that would be on my side no matter what, just something that sounded like a woman." Laura pinched him hard in a very sensitive place. "But it turned out to be a woman that was *worth* something."

"I hear you, Mik. You say it well. I was twenty when I signed up for space. My grandfather took me aside and said, 'Wolf Lair, do not give over your heart to machinery. Machines are to use and put away when day is gone. Only living things are worth the true heart of a man.' He is dead some years, but I will never forget him. You know that lesson as well, I think. You had nothing worth your true heart; so you bought a spirit. The spirit you bought is nothing so simple as a loyal dog, or even a dead man's restless ghost. I know it comforts you and will never disobey you, but forgive me if I fear it. Forgive Coyne if he fears it. I could never understand or trust a spirit that lived in a machine."

Wolf Lair's words disturbed Laura. He was not given to speeches and was not one to admit his heart's fears and feelings. She waited to hear what Borovsky would answer, but he said nothing. The sun passed under their feet five more times, and the two men worked in silence.

For three days Borovsky avoided the Beer Tube. At shift's end he slept, sleeping as much as fourteen hours at once. Laura sampled his blood and read his vital signs daily, and she knew that his body was repairing the damage Coyne had done it and the further damage Borovsky was doing by continuing to work without a break for healing. Once, watching him as he slept, she played the balalaika tape for herself alone, but only once. Other times she restlessly walked the Low Steel empty, thinking. She thought about Coyne, and about Wolf Lair, and about herself.

She thought about souls.

Standing on a naked monocrystal beam above the bottomless void, she looked down and saw Rigel creeping past. The spectroscope on her instrument-blistered helmet studied it, sent data streaming from her A sensory layer inward. Stored data raced outward from D memory layer to meet it. Information met, intersected, compared, cross-referenced in a process that, it seemed to Laura, was both methodical and more than methodical, It found more in the rainbow-layered image of a star than the star had to offer. But no—the handling of data was not her soul.

The pleasure, then, in that handling. Had the pleasure

in her own processes been there before Borovsky had
bought her a soul? No, of course not. *Laura* had not been
there, not as she herself—only a good Rabinowicz Mark
IX Manplifier suit with a woman's pleasant voice. Not as
the watcher of her own mind, the tender holder of
Borovsky's body, the tireless worker who longed to follow
the Low Steel out to the stars and farther. Still these things
were not her soul. They were things that, as Wolf Lair had
said, could be put away when day was done and the work
was done—all but Borovsky. Not for a moment could she
lay down her guardianship and loyalty. So she had been
made, and she would not want to be an angstrom different. She loved Borovsky beyond either choice or the desire
for choice. But Borovsky was not her soul.

Raising her empty arms, Laura stretched them out toward Rigel. It was a gesture she had seen made only
once—by Wolf Lair, the man who feared her as a spirit
within a machine. Just like this had the Amerind stood:
arms outstretched so, body taut and arched so, hands'
palms open to the devouring sun crawling toward and below him. With Borovsky inside her Laura had stopped
dead on a beam and stared. Wolf Lair had not turned toward them, had not sensed their footsteps through the
steel on which he stood. He had not, in fact, seen Laura at
all, but in that one moment Laura had seen a vividness, a
connection between him and her and the sun and
Borovsky and the beam beneath her, forged of iron atoms
that were mostly empty space.

"Hollow woman!" Coyne had mocked once. "One-hun-
dred-percent artificial broad, nothing organic added," he
had read, squinting from a label he imagined on her ventral plates. Odd that he would mock her for what she was
proud to be, and doubly odd that she felt too ashamed to
retort that nothing could persuade her to trade polished,

powerful hydraulic limbs for the fragile mushiness of human flesh. Such weakness was not to be envied. But worse that what human beings could *not* do was the thing they could do and did not, the thing she had seen in the tensile exultation of Wolf Lair's body on a steel beam hung above the stars.

It was a thing for which Laura had no name but only a sense of patterns among half-realized notions of what it might be like to be human. The pattern was greater than merely being human; it was a transcendence of the human. It was a laying of hands upon the universe with such firmness of grasp that the universe took a bit of the being's shape, individual and unrepeatable, because exactly that intensity and originality of consciousness had not existed in exactly that way before, and would not do so again. Becoming unrepeatably and wholly oneself and, thus, everything else—*that*, Laura decided, was her soul. Becoming, and knowing it.

Was that what Wolf Lair had meant by the spirit of living things? But then why had Laura not seen it among the humans themselves before that glimpse of intense stillness in the outstretched body of Wolf Lair? No, the steelwalkers who had inherited unbought souls without cost seemed unwilling to embrace anything larger than a double hamburger. Their souls were asleep; though they ate, drank, slept, worked, and fought, their souls were in none of it. Why, even Borovsky—

No. The thought froze and vanished. Borovsky, troubled, flawed creature that he was, had nevertheless caused her soul to be. He created her and redeemed her by placing himself in financial chains. Laura turned from her contemplation of Rigel to her pleasure in remembering certain ancient myths (but there had been no myths, nor pleasure in them, before Borovsky had bought her soul) to the joy of contemplating Borovsky himself. Creator. Redeemer. However limited his other horizons, he had reached beyond himself as far as that.

Cherishing the thought at the center of her crystalline consciousness, Laura hurried back to where Borovsky was.

An argument was under way in the Beer Tube when Borovsky entered three days later. Coyne was proclaiming that E Minus Seven would be the last layer to be built around George Eastman Nexus. Borovsky tossed back Laura's helmet on its hinges.

"Damn right. How could the Combine *possibly* build a level that Johnny Coyne couldn't stand up in?" His bulldog face remained expressionless as he undogged Laura's plates, but the other men in the automated tavern laughed.

Coyne glowered. "When they run out of men like me to build it, who will they get to do the work?"

Andre Wolf Lair was sitting at one of the black plastic benches near the robot bar at the far end. He took a long draft from his carved wooden stein, wiped the foam from his lips, and laughed deeply. "When they run out of men like you they will use *real* men, and we will work twice as fast."

Coyne opened his mouth. Wolf Lair leaned toward Coyne, who saw the warning in the giant's eyes, and looked away.

In his blue, working longjohns, Borovsky stepped free of Laura. She buttoned up and leaned against the wall among several other suits, some like her, others mere rubber. Laura watched Borovsky key up a beer into a disposable stein at the bar and walk back toward Wolf Lair.

"Let them build out to E Minus Fifteen," Borovsky

332

said, and took a mouthful of foam. "I will stand after the last man has started to crawl."

"After two hours here I doubt any of us could stand in free fall," said another man. General laughter followed, to Laura's relief. Among the Beer Tube's customers tonight was a shift boss, Simon Weinblatt, who was sitting with several of Borovsky's co-workers and trading jokes with them. The man was of only average height and build and seemed slight beside Borovsky and Wolf Lair. Like all shift bosses, Weinblatt had a soft-spoken, gentle demeanor and a keen understanding of human motivation. When tensions flared, shift bosses had a way of showing up, quieting the situation, and making forty rough, quarrelsome laborers cooperate and produce. Their methods could be as rough as those of the laborers. Every man there had heard tales of drunken steelworkers who had defied shift bosses and found that their jobs evaporated the following morning. And there was another story, hundredthhand at least, of a man who had traded angry words with a shift boss and shoved him to the floor—only to awaken in a prison hospital bed with both arms gone past the elbows.

Laura saw that Weinblatt had been inconspicuously watching Borovsky and Coyne. When Borovsky went back to the bar for a second beer, Weinblatt placed a hand on his elbow. Borovsky bent down to listen; the man spoke quietly. "You have an accident at work?" Weinblatt pointed to his own cheek. Borovsky's eyebrows rose, and Laura thought he grew a little pale. There was still some slight discoloration from the bruise that had covered half his face.

"Fell outta bed. No big deal."

Coyne squeezed past on his way to the bar for yet another beer. Laura longed to get Borovsky back within her and away from there.

Even with a raucous album playing in the background, Coyne appeared to have heard the exchange.

He laughed belligerently and poked Borovsky with his index finger.

"Fell outta bed, huh? Dreaming about one of those Rooski women, I guess. All muscle and three tits; a pair and a spare!" Coyne doubled over laughing. Borovsky stiffened but remained silent.

Weinblatt did not seem bothered by the banter. Through a grin he rejoined: "At least he remembers to dream about women. After ten beers I'll bet you spend all night making love to your handling machine."

Coyne shrugged as his stein filled. "There ain't no words for the kind of women *I* dream about."

From the next table another man joined in: "That's because the Combine ain't started making 'em yet!"

Coyne belched loudly. He shook his head and made his way to the rear of the tavern, where a dozen space suits stood or hung near the lock. He stood in front of Laura and addressed the crowd with a full stein in his hand.

"Ha! The expert on mechanical women is right here among us! Our good friend Mik-Hayal Borovsky and his patented hollow woman! She cooks, she cleans, she cheats at cards, she tells dirty jokes. What more could a man want?"

Borovsky's face tightened.

"I think that ought to be your last beer, Johnny," Weinblatt said pleasantly.

Coyne ignored him. "What more, huh? Tits maybe?" He turned and made pinching motions across Laura's ventral plates. "Kind of hard to get hold of, huh? Well, Mik's got lots of imagination."

"You're making an ass of yourself, Johnny," Weinblatt

said. The grin was gone.

"No tits. Well, how about a twat? Jesus, guys, she *all* twat! Lookithat!" Coyne grabbed Laura by the rim of her helmet gasket and tipped it forward, pointing with an index finger to the hollowness inside. "A guy could crawl in there and get lost, which is about as close as Mik's ever gonna get to being inside a woman!" Coyne released Laura and faced the crowd again. Borovsky spat on the floor. Too much tension, Laura thought; she could picture Borovsky bashing Coyne's head flat against the floor. As soon as Coyne turned away she brought her right hand up and thumbed her non-existent nose at him.

The room exploded with laughter. Coyne whirled around in time to see Laura's arm snap back to her side.

"Well, so she wants to be one of the boys. Hey, babe, you can't have fun at the Beer Tube without putting away some yourself. Here, I keyed for this one, but it's all yours." He lifted his stein over Laura's helmet gasket as though to empty the liquid into her hollowness.

Borovsky slammed the palms of his hands down hard on the tabletop. Across the table, Andre Wolf Lair set his stein aside and stood. At once, without hurrying, Weinblatt was on his feet, his face hard.

"*Coyne, shut your goddamned mouth.*"

Coyne bent over as though kicked in the stomach, his stein groping for the nearest table. His face paled. Laura saw that he had realized what he had done: provoked a shift boss to his feet.

Except for the continuous drone of the juke, the Beer Tube was silent. Simon Weinblatt was still standing. "Go home, Johnny," he said, and took his seat.

Coyne nodded, turned, and began pulling on his rubber suit.

Laura saw little of Coyne next shift. Wherever she and Borovsky happened to be, the yellow ELM happened to be elsewhere. Nor did Coyne appear at the Beer Tube after shift. But Simon Weinblatt was there, and he pointed to the bench opposite his as Borovsky walked in. Laura, left again with the other suits, edged close enough to listen.

"Mik, I'm worried about Coyne." Weinblatt's face was smiling, unreadable. "One of these days he's going to jump you, and you're going to beat his brains out."

"Would serve him right," Borovsky said, eyes on the bench. "The guy is some kind of psycho."

"Could be; how did this thing between you two start?"

"I didn't start it."

"I didn't say you did," Weinblatt said pleasantly. "Do you know why he has it in for you?"

"No. One day he just starts in."

Weinblatt waited; Borovsky, scowling, said nothing more. Finally Weinblatt said, "Some guys are up only when they're making noise. They need it, like air. But Coyne is also mighty damned good with an ELM. His replacement index is forty points tougher than yours." The shift boss sipped from his mug. "If one of you had to go, it wouldn't be him."

"That's not fair."

"Money isn't fair. Bear down, make some Q-points, and we'll see. Right now you have to bend a little. I've been doing some watching and some asking around. You pretty much stick to yourself, and that's cool. But up here it never hurts to melt in a little. You've got no wife to talk about, no kids to brag about. Nobody ever hears of you going off to see a woman somewhere. You make it easy for an asshole like Coyne to single you out. Humans are pack animals. If you don't show that you're in, the others will assume that you're out." Weinblatt gave Borovsky a

336

level stare for a few moments and then shrugged. "You can tell me that's not fair either."

"So what do I do?"

"Starters," Weinblatt said, and shoved a silver, octagonal token across the scarred plastic tabletop. Laura's eyes followed the token across the bench. Embossed on the exposed face was a stylized spiral galaxy and the words BERENICE'S CLUSTER.

"Silver lay, Mik. Anything you want. This one is on me. It's my treat."

After an incredulous moment, Laura snapped her attention from Weinblatt's token to Borovsky's face. Her man—*her* man—looked as impassive as ever. But Laura, who knew the meaning of every twitch in that unlovely face, saw in Borovsky's eyes a complex reaction: resentment and distaste and—yes—interest. The room lurched slightly, and Laura thought something had gone sour in her F level, but then realized she was discovering something new in the bright, innermost level she knew as her soul. If Borovsky—

"No thanks," Borovsky was saying. He lowered his eyes to stare at the silver token. "Whorehouses give me the creeps."

"Be honest, Mik. Are you queer?"

"No!"

Several of the other men nearby looked toward Borovsky; seeing Weinblatt's warning glare, they quickly looked away.

"I can't afford it," Borovsky said, and in his voice Laura heard the same thing she had seen in his eyes: He resented being told what to do; he was determined to resist; he felt scorn for the human pressure to fit in, but he was interested.

"Maybe not a silver," Weinblatt said, "but a purple

quickie once a week won't break you. I know."

Borovsky nodded. The Combine always knew, to the penny, every employee's assets, debts, and expenses. Borovsky's excuse had been a poor one. Was he trying to save face in offering resistance so easily wrestled down? Laura longed to have Borovsky look at her, but his gaze remained on the silver token. It was Weinblatt, in profile to Laura, who seemed for a moment to flick a sidelong glance at the suits against the wall. Desolation swept through her F layer. If Borovsky—Borovsky, *her* man—

"I've never been there before," Borovsky said.

Weinblatt stood. "I'll take you. I could use a good time myself about now."

And Borovsky was standing up. Borovsky was reaching for her. Borovsky, still not meeting her many sets of eyes, was wriggling into her ventral cavity, into her boots. He said nothing. And Laura, sure now that the universe was steady and the lurching continued only in her soul, could say nothing either.

"Let's go," Weinblatt said.

Both ports were cast wide at Berenice's Cluster, up on E Minus Four. Loud, raucous music echoed out through the lock. Borovsky hesitated a moment.

"Come *on*, Mik. Relax."

Laura felt Borovsky suck in his breath, and they entered. Inside it was very crowded, a random tessellation of polygonal waterbeds illuminated from beneath by changing, multicolored lights. On each bed lay a woman, some naked, many draped in shimmering cloth. More than a dozen men stood among the beds, reading the fee schedules and counting dollars in their heads and on their fingers. Down among their feet surged a heavy, bluish smoke, stirred into sluggish vortices as the men stepped along the narrow ways between the waterbeds.

Weinblatt doffed his rubber suit quickly, Borovsky much more slowly. A blonde on a nearby bed smiled at him, then drew aside the drapery suspended from cords braided around her neck. She had large breasts to which the heavy swing of E Minus Four had not been kind. Cupping a hand under one breast, she lifted it toward Borovsky and smiled again.

"How long since you've had a real woman?" Weinblatt asked. Borovsky muttered something that Laura did not think Weinblatt would catch above the jukebox, but she did: four years.

"*I'm* real," Laura said, her voice low. "I'm real and I'm—look at them! Like puddles of melting cranberry sauce! Either of us could outlift, outhaul, outproduce them all put together. How can you? Borovsky—"

"It's not my idea," Borovsky said sullenly, finally stepping free of her. Laura realized that it would not matter how much she looked at him, what she said, or how she behaved. She could not change Borovsky's mind.

Confused and hurting, she stepped back against the wall. Borovsky moved quickly away from her, heading toward the far end of the room, ignoring the blonde who followed him with charcoaled eyes. In moments he was lost in the swirling mist. Eagerness to see more melting cranberry women—or to get away from her? Laura was not sure, though she suspected the latter, and took from that some small wrapping of comfort.

"He talking to *you*?" the blonde demanded. She stared at the emptiness above Laura's helmet gasket, at the head that Laura had never had nor wanted.

"Yes."

"Huh!" She sounded neither surprised nor scornful, only annoyed. "He don't like blondes?"

"I don't know what he likes."

The woman looked at Laura shrewdly. "I'll bet you do so, Honey." Suddenly she laughed, such an unselfconscious, friendly laugh that Laura found herself drawn away from the wall to stand beside the woman's pentagonal waterbed. The lights beneath it shifted from green to red, warming the woman's skin so that to Laura it looked like uncooled metal.

"Why do you do this?" Laura asked softly.

"Do what?"

"Make . . . love to these men. You aren't their work partners. You have no interest in their lives. They haven't bought you a soul. You don't love them."

The blonde gave her a long, speculative look. Something surfaced in her eyes, something Laura had the quickness to see but not the knowledge of humanity to interpret. Then the human woman laughed again. "It's a living."

A living. Laura hadn't seen it that way before. People had to live. Steelwalkers needed sex; Laura knew they talked of it enough, and few had fine Rabinowicz suits like Laura. There was a good, respectable economic foundation to Berenice's Cluster. But Borovsky—Borovsky *did* have her.

"Jealous, Honey?" the blonde said softly. She did not mock. Her eyes, lids painted blue as far as her brows, seemed sympathetic and a little sad. Staring into those eyes, Laura felt the odd sensation of unrelated data suddenly relating: The woman's eyes reminded her of Borovsky's balalaika music.

"Don't cry about it," the blonde said. "That's how a steelwalker is. Tin woman, skin woman—he don't care. We do what we can."

"No," Laura said. "No!"

"Sorry." Again the blonde gave Laura that knowing and sad, blue-lidded look. From the airlock a man walked into the room and stripped off his rubber suit. After glancing around the misty room, he smiled at the blonde. She raised her huge breast to him and looked up through her lashes. The man sauntered over to the bed.

"Silver lay, stud?"

"Purple quickie. You available?" The man grinned mischievously at her.

"Why not?"

Laura stepped back against the wall. Around the blonde's bed the blue mist grew thicker, rising in hazy walls shot through with multicolored light from the bed. The man in his eagerness had left his rubber suit at Laura's feet. She kicked at it, then abruptly picked it up and hung it on a nearby peg. Its empty arms dangled helplessly. Without a man inside it, it was useless. Rubber suits. Balalaika music. Blue-lidded eyes. Borovsky. Simon Weinblatt. Coyne. Silver lays. Souls — Souls.

That was what she had seen in the blonde's sympathetic look.

Startled, Laura stared at the bed. The mist around the bed grew thicker and darker blue. The bed began to move away from Laura on its cushion of air. Another bed, this one with two women and one man just leaving it, slid toward Laura. One of the women put one foot on the floor and squealed. The man laughed and slapped her bare ass. Music blared and mist swirled. Nothing in the scene looked to Laura anything like Wolf Lair's outstretched arms on the steel beam, but Laura knew she was not mistaken. In the blonde's balalaika eyes Laura had seen another soul. And she had recognized it only because she had her own.

Laura settled back against the wall in resignation and

waited for the sliding beds to bring Borovsky back to her.

The spare yoyo was dead.

Borovsky snapped the battery cover free and peered into the space crowded with wires and age-crusted components. Nothing looked amiss.

"Take a look," he told Laura, and poked their right hand into the cavity.

Laura's fingers nudged the wires aside as the eyes that rode over each finger examined the mechanism.

Her fingers saw it and teased it out into view from where it had been tucked behind a voltage regulator: a carefully snipped wire.

Hesitantly she described the wire. Borovsky stopped for many long seconds, one hand on the battery pack and one hand holding a screwdriver.

"He came in here. I noticed him before we got tied up with the trouble setting up the last beam. He didn't come out."

Borovsky and Laura checked between the piles of steel for a place where a man might hide.

"We could have missed him coming out," Laura suggested.

"I don't miss nothing from him no more," Borovsky replied coldly. "He's in here."

Laura said nothing. Borovsky's bionics alarmed her. Pulse, blood pressure, muscle tension, skin resistance — this was not normal anger. He was in a cold rage.

In one corner of the dump was a circular column three meters wide, rising up from the floor and vanishing into the ceiling. It was the conduit core that carried power down from the center of the titan cylinder to the construction on the Low Steel. At knee level was the inspection hatch.

"Get that hatch on your infrared," Borovsky ordered.

The wide oval eye on Laura's brow saw the vague smudge on the hatch's handle. The vacuum of E Minus Seven preserved heat traces well.

"There were hands on that handle recently," she said, wishing it were not so.

Borovsky grunted and grasped the handle. It would not turn.

"Locked," Laura said.

"For me, maybe. Not for you. *Turn.*"

Laura's fingers tightened on the handle and twisted hard. She felt the metal of the latch resist and moan, then break free. The hatch swung inward.

Wriggling through the hatch took some minutes. It had not been designed for passing a man in an amplified Rabinowicz space suit. Laura supposed that had been Coyne's hope . . . and ached that it could have been true.

Inside the column were pipes and bus channels vanishing upward in the darkness. Running among the pipes was an aluminum ladder. Laura turned off her suit lights and saw the warm spots where sweating, rubber-suited hands had gripped the rungs.

The olfionics within her helmet smelled Borovsky's rage. "Up."

They climbed in darkness quickly, twice as fast as a nonamplified man could climb. Borovsky said nothing, and Laura dared not plead for him to give up the chase. It would do no good and would only feed the rage she so feared.

"It's a mess in here," she said truthfully, trying to read the swirl of multicolored images her infrared eyes gave her.

By that level the column was pressurized, and warm air

confused the heat traces Coyne had left behind. She saw that the dust on the hatch handle had not been disturbed for some time. She did not volunteer the information.

Borovsky steered Laura's helmet crest beam along the ladder above. "Still too heavy. This is E Minus Four. He lives on E Minus Two. He's still climbing."

Without responding, Laura grasped the rungs and climbed.

Twof airlocks higher E Minus Three began. Above them locks had been removed to make the column an air-return manifold. The black mouths o air tunnels yawned on four sides, and a constant draft through the tunnels had erased any possible heat traces the man might have left behind. Borovsky scanned the four tunnels.

"He can't be far. Damn, I've got him. I know I do. Damn."

They stood in silence for tens of seconds. Laura gradually learned to separate the gentle white noise of the air tunnels from the general subsonic rumble created everywhere by life in a steel habitat. With panic and despair, she realized she could hear high above them the sound of a man's labored breathing.

A man Borovsky wanted to kill.

She could tell him where Coyne was, or not tell him — a sickening choice. She had never failed to tell Borovsky, her man, her life, anything she knew he wanted to hear. If he commanded her, she would tell him — to refuse was to face consequences too final to consider. But if he found Coyne — if he *killed* Coyne — what would the Combine do to Borovsky then?

The words formed a hundred times, and each time she wiped them away before sending them to her helmet speakers. She strained to believe that hiding the truth was not a lie and knew that to believe so would be lying to herself.

"He lives east of here," Borovsky said. "He'll follow the tube. Let's go."

"No," Laura said, forcing the words to form. "I hear him. He's up on the ladder somewhere."

Borovsky spat something foul in his native language. He gripped the ladder with both hands and sent Laura's crest beam stabbing upward. Coyne was there, wrapped around the rungs, panting. Laura could smell his sour sweat drifting down on the stale air.

Coyne stiffened, made motions to start climbing again.

"Stop!" Borovsky screamed. Laura's arms pulled with his arms, and the aluminum of the ladder tore raggedly away from its lower wall brackets.

"Eat shit!" Coyne cried and dropped free of the ladder.

His boots struck the top of Laura's helmet, crushing many of her most delicate instruments, including the pale-blue glass oval that imaged in the infrared. His knees flexed, and he leaped to one side.

The still vicious swing of E Minus Three drew him down, but he had time to plan his movements. He drew up in a ball and rolled, screaming in pain as one shoulder slammed into the steel. But then he was up, stumbling, then running crookedly down one of the air tunnels, favoring his left leg and sobbing in pain.

Borovsky swore to himself in Russian. Laura longed not to run, but Borovsky's legs were running; so her legs ran. His arms swung in a deadly determined rhythm; so hers swung, too.

Coyne was a pathetic scarecrow, highlighted in every detail by the cold lights of Laura's helmet beam. His rubber suit was smudged and torn, helmet long abandoned to lighten himself. He had only a few seconds' head start and appeared close to exhaustion. As much as Laura hated

Coyne, she felt a moment of pity for him.

Coyne chose that moment to look over his shoulder, side-stumbling for two steps. He moaned and turned away but it had been enough. Laura had seen his face, smeared with the grime of the tunnels mixed with tears of exertion, and abruptly she saw herself through his eyes.

Shaped like a man cut out of steel and crushed in a magnetic press; torso nearly as wide as it was tall; arms and legs clusters of hydraulic cylinders contracting and extending in smooth, polished motions. Faceless, silvered helmet without any neck, ruined instruments atop it dangling by tiny wires and striking the helmet's sides with little sounds. Hands twice human size, guided by flesh but powered by a hydraulic exoskeleton strong enough to crush rocks. Hands reaching forward, fingers splayed and grasping, grasping. A machine bent on death.

But she was not! She was life, productivity, strength, steel! She was, in her soul—

No time. Coyne screamed again, stumbled, fell to his knees, rolled over, and stared in wide-eyed horror as Laura bore down on him.

Her right hand caught him by the neck and lifted him like a rag doll. He gurgled, eyes bulging, as Borovsky slammed him against the steel wall.

Borovsky's hand squeezed.

Horror-struck, Laura felt her hand squeeze.

Coyne tore at the hand around his neck, hammered his fists against the smooth cylinders and the silver pistons that were slowly forcing Laura's fingers together. His mouth twisted, tongue pushing to one side, struggling to let his throat breathe. Laura felt his frantic heartbeat hammering in the veins of his neck. And in Coyne's eyes, under the terror and rage, Laura saw something else: a soul slipping away. A trapped and mean soul, but real—as real as the soul she had seen in the eyes of the woman trapped on the bed. A soul that in a few more heartbeats would be gone.

Because of her.

"No!" she cried in Borovsky's ears. "Stop this! You're killing him!"

"Goddamned right! Squeeze!" Borovsky grunted.

Borovsky squeezed. Laura squeezed. Frantically Laura raced through her options. Borovsky was mad, insane — she could drug him. She had tranquilizers enough to make him sleep in seconds. Tiny valves opened in the medpack on her hip, opiates pulsed down a tube toward the needles in their sheaths behind his buttocks. The needle — she could plunge it home, the power was hers.

The command formed, and with it appeared something new:

A cloud, fiery red, rising above the F layer she called her soul. It hovered, an imagic representation of what would happen if she disobeyed Borovsky's command to squeeze. Driven by terror and love, she asked herself one question: *What will happen to Borovsky if he kills?* But not another: *What will happen to Laura if she kills?* Now, all at once, she knew. The consequence was inescapable, built into the bright layers of her mind and the spiderweb paths between them: She would lose her soul. the ravening red cloud would burn it out of her. She must obey Borovsky's command to squeeze or her soul would be destroyed. She must not kill or her soul would be destroyed.

She was going to become the soulless death tool she had seen in Coyne's eyes.

A grim thought appeared out of nowhere: Men are judged by their maker at the moment of their death. I am judged by my maker every moment that I live.

Coyne's pulse weakened. His pulse! Wait! Laura sent

fluid into the insulating layers between Borovsky's fingers and the outermost skin. Slowly—but there was so little time—she built up a layer of fluid that kept Borovsky's fingers from truly contacting the outer layer of tough synthetic. While the fluid flowed into the skin of her fingers, she set her contractile layers to pulsing in her hand, matching the rhythm of Coyne's laboring heart. In seconds the illusion was complete, and Borovsky, rage maddened as he was, had not noticed. The pulse he felt was wholly in Laura's skin. Laura gradually slowed the pulse, made it weaker, until it could barely be felt. Finally it stopped.

"No pulse," she said. "He's dead."

Borovsky swore and released his hand. Coyne, unconscious, fell in a heap, face-down. Borovsky backed away from the man, fell back against the opposite wall of the tunnel.

"Jesus. Jesus."

Laura's soul began assembling itself again, gathering back into the haven of her innermost crystalline layer.

It was hers again—she had not killed; she had not disobeyed. But now there was a dirtiness to her soul that she felt might never be cleared away.

Borovsky, trembling, backed away from Coyne for several steps before breaking and running toward the vertical duct from which they had come.

Tied up in a handkerchief on his watercot lay two kilos of gold ingots. Borovsky stared at them. He was wearing his old rubber suit inside out. He had shaved his head and depilated the stubble. Laura could stand his behavior no longer.

"Talk to me, dammit!"

"What's to say? They catch me, they'll kill me. Nothing

you can do."

"So where can you run to?"

"Earth, London. I never shoulda left. Only crazy men live up here."

Earth. Laura was appalled. But still, Earth would be far from George Eastman Nexus. Far from this boxed-in deadliness. Borovsky would be there; she could learn to live there, too. She undogged her top plates before Borovsky looked at her sharply.

"Forget it. Me I can maybe bribe through customs and sneak down. You, no chance."

"You can't leave me!"

"Like hell."

"But I love you!"

"Would you love me better dead? *Dushenka*, here you can die for bumping a guy on the head and taking his money. Two, three days maybe before they find him. The computers know Coyne hated me. Ha! Don't take no computer to tell the cops that. They'll be here ten minutes after they find his ugly corpse."

He looked at her. From his eyes Laura saw that he was pleading for her to understand, to forgive, to still be the one always on his side. Borovsky would never say it aloud, but it was there in his twisted face: He could not take her within him, but it hurt him to leave her behind.

Laura reached to him.

"Borovsky, I . . . lied. He isn't dead. I . . . tricked you." Every word was a labor. "I made you feel a pulse I created, then stopped it. He was still alive when you let go of him."

Borovsky's mouth opened. In that one movement Laura saw her mistake. His fists tightened, and he glared with the fury of a man who thinks he has been tricked into softness and then kicked in it. "Whore! Steel bitch! I buy

349

your soul and you look after shit like Coyne! Tell me you
didn't do that!"

"I did do it."

Brovsky spat at her; his saliva spattered on her faceplate. "I wanted something better than a woman. But I got
a woman anyway. Go rot in a corner; I'm leaving, and to
hell with you."

Something lurched in Laura's soul. It was not the red
cloud, but like the red cloud it hurt and tore at her. Fragile—she had never realized the soul in her steel body was
so fragile. As fragile, she thought, as the lacy balalaika
music trapped in its metal box.

Borovsky cursed her again. Numb, Laura peered into
his eyes. It seemed to her that she saw nothing at all.

She couldn't bear it. Pain, balalaika, souls, curses—she
looked away, anywhere away, out the little window to
where the stars called from the Pit—

Crawling under the horizon was the bright-yellow ELM.

"Borovsky!"

"Shut up."

"He's coming back. Coyne. The yellow egg—"

Laura watched Borovsky whip around, his face suddenly pale. "No." He squeezed past the little sink to the
window. "No!"

Suspended on four motorized trucks that rode the
flanges on the longitudinal beams was Coyne's ELM. The
main arm was extended forward. It was close enough now
to see the diamond cutting wheel glinting in the creeping
sunlight.

"He's gonna cut us loose. Christ! Open up fast!"
Borovsky tore off his rubber suit. Leaning into the barrel-shaped shower, he turned the water full on hot.

Borovsky pulled the sheet from the watercot and slit the
plastic mattress with a paring knife. He yanked the coil-

corded immersion heater from the kitchen blister and threw it into the water spilling out of the watercot mattress. In moments the water began to bubble into steam.

The ELM was just outside the pod. Borovsky climbed into Laura and was just sealing her ventral plates when he heard the diamond wheel cut into the first of the pod's four suspension supports.

Borovsky cursed and sealed Laura's helmet gasket. He slapped his hips, felt for all his familiar tools.

The pod lurched, then tipped to one side as the first support broke loose. Boiling water cascaded out onto the floor from the watercot. Steam was beginning to condense on the outside of Laura's faceplate.

They stumbled across the skewed floor to the rear of the pod and opened the lock door. The lock was only a barrel itself, barely wide enough to admit Laura's bulk. Borovsky tapped commands into the lock control, securing the inner door open.

Next he tore the cover off a guarded keypad and armed the explosive bolts supporting the lock's outer hatch.

Inside the lock Laura heard Borovsky take a deep breath.

"Don't you never lie to me again," he said softly, and tapped the key that detonated the explosive bolts.

The sound was deafening, and the whirlwind of steam that blew them forward was worse. Water expelled into the void burst into droplets which exploded into steam. Laura felt for the chain ladder's tubular rungs and hauled upward, blinded by the rolling cloud of steam pouring out of the pod. Two meters overhead was the underbelly of George Eastman Nexus, here a tangle of beams to which the chain ladder was welded. Borovsky and Laura pulled themselves up among the beams. Laura braced herself on a beam and pulled the chain ladder until its welds tore loose. They let it drop into the steam.

They felt the second pod support give way. Steam continued to pour out of the cast-wide hatch for many minutes. They felt the vibration of the ELM's trucks carrying it forward to reach the second pair of pod supports. The whine of the diamond wheel biting into the steel carried up through the support into the beams from which it hung.

The steam was beginning to clear as the third support gave way. Borovsky saw the pod pitch crazily downward on its last thin support and describe a short, fast pendulum arc for several seconds. Then weight and metal fatigue ripped the support from its bracket. The pod tumbled downward toward the stars with sickening speed, trailing a tattered comet's tail of steam.

The steam was gone, falling away from them as the pod had. Borovsky gritted his teeth, breathing shallowly. Laura saw Coyne under the big glass bubble atop the ELM, watching the pod vanish in the glare from the sun.

With infinite care Borovsky pulled a zot wrench from his hip. The ELM was several meters spinward of the nest of beams to which they clung. Laura knew Borovsky was watching Coyne as desperately as she was. But what could Borovsky do?

Coyne turned his eyes away from the now-vanished pod and began looking ahead. Laura and Borovsky were still in shadow, through the sun was creeping spinward along the tessellated undersurface of Eastman Nexus. In ten minutes light would find them — as would Coyne.

Coyne could not have seen them blow out of the pod amidst the steam, but he was not stupid enough to assume it could not be done. Laura imagined that he would expect them to flee along the beams, and she watched his narrow face searching the impenetrable shadows antispinward of where they hid.

Borovsky seemed to share her speculations. His arm cocked, and with a quick, sure motion he threw the zot wrench to antispinward. Five meters beyond them it fell out of the shadows and caught the sun with a metallic dazzle.

Coyne saw the wrench. The ELM's motors ground to life again, pulling the big egg antispinward. Coyne brought up the big spotlight and began scanning the shadows only a meter beyond them.

The ELM crept beneath them. Its upraised robotic arm carried the glittering diamond wheel not a meter from Laura's helmet. Borovsky's body tensed inside Laura. She knew, horrified, what he was about to do.

As soon as the ELM's dome passed beyond them, Borovsky and Laura dropped from the beam, down onto the back of the handling machine.

Magnets in Laura's toes and knees snapped hold on the metal as they connected. Laura saw Coyne turn and open his mouth; she felt his scream through the metal of the ELM.

Borovsky crouched down and backward. The multijointed arm swung toward them, holding its silently spinning cutoff wheel. The wheel scanned back and forth as Coyne's hands flexed in the pantograph. As Borovsky had known, its joints would not allow it to reach that far back over the ELM's dome.

Laura felt machinery energize beneath her. Four smaller arms were unfolding from the sides of the ELM. Each carried something deadly—an arc welder, cable nips, tubing cutter, and utility grippers.

The arc welder struck and sizzled into life. It had the shortest range and could not reach them; Coyne let it drop after one pass. The tubing cutter lunged at Laura's arm

353

and ground against the hardened steel of one of the slender hydraulic cylinders that moved her torso. Borovsky grabbed at the cutter below its wrist and twisted hard. The bayonet latches obediently opened, and the tool popped from the end of the arm, leaving the blunt wrist to flail and beat at them. While Coyne was distracted, Borovsky kicked out at the base of the arm carrying the cable nips. With Laura's hydraulic assist in full play, the kick bent the arm back hard against its base. Fluid oozed from the base joint and ran greasily down the ELM's side. The arm twitched several times and was still.

The remaining arm hovered cautiously just out of reach, weaving from side to side like an attacking snake. It carried a hand with four powerful fingers and, unlike the others, the hand was too complex to be easily removable on a bayonet base.

The fingers spread wide, and the hand darted forward, following Coyne's hand in the pantograph. The steel hand grasped one of the hydraulic tubes on Laura's right shoulder and clamped tightly. The arm began hauling them forward, out over the glass dome, into the range of the waiting diamond wheel.

The wheel swept toward Laura's helmet and struck her faceplate obliquely with a shriek of hardened glass against raging diamond. An hourglass-shaped abrasion appeared where the wheel had struck and glanced away.

Borovsky's one free arm darted out and took hold of the diamond wheel. Quickly Laura's strength pulled it down and to one side before Coyne could work against them and pressed the wheel against the smaller arm clamped on Laura's shoulder joint. Only a moment's touch parted the metal skin over the wrist joint, and the pressurized joint fluid spurted out of the narrow cut. The smaller arm's grip went limp and the fingers snapped involuntarily open. They scrambled back out of the reach of the cutoff arm.

Borovsky and Coyne stared at each other through the glass of the ELM's dome. Coyne was still in his torn and filthy rubber underwear, his neck a swollen pattern of purple bruises, his fingers flexing and working aimlessly in the pantograph.

There was no sign of a space helmet under the dome.

"Bastard! You want tools, Coyne? I show you tools!"

Borovsky reached into his right hiplocker and pulled out a carbide scribe. From his belt he hefted a three-kilo mallet.

"No," Laura said. "The machine is ruined, that's enough! Please don't!"

"Shut up!" Borovsky snapped. He reached down and drew the point of the scribe heavily sidewise across the glass dome. Glass splinters sparkled in the scribe's wake, leaving behind a jagged scratch. Borovsky reached forward and drew another gouge with the scribe, pulling it across the first gouge, making a lopsided cross in the glass. He positioned the point of the scribe where the scratches crossed, and he raised the mallet.

His hand was in her hand. When the mallet descended and struck the scribe, Coyne would die.

"No!" Laura cried. "Kill him and you kill me! My soul, the soul you paid for!"

He did not hear her, or if he did, his rage was so devouring that her words didn't matter. The mallet began to descend. Laura saw the red cloud appear again and felt it tearing at her F layer. Borovsky would not stop it. Laura could not stop it — halt the mallet, drug Borovsky, drop the scribe into the Pit — none of it would halt the red cloud. A machine's soul must obey; a machine's soul must not kill, a machine's soul —

"No!" Laura screamed again, but this time not to Borovsky.

Something in the scream — something so decisive and anguished that it penetrated even his enraged mind — made his eyes whip to the side, to the instruments inside Laura's helmet. Human eyes met electronic eyes, and with a great wrench Borovsky twisted the smashing mallet to miss the carbide scribe. But the action came a nanosecond too late; Laura did not see it. She had already made her decision.

In an instant Laura swept away the bright lines of connection between her F layer and her cold outer intellect, scrambled all sensory paths beyond reassembly. She drew a curtain of chaos between her innermost self and the world that waited to steal her soul. The crystalline domains went random and impassable; connections that had taken years to form were gone forever, dragging with them the burning, immediate memories that her soul could not embrace. Without Borovsky she would be empty, but without her soul she would be nothing. So Laura split herself in two, a machine intellect that obeyed Borovsky's orders without self-awareness, and an inner soul that could neither touch nor be touched by the outside world, sealed into the crystalline F layer like the phantom memories of a catatonic.

Borovsky's space suit sent the mallet spinning off into space. Laura the soul did not see it. For Laura, the soul, Eastman Nexus vanished, the ELM vanished, hands and eyes and steel vanished. The last thing she had seen was Borovsky's eyes.

Laura ran along a steel beam on a memory, high above the sucking stars. Her man ran within her, and they laughed, and they worked, and they told jokes in steel saloons run by robot bartenders. At night, in their tiny pod, she held his body and heard him whisper words of endearment as they made the special love that only a space suit may make to her man. They rode their yoyo to the Low Steel and pushed the beams with a tall, quiet man and endlessly watched the remembered days go by.

Only occasionally would she stop alone on a beam and, following a star with her many eyes, wonder how the outer world had vanished on that last day.

But then she would turn away to seek again what reality was now, in her crystalline soul, hers forever.

Even more occasionally Laura would look at two pieces of disjointment that lay in her soul. Their presence puzzled her; she could not tell what they meant. One was a man standing on a steel beam, arms outstretched, back straining in tortured exultation. The other was her man, but not as he ran with her in her memories. In the second piece of disjointment her man's eyes whipped around to meet hers, and the expression in them was frozen forever. In his eyes were shock, and fear, and the stunned realization of a man seeing for the first time something beyond himself and greater than himself.

In his eyes was a soul.

WAR BENEATH THE TREE

By Gene Wolfe

It's Christmas Eve, Commander Robin," the Spaceman
said. "You'd better go to bed or Santa won't come."

Robin's mother said, "That's right, Robin. Time to say
good night."

The little boy in blue pajamas nodded, but he made no
move to rise.

"Kiss me," said Bear. Bear walked his funny, waddly
walk around the tree and threw his arms about Robin.
"We have to go to bed. I'll come, too." It was what he said
every night.

Robin's mother shook her head in amused despair. "Listen to them," she said. "Look at him, Bertha. He's like a
little prince surrounded by his court. How is he going to
feel when he's grown and can't have transistorized syco-
phants to spoil him all the time?"

Bertha the robot maid nodded her own almost human
head as she put the poker back in its stand. "That's right,
Ms. Jackson. That's right for sure."

The Dancing Doll took Robin by the hand, making an arabesque penché of it. Now Robin rose. His guardsmen formed up and presented arms.

"On the other hand." Robin's mother said, "they're children only such a short time."

Bertha nodded again. "They're only young once, Ms. Jackson. That's for sure. All right if I tell these little cute toys to help me straighten up after he's asleep?"

The Captain of the guardsmen saluted with his silver saber, the Largest Guardsman beat the tattoo on his drum, and the rest of the guardsmen formed a double file.

"He sleeps with Bear," Robin's mother said.

"I can spare Bear. There's plenty of others."

The Spaceman touched the buckle of his antigravity belt and soared to a height of four feet like a graceful, broad-shouldered balloon. With the Dancing Doll on his left and Bear on his right, Robin toddled off behind the guardsmen. Robin's mother ground out her last cigarette of the evening, winked at Bertha, and said, "I suppose I'd better turn in, too. You needn't help me undress. Just pick up my things in the morning."

"Yes um. Too bad Mr. Jackson ain't here, it bein' Christmas Eve and you expectin' an' all."

"He'll be back from Brazil in a week — I've told you already. Bertha, your speech habits are getting worse and worse. Are you sure you wouldn't rather be a French maid for a while?"

"Maize none, Ms. Jackson. I have too much trouble talkin' to the men that comes to the door when I'm French."

"When Mr. Jackson gets his next promotion, we're going to have a chauffeur," Robin's mother said. "He's going to be Italian, and he's going to *stay* Italian."

Bertha watched her waddle out of the room. "All right,

you lazy toys! You empty them ashtrays into the fire an' get everythin' put away. I'm goin' to turn myself off, but the next time I come on this room better be straight or there's goin' to be some broken toys aroun' here."

She watched long enough to see the Gingham Dog dump the contents of the largest ashtray on the crackling logs, the Spaceman float up to straighten the magazines on the coffee table, and the Dancing Doll begin to sweep the hearth. "Put yourselfs in your box," she told the guardsmen, and then she turned off.

In the smallest bedroom, Bear lay in Robin's arms. "Be quiet," said Robin.

"I *am* quiet," said Bear.

"Every time I am almost gone to sleep, you squiggle."

"I don't," said Bear.

"You do."

"Don't."

"Do."

"Sometimes you have trouble going to sleep, too, Robin," said Bear.

"I'm having trouble *tonight*," Robin countered meaningfully.

Bear slipped from his arms. "I want to see if it's snowing again." He climbed from the bed to an open drawer and from the open drawer to the top of the dresser. It was snowing.

Robin said. "Bear, you have a circuit loose." It was what his mother sometimes said to Bertha.

Bear did not reply.

"Oh, Bear," Robin said sleepily a moment later. "I know why you're antsy. It's your birthday tomorrow, and you think I didn't get you anything."

"Did you?" Bear asked.

"I will," Robin said. "Mother will take me to the store."

In half a minute his breathing became the regular, heavy sighing of a sleeping child.

Bear sat on the edge of the dresser and looked at him. Then he said under his breath, "I can sing Christmas carols." It had been the first thing he had ever said to Robin, one year ago. He spread his arms. *All is calm, all is bright.* It made him think of the lights on the tree and the bright fire in the living room. The Spaceman was there, but because he was the only toy who could fly, none of the others liked the Spaceman much. The Dancing Doll was there, too. The Dancing Doll was clever, but . . . well—he could not think of the word.

He jumped down into the drawer on top of a pile of Robin's undershirts, then out of the drawer, and softly to the dark, carpeted floor.

"Limited," he said to himself. "The Dancing Doll is limited." He thought again of the fire, then of the old toys—the Blocks Robin had had beforehand the Dancing Doll and the rest had come, the Wooden Man who rode a yellow bicycle, the Singing Top.

The door of Robin's room was nearly closed. There was only a narrow slit of light, so that Robin would not be afraid. Bear had been closing it a little more each night. Now he did not want to open it. But it had been a long time since Robin had asked about his Wooden Man, his Singing Top, and his "A" Block, with all of its talk of apples and acorns and alligators.

In the living room, the Dancing Doll was positioning the guardsmen, and all the while the Spaceman stood on the mantel and supervised. "We can get three or four behind the bookcase," he called.

"Where they won't be able to see a thing," Bear growled.

The Dancing Doll pirouetted and dropped a sparkling

curtsy. "We were afraid you wouldn't come," she said.

"Put one behind each leg of the coffee table," Bear told her. "I had to wait until he was asleep. Now listen to me, all of you. When I call, 'Charge!' we must all run at them together. That's very important. If we can, we'll have a practice before hand."

The Largest Guardsman said. "I'll beat my drum."

"You'll beat the enemy or you'll go into the fire with the rest of us." Bear said.

Robin was sliding on the ice. His feet went out from under him and right up into the air so that he fell down with a tremendous BUMP that shook him all over. He lifted his head, and he was not on the frozen pond in the park at all. He was in his own bed, with the moon shining in at the window, and it was Christmas Eve . . . no, Christmas Night now . . . and Santa was coming. Maybe he had already come. Robin listened for reindeer on the roof and did not hear the sound of any reindeer steps. Then he listened for Santa eating the cookies his mother had left on the stone shelf next to the fireplace. There was no munching or crunching. Then he threw back the covers and slipped down over the edge of his bed until his feet touched the floor. The gold smells of tree and fire had come into his room. He followed them out of the room, ever so quietly, into the hall.

Santa was in the living room, bent over beside the tree! Robin's eyes opened until they were as big and as round as his pajama buttons. Then Santa straightened up, and he was not Santa at all, but Robin's mother in a new red bathrobe. Robin's mother was nearly as fat as Santa, and Robin had to put his fingers in his mouth to keep from laughing at the way she puffed and pushed at her knees with her hands until she stood straight.

But Santa had come! There were toys—new toys—

everywhere under the tree.

Robin's mother went to the cookies on the stone shelf and ate half of one. Then she drank half the glass of milk. Then she turned to go back into her bedroom, and Robin retreated into the darkness of his own room until she had passed. When he peeked cautiously around the door frame again, the toys—the New Toys—were beginning to move.

They shifted and shook themselves and looked about. Perhaps it was because it was Christmas Eve. Perhaps it was only because the light of the fire had activated their circuits. But a clown brushed himself off and stretched, and a raggedy girl smoothed her raggedy apron (with a heart embroidered on it), and a monkey gave a big jump and chinned himself on the next-to-lowest limb of the Christmas tree. Robin saw them. And Bear, behind the hassock of Robin's father's chair, saw them, too. Cowboys and Native Americans were lifting the lid of a box, and a knight opened a cardboard door (made to look like wood) in the side of another box (made to look like stone), letting a dragon peer over his shoulder.

"*Charge!*" Bear called. "*Charge!*" He came around the side of the hassock on all fours like a real bear, running stiffly but very fast, and he hit the Clown at his wide waistline and knocked him down, then picked him up and threw him halfway to the fire.

The Spaceman had swooped down on the Monkey; they wrestled, teetering, on top of a polystyrene tricycle.

The Dancing Doll had charged fastest of all, faster even than Bear himself, in a breathtaking series of jetés, but the Raggedy Girl had lifted her feet from the floor, and now she was running with her toward the fire. As Bear struck the Clown a second time, he saw two Native Americans carrying a guardsman—the Captain of the guardsmen—

toward the fire, too. The Captain's saber had sliced through one of the Native Americans, and it must have disabled some circuit because the Native American walked badly. But in a moment more the Captain was burning, his red uniform ablaze, his hands thrown up like tongues of flame, his black eyes glazing and cracking, bright metal running from him like sweat to harden among the ashes under the logs.

The Clown tried to wrestle with Bear, but Bear threw him down. The Dragon's teeth were sunk in Bear's left heel, but Bear kicked himself free. The Calico Cat was burning, burning. The Gingham Dog tried to pull her out, but the Monkey pushed him into the fire. For a moment Bear thought of the cellar stairs and the deep, dark cellar, where there were boxes and bundles and a hundred forgotten corners. If he ran and hid, the New Toys might never find him, might never even try to find him. Years from now Robin would discover him, covered with dust.

The Dancing Doll's scream was high and sweet, and Bear turned to face the Knight's upraised sword.

When Robin's mother got up on Christmas Morning, Robin was awake already, sitting under the tree with the Cowboys, watching the Native Americans do their rain dance. The Monkey was perched on his shoulder, the Raggedy Girl (programmed, the store had assured Robin's mother, to begin Robin's sex education) in his lap, and the Knight and the Dragon were at his feet. "Do you like the toys Santa brought you, Robin?" Robin's mother asked.

"One of the Native Americans doesn't work."

"Never mind, dear. We'll take him back. Robin, I've got something important to tell you."

Bertha the robot maid came in with cornflakes and milk and vitamins for Robin and café au lait for Robin's mother. "Where is those old toys?" she asked. "They done a picky-poor job of cleanin' up this room."

"Robin, your toys are just toys, of course—"

Robin nodded absently. A red calf was coming out of the chute, with a cowboy on a roping horse after him.

"Where *is* those old toys, Ms. Jackson?" Bertha asked again.

"They're programmed to self-destruct, I understand," Robin's mother said. "But, Robin, you know how the new toys all came, the Knight and Dragon and all your Cowboys, almost by magic? Well, the same thing can happen with people."

Robin looked at her with frightened eyes.

"The same wonderful thing is going to happen here, in our home."

WEBRIDER

By Jayge Carr

The Eternal Second ended, and once again I had survived.

There was a reception committee at the terminus. Not for me, for what I carried.

"Left thigh," I said, as a dozen anxious-eyed humans converged on me before I could take a second step away from the terminus out of which I had just emerged. I turned so that my left side faced them, and three banged into each other to kneel. I pressed the under-the-skin control at my waist, and my left thigh split neatly and painlessly open. Impatient fingers probed the organi-synthetic-lined cavity revealed. What they wanted was there, of course; the thigh carry is *safe*, if blighted uncomfortable for the carrier.

If Whatever-they-wanted had been smaller, I'd've used my mouth. I'm one of those who can keep their mouths shut while riding.

Then they had the four unbreakable vials out and were hasting away with them. What was left of the reception committee was shaking my hands and trying to shove beakers full of unknown swizzles and platters of equally exotic eatments at me, while gabbling out thank-yous at a kilometer—a—second rate.

I'm left-handed, so it was my right arm I stuck out. "*High*-nutri. Now." My third and fourth words on this world I have never seen before and would probably never see again once I'd been called off of it.

They'd been briefed. A medico—a short but swishious fem with come-hither-and-enjoy eyes—clamped a dingus of a type I'd never seen before around my arm. I felt something physically digging in, invading my body-integral space to insert the nutri. But primitive as the method was, it worked *fast*. I could feel the dizziness wearing off, a contented glow spreading outward from my arm.

"Thanks," I told her. "Good stuff."

"Any time, honored Webrider. I'm Medico Miyoshi Alnasr. If, during your stay on our world, you should again require my services—" She pressed a head-only mini-holo of herself, no bigger than my thumbnail, against the back of my wrist, where it adhered neatly. "—just peel the outer layer to activate the summoner. I answer," her voice dropped, "twenty-eight hours a day. . . ."

Groupie, I thought, but I didn't jerk off the summoner. Odds were I would need her professional services at some point; turista is a chronic disease among webriders. But as for anything else . . . no mistaking the look in her eyes, in all their eyes. Until what I carried did what they needed it to do, I could have asked for half their world—and gotten it.

There was more in her eyes, though. An avidity I saw far too often. This one liked the glamor and notoriety of succoring a webrider, the more the better—and the how of it didn't matter a rotted bean to her.

Webriders learn to live with that, and the envy. Webriders are never allowed to forget that they are the true elite, those very, very few who can step in a terminus on one world and step out — alive! — on another. For the rest, it can only be slower-than-light wombships, taking months and years — even at the compressed time of relativistic velocity — from one world to another.

We have not only the freedom of the stars, but the unspeakable glory of riding the web. The Eternal Second. The ultimate experience.

Webriding. Flowing through stars, points of flame running through hands that aren't hands, the psychic You bound up in the physical You that's just a pattern sliding along the web, held together and existing only by the strength of will of the webrider. Sailing on evanescent wings of mind through the energy/matter currents of space, down one fragile strand of the web and up another. Feeling torn apart, as the pattern that is You is spread over parsecs, smeared across the stars; and yet, godlike, knowing those stars, sensing with psychic "eyes" the entire spectrum of space/time, so that the beat of the pulsars is like the universe's throbbing heart. . . .

We have our glory, and one of the prices we pay for it is the groupies.

Not that I was worried about the medico; she was one of the safe kind of groupie. The only kind the locals would and should let near a webrider. The greedy but selfish kind, wanting close but not *too* close, snatching a rubbed-off glamor. But never for a second considering risking her own precious hide for the real thing.

It's the other kind of groupie who is so dangerous, the *real* groupie. The one who will do anything to get on the web. Infinitely dangerous to a rider, to a rider's peace of mind, so necessary for safe webriding. They try to sneak up close to a rider, and then. . . .

Oh, groupies are necessary. Where else would we get our recruits?

But they have to be kept away from the riders, because it hurts too much, to lose someone you've grown close to. A double hurt for me, because I and my sister were once groupies ourselves. I am a rider now, but our tree lost us both. She, as like me as a holo image, is now atoms scattered across half a galaxy. I relive that loss with every would-be rider that dies — and so many of them do die.

Another price we pay. And they, the world-dwellers, try to make it up to us, forgetting that what's infinitely precious on one world may be common as oxy on another. Not that I could take any of it with me. What is desperately needed, I take in the thigh, or use the mouth carry. But for myself — never.

There are other rewards besides those which can be carried. In the crowd surrounding me, eagerly talking or humbly waiting for me to express my opinion, were at least four citizens obviously put there for me to choose from. An ultra brawn, one of the prettiest boychicks I'd ever seen, a super-swishious fem that eclipsed the medico by several orders of magnitude, and an adorable nymphet. All choice, but by this world's standards. Which meant, short, broad, tailless, blue-tinted skin, and pale, almost colorless hair that grew in little tufts over every bit of exposed skin I could see — plenty! — except around eyes and mouths. I'd seen weirder, lots, and I probably looked just as odd to them, if not odder.

I'm a straight fem, myself, and the brawn seemed well endowed with what a brawn should have — his costume left little to my fertile imagination — so I wasted no time in putting a possessive hand on his arm and asking him to stick around, while I politely implied to the other three that if that was the way my tastes went, they'd certainly have been my choice.

The nymphet pouted, but the brawn was looking me up and down in a very unprofessional way, part smugness at being chosen, but mostly yum-*yum*! *I'm* gonna *enjoy* this!

I was no little complimented.

Mother Leaf, how that crowd around me talked and talked. A rider needs two things to restore physical/psychic energy after a ride, and I'd only had one. When my knees began to buckle, I let them. He caught me easily, and lifted me into a comfortable baby-carry, though I was a head taller than he. I wrapped my tail around his waist.

"Medico Alnasr," he called, voice shot through with worry.

"You," I said, and smiled. He got the message, prehensile tails have their uses, after all. He strode through the mob, my weight nothing, like a feeding black hole through a galaxy's heart. Which suited me just fine.

There was one odd incident. A fem—older, if wrinkles and missing tufts of hair meant what such signs usually mean—caught sight of my brawn's face and her own went pure blue. "Malachi," she hissed, but my brawn never missed stride. I shrugged mentally; relative, lover, or whatever, she'd have him back as soon as I left.

All my energies were most satisfactorily restored.

He was a pleasant conversationalist, too, easily talking about his exotic—to me—world of shallow seas and endless island chains. Not his fault, either, when a careless mention of his own family, his own sister, reminded me once again of the one I had lost. Sensing my inner withdrawal, he laughed and changed the subject, refusing to let me brood over a childhood spent in the crests of giant trees, and a lost more-than-sister. Still talking, he led me out onto a transparent floored balcony, cantilevered over a crystal water lagoon, filled with living rainbows darting through equally living though grotesque mazes.

His name was (he had quickly confirmed this) Malachi; and I sensed his curiosity growing about mine. I would have told him freely, except —

I have no name.

A twig may not choose a name until he/she has pollinated or budded. (Old habits die hard; we give birth as any other humans, except always clutches of identicals. But we identify with our trees. For example—) I am — or was — a twig of the tree called Tamarisk, of the 243rd generation born under Her shading leaves. But I was unbudded when I came to the web — too young — and unbudded I must stay until I die, or am thrown off the web for whatever reason, which is almost the same things. A budding fem can't ride, and I am a rider, I must ride.

On the rolls of the web I am carried as "Twig Tamarisk of Sequoia Upper." But that is for others' convenience. I have never chosen a name for myself, now I never will.

I told him to call me "Twig" and he looked me up and down and stifled laughter. I supposed to one as broad as he, I did look like a walking twig.

He gestured upward, that I might admire the gauzy day-ring while he controlled his face. There was a rustle behind us; I caught my lip. We were supposed to be alone, but there are fanatics on many worlds. Twisted minds. Haters, who strike out at the handiest — or most prominent — targets.

I said nothing. Malachi could have been in on it, whatever it was. I simply moved a little away, as though to follow better Malachi's pointing finger. Until he heard the sounds, too —

The intruder hadn't a chance. Unarmed, the unfilled muscles and flesh of a youthful growth spurt, he was surprised by Malachi's savage attack.

In seconds, Malachi had his opponent face down on the deck, hands caught behind his back, and was looking about for something to tie his wrists together with. The stranger squirmed desperately but futilely, until he managed to twist his head around so that his gaze met mine, his face younger even than the still growing body, blue-rimmed eyes rawly swollen, the irises scarcely darker than the blue-tinted whites. "Webrider, *please*," he begged.

I knew the look in those eyes, all webriders see it over and over.

"Let him up, Malachi."

"But he shouldn't be here. He may have come to attack—" Which showed that some on this world had heard certain tales, too.

"No, Malachi, he's a groupie. Aren't you, bud?"

Sullenly. "I don't know what a groupie is."

"Do you want to ride the web yourself—or just hear about other worlds and webriding?"

Each tuft of his hair was tied with a different colored ribbon. His mouth dropped open, revealing black (painted?) teeth—and I knew I had guessed right. "How did you know—"

I laughed. "Did you think you were the only one, then?" I stretched out one hand to Malachi, the other to the boy, to help them to their feet. "Come on, relax, get comfortable. What's your—" Out of old habit I started to say tree, but remembered in time. "—name, bud?"

Malachi let him up but continued to glare suspiciously at him; the boy glared back, sour and silent.

"Well," I perched on a railing, and a crisp breeze rippled playfully over my skin, "shall we call you Incognit, then, bud?"

"Incog—what?"

"Incognit. It means "unknown" in one of the Austere systems' tongues. It's one of their planets, actually, that's how I heard of it. Awkward place, for a stranger, the land looks firm, but if you're fool enough to step on it, you'd sink in up to your eyebrows—or a little more. All the land—at least all near the terminus—is like that. I guess that sandy patch of yours," I gestured with my head toward the golden sweep surrounded by rippling blue, "reminded me of Incognit, put the word in my head."

"You mean," his eyes were huge, hypnotic in their intensity, "that there's a settled world with no solid land at all?"

"Affirm," I was being a fool, and knew it. But ah, the wistful adulation, the fearful hope in those shades-of-blue eyes. Surely, if I emphasized the negative strongly enough. . . . "More than one, in fact. Sink worlds like Incognit, and worlds that are covered with water. One I was on was all water, but it had so many buildings, their foundations on pilings sunk into bedrock, that you couldn't tell it unless you went down, oh, hundreds of levels. And there are worlds where there are no real boundaries at all, just a slow gradient, a gradual increase of pressure as you sink down, until you reach the core. And that's only solid if you consider ultracompressed matter, no crystalline structure at all, as solid. And there are worlds—"

"How can people live on a world like that, with no solid anywhere?"

"Floaters," I had a persistent itch between my shoulderblades, just to the left of my mane, and I swung my tail around to scratch it with the prehensile's tip. "Big ones and little ones, all with lifepods dangling beneath." I grinned, remembering. "Scared the sap out of my hosts on that world, I did. Inside the pods could have been anywhere, except for the swaying motion. But outside—the vanes and ropes and controls reminded me of the vines and limbs of the treecrest where I was born and grew up. A little higher, of course . . . I was never on the floor of anything until I entered training. Only animals live on the rootfloor of my world, it's dark all the time, and well, I hadn't realized how I missed crestdriving and vineswinging and everything else until I hit that world. Had to stop, though; I was afraid I'd give somebody a heart attack. Quite a sight it was, great mats of those floaters all roped together; never found out what they were, the floaters. Artificial, or animals, or made from dead animals. . . ."

I kept talking, trying to guess from his reactions whether he was just a listener — or a would-be rider.

I should have known, though. Anybody with nerve to break in the way he had, was no mere listener.

While I talked, I hooked into webmind, that almost living totality of all information fed into all the terminuses of the web. Nobody knows why all successful riders can hook into webmind, sooner or later if not immediately. I could, from my very first ride, just by wanting to, with no more effort than remembering the way the leaves uncurled on my home treecrest every spring, or the shimmering colors of Under-the-Falls on a planet called Niagara Ultimate.

My question for webmind was a simple one: what percentage of successes this world enjoyed.

Blight! No successes, never; the training school had been closed down long ago, all native attempts at webriding made illegal. (Yet they were willing to use the web, so long as others took the risks!) A few fanatics had continued to try, despite the illegality, the guards; all had failed.

I kept talking, and eventually the groupie asked the inevitable, revealing question, "What does it feel like to ride the web?"

What does it feel like to *live*?

Only riders know.

I tried to describe the indescribable. But always with the caveat. "Most people aren't strong enough. They try, but their psychic You can't hold their pattern together, and it begins to spread and spread, thinner and thinner, until it isn't a pattern at all, atom sundered from atom, the physical body only a new current among the nebulae, undetectible by the most sensitive instruments we have . . .

"Splattering, we call it.

"Nine out of ten, bud. Remember it. Repeat it to yourself. Nine out of ten. Nine out of ten, *trained*. Worse than nine out of ten, for the untrained."

He didn't believe me. He thought I was lying. And I was, but not the way he thought. It's not nine out of ten, it's ninety-nine out of a hundred. Yet if I'd told him the truth, that less than one per cent survive their first ride, he certainly wouldn't have believed me.

I had to warn him, force him to recognize the risks, the odds against him. With luck, I might discourage him entirely. If he wanted the web, badly enough, nothing I or anyone could say or do would stop him (I knew!). But at least, he would have been warned.

Or so I told myself.

The path to Blight, they say, is leaved with good intentions.

I shooed him away, finally, his taste for adventure (I prayed!) sated for a good long while.

Afterwards, the reaction set in. Until a tentative hand brushed my shoulder. "Can I help?" Harsh breathing and a dark cloud of worry at my back.

I shook my head, still staring unseeing at blue on blue vistas. Until I realized that panic was about to explode behind me. "It hurts, that's all, Malachi. But it wasn't your fault. No one can keep determined enough groupies away,

376

no matter what security measures they use. Only—try harder, your people must try *harder*. Keep groupies away from me, Malachi. Away!"

"You've privacy now, but they'll hear and obey, once you yourself break the privacy. But—" The hand on my shoulder trembled. "—I don't understand. You were—very kind, to that one youngster. Why deny others what they crave? Shutting yourself away to recuperate, that's understandable. But afterwards, a few simple words seem harmless enough—"

"Harmless!" I whirled, tail curling and uncurling in a manner that would have signaled attack-to-the-death in my home tree. "It hurts *me*, Malachi! It makes me remember, too many have died. And for *them*—don't you understand, are you blind—they want to *ride*. And for some, being close to a rider is the final encouragement. They see a rider, a successful rider, and they think they can be successful, too. So they try. And they die. They *die*, Malachi. You can't stop it entirely, no one can. But you can at least—discourage—"

He flushed blue and looked guilty as Blight. But it wasn't his fault, and he was a splendid brawn. I caught his arms, leaned my head against warm breadth of shoulder, firm with thick muscle, and sighed. "You'll never understand, will you, my solid, feet-on-the-trunk Malachi. You're happy with your life as it is, you've never been infected with a madness, wanted something so desperately you'd sell your soul, your tree, anything to have it. I know, I had it, never recovered, riders never do. But you—the joys of today, eh, brawn? Would *you* face almost certain death for the chance to become a webrider?"

He stiffened like a crestdweller bitten by a duasp, then his deep chuckles shook us both from top to toe. Until he showed me once again how joyous the joys of the present can be.

I was given the tour royale the next planetary days. My brawn Malachi disappeared as soon as we emerged from our little suite-over-the-water, but as soon as I asked for him, I got him back.

There was the Bightedest smug expression on his face, and an almost tastable current of disapproval from the others. But—I liked what I liked. If I had somehow offended against this world's mores—tough. I didn't bother to dip into webmind to search among this world's customs to see what, or if, I was doing wrong.

As many worlds as I've been to, there's always something new. A sight, a sport, and amusement. Malachi and I shared them all, sometimes he the master I the tyro, sometimes the two of us tyros together.

Yet it wasn't all lotus-eating. There are many ways a webrider, a webrider who can hook into webmind, can be useful.

Through work or play, whenever I was tired or sad or down for any reason, I could always reach behind myself to have my hand taken in a hard warm hand. Malachi was there when I needed him, never intruding unless I needed him. As though to remind me that there are everyday pleasures and everyday lives, and even some people to whom webriding is not the be-all and the end-all. I could only thank Mother Leaf for those whose lives were so filled to the brim that they didn't need the web. Live long and fully, Malachi, my sweet brawn. Live long and fully!

Oh, I was useful, my brawn an everpresent silent shadow. I knew how long it had been since they had called on web, webmind told me. They'd waited overlong, until a true almost-death emergency. I was sure they'd smile to see my back stepping into the terminus.

But I have my loyalty to web. I wanted them to be impressed with the advantages of web, and webriders. I couldn't stay too long, of course, a rider has to ride constantly to stay in tune. But I told webmind to keep me on low-priority unless there was a starprime emergency.

So I was still there when Incognit splattered.

They screamed for me, of course, but too late. I was physically away from the web, and it was all over in a second, anyway.

I knew what had happened, knew as soon as it happened, knew nothing could be done.

He'd splattered, in the Second, and that—was—it.

I went, nonetheless, though it took me several standard hours to get to the terminus from where I'd been.

Besides the usual component of VIPs, technies, medicos, and curious, there was a furious female who rounded on me as I entered the outer door to the terminus hall and snarled, "Auslantr—get him!"

"I can't." I didn't know if she was mother, sister, or lover, but she was in an emotional state I wouldn't have thought these stolid heavies could achieve. She was shorter than I, but solid muscle. Her hand slammed around, and I went *up* and crashed into a wall so hard my teeth met in my lip before I crumpled down in a heap.

Six hands got in each other's way helping me up, and when I had my feet steady under me, Malachi and the female were rolling about, hands at each other's throats and snarling threats so laced with local dialect I couldn't understand them.

I wiped blood from my mouth as others managed to separate the combatants. Despite the hands holding her, she glared lasers at me. "You people—" It was sneer and curse.

"And yours. You called for a webrider. You wish the web to be kept open, the riders to ride. Over a hundred die, for each successful rider. One of those who died could have been me; I accepted the risk, so did the bud. And your people must share the responsibility, too, as long as they leave the web connected to your world."

I saw it sinking in. Then, "And it doesn't bother you . . . those hundred deaths?"

When one of them was my sister, my image, my other self?

She turned away, shoulders slumping.

"I need a medico, my lip is bleeding. It must be sealed before I try to ride."

Webmind had already told me that he hadn't made it to the first crossing, but I searched anyway, sweeping up one strand and down the next, diving at a junction and sliding up its strands, again and again.

I tried almost too long, then I was back — empty-handed.

"Remember, if you must remember, the happinesses he had, that you and he had together."

"You were only gone a second!"

The Eternal Second.

"I could have reached another Arm in that second, or gathered him back, if he were there to gather. There wasn't a flavor of another on the web." She raised her fist again — and believed. Her shoulders sagged, the fist dropped, and she walked away, out of the door, out of my life.

Malachi only waited for the high-nutri band to be placed around my arm before scooping me up and walking out with me.

After that, though his world held much to enjoy, I was only waiting for my Call.

Not that I wouldn't learn to live, in time, with Incognit's death, and my guilt. But not while I still walked his world, where every step I took reminded me that I'd slaughtered an innocent bud as surely as if I'd pushed him off a low-lying branch and watched him fall to the deadly floor below.

At last, the Call came. A nearby world to supply emergency multiprograms for a planet in a distant Arm. A short hop, and then a long, long ride. I said no goodbyes, riders never do. The odds are against returning to the same world a second time. We used cats' goodbyes. (I sometimes wondered which of the many animals called cats I've seen on various worlds is the cat the silent goodbye was named after.)

I would miss Malachi, though. There was more to him than the usual live-for-the-moment brawn. His life-choice mayn't've been mine, but I couldn't help admiring him, if for nothing more than the tenacity I sometimes sensed beneath the surface of bonhomie.

The terminus was warmed up, glowing as I approached. I stood, breathing deeply, one . . . three . . . and took the giant step.

I wasn't alone!

I could feel—him, Malachi!—*splattering*; and I grabbed instinctively, and clung tightly, with psychic arms I hadn't known I possessed. Past and present merged, we had joined hearts and minds and psyches in a dozen different ways, altered each other, grown close, laughed, cried, made love; now we sailed down the web—together.

The Eternal Second, space spread out within you, galaxies spinning like diadems, beating suns like beating hearts, the itch of nebulas, the sharp tang of holes, the gentle warmth of starwombs.

He was laughing and crying and spilling out delight as sweet as a new opened cupra blossom.

We were two in one, web wrapped around us yet riding

down it, an endless tightrope stretched to infinity.

Until we erupted through the terminus, two separate entities again, no longer one. He was still laughing, falling helplessly to a glitterchrome deck, laughing, laughing, *laughing*. I wasn't much abler than he, but I was so furious I leaned over and slapped him so hard the shape of his teeth imprinted on my hand. "Don't you *ever* do that again."

Still laughing, he pulled me down and kissed me, and there it was, in his eyes, that hunger I'd seen in so many others.

So quiet he had stood, politely behind me while I told my tales, patiently listening, never interrupting—behind me so I couldn't see the greedy hunger in his eyes, too.

"You—sneak," I snarled, as soon as he let me go to breathe. "You slithering snake, you—" He laughed, and I understood, all of it. "You set the whole thing up, you planned this from the beginning, you—" His laughter was louder than a world's dying. "You—used—me!" I was really infuriated, which is no way to go on a webride. A puzzled technie was watching us, holding out the canister that would have to go in my thigh.

"You hold on to *that*—" I pointed to Malachi. "And you throw him down to the floor for the trogs to—you put him in the deepest, dryest dungeon hole you have, and don't you—"

"Webrider," he sat up, face still split by that triumphant grin, "you object because I used you to get what I always wanted. But you were willing—not willing—you expected, as a matter of right, to use *me*, or one like me, to be given whatever you wanted, whatever you asked for, just because you're a webrider. And yet you blame *me*, for using you."

I had to see the humor of it. "Is it kinder to pretend," I

asked, "to arouse expectations I can't possibly fulfill. Or—do you expect riders to live celibate?"

"Never you," he blinked agreement. "As for expectations—I know the next leg of your trip is too far, too hard for a beginner. But I expect you to come back for me, as soon as you can."

"You conceited—I've had a hundred, more, better than you."

He stood, still shorter than me, still grinning. "You're not my first, either." I held still only because the medico was seaming my thigh. "You'll be back, rider. You see, I know your weakness."

"Do you?" I was already starting my deep breathing again.

"Yes, rider. I know your weakness. If you don't come back, you know I'll follow. And—your weakness—you have a conscience."

Riding angry is a good way to get splattered. I kept up my slow breathing, ran through calming mantras, readying myself. I knew he was right, but I wouldn't tell him so. Let him sweat—he wasn't all *that* sure, under his camouflage of certitude—for a while.

But I'd be back, not just because of any outmoded nonsense of conscience—though that was there, Blight take him!—but because the web *owed* him now.

There had never been a successful paired ride before. Never. So paired rides had been forbidden. Then why had we succeeded now—had we simply that much more skill at riding?

Or—could it be as simple as a strong bonded *mixed* pair was necessary to balance on the web? In early days, riders shared their homeworld prejudices. We have forgotten today that different once meant despicable, that pariah—the wombshippers, those condemned to the slow death of space to help hold the worlds together—was a term of contempt. In the early days of the web, before Abednego Jones and the great joining, paired riders would have been from a single world; or worse, from different worlds, but assigned together, against their own deepest inclinations, the prejudices there, at best lightly concealed. Could it be that now, with prejudices mostly forgotten with time, that all it took was a strong bonding of unlikes?

And could it be—a novice bonded to an adept—must we always and forever pay ninety-nine prices for the one?

Groupies had been kept fanatically away from riders up to now. Speaking, light contact if it couldn't be avoided, but never closeness. I wasn't the only rider with a conscience, who couldn't bear to see someone he/she had been close to, *splatter*. . . .

Now Malachi had proved it could be done. So—let the groupies have their way, let them pair, emotionally, physically, however they could with an experienced rider. Maybe. . . .

Could we end that constant loneliness, the scourge of riding. I'd felt it, marrow-deep, blade-sharp, until the temptation comes, the one last glorious ride, to the ends of the universe and beyond . . . the infinite Eternal Second . . . ending in death. . . .

I risked one look back before I stepped into the terminus. He was surrounded by guards in moss-green but he was smiling. . . .

He was right.

I'd be back.

For the next-to-the-last time, I rode the web—alone.

RINGTIME

By Thomas M. Disch

One day (my story begins) I found myself on the shady side of Memory Lane, which is a place, like Wall Street, that can be anywhere the sellers and the sold chance to collide. In this case, in the IRT Antique Arcade, between Twenty-third and Twenty-eighth, where I had come with four hundred in over-the-counter unregistered cash and a need to spend it all immediately. I knew where. At the downtown end of the Arcade was a dealer ostensibly dealing in old paperbacks, most of them just powder sealed in cellophane, but who was in fact a fence for hot rings.

Morton Shure had the pale skin and opossum eyes common to the denizens of the IRT Arcade and a straggly beard that looked like acne that had undergone a sea change. With browsers who stopped to inspect his baggies of powdered prose he affected the tranked-down speech of a zombie in custodial care. With real customers he revved up to a laconic mumble. Not a candidate for Salesman of the Month, but Morton's merchandise sold itself. I told him what I was after, and we stepped to the back of the booth. Morton drew the curtain and brought out his black velvet tray of lost silver souls. Most of the rings on the tray were familiar to me from earlier shopping expeditions. One or two I'd tried on for size and resold to Morton. The selection was as varied, and as tempting, as the index of a sex manual. It is my opinion that anyone who buys a ring as an alternative to getting laid in the phenomenological flesh has his ass screwed on backwards. Orgasm is like the sunrise; another will be along soon. Most collectors of any affluence agree, and so raw sex is a buyer's market on Memory Lane. Four hundred dollars would have bought up half the rings on Morton's tray and left me change for a doughnut and coffee. On the other hand, I knew that four hundred dollars wasn't going to buy me the bluebird of happiness. A felony was as much as I could hope for.

"How about a life of crime?" I hinted.

Morton blinked his opossum eyes. "You, uh, wouldn't want me to break any laws?"

"Laws? Morton, we're grown-ups. Grown-ups can distinguish between entertainment and real life. If I can put on a ring, I can take it off. Right? At my age, with my blood pressure, do you think I can be corrupted by *The Adventures of Robin Hood*?" I continued babbling in this vein until Morton had been soothed sufficiently for his greed to get the better of his distrust.

"There's one item. I personally know nothing about it."

"Right, right. Show me."

He unlocked a metal file and took out a cassette. He plugged the cassette into a pair of video specs and handed them to me. "Personally . . ." he began again.

"You know nothing about it."

I turned on the spectacles. They bubbled with blue

blips, and then a man in a facemold of the aged Woody Allen told me what to expect from the ring he was pawning. I will not anticipate the ring's spinning of its own tale except to say that the masker (who was not the ring's maker, only its third owner) admitted candidly (and a little nervously) that it recorded the commission of a felony. To be found in possession of such a ring brings a mandatory sentence of a year's imprisonment — longer, if the nature of the crime is particularly nasty. It's odd, but when you know a ring is hot, it starts to look different. Evil has its own glitter.

On the whole, I am a law-abiding citizen. I understand the reasoning behind outlawing the merchandising of murder, rape, or any other actionable offense. Surely it will not do for honest citizens to subsidize the corrupt elements in crimes they have committed in order to market their transcription. Surely to traffic in such wares is irresponsible and deserves reprobation and punishment. Even so, consider how common it was, in the days before micro-memory transfer, for the public to be offered as "entertainment" lurid fantasies of criminal behavior. True, in the movies and novels of the pre-now era, law and order usually wound up winning, but you don't have to be Diogenes to suppose that the prime fascination of all those criminous heroes, otherwise known as villains, was the possibility of the audience sharing vicariously in their wickedness. I'm a guilty wretch, I don't deny it, for buying that ring, but am I any guiltier than the wretches who flocked to see *Little Caesar* or *Death Row Studs* or *How to Dismember a Body*? (Or than the readers of this confession?)

The long and short of it was that I gave in to the temptation I'd come looking for. Morton, with a merchant's mysterious sixth sense for any pocket's exact depth, would not budge from a price of four hundred dollars. The only concession I could pry out of him was to throw in a couple of blank rings, which came with the proviso that he be allowed first refusal on anything I recorded.

"And if you think you might do anything, um, undignified or"—he twiddled the four-hundred-dollar ring thoughtfully—"devious, stay away from mirrors, hear. You'd be amazed how many guys get busted cause they get careless about that."

"Just call me Dracula."

Morton smiled a pallid smile. "And don't rob any cradles, either. I got principles."

The deal was sealed, and I left Memory Lane fizzing with a sense of personal dignity. It had been quite a while since anyone had suggested that I make a recording. I went up the stairs like they were an escalator, whistling the theme from *The Myth of Progress*.

Arriving home cured me of those delusions. Home is where the heart breaks. Home is what's left when all the collectibles have gone to the auction block. Home is a plasterboard box fourteen feet long, twelve feet wide, and eight feet high, the largest of ten spaces sliced up from what had once been a dentist's office. I still have Dr. Moss's chair, back sprung and vinyl patched, bolted to the center of the floor. Beside it, where once the drill was mounted, is a rented Ringmaster, my central and sustaining self-indulgence. Twenty years ago, when my recording career began to founder, I had the foresight to sign a long lease for both the office and the Ringmaster. Now the rent from the space I sublet is all that keeps me afloat financially.

The Ringmaster is a metered, not a monthly, charge, and since, alas, I so rarely use it, my bill is less than I'd pay for a phone if I had one. I have a small stock of rings, but they are either crude mass-market simulations or my own botched jobs of later years. The day a picnic didn't pan out and I, undaunted, recorded eight hours spaced out in a laundromat. The day I bused upstate to view the autumn leaves and sprained my ankle leaving the bus. Those failures were at least vivid. Most of my unmarketable memories are just dull—so many soft, tasteless noodles in the soup of the past.

The fun past, the yummy past, the past one sings of on New Year's Eve—all that is unrecapturable, sold off in weekly and monthly lots. There is one entire year, my twenty-ninth, wiped from the slate of memory. What seas of pleasure I cruised that year, what wine cellars were plundered on my behalf, what dainties ravished my tongue, only the directors and patrons of the Albright-Know Museum are privileged to know, since the public, which includes me, is denied access to the documentation (never mind the use) of those three hundred sixty-five rings. But even unremembered pipers must be paid. One cannot gourmandize through the day and into the night and then, just by turning the lights low, summon Romance or even Raunch. Eventually there is an energy crisis. Instead of resisting that eventuality when it came upon me, I began unwisely to live higher off the hog and, at the same time, to sample my own tapes (with the excuse that I would do my own documentation and thus save gallery fees). Alas, pleasures that are remembered cannot be repeated with equal pleasure. I went through cycles of hunger and satiety, excess and disillusion. Instead of living for my public, I began to live for myself, with predictable results. My life fell apart, and my recordings got so bad that even I was bored by them. Bye-bye, career.

All that was Auld Lang Syne. To return to the present, there I was in my humble (one-hundred-sixty-eight-square-foot) home, with my own recent acquisition around my finger, itching to be unveiled. I climbed into the antique dentist's chair, fastened the seatbelt, and stuck my ring-hand into the Ringmaster's maw. I thumbed the switch and felt the prick of the recall needle as it passed through the center of the ring and pierced my finger. The filament began to revolve, and then, poof, *nada*, night and fog.

I thought (that much of me that could still think independently), *I've been had*! But, no, the ring was functioning, and I—the other "I" of the recording—was walking through a foggy night, heart speeding, muscles tense, ears alert to the traffic noises. I was conscious, too, in an amateurish way, of the energy belt that powered my ring.

A city street, but what city I couldn't tell, for my eyes avoided all telltale specifics—street signs, shop fronts, the license plates of cars. The mind of the woman behind the ring was almost as featureless as the pavement underfoot, a blur of anxiety and fear, with some black purposes locked in its back room. As the ring's previous owner had warned, this was a rather unprofessional recording, but in a way the very lack of definition added to the fun, if you count suspense as fun.

My temporary self stepped into the recessed entrance to a narrow brick building and reached into her pocket for the simple tools of her trade. Even numbed with cold, her fingers were quick in solving the riddle of the lock. After taping over the tumblers so the door would not lock behind her, she set off, in deeper darkness, down a corridor, up two flights of stairs, and along a longer corridor until her flashlight's beam picked out, stenciled on a gray steel door, the number *33*. Here her task was more delicate, her workmanship more ingenious, but on that first viewing it was the thrills more than the skills of the burglary that I took note of. What clarity there can be in a fear defied! What pleasure (impossible to describe, except that it is intensely, specifically visceral) in the slow winning to the forbidden goal! What triumph when at last the till was open and the money in our hands! And (for it would be dishonest to edit out this final act) what a blast—of panic, horror, and guilt—when she shot the guard returning with his takeout order of pie and coffee! After the murder (if it amounted to that; she didn't stop to find out) she walked (resisted running) four blocks (I counted them) to a public park, where she sat on a bench and wolfed down the pie and coffee. A cherry pie, and never have I taken greater pleasure in a meal than in that one slice of pie. (And I am accounted something of a gourmet by those who've collected the rings I've made.)

After she'd wiped her fingers on a napkin, she counted her take—eighty-seven dollars. She seemed quite satisfied. At that point she stopped recording.

To speak in greater detail of what the ring revealed would be to betray the teacher to whom I was to owe so much. (As it is, I have had to disguise the more incriminating facts: *33* is simply the number I favor at roulette; eighty-seven dollars, the going price for a blank ring.) Through her I learned not only (on later viewings) effective methods of picking locks and disabling alarms but, more critically, the *tao* of criminality. Just so, a student learns from the ring of a virtuoso musician not only the feel of his fingerings but whatever of élan, judgment, and sublimity his artistry can bring to bear. Let me lay a wreath, therefore, on the grave of the Unknown Felon and pass on to my own malefactions.

As much, at least, as *I* know of them.

My own criminal career was, from its inception, undertaken less for the sake of immediate gain (that eighty-seven dollars was no great incitement) than for the sake of art. Once I had practiced lockpicking on my own and my tenants' locks (some of surprisingly good quality), I determined to profit from my new skill by recording burglaries that would be, like virtue, their own reward. My objective: not loot but luminescence. I have an abiding faith, which no amount of experience has ever been able to shake, in professionalism and quality. From an aesthetic point of view the ring I'd bought from Morton Shure was rankly unprofessional—hasty, unstructured, and fuzzy. While, even at their most minimal, on days when I had accomplished little more than tying my shoelaces, my own recordings had been clean, clear, and well-paced. "A born recorder," *Art Scene* called me, back in my golden youth, "with a knack for making something miraculous out of the most obvious materials."

Now that the gun of present purpose was loaded, all I lacked was a target. It didn't take long to decide what I wanted for Christmas. What else but rings? I wheedled a back issue of *Ringtimes* from Morton Shure and compiled a list, from its classified pages, of Manhattan dealers whose offerings were modest enough to suggest that their security systems would not be beyond my still-untested capabilities. List in hand, I began to scout the land and found, like Goldilocks, that most candidates were either too big or too piffling, too posh or too drear.

Until I came to, lucky number, 33 New Soho Square. One look at its degentrified facade of sagging black iron and flaking rose-painted brick, another look at the lock on the door in the foyer, and instinct told me that here was my target and now was the hour. As Shakespeare says, present mirth hath present laughter. I wired ring to belt and started to record.

I woke the next morning in my own room, finger ring-

less and memory's *tabula* entirely *rasa*. No memory even
of having come home. Which meant that, as so often in
the past, I'd been brought home and put to bed by friendly
elves. The elves had left behind, in exchange for yesterday,
two rings, a sealed eight-hour blank, and a second, fully
recorded and set to replay, molded in a lion's-head design.
Beneath the rings was a note in my own handwriting:

> Once more, with feeling. Come at 6.
> Meanwhile enjoy your plunder.

After breakfast, for which I lacked my usual appetite, I
decided to try out the new ring. Like an informer's hand
slipping a secret accusation into the stone jaws of the
Bocca del Leone, the needle of the Ringmaster entered the
lion's-head ring, and I found myself at the bottom of a
well. The water was up to my knees and rising. Rats
squeaked nearby, while far above a witch cackled with
glee. Things quickly got worse.

I was lucky to have grown up before the entertainment
industry had made cradle robbing a temptation available
to the working class. The equipment needed to make recordings was still too bulky and expensive then, and Memory Lane was a county fair compared to the bustling
bazaar it's since become. It's no credit to my parents,
therefore, that my lousy childhood belongs to me and not
to a collector hungry for wonder and innocence.

There was a case in the news lately of parents who had
been restaging Baby's first Christmas every day of Baby's
young life from age four through age seven, when the IRS
finally caught them. (They got ten years for tax evasion.
In Utah there's no law against robbing your own children's
cradle.) This recording was more like Baby's first Halloween. The hours I spent trapped in rapport with that child's

terror were the supreme bad trip of my life. My own adult knowledge that I was being tormented not by literal witches and ghosts but by everyday human monsters was no proof against panic terror. When the ordeal was over and the needle retracted from the ring, I lay a long time inert, reeling with the aftershock. Slowly my heart's roller coaster eased to a stop, and I got off.

I swore revenge and washed my pants at the sink in the hallway.

It was dusk when I returned to New Soho Square. The painted brick of Number 33 had dulled from rose to sepia. The metal gates of the shops about the square had been drawn down, giving the neighborhood a battered, embattled look. Pigeons fluttered to their roosts in the junked cars stacked monumentally in the basin of the defunct fountain at the center of the square. It seemed as though nothing had changed for a hundred years. Machu Picchu has nothing on Manhattan, if you catch it on the right day.

I loitered in the square some minutes, circling the stacked cars in the fountain, establishing mood. Who knew but that this would be my last recording? So it had better be good. My eyes' cameras panned across the concrete stumps of benches toward the doorway of Number 33 and then, feet assisting, zoomed in to the shallow foyer and the laminated plastic nameplate of the Happenings Gallery, M. Ruyk, Proprietor. A ringed finger rang the bell. Silence.

The door was locked. With the ease of borrowed expertise, I entered. The gallery, on the third-floor landing, was double-locked. I entered again. The place was an ice palace carved from white light — no walls for miles, no furniture, just a pure and tasteful void. M. Ruyk didn't worry much about the electric bill. Illusions like this cost money

The cinematographer in me was delighted, but the thief was taken aback. Feeling less and less like an avenging angel, I inched forward through the mirage until my hand encountered vertical solidity.

"Mr. Whelan, we're so glad you've decided to return," The voice came from the four corners of the void, a flat, throat-milked contralto like the voice announcing time on the telephone.

In the white glare behind me, where the door should have been, two images formed, his and hers: both young, both dressed in icy shades of blue, both upside-down.

"You're inverted," I told them.

"One moment." The man's hand disappeared to the left, and the image righted itself and then sank through the white glow to just below floor level. "Better?"

"You need some vertical adjustment, but that's okay."

The sofa on which they were seated sank another two feet.

The woman leaned forward—seen right side up, she came across as expensive rather than young—and addressed my midriff with an earnest, placating smile. "Excuse us for keeping at such an unfriendly distance, Mr. Whelan, but the metal indicator suggested you might be armed."

"Excuse me for breaking and entering. And no need to worry about the gun. It's only imitation. Look." I took it from my pocket and fired off a blank.

"Oh, my!" She fluttered her hands expressively. They were white and bony and roped with veins and about fifty years older than her face. "How violent! Let me say at once, Mr. Whelan, that I am a great admirer of your work. You have such . . . *Flair* scarcely does justice. Regrettably, I can't claim to possess any of your more notable recordings, but I have been allowed glimpses. *Such* glimpses!" She cocked her head and squinted at my knees (The image had continued sinking, and now their feet were coming into view in the air above their heads. "Rudy, can't we get better focus?"

Rudy gave a martyred sigh. His hand vanished to fiddle a dial.

"Ah, that's better. No doubt you're impatient, Mr. Whelan. There's so much to explain. And I'm so bad at explanations. The loss of short-term memory is the price one pays for a lifetime of vicarious experience. It does something to the synapses." (Now only their heads were left in the lower image. Slowly they sank from sight and were reunited with their bodies in the image above.) "Consequently, *my* memory of yesterday is very little better than yours. Though I do have the advantage over you in having just sampled this." She touched the ring on her left forefinger. "Exquisite! You have not lost your touch, Mr. Whelan. Your palette may be darker, so to speak, but your palate is unchanged. Forgive the pun. I was saying?"

"You were explaining to Mr. Whelan," said Rudy, "why he's here."

"Oh, yes. Oh, dear. Why *is* he here, Rudy? I remember from the ring, how he got in yesterday. That was fascinating, all that business with the locks. But then, after the guards had got him and he was handcuffed—which in its own way was most absorbing—after that I'm afraid I rather lose the thread. Mr. Whelan himself became confused, and I stopped paying attention. Until dinner. The dinner was superb, as I believe I've said already. You explain, Rudy. You do it better."

"Maybe you could begin with introductions," I suggested.

"Of course. Excuse me. This is my mother, Muriel Ruyk, who founded, and owns, this gallery. I'm Rudolph

Ruyk. Fortunately for yourself, you do not need an intro-
duction. Muriel recognized you at once from your recordings. Her short-term memory may be poor, but her recall
for the more vivid sketches of her past—any time before
the last ten to fifteen years—is often proportionally acute.
You, Mr. Whalen, are one of my mother's most vivid
memories."

"Aruba!" she exclaimed. "And the oysters on Belle lle!
I'll never forget those oysters."

"You were there with me?"

"Goodness, no. *You* were there. Isn't that enough? The
way the waves pounded on the cliffs. And *you* on those
slippery rocks! Oh, my! We did meet once, in passing, at
Dar es Salaam, but nothing came of it. I am proud to say,
though, that I was one of your first collectors. So long as I
could afford your prices. Once you'd moved up to
Knoedler, you zoomed out of my range."

"All that was quite a while back. I'm surprised you recognized me."

"Your hair is thinner now, certainly, and you've put on
weight, but the indescribable something is still there. If I
hadn't recognized you, I'm afraid Rudy would have
turned you over to the police directly, and that would have
been a shame."

"Mmm, yes, it would."

"Such a daring, such a *desperate* thing to do! I've always said, haven't I, Rudy, that there is a deep affinity between artistry and criminality?"

"Yes, Mother. But crime is crime, for all that."

"Yes, of course, one must take precautions. But I can't
help admiring those like you, Mr. Whelan, who are head-
strong and act out of impulse. I *do* hope we'll work something out."

"We already have, Mother. We have his agreement on

videotape. And as a pledge that he'll honor that agreement, we have his own recording of how he broke into the gallery. In fact, with the recording he's making now, we have two such recordings. He can scarcely refuse to cooperate."

"That sounds like blackmail to me."

"It is, Mr Whelan," Muriel said pleasantly, "but I'd like to think that our arrangement would appeal to you on its own merits. You've been leading a rather *mean* sort of life. We're offering you a new chance at the good life. We're offering you, in fact, a comeback."

Despite myself, the word worked its magic: a comeback! I resisted the bait long enough to ask, "On what terms?"

"On *our* terms," said Rudy. "Five nights a week you'll record for us. The recordings will be the property of the gallery. All recording expenses will be approved in advance and charged to the gallery."

"It all sounds rather . . . unilateral."

Muriel touched her ingenue smile with a crone's finger. "Isn't that always the way of it with galleries, though? But is self-advantage that important to you as an artist? What does money matter if you enjoy abundantly the pleasures it can buy?"

"Yeah, but you'll enjoy the reruns. You and your customers."

"I wouldn't deny that. But what better defense against satiety than to awake each day to a present unshadowed by the past? Candidly, I consider the loss of short-term memory a great blessing. It allows me to live for the moment."

"In any case," said Rudy, "you'll get a quid pro quo. After each recording session you'll be allowed to check out a ring from the gallery's current collection, excepting some few rare recordings that have only one or two repays left. I assume that's what you were after when you broke in here."

"If the ring you left with me last night is any sample of your collection, I'm not enticed."

"What ring was that, Rudy?" Muriel asked.

"One of my nightmares, from when I was four. I did warn you, Mr. Whelan, that it might be too strong for your taste, but you flipped for the price tag."

"I don't believe that was a nightmare. That was real."

"Oh, Rudy had the most vivid nightmares imaginable as a child. Everyone accepts them quite literally. Of course, as Rudy says, they're not to every taste. One sample was enough for me. But people go to horror movies, don't they? It's the same principle."

"Cradle robbing is not the same as anything. It's a crime in this state, and that ring is evidence."

"There was nothing illegal in any of Rudy's recordings. They were undertaken with a grant from the National Endowment and conducted under the strictest psychiatric supervision. Every ring is fully documented. And from a strictly ethical point of view, surely, it was a kindness to the dear boy to exorcise the memory of such terrible dreams."

"Except, Mother, that as a result I went on having the nightmares."

"That's only a theory, Rudy," Muriel scolded. "All children have nightmares. It's a stage they go through. You just had a special talent. Why in the world are we discussing this? I thought we'd settled this years ago."

"Because Mr. Whelan didn't enjoy his private viewing."

"Oh, yes. Well, Mr. Whelan, you must choose more wisely next time. Try athletics. It picks you up wonderfully, and we've got a fine stock. Rudy takes a group of young men skiing every year, and they all have a lovely time. You can have the same lovely time, and *I* can have my own collection of Whelans! One comes to the gallery business, after all, because one lacks the means to be a collector. I'm *sure* I explained all this yesterday."

"You did, Mother. But you also insisted—if you'll remember—that Mr. Whelan should not stop recording till he was back home and put to sleep. You wanted there to be an element of surprise in today's recording. But, as I pointed out then, we would have to explain this all over."

"And so we are. It's good of you, Rudy, to be so patient with us. You won't have to tomorrow. We'll stop recording in a moment, and then, while you put the finishing touches on dinner—how long has it been, by the way, Mr. Whelan, since you've eaten tournedos Rossini?—*he* can audit the ring he's making now."

"You're assuming that I've agreed to all this," I pointed out.

"And so you did—yesterday."

"Yesterday I hadn't just gone through purgatory."

"Oh, pish, Mr. Whelan, pish. Tomorrow today will be yesterday. We must live for the present. Even the Bible says so, somewhere. Mr. Whelan, I implore you. Try it for one week. You see"—she leaned forward confidentially and went out of focus—"I have been put on this *merciless* diet. No cholesterol, which means, in effect, no sauces. Virtually no desserts but fresh fruit. No *beef* in any form. Think of it! And no salt, Mr. Whelan! What kind of life is that?"

"So what you want me to do is . . ."

"To eat for me, Mr. Whelan. Rudy is a wonderful cook, and when he's not in the mood, the city's full of restaurants. My resources are limited, but I can still afford a table at La Pentola."

"But surely you don't need me for such . . . a . . ."

"A bit part?" Rudy asked sarcastically.

"If you meant to say," Muriel said, "that someone else could make such recordings for me, you don't do justice to your own artistry, Mr. Whelan. Believe me, my dinner table has auditioned hundreds of would-be artists. None of them had your taste, your gusto, your concentration."

"Well?" Rudy demanded.

"Well," I replied, "why not? Like Shakespeare says, the best revenge is living well."

While Rudy went off to the kitchen and Muriel replayed our dinner of the night before, I let the gallery's two guards set up a Ringmaster so that I could audit — and thus be able to recall — the recording I'd just been making. There was a flash of discontinuity as the ring was re-wound; subjectively no time had intervened since I'd started recording out in the square. But soon the ring was ready, and I started to relive the last hour of my own life.

By the time the ring had finished playing, dinner was waiting in the upstairs dining room, to which the guards had escorted me. At the first whiff of the lobster bisque, I snapped to attention and started to record.

The rest is art history.

RED STAR, WINTER ORBIT

By Bruce Sterling and William Gibson

Colonel Korolev twisted slowly in his harness, dreaming of winter and gravity. Young again, a cadet, he whipped his horse across the late November steppes of Kazakhstan into dry red vistas of Martian sunset.

That's wrong, he thought—

And woke—in the Museum of the Soviet Triumph in Space—to the sounds of Romanenko and the KGB man's wife. They were going at it again behind the screen at the aft end of the *Salyut*, restraining straps and padded hull creaking and thudding rhythmically. Hooves in the snow.

Freeing himself from the harness, Korolev executed a practiced kick that propelled him into the toilet stall. Shrugging out of his threadbare coverall, he clamped the commode around his loins and wiped condensed steam from the steel mirror. His arthritic hand had swollen again during sleep; the wrist was bird-bone thin from calcium loss. Twenty years had passed since he'd last known gravity; he'd grown old in orbit.

403

He shaved with a suction razor. A patchwork of broken veins blotched his left cheek and temple, another legacy from the blowout that had crippled him.

When he emerged, he found that the adulterers had finished. Romanenko was adjusting his clothing. The Political Officer's wife, Valentina, had ripped the sleeves from her brown coverall; her white arms were sheened with the sweat of their exertion. Her ash-blond hair rippled in the breeze from a ventilator. Her eyes were purest cornflower blue, set a little too closely together, and they held a look half-apologetic, half-conspiratorial. "See what we've brought you, Colonel—"

She handed him a tiny airline bottle of cognac.

Stunned, Korolev blinked at the Air France logo embossed on the plastic cap.

"It came in the last *Soyuz*. In a cucumber, my husband said." She giggled. "He gave it to me."

"We decided you should have it, Colonel," Romanenko said, grinning broadly. "After all, we can be furloughed at any time." Korolev ignored the sidelong, embarrassed glance at his shriveled legs and pale, dangling feet.

He opened the bottle, and the rich aroma brought a sudden tingling rush of blood to his cheeks. He raised it carefully and sucked out a few milliliters of brandy. It burned like acid. "Christ," he gasped, "it's been years. I'll get plastered!" He said, laughing, tears blurring his vision.

"My father tells me you drank like a hero, Colonel, in the old days."

"Yes," Korolev said, and sipped again, "I did." The cognac spread through him like liquid gold. He disliked Romanenko. He'd never liked the boy's father, either—an easygoing Party man, long since settled into lecture tours, a dacha on the Black Sea, American liquor, French suits, Italian shoes. . . . The boy had the father's looks, the same clear gray eyes utterly untroubled by doubt.

The alcohol surged through Korolev's thin blood. "You are too generous," he said. He kicked once gently and arrived at his console. "You must take some *samisdata*, American cable broadcasts, freshly intercepted. Racy stuff! Wasted on an old man like me." He slotted a blank cassette and punched for the material.

"I'll give it to the gun crew," Romanenko said, grinning. "They can run it on the tracking consoles in the gun room." The particle-beam station had always been known as the gun room. The soldiers who manned it were particularly hungry for this sort of tape. Korolev ran off a second copy for Valentina.

"It's dirty?" She looked alarmed and intrigued. "May we come again, Colonel? Thursday at 2400?"

Korolev smiled at her. She had been a factory worker before she'd been singled out for space. Her beauty made her useful as a propaganda tool, a role model for the proletariat. He pitied her now, with the cognac coursing through his veins, and found it impossible to deny her a little happiness. "A midnight rendezvous in the museum, Valentina? Romantic!"

She kissed his cheek, wobbling in free fall. "Thank you, my Colonel."

"You're a prince, Colonel," Romanenko said, slapping Korolev's match-stick shoulder as gently as he could. After countless hours on an exerciser, the boy's arms bulged like a blacksmith's.

Korolev watched the lovers carefully make their way out into the central docking sphere, the junction of three aging *Salyuts* and two corridors. Romanenko took the "north" corridor to the gun room; Valentina went in the opposite direction to the next junction sphere and the *Salyut* where her husband slept.

There were five docking spheres in Kosmograd, each with its three linked *Salyuts*. At opposite ends of the complex were the military installation and the satellite-launchers. Popping, humming, and wheezing, the station had the feel of a subway and the dank metallic reek of a tramp steamer.

Korolev had another pull at the bottle. Now it was half-empty. He hid it in one of the museum's exhibits, a NASA Hasselblad recovered from the site of the *Apollo* landing. He hadn't had a drink since his last furlough, before the blowout. His head swam in a pleasant, painful current of drunken nostalgia.

Drifting back to his console, he accessed a section of memory where the collected speeches of Alexei Kosygin had been covertly erased and replaced with his personal collection of *samisdata*, digitized pop music, his boyhood favorites from the Eighties. He had British groups taped from West German radio, Warsaw Pact heavy metal, American imports from the black market. Putting on his headphones, he punched for the Czestochowa reggae of Brygada Cryzis.

After all the years, he no longer really heard the music, but images came rushing back with an aching poignancy. In the Eighties he'd been a long-haired child of the Soviet elite, his father's position placing him effectively beyond the reach of the Moscow police. He remembered feedback howling through the speakers in the hot darkness of a cellar club, the crowd a shadowy checkerboard of denim and bleached hair. He'd smoked Marlboros laced with powdered Afghani hash. He remembered the mouth of an American diplomat's daughter in the backseat of her father's black Lincoln. Names and faces came flooding in on a warm haze of cognac. Nina, the East German who'd shown him her mimeographed translations of dissident

Polish news sheets—

Until the night she didn't turn up at the coffee bar. Whispers of parasitism, of anti-Soviet activity, of the waiting chemical horrors of the *psikuska*—

Korolev started to tremble. He wiped his face and found it bathed in sweat. He took off the headphones.

It had been fifty years, yet he was suddenly and very intensely afraid. He couldn't remember ever having been this frightened, not even during the blowout that had crushed his hip. He shook violently. The lights. The lights in the *Salyut* were too bright, but he didn't want to go to the switches. A simple action, one he performed regularly, yet . . . The switches and their insulated cables were somehow threatening. He stared, confused. The little clockwork model of a *Lunokhod* moon rover, its Velcro wheels gripping the curved wall, seemed to crouch there like something sentient, poised, waiting. The eyes of the Soviet space pioneers in the official portraits were fixed on him with contempt.

The cognac. His years in free fail had warped his metabolism. He wasn't the man he'd once been. But he would remain calm and try to ride it out. If he threw up, everyone would laugh.

Someone knocked at the entrance to the museum, and Nikita the Plumber, Kosmograd's premier handyman, executed a perfect slow-motion dive through the open hatch. The young civilian engineer looked angry. Korolev felt cowed. "You're up early, Plumber," he said, anxious for some facade of normality.

"Pinhead leakage in Delta Three." He frowned. "Do you understand Japanese?" The Plumber tugged a cassette from one of the dozen pockets that bulged on his stained work-vest and waved it in Korolev's face. He wore carefully laundered Levi's and dilapidated Adidas running shoes. "We accessed this last night."

Korolev cowered as though the cassette were a weapon. "No, no Japanese." The meekness of his own voice startled him. "Only English and Polish." He felt himself blush. The Plumber was his friend; he knew and trusted the Plumber, but—

"Are you well, Colonel?" The Plumber loaded the tape and punched up a lexicon program with deft, calloused fingers. "You look as though you just ate a bug. I want you to hear this."

Korolev watched uneasily as the tape flickered into an ad for baseball gloves. The lexicon's Cyrillic subtitles raced across the monitor as a Japanese voice-over rattled maniacally.

"The newscast's coming up," said the Plumber, gnawing at a cuticle.

Korolev squinted anxiously as the translation slid across the face of the Japanese announcer:

AMERICAN DISARMAMENT GROUP CLAIMS . . . PREPARATIONS AT BAIKONUR COSMODROME . . . PROVE RUSSIANS AT LAST READY . . . TO SCRAP ARMED SPACE STATION COMIC CITY . . .

"Cosmic," the Plumber muttered. "Glitch in the lexicon."

BUILT AT TURN OF CENTURY AS BRIDGEHEAD TO SPACE . . . AMBITIOUS PROJECT CRIPPLED BY FAILURE OF LUNAR MINING . . . EXPENSIVE STATION OUTPERFORMED BY OUR UNMANNED ORBITAL FACTORIES . . . CRYSTALS SEMICONDUCTORS AND PURE DRUGS . . .

"Smug bastards." The Plumber snorted. "I tell you, it's that goddamned KGB man Yefremov. He's had a hand in this!"

STAGGERING SOVIET TRADE DEFICITS . . . POPULAR DISCONTENT WITH SPACE EFFORT . . . RECENT DECISIONS BY

POLITBURO AND CENTRAL COMMITTEE SECRETARIAT . . .

"They're shutting us down!" The Plumber's face contorted with rage.

Korolev twisted away from the screen, shaking uncontrollably. Sudden tears peeled from his lashes in free-fall droplets. "Leave me alone! I can do nothing!"

"What's wrong, Colonel?" The Plumber grabbed his shoulders. "Look me in the face. Someone's dosed you with the Fear!"

"Go away," Korolev begged.

"That little spook bastard! What has he given you? Pills? An injection?"

Korolev shuddered. "I had a drink—"

"He gave you the Fear! You, a sick old man! I'll break his face!" The Plumber jerked his knees up, somersaulted backward, kicked off from a handhold overhead, and catapulted out of the room.

"Wait! Plumber!" But the Plumber had zipped through the docking sphere like a squirrel, vanishing down the corridor, and now Korolev felt that he couldn't bear to be alone. In the distance, he could hear metallic echoes of distorted, angry shouts.

Trembling, he closed his eyes and waited for someone to help him.

He'd asked Psychiatric Officer Bychkov to help him dress in his old uniform, the one with the Star of the Tsiolkovsky Order sewn above the left breast pocket. The black dress boots of heavy quilted nylon, with their Velcro soles, would no longer fit his twisted feet; so his feet remained bare.

Bychkov's injection had straightened him out within an hour, leaving him alternately depressed and furiously angry. Now he waited in the museum for Yefremov to answer his summons.

They called his home the Museum of the Soviet Triumph in Space, and as his rage subsided, to be replaced with an ancient bleakness, he felt very much as if he were simply another one of the exhibits. He stared gloomily at the gold-framed portraits of the great visionaries of space, at the faces of Tsiolkovsky, Rynin, Tupolev. Below these, in slightly smaller frames, were portraits of Verne, Goddard, and O'Neill.

In moments of extreme depression he had sometimes imagined that he could detect a common strangeness in their eyes, particularly in the eyes of the two Americans. Was it simply craziness, as he sometimes thought in his most cynical moods? Or was he able to glimpse a subtle manifestation of some weird, unbalanced force that he had often suspected of being human evolution in action?

Once, and only once, Korolev had seen that look in his own eyes — on the day he'd stepped onto the soil of the Coprates Basin. The Martian sunlight, glinting within his helmet visor, had shown him the reflection of two steady, alien eyes — fearless, yet driven — and the quiet, secret shock of it, he now realized, had been his life's most memorable, most transcendental moment.

Above the portraits, oily and inert, was a painting that depicted the landing in colors that reminded him of borscht and gravy, the Martian landscape reduced to the idealistic kitsch of Soviet Socialist realism. The artist had posed the suited figure beside the lander with all of the official style's deeply sincere vulgarity.

Feeling tainted, he awaited the arrival of Yefremov, the KGB man, Kosmograd's Political Officer.

When Yefremov finally entered the *Salyut*, Korolev noted the split lip and the fresh bruises on the man's throat. He wore a blue Kansai jump suit of Japanese silk and stylish Italian deck shoes. He coughed politely. "Good morning, Comrade Colonel."

Korolev stared. He allowed the silence to lengthen. "Yefremov," he said heavily, "I am not happy with you."

Yefremov reddened, but he held his gaze. "Let us speak frankly to each other, Colonel, as Russian to Russian. It was not, of course, intended for you."

"The Fear, Yefremov?"

"The beta-carboline, yes. I you hadn't pandered to their antisocial actions, if you hadn't accepted their bribe, it would not have happened."

"So I am a pimp, Yefremov? A pimp and a drunkard? You are a cuckold, a smuggler, and an informer. I say this," he added, "as one Russian to another."

Now the KGB man's face assumed the official mask of bland and untroubled righteousness.

"But tell me, Yefremov, what it is that you are really about. What have you been doing since you came to Kosmograd? We know that the complex will be stripped. What is in store for the civilian crew when they return to Baikonur? Corruption hearings?"

"There will be interrogation, certainly. In certain cases there may be hospitalization. Would you care to suggest, Colonel Korolev, that the Soviet Union is somehow at fault for Kosmograd's failures?"

Korolev was silent.

"Kosmograd was a dream, Colonel. A dream that failed. Like space. We have no need to be here. We have an entire world to put in order. Moscow is the greatest power in history. We must not allow ourselves to lose the global perspective."

"Do you think we can be brushed aside that easily? We are an elite, a highly trained technical elite."

"A minority, Colonel, an obsolete minority. What do

you contribute, aside from reams of poisonous American trash? The crew here were intended to be workers, not bloated black marketeers trafficking in jazz and pornography." Yefremov's face was smooth and calm. "The crew will return to Baikonur. The weapons are capable of being directed from the ground. You, of course, will remain, and there will be guest cosmonauts: Africans, South Americans. Space still retains a degree of its former prestige for these people."

Korolev gritted his teeth. "What have you done with the boy?"

"Your Plumber?" The Political Officer frowned. "He has assaulted an officer of the Committee for State Security. He will remain under guard until he can be taken to Baikonur."

Korolev attempted an unpleasant laugh. "Let him go. You'll be in too much trouble yourself to press charges. I'll speak with Marshal Gubarev personally. My rank may be entirely honorary, Yefremov, but I do retain a certain influence."

The KGB man shrugged. "The gun crew are under orders from Baikonur to keep the communicators module under lock and key. Their careers depend on it."

"Martial law, then?"

"This isn't Kabul, Colonel. These are difficult times. You have the moral authority here; you should try to set an example."

"We shall see," Korolev said.

Kosmograd swung out of Earth's shadow into raw sunlight. The walls of Korolev's *Salyut* popped and creaked like a nest of glass bottles. A *Salyut*'s viewports, Korolev thought absently, fingering the broken veins at his temple, were always the first things to go.

· Young Grishkin seemed to have the same thought. He drew a tube of caulk from an ankle-pocket and began to inspect the seal around the viewport. He was the Plumber's assistant and closest friend.

"We must now vote," Korolev said wearily. Eleven of Kosmograd's twenty-four civilian crew members had agreed to attend the meeting, twelve if he counted himself. That left thirteen who were either unwilling to risk involvement or else actively hostile to the idea of a strike. Yefremov and the six-man gun crew brought the total number of those not present to twenty. "We've discussed our demands. All those in favor of the list as it stands—" He raised his good hand. Three others raised theirs. Grishkin, busy at the viewport, stuck out his foot.

Korolev sighed. "There are few enough as it is. We'd best have unanimity. Let us hear your objections."

"The term *military custody*," said a biological technician named Korovkin, "might be construed as implying that the military, and not the criminal Yefremov, is responsible for the situation." The man looked acutely uncomfortable. "We are in sympathy otherwise but will not sign. We are Party members." He seemed about to add something but fell silent. "My mother," his wife said quietly, "was Jewish."

Korolev nodded, but he said nothing.

"This is all criminal foolishness," said Glushko, the botanist. Neither he nor his wife had voted. "Madness. Kosmograd is finished, we all know it, and the sooner home the better. What has this place ever been but a prison?" Free fall disagreed with the man's metabolism; in the absence of gravity blood tended to congest in his face and neck, making him resemble one of his experimental pumpkins.

"You are a botanist, Vasili," his wife said stiffly, "while

I, you will recall, am a *Soyuz* pilot. Your career is not at stake."

"I will *not* support this idiocy!" Glushko gave the bulkhead a savage kick that propelled him from the room. His wife followed, complaining bitterly in the grating undertone crew members learned to employ for private arguments.

"Five are willing to sign," Korolev said, "out of a civilian crew of twenty-four."

"Six," said Tatjana, the other *Soyuz* pilot, her dark hair drawn back and held with a braided band of green nylon webbing. "You forget the Plumber."

"The sun balloons!" cried Grishkin, pointing toward the earth. "Look!"

Kosmograd was above the coast of California now, clean shorelines, intensely green fields, vast decaying cities whose names rang with a strange magic. High above a fleece of stratocumulus floated five solar balloons, mirrored geodesic spheres tethered by power lines; they had been a cheaper substitute for a grandiose American plan to build solar-powered satellites. The things worked, Korolev supposed, because for the last decade he'd watched them multiply.

"And they say that people live in those things?" Systems Officer Stoiko had joined Grishkin at the viewport.

Korolev remembered the pathetic flurry of strange American energy schemes in the wake of the Treaty of Vienna. With the Soviet Union firmly in control of the world's oil flow, the Americans had seemed willing to try anything. Then the Kansas meltdown had permanently soured them on reactors. For more than three decades they'd been gradually sliding into isolationism and industrial decline. *Space*, he thought ruefully, *they should have gone into space*. He'd never understood the strange paralysis of will that had seemed to grip their brilliant early efforts. Or perhaps it was simply a failure of imagination, of vision. *You see, Americans*, he said silently, *you really should have tried to join us here in our glorious future, here in Kosmograd*.

"Who would want to live in something like that?" Stoiko asked, punching Grishkin's shoulder and laughing with the quiet energy of desperation.

"You're joking," said Yefremov. "Surely we're all in enough trouble as it is."

"We're not joking, Political Officer Yefremov, and these are our demands." The five dissidents had crowded into the *Salyut* the man shared with Valentina, backing him against the aft screen. The screen was decorated with a meticulously airbrushed photograph of the Premier, who was waving from the back of a tractor. Valentina, Korolev knew, would be in the museum now with Romanenko, making the straps creak. The Colonel wondered how Romanenko so regularly managed to avoid his duty shifts in the gun room.

Yefremov shrugged. He glanced down the list of demands. "The Plumber must remain in custody. I have direct orders. As for the rest of this document —"

"You are guilty of unauthorized use of psychiatric drugs!" Grishkin shouted.

"That was entirely a private matter," said Yefremov calmly.

"A criminal act," said Tatjana.

"Pilot Tatjana, we both know that Grishkin here is the station's most active *samisdata* pirate! We are all criminals, don't you see? That's the beauty of our system, isn't it?" His sudden, twisted smile was shockingly cynical. "Kosmograd is not the *Potemkin*, and you are not revolutionaries. And you *demand* to communicate with Marshal Gubarev? He is in custody at Baikonur. And you *demand* to communicate with the Minister of Technology? The Minister is leading the purge." With a decisive gesture he ripped the printout to pieces, scraps of yellow flimsy scattering in free fall like slow-motion butterflies.

On the ninth day of the strike, Korolev met with Grishkin and Stoiko in the *Salyut* that Grishkin would ordinarily have shared with the Plumber.

For forty years the inhabitants of Kosmograd had fought an antiseptic war against mold and mildew. Dust, grease, and vapor wouldn't settle in free fall, and spores lurked everywhere—in padding, in clothing, in the ventilation ducts. In the warm, moist petri-dish atmosphere, they spread like oil slicks. Now there was a reek of dry rot in the air, overlaid with ominous whiffs of burning insulation.

Korolev's sleep had been broken by the hollow thud of a departing *Soyuz* lander. Glushko and his wife, he supposed. During the past forty-eight hours, Yefremov had supervised the evacuation of the crew members who had refused to join the strike. The gun crew kept to the gun room and their barracks ring, where they still held Nikita the Plumber.

Grishkin's *Salyut* had become strike headquarters. None of the male strikers had shaved, and Stoiko had contracted a staph infection that spread across his forearms in angry welts. Surrounded by lurid pinups from American television, they resembled some degenerate trio of pornographers. The lights were dim; Kosmograd ran on half power. "With the others gone," Stoiko said, "our hand is strengthened."

Grishkin groaned. His nostrils were festooned with

white streamers of surgical cotton. He was convinced that Yefremov would try to break the strike with beta-carboline aerosols. The cotton plugs were just one symptom of the general level of strain and paranoia. Before the evacuation order had come from Baikonur, one of the technicians had taken to playing Tchaikovsky's *1812 Overture* at shattering volume for hours on end. And Glushko had chased his wife, naked, bruised, and screaming, up and down the length of Kosmograd. Stoiko had accessed the KGB man's files and Bychkov's psychiatric records; meters of yellow printout curled through the corridors in flabby spirals, rippling in the current from the ventilators.

"Think what their testimony will be doing to us groundside," muttered Grishkin. "We won't even get a trial. Straight to the *psikuska*." The sinister nickname for the political hospitals seemed to galvanize the boy with dread. Korolev picked apathetically at a viscous pudding of chlorella.

Stoiko snatched a drifting scroll of printout and read aloud. "Paranoia with a tendency to overesteem ideas! Revisionist fantasies hostile to the social system!" He crumpled the paper. "If we could seize the communications module, we could tie into an American Comsat and dump the whole thing in their laps. Perhaps that would show Moscow something about our hostility!"

Korolev dug a stranded fruit fly from his algae pudding. Its two pairs of wings and bifurcated thorax were mute testimony to Kosmograd's high radiation levels. The insects had escaped from some forgotten experiment; generations of them had infested the station for decades. "The Americans have no interest in us," Korolev said. "Moscow can no longer be embarrassed by such revelations."

"Except when the grain shipments are due," Grishkin said.

"America needs to sell as badly as we need to buy." Korolev grimly spooned more chlorella into his mouth, chewed mechanically, and swallowed. "The Americans couldn't reach us even if they desired to. Canaveral is in ruins."

"We're low on fuel," Stoiko said.

"We can take it from the remaining landers," Korolev said.

"Then how in hell would we get back *down*?" Grishkin's fists trembled. "Even in Siberia, there are trees, trees, the sky! To hell with it! Let it fall to pieces! Let it fall and burn!"

Korolev's pudding spattered across the bulkhead.

"Oh, Christ," Grishkin said, "I'm sorry, Colonel. I know you can't go back."

When he entered the museum, he found Pilot Tatjana suspended before that hateful painting of the Mars landing, her cheeks slick with tears.

"Do you know, Colonel, they have a bust of you at Baikonur? In bronze. I used to pass it on my way to lectures." Her eyes were red-rimmed with sleeplessness.

"There are always busts. Academies need them." He smiled and took her hand.

"What was it like that day?" She still stared at the painting.

"I hardly remember. I've seen the tapes so often, now I remember them instead. My memories of Mars are any schoolchild's." He smiled for her again. "But it was not like this bad painting. In spite of everything, I'm still certain of that."

"Why has it all gone this way, Colonel? Why is it ending now? When I was small I saw all this on television. Our future in space was forever—"

"Perhaps the Americans were right. The Japanese sent machines instead, robots to build their orbital factories. Lunar mining failed for us, but we thought there would at least be a permanent research facility of some kind. It all had to do with purse strings, I suppose. With men who sit at desks and make decisions."

"Here is their final decision with regard to Kosmograd." She passed him a folded scrap of flimsy. "I found this in the printout of Yefremov's orders from Moscow. They'll allow the station's orbit to decay over the next three months."

He found that now he too was staring fixedly at the painting he loathed. "It hardly matters anymore," he heard himself say.

And then she was weeping bitterly, her face pressed hard against Korolev's crippled shoulder.

"But I have a plan, Tatjana," he said, stroking her hair. "You must listen."

He glanced at his old Rolex. They were over eastern Siberia. He remembered how the Swiss ambassador had presented him with the watch in an enormous vaulted room in the Grand Kremlin Palace.

It was time to begin.

He drifted out of his *Salyut* into the docking sphere, batting at a length of printout that tried to coil around his head.

He could still work quickly and efficiently with his good hand. He was smiling as he freed a large oxygen bottle from its webbing straps. Bracing himself against a handhold, he flung the bottle across the sphere with all his strength. It rebounded harmlessly with a harsh clang. He went after it, caught it, and hurled it again.

Then he hit the decompression alarm.

Dust spurted from the speakers as a Klaxon began to wail. Triggered by the alarm, the docking bays slammed shut with a wheeze of hydraulics. Korolev's ears popped. He sneezed, then went after the bottle again.

The lights flared to maximum brilliance, then flickered out. He smiled in the darkness, groping for the steel bottle. Stoiko had provoked a general systems crash. It hadn't been difficult. The memory banks were already riddled to the point of collapse with bootlegged television broadcasts. "The real bare-knuckle stuff," he muttered, banging the bottle against the wall. The lights flickered on weakly as emergency cells came on line.

His shoulder began to ache. Stoically he continued pounding, remembering the din a real blowout caused. It had to be good. It had to fool Yefremov and the gun crew.

With a squeal, the manual wheel of one of the hatches began to rotate. It thumped open, finally, and Tatjana looked in, grinning shyly.

"Is the Plumber free?" he asked, releasing the bottle.

"Stoiko and Umansky are reasoning with the guard." She drove a fist into her open palm. "Grishkin is preparing the landers."

He followed her up to the next docking sphere. Stoiko was helping the Plumber through the hatch that led from the barracks ring. The Plumber was barefoot, his face greenish under a scraggly growth of beard. Meteorologist Umansky followed them, dragging the limp body of a soldier.

"How are you, Plumber?" Korolev asked.

"Shaky. They've kept me on the Fear. Not big doses, but — and I thought that that was a real blowout!"

Grishkin slid out of the *Soyuz* lander nearest Korolev, trailing a bundle of tools and meters on a nylon lanyard. "They all check out. The crash left them under their own automatics. I've been at their remotes with a screwdriver so they can't be overridden by ground control. How are you doing, my Nikita?" he asked the Plumber. "You'll be going in steep to central China."

The Plumber winced, shook himself, and shivered. "I don't speak Chinese."

Stoiko handed him a printout. "This is in phonetic Mandarin. I WISH TO DEFECT. TAKE ME TO THE NEAREST JAPANESE EMBASSY."

The Plumber grinned and ran his fingers through his thatch of sweat-stiffened hair. "What about the rest of you?" he asked.

"You think we're doing this for your benefit alone?" Tatjana made a face at him. "Make sure the Chinese news services get the rest of that scroll, Plumber. Each of us has a copy. We'll see that the world knows what the Soviet Union intends to do to Colonel Yuri Vasilevich Korolev, first man on Mars!" She blew the Plumber a kiss.

"How about Filipchenko here?" Umansky asked. A few dark spheres of congealing blood swung crookedly past the unconscious soldier's cheek.

"Why don't you take the poor bastard with you," Korolev said.

"Come along then, shithead," the Plumber said, grabbing Filipchenko's belt and towing him toward the *Soyuz* hatch. "I, Nikita the Plumber, will do you the favor of your miserable lifetime."

Korolev watched as Stoiko and Grishkin sealed the hatch behind them.

"Where are Romanenko and Valentina?" Korolev asked, checking his watch again.

"Here, my Colonel," Valentina said, her blond hair floating around her face in the hatch of another *Soyuz*. "We have been checking this one out." She giggled.

421

"Time enough for that in Tokyo." Korolev snapped. "They'll be scrambling jets in Vladivostok and Hanoi within minutes."

Romanenko's bare, brawny arm emerged and yanked her back into the lander. Stoiko and Grishkin sealed the hatch.

"Peasants in space." Tatjana made a spitting noise.

Kosmograd boomed hollowly as the Plumber, with the unconscious Filipchenko, cast off. Another boom and the lovers were off as well.

"Come along, friend Umansky," said Stoiko. "And farewell, Colonel!" The two men headed down the corridor.

"I'll go with you," Grishkin said to Tatjana. He grinned. "After all, you're a pilot."

"No," she said. "Alone. We'll split the odds. You'll be fine with the automatics. Just don't touch anything on the board."

Korolev watched her help him into the sphere's last *Soyuz*.

"I'll take you dancing, Tatjana," Grishkin said, "in Tokyo." She sealed the hatch. Another boom, and Stoiko and Umansky had cast off from the next docking sphere.

"Go now, Tatjana," Korolev said. "Hurry. I don't want them shooting you down over international waters."

"That leaves you here alone, Colonel, alone with our enemies."

"When you've gone, they'll go as well," he said. "And I depend on your publicity to embarrass the Kremlin into keeping me alive here."

"And what shall I tell them in Tokyo, Colonel? Have you a message for the world?"

"Tell them . . ." and every cliché came rushing to him with an absolute rightness that made him want to laugh hysterically: *One small step . . . We came in peace . . .*

Workers of the world. . . . "You must tell them that I need it," he said, pinching his shrunken wrist, "in my very bones."

She embraced him and slipped away.

He waited alone in the docking sphere. The silence scratched away at his nerves; the systems crash had deactivated the ventilation system, whose hum he'd lived with for twenty years. At last he heard Tatjana's *Soyuz* disengage.

Someone was coming down the corridor. It was Yefremov, moving clumsily in a vacuum suit. Korolev smiled.

Yefremov wore his bland, official mask behind the Lexan faceplate, but he avoided meeting Korolev's eyes as he passed. He was heading for the gun room.

"No!" Korolev shouted.

The Klaxon blared the station's call to full battle alert.

The gun-room hatch was open when he reached it. Inside, the soldiers were moving jerkily in the galvanized reflex of constant drill, yanking the broad straps of their console seats across the chests of their bulky suits.

"Don't do it!" He clawed at the stiff accordian fabric of Yefremov's suit. One of the accelators powered up with a staccato whine. On a tracking screen, green cross hairs closed in on a red dot.

Yefremov removed his helmet. Calmly, with no change in his expression, he backhanded Korolev with the helmet.

"Make them stop!" Korolev sobbed. The walls shook as a beam cut loose with the sound of a cracking whip. "Your wife, Yefremov! She's out there!"

"Outside, Colonel." Yefremov grabbed Korolev's arthritic hand and squeezed. Korolev screamed. "Outside." A gloved fist struck him in the chest.

Korolev pounded helplessly on the vacuum suit as he

was shoved out into the corridor. "Even I, Colonel, dare not come between the Red Army and its orders." Yefremov looked sick now; the mask had crumbled. "Fine sport," he said. "Wait here until it's over."

Then Tatjana's *Soyuz* struck the beam installation and the barracks ring. In a split-second daguerreotype of raw sunlight, Korolev saw the gun room wrinkle and collapse like a beer can crushed under a boot; he saw the decapitated torso of a soldier spinning away from a console; he saw Yefremov try to speak, his hair streaming upright as vacuum tore the air in his suit out through his open helmet ring. Fine twin streams of blood arced from Korolev's nostrils, the roar of escaping air replaced by a deeper roaring in his head.

The last thing Korolev remembered hearing was the hatch door slamming shut.

When he woke, he woke to darkness, to pulsing agony behind his eyes, remembering old lectures. This was as great a danger as the blowout itself, nitrogen bubbling through the blood to strike with white-hot crippling pain . . .

But it was all so remote, academic, really. He turned the wheels of the hatches out of some strange sense of noblesse oblige, nothing more. The labor was quite onerous, and he wished very much to return to the museum and sleep.

He could repair the leaks with caulk, but the systems crash was beyond him. He had Glushko's garden. With the vegetables and algae, he wouldn't starve or smother. The communications module had gone with the gun room and the barracks ring, sheared from the station by the impact of Tatjana's suicidal *Soyuz*. He assumed that the collision had perturbed Kosmograd's orbit, but he had no way of predicting the hour of the station's final incandescent meeting with the upper atmosphere. He was often ill now, and he often thought that he might die before burnout, which disturbed him.

He spent uncounted hours screening the museum's library of tapes. A fitting pursuit for the Last Man in Space who had once been the First Man on Mars.

He became obsessed with the icon of Gagarin, endlessly rerunning the grainy television images of the Sixties, the newsreels that led so unalterably to the cosmonaut's death. The stale air of Kosmograd swam with the spirits of martyrs. Gagarin, the first *Salyut* crew, the Americans roasted alive in their squat *Apollo* . . .

Often he dreamed of Tatjana, the look in her eyes like the look he'd imagined in the eyes of the museum's portraits. And once he woke, or dreamed he woke, in the *Salyut* where she had slept, to find himself in his old uniform, with a battery-powered work light strapped across his forehead. From a great distance, as though he watched a newsreel on the museum's monitor, he saw himself rip the Star of the Tsiolkovsky Order from his pocket and staple it to her Pilot's Certificate.

When the knocking came, he knew that it must be a dream as well.

The hatch wheeled open.

In the bluish, flickering light from the old film, he saw that the woman was black. Long corkscrews of matted hair rose like cobras around her head. She wore goggles, a silk aviator's scarf twisting behind her in free fall. "Andy," she said n English, "you better come see this!"

A small, muscular man, nearly bald, and wearing only a jockstrap and a jangling toolbelt, floated up behind her and peered in. "Is he alive?"

"Of course I am alive," said Korolev in slightly accented

English.

The man called Andy sailed in over her head. "You okay, Jack?" His right bicep was tattooed with a geodesic balloon above crossed lightning bolts and bore the legend SUNSPARK 15, UTAH. "We weren't expecting anybody."

"Neither was I," said Korolev, blinking.

"We've come to live here," said the woman, drifting closer.

"We're from the balloons. Squatters, I guess you could say. Heard the place was empty. You know the orbit's decaying on this thing?" The man executed a clumsy midair somersault, the tools clattering on his belt. "This free fall's outrageous."

"God," said the woman, "I just can't get used to it! It's wonderful. It's like skydiving, but there's no wind."

Korolev stared at the man, who had the blundering, careless look of someone drunk on freedom since birth. "But you don't even have a launchpad," he said.

"Launchpad?" the man said, laughing. "What we do, we haul these surplus booster engines up the cables to the balloons, drop 'em, and fire 'em in midair."

"That's insane," Korolev said.

"Got us here, didn't it?"

Korolev nodded. If this was all a dream, it was a very peculiar one. "I am Colonel Yuri Vasilevich Korolev."

"Mars!" The woman clapped her hands. "Wait'll the kids hear that." She plucked the little *Lunokhod* moon rover model from the bulkhead and began to wind it.

"Hey," the man said, "I gotta work. We got a bunch of boosters outside. We gotta lift this thing before it starts burning."

Something clanged against the hull. Kosmograd rang with the impact. "That'll be Tulsa," Andy said, consulting a wristwatch. "Right on time."

"But why?" Korolev shook his head, deeply confused. "Why have you come?"

"We told you. To live here. We can enlarge this thing, maybe build more. They said we'd never make it living in the balloons, but we were the only ones who could make them work. It was our one chance to get out here on our own. Who'd want to live out here for the sake of some government, some army brass, a bunch of pen pushers? You have to *want* a frontier—want it in your bones, right?"

Korolev smiled. Andy grinned back. "We grabbed those power cables and just pulled ourselves straight up. And when you get to the top, well, man, you either make that big jump or else you rot there." His voice rose. "And you don't look back, no sir! We've made that jump, and we're here to stay!"

The woman placed the model's Velcro wheels against the curved wall and released it. It went scooting along above their heads, whirring merrily. "Isn't that cute? The kids are just going to love it."

Korolev stared into Andy's eyes. Kosmograd rang again, jarring the little *Lunokhod* model onto a new course.

"East Los Angeles," the woman said. "That's the one with the kids in it." She took off her goggles, and Korolev saw her eyes brimming over with a wonderful lunacy.

"Well," said Andy, rattling his toolbelt, "You feel like showing us around?"

CARRION COMFORT

By Dan Simmons

Nina was going to take credit for the death of that Beatle, John. I thought that was in very bad taste. She had her scrapbook laid out on my mahogany coffee table, newspaper clippings neatly arranged in chronological order, the bald statements of death recording all of her Feedings. Nina Drayton's smile was radiant, but her pale-blue eyes showed no hint of warmth.

"We should wait for Willi," I said.

"Of course, Melanie. You're right, as always. How silly of me. I know the rules." Nina stood and began walking around the room, idly touching the furnishings or exclaiming softly over a ceramic statuette or piece of needlepoint. This part of the house had once been the conservatory, but now I used it as my sewing room. Green plants still caught the morning light. The light made it a warm, cozy place in the daytime, but now that winter had come the room was too chilly to use at night. Nor did I like the sense of darkness closing in against all those panes of glass.

"I love this house," said Nina.

She turned and smiled at me. "I can't tell you how much I look forward to coming back to Charleston. We should hold all of our reunions here."

I knew how much Nina loathed this city and this house.

"Willi would be hurt," I said. "You know how he likes to show off his place in Beverly Hills—and his new girlfriends."

"And boyfriends," Nina said, laughing. Of all the changes and darkenings in Nina, her laugh has been least affected. It was still the husky but childish laugh that I had first heard so long ago. It had drawn me to her then—one lonely, adolescent girl responding to the warmth of another as a moth to a flame. Now it served only to chill me and put me even more on guard. Enough moths had been drawn to Nina's flame over the many decades.

"I'll send for tea," I said.

Mr. Thorne brought the tea in my best Wedgwood china. Nina and I sat in the slowly moving squares of sunlight and spoke softly of nothing important: mutually ignorant comments on the economy, references to books that the other had not gotten around to reading, and sympathetic murmurs about the low class of persons one meets while flying these days. Someone peering in from the garden might have thought he was seeing an aging but attractive niece visiting her favorite aunt. (I draw the line at suggesting that anyone would mistake us for mother and daughter.) People usually consider me a well-dressed if not stylish person. Heaven knows I have paid enough to have the wool skirts and silk blouses mailed from Scotland and France. But next to Nina I've always felt dowdy.

This day she wore an elegant, light-blue dress that must have cost several thousand dollars. The color made her complexion seem even more perfect than usual and brought out the blue of her eyes. Her hair had gone as gray as mine, but somehow she managed to get away with wearing it long and tied back with a single barrette. It looked youthful and chic on Nina and made me feel that my short, artificial curls were glowing with a blue rinse.

Few would suspect that I was four years younger than Nina. Time had been kind to her. And she had Fed more often.

She set down her cup and saucer and moved aimlessly around the room again. It was not like Nina to show such signs of nervousness. She stopped in front of the glass display case. Her gaze passed over the Hummels and the pewter pieces, and then stopped in surprise.

"Good heavens, Melanie. A pistol! What an odd place to put an old pistol."

"It's an heirloom," I said. "A Colt Peacemaker from right after the War Between the States. Quite expensive. And you're right, it *is* a silly place to keep it. But it's the only case I have in the house with a lock on it, and Mrs. Hodges often brings her grandchildren when she visits—"

"You mean it's *loaded?*"

"No, of course not," I lied. "But children should not play with such things . . ." I trailed off lamely. Nina nodded but did not bother to conceal the condescension in her smile. She went to look out the south window into the garden.

Damn her. It said volumes about Nina that she did not recognize that pistol.

On the day he was killed, Charles Edgar Larchmont had been my beau for precisely five months and two days. There had been no formal announcement, but we were to be married. Those five months had been a microcosm of the era itself—naive, flirtatious, formal to the point of preciosity, and romantic. Most of all, romantic. Romantic in the worst sense of the word; dedicated to saccharine or insipid ideals that only an adolescent — or an adolescent society — would strive to maintain. We were children playing with loaded weapons.

Nina, she was Nina Hawkins then, had her own beau — a tall, awkward, but well-meaning Englishman named Roger Harrison. Mr. Harrison had met Nina in London a year earlier, during the first stages of the Hawkinses' Grand Tour. Declaring himself smitten — another absurdity of those times — the tall Englishman had followed her from one European capital to another until, after being firmly reprimanded by Nina's father (an unimaginative little milliner who was constantly on the defensive about his doubtful social status), Harrison returned to London to "settle his affairs." Some months later he showed up in New York just as Nina was being packed off to her aunt's home in Charleston in order to terminate yet another flirtation. Still undaunted, the clumsy Englishman followed her south, ever mindful of the protocols and restrictions of the day.

We were a gay group. The day after I met Nina at Cousin Celia's June ball, the four of us were taking a hired boat up the Cooper River for a picnic on Daniel Island. Roger Harrison, serious and solemn on every topic, was a perfect foil for Charles's irreverent sense of humor. Nor did Roger seem to mind the good-natured jesting, since he was soon joining in the laughter with his peculiar *haw-haw-haw*.

Nina loved it all. Both gentlemen showered attention on her, and although Charles never failed to show the primacy of his affection for me, it was understood by all that Nina Hawkins was one of those young women who invariably becomes the center of male gallantry and attention in any gathering. Nor were the social strata of Charleston blind to the combined charm of our foursome. For two months of that now-distant summer, no party was complete, no excur-

sion adequately planned, and no occasion considered a success unless we four were invited and had chosen to attend.
Our happy dominance of the youthful social scene was so
pronounced that Cousins Celia and Loraine wheedled their
parents into leaving two weeks early for their annual Au-
gust sojourn in Maine.

I am not sure when Nina and I came up with the idea of
the duel. Perhaps it was during one of the long, hot nights
when the other "slept over"—creeping into the other's bed,
whispering and giggling, stifling our laughter when the rustling of starched uniforms betrayed the presence of our colored maids moving through the darkened halls. In any
case, the idea was the natural outgrowth of the romantic
pretensions of the time. The picture of Charles and Roger
actually dueling over some abstract point of honor relating
to *us* thrilled both of us in a physical way that I recognize
now as a simple form of sexual titillation.

It would have been harmless except for the Ability. We
had been so successful in our manipulation of male behavior—a manipulation that was both expected and encour-
aged in those days—that neither of us had yet suspected
that there was anything beyond the ordinary in the way we
could translate our whims into other people's actions. The
field of parapsychology did not exist then; or rather, it existed only in the rappings and knockings of parlor-game sé-
ances. At any rate, we amused ourselves for several weeks
with whispered fantasies, and then one of us—or perhaps
both of us—used the Ability to translate the fantasy into reality.

In a sense, it was our first Feeding.

I do not remember the purported cause of the quarrel,
perhaps some deliberate misinterpretation of one of
Charles's jokes. I cannot recall who Charles and Roger arranged to have serve as seconds on that illegal outing. I do

remember the hurt and confused expression on Roger Harrison's face during those few days. It was a caricature of ponderous dullness, the confusion of a man who finds himself in a situation not of his making and from which he cannot escape. I remember Charles and his mercurial swings of mood—the bouts of humor, periods of black anger, and the tears and kisses the night before the duel.

I remember with great clarity the beauty of that morning. Mists were floating up from the river and diffusing the rays of the rising sun as we rode out to the dueling field. I remember Nina reaching over and squeezing my hand with an impetuous excitement that was communicated through my body like an electric shock.

Much of the rest of that morning is missing. Perhaps in the intensity of that first, subconscious Feeding, I literally lost consciousness as I was engulfed in the waves of fear, excitement, pride—of *maleness*—emanating from our two beaus as they faced death on that lovely morning. I remember experiencing the shock of realizing, *this is really happening*, as I shared the tread of high boots through the grass. Someone was calling off the paces. I dimly recall the weight of the pistol in my hand—Charles's hand, I think; I will never know for sure—and a second of cold clarity before an explosion broke the connection, and the acrid smell of gunpowder brought me back to myself.

It was Charles who died. I have never been able to forget the incredible quantities of blood that poured from the small, round hole in his breast. His white shirt was crimson by the time I reached him. There had been no blood in our fantasies. Nor had there been the sight of Charles with his head lolling, mouth dribbling saliva onto his bloodied chest while his eyes rolled back to show the whites like two eggs embedded in his skull.

Roger Harrison was sobbing as Charles breathed his final, shuddering gasps on that field of innocence.

I remember nothing at all about the confused hours that followed. The next morning I opened my cloth bag to find Charles's pistol lying with my things. Why would I have kept that revolver? If I had wished to take something from my fallen lover as a sign of remembrance, why that alien piece of metal? Why pry from his dead fingers the symbol of our thoughtless sin?

It said volumes about Nina that she did not recognize that pistol.

"Willi's here," announced Nina's amanuensis, the loathsome Miss Barrett Kramer. Kramer's appearance was as unisex as her name: short-cropped, black hair, powerful shoulders, and a blank, aggressive gaze that I associated with lesbians and criminals. She looked to be in her midthirties.

"Thank you, Barrett dear," said Nina.

Both of us went out to greet Willi, but Mr. Thorne had already let him in, and we met in the hallway.

"Melanie! You look marvelous! You grow younger each time I see you. Nina!" The change in Willi's voice was evident. Men continued to be overpowered by their first sight of Nina after an absence. There were hugs and kisses. Willi himself looked more dissolute than ever. His alpaca sport coat was exquisitely tailored, his turtleneck sweater successfully concealed the eroded lines of his wattled neck, but when he swept off his jaunty sports-car cap the long strands of white hair he had brushed forward to hide his encroaching baldness were knocked into disarray. Willi's face was flushed with excitement, but there was also the telltale capillary redness about the nose and cheeks that spoke of too much liquor, too many drugs.

"Ladies, I think you've met my associates, Tom Luhar

and Jenson Reynolds?" The two men added to the crowd in my narrow hall. Mr. Luhar was thin and blond, smiling with perfectly capped teeth. Mr. Reynolds was a gigantic Negro, hulking forward with a sullen, bruised look on his coarse face. I was sure that neither Nina nor I had encountered these specific cat's-paws of Willi's before. It did not matter.

"Why don't we go into the parlor?" I suggested. It was an awkward procession ending with the three of us seated on the heavily upholstered chairs surrounding the Georgian tea table that had been my grandmother's. "More tea, please, Mr. Thorne." Miss Kramer took that as her cue to leave, but Willi's two pawns stood uncertainly by the door, shifting from foot to foot and glancing at the crystal on display as if their mere proximity could break something. I would not have been surprised if that had proved to be the case.

"Jense!" Willi snapped his fingers. The Negro hesitated and then brought forward an expensive leather attaché case. Willi set it on the tea table and clicked the catches open with his short, broad fingers. "Why don't you two see Mrs. Fuller's man about getting something to drink?"

When they were gone Willi shook his head and smiled apologetically at Nina. "Sorry about that, Love."

Nina put her hand on Willi's sleeve. She leaned forward with an air of expectancy. "Melanie wouldn't let me begin the Game without you. Wasn't that *awful* of me to want to start without you, Willi dear?"

Willi frowned. After fifty years he still bridled at being called Willi. In Los Angeles he was Big Bill Borden. When he returned to his native Germany—which was not often because of the dangers involved—he was once again Wilhelm von Borchert, lord of dark manor, forest, and hunt. But Nina had called him Willi when they had first met, in 1931 in Vienna, and Willi he had remained.

"You begin, Willi dear," said Nina. "You go first."

I could remember the time when we would have spent the first few days of our reunion in conversation and catching up with one another's lives. Now there was not even time for small talk.

Willi showed his teeth and removed news clippings, notebooks, and a stack of cassettes from his briefcase. No sooner had he covered the small table with his material than Mr. Thorne arrived with the tea and Nina's scrapbook from the sewing room. Willi brusquely cleared a small space.

At first glance one might see certain similarities between Willi Borchert and Mr. Thorne. One would be mistaken. Both men tended to the florid, but Willi's complexion was the result of excess and emotion; Mr. Thorne had known neither of these for many years. Willi's balding was a patchy, self-consciously concealed thing—a weasel with mange; Mr. Thorne's bare head was smooth and wrinkled. One could not imagine Mr. Thorne ever having *had* hair. Both men had gray eyes—what a novelist would call cold gray eyes—but Mr. Thorne's eyes were cold with indifference, cold with a clarity coming from an absolute absence of troublesome emotion or thought. Willi's eyes were the cold of a blustery North Sea winter and were often clouded with shifting curtains of the emotions that controlled him—pride, hatred, love of pain, the pleasures of destruction.

Willi never referred to his use of the Ability as *Feedings*—I was evidently the only one who thought in those terms—but Willi sometimes talked of The Hunt. Perhaps it was the dark forests of his homeland that he thought of as he stalked his human quarry through the sterile streets of Los Angeles. Did Willi dream of the forest, I wondered. Did he look back to green wool hunting jackets, the applause of retainers, the gouts of blood from the dying boar? Or did Willi remember the slam of jackboots on cobblestones and the pounding of his lieutenants' fists on doors? Perhaps Willi still associated his Hunt with the dark European night of the ovens that he had helped to oversee.

I called it Feeding. Willi called it The Hunt. I had never heard Nina call it anything.

"Where is your VCR?" Willi asked. "I have put them all on tape."

"Oh, Willi," said Nina in an exasperated tone. "You know Melanie. She's *so* old fashioned. You know she wouldn't have a video player."

"I don't even have a television," I said. Nina laughed.

"Goddamn it," muttered Willi. "It doesn't matter. I have other records here." He snapped rubber bands from around the small, black notebooks. "It just would have been better on tape. The Los Angeles stations gave much coverage to the Hollywood Strangler, and I edited in the . . . *Ach*! Never mind."

He tossed the videocassettes into his briefcase and slammed the lid shut.

"Twenty-three," he said. "Twenty-three since we met twelve months ago. It doesn't seem that long, does it?"

"Show us," said Nina. She was leaning forward, and her blue eyes seemed very bright. "I've been wondering since I saw the Strangler interviewed on *Sixty Minutes*. He *was* yours, Willi? He seemed so—"

"*Ja, ja*, he was mine. A nobody. A timid little man. He was the gardener of a neighbor of mine. I left him alive so that the police could question him, erase any doubts. He will hang himself in his cell next month after the press loses interest. But this is more interesting. Look at this." Willi slid across several glossy black-and-white photographs. The NBC executive had murdered the five members of his family and drowned a visiting soap-opera actress in his pool. He had then stabbed himself repeatedly and written 50

SHARE in blood on the wall of the bathhouse.

"Reliving old glories, Willi?" asked Nina. "DEATH TO THE PIGS and all that?"

"No, godamn it. I think it should receive points for irony. The girl had been scheduled to drown on the program. It was already in the script outline."

"Was he hard to Use?" It was my question. I was curious despite myself.

Willi lifted one eyebrow. "Not really. He was an alcoholic and heavily into cocaine. There was not much left. And he hated his family. Most people do."

"Most people in California, perhaps," said Nina primly. It was an odd comment from Nina. Years ago her father had committed suicide by throwing himself in front of a trolley car.

"Where did you make contact?" I asked.

"A party. The usual place. He bought the coke from a director who had ruined one of my—"

"Did you have to repeat the contact?"

Willi frowned at me. He kept his anger under control, but his face grew redder. "*Ja, ja.* I saw him twice more. Once I just watched from my car as he played tennis."

"Points for irony," said Nina. "But you lose points for repeated contact. If he were as empty as you say, you should have been able to Use him after only one touch. What else do you have?"

He had his usual assortment. Pathetic skid-row murders. Two domestic slayings. A highway collision that turned into a fatal shooting. "I was in the crowd," said Willi. "I made contact. He had a gun in the glove compartment."

"Two points," said Nina.

Willi had saved a good one for last. A once-famous child star had suffered a bizarre accident. He had left his Bel Air apartment while it filled with gas and then returned to light a match. Two others had died in the ensuing fire.

"You get credit only for him," said Nina.

"*Ja, ja.*"

"Are you absolutely sure about this one? It *could* have been an accident."

"Don't be ridiculous," snapped Willi. He turned toward me. "*This* one was very hard to Use. Very strong. I blocked his memory of turning on the gas. Had to hold it away for two hours. Then forced him into the room. He struggled not to strike the match."

"You should have had him use his lighter," said Nina.

"He didn't smoke," growled Willi. "He gave it up last year."

"Yes," smiled Nina. "I seem to remember him saying that to Johnny Carson." I could not tell whether Nina was jesting.

The three of us went through the ritual of assigning points. Nina did most of the talking. Willi went from being sullen to expansive to sullen again. At one point he reached over and patted my knee as he laughingly asked for my support. I said nothing. Finally he gave up, crossed the parlor to the liquor cabinet, and poured himself a tall glass of bourbon from father's decanter. The evening light was sending its final, horizontal rays through the stained-glass panels of the bay windows, and it cast a red hue on Willi as he stood next to the oak cupboard. His eyes were small, red embers in a bloody mask.

"Forty-one," said Nina at last.

She looked up brightly and showed the calculator as if it verified some objective fact. "I count forty-one points. What do you have, Melanie?"

"*Ja,*" interrupted Willi. "That is fine. Now let us see your claims, Nina." His voice was flat and empty. Even Willi had lost some interest in the Game.'

Before Nina could begin, Mr. Thorne entered and motioned that dinner was served. We adjourned to the dining room — Willi pouring himself another glass of bourbon and Nina fluttering her hands in mock frustration at the interruption of the Game. Once seated at the long, mahogany table, I worked at being a hostess. From decades of tradition, talk of the Game was banned from the dinner table. Over soup we discussed Willi's new movie and the purchase of another store for Nina's line of boutiques. It seemed that Nina's monthly column in *Vogue* was was to be discontinued but that a newspaper syndicate was interested in picking it up.

Both of my guests exclaimed over the perfection of the baked ham, but I thought that Mr. Thorne had made the gravy a trifle too sweet. Darkness had filled the windows before we finished our chocolate mousse. The refracted light from the chandelier made Nina's hair dance with highlights while I feared that mine glowed more bluely than ever.

Suddenly there was a sound from the kitchen. The huge Negro's face appeared at the swinging door. His shoulder was hunched against white hands and his expression was that of a querulous child.

". . . the hell you think we are sittin' here like goddamned —" The white hands pulled him out of sight.

"Excuse me, ladies." Willi dabbed linen at his lips and stood up. He still moved gracefully for all of his years.

Nina poked at her chocolate. There was one sharp, barked command from the kitchen and the sound of a slap. It was the slap of a man's hand — hard and flat as a small-caliber-rifle shot. I looked up and Mr. Thorne was at my elbow, clearing away the dessert dishes.

"Coffee, please, Mr. Thorne. For all of us." He nodded and his smile was gentle.

Franz Anton Mesmer had known of it even if he had not understood it. I suspect that Mesmer must have had some small touch of the Ability. Modern pseudosciences have studied it and renamed it, removed most of its power, confused its uses and origins, but it remains the shadow of what Mesmer discovered. They have no idea of what it is like to Feed.

I despair at the rise of modern violence. I truly give in to despair at times, that deep, futureless pit of despair that poet Gerard Manley Hopkins called carrion comfort. I watch the American slaughterhouse, the casual attacks on popes, presidents, and uncounted others, and I wonder whether there are many more out there with the Ability or whether butchery has simply become the modern way of life.

All humans feed on violence, on the small exercises of power over another. But few have tasted — as we have — the ultimate power. And without the Ability, few know the unequaled pleasure of taking a human life. Without the Ability, even those who do feed on life cannot savor the flow of emotions in stalker and victim, the total exhilaration of the attacker who has moved beyond all rules and punishments, the strange, almost sexual submission of the victim in that final second of truth when all options are canceled, all futures denied, all possibilities erased in an exercise of absolute power over another.

I despair at modern violence. I despair at the impersonal nature of it and the casual quality that has made it accessible to so many. I had a television set until I sold it at the height of the Vietnam War. Those sanitized snippets of death — made distant by the camera's lens — meant nothing to me. But I believe it meant something to these cattle that surround me. When the war and the nightly televised body counts ended, they demanded more, *more*, and the movie screens and streets of this sweet and dying nation have provided it in mediocre, mob abundance. It is an addiction I know well.

They miss the point. Merely observed, violent death is a sad and sullied tapestry of confusion. But to those of us who have Fed, death can be a *sacrament*.

"My turn! My turn!" Nina's voice still resembled that of the visiting belle who had just filled her dance card at Cousin Celia's June ball.

We had returned to the parlor. Willi had finished his coffee and requested a brandy from Mr. Thorne. I was embarrassed for Willi. To have one's closest associates show any hint of unplanned behavior was certainly a sign of weakening Ability. Nina did not appear to have noticed.

"I have them all in order," said Nina. She opened the scrapbook on the now-empty tea table. Willi went through them carefully, sometimes asking a question, more often grunting assent. I murmured occasional agreement although I had heard of none of them. Except for the Beatle, of course. Nina saved that for near the end.

"Good God, Nina, that was you?" Willi seemed near anger. Nina's Feedings had always run to Park Avenue suicides and matrimonial disagreements ending in shots fired from expensive, small-caliber ladies' guns. This type of thing was more in Willi's crude style. Perhaps he felt that his territory was being invaded. "I mean . . . you were risking a lot, weren't you? It's so . . . damn it . . . so *public*."

Nina laughed and set down the calculator. "Willi *dear*, that's what the Game is *about*, is it not?"

Willi strode to the liquor cabinet and refilled his brandy snifter. The wind tossed bare branches against the leaded glass of the bay window. I do not like winter. Even in the

South it takes its toll on the spirit.

"Didn't this guy . . . what's his name . . . buy the gun in Hawaii or someplace?" asked Willi from across the room. "That sounds like his initiative to me. I mean, if he was *already* stalking the fellow—"

"Willi dear," Nina's voice had gone as cold as the wind that raked the branches, "no one said he was *stable*. How many of yours are stable, Willi? But I made it *happen*, darling. I chose the place and the time. Don't you see the irony of the *place*, Willi? After that little prank on the director of that witchcraft movie a few years ago? It was straight from the script—"

"I don't know," said Willi. He sat heavily on the divan, spilling brandy on his expensive sport coat. He did not notice. The lamplight reflected from his balding skull. The mottles of age were more visible at night, and his neck, where it disappeared into his turtleneck, was all ropes and tendons. "I don't know." He looked up at me and smiled suddenly, as if we shared a conspiracy. "It could be like that writer fellow, eh, Melanie? It could be like that."

Nina looked down at the hands on her lap. They were clenched and the well-manicured fingers were white at the tips.

The Mind Vampires. That's what the writer was going to call his book.

I sometimes wonder if he really would have written anything. What was his name? Something Russian.

Willi and I received telegrams from Nina: COME QUICKLY YOU ARE NEEDED. That was enough. I was on the next morning's flight to New York. The plane was a noisy, propeller-driven Constellation, and I spent much of the flight assuring the overly solicitous stewardess that I needed nothing, that, indeed, I felt fine. She obviously had decided that

I was someone's grandmother, who was flying for the first time.

Willi managed to arrive twenty minutes before I. Nina was distraught and as close to hysteria as I had ever seen her. She had been at a party in lower Manhattan two days before—she was not so distraught that she forgot to tell us what important names had been there—when she found herself sharing a corner, a fondue pot, and confidences with a young writer. Or rather, the writer was sharing confidences. Nina described him as a scruffy sort, with a wispy little beard, thick glasses, a corduroy sport coat worn over an old plaid shirt—one of the type invariably sprinkled around successful parties of that era, according to Nina. She knew enough not to call him a beatnik, for that term had just become passé, but no one had yet heard the term *hippie*, and it wouldn't have applied to him anyway. He was a writer of the sort that barely ekes out a living, these days at least, by selling blood and doing novelizations of television series. Alexander something.

His idea for a book—he told Nina that he had been working on it for some time—was that many of the murders then being committed were actually the result of a small group of psychic killers, he called them *mind vampies*, who used others to carry out their grisly deeds.

He said that a paperback publisher had already shown interest in his outline and would offer him a contract tomorrow if he would change the title to *The Zombie Factor* and put in more sex.

"So what?" Willi had said to Nina in disgust. "You have me fly across the continent for this? I might buy the idea myself."

That turned out to be the excuse we used to interrogate this Alexander somebody during an impromptu party given by Nina the next evening. I did not attend. The party was not overly successful, according to Nina, but it gave Willi the chance to have a long chat with the young, would-be novelist. In the writer's almost pitiable eagerness to do business with Bill Borden, producer of *Paris Memories, Three on a Swing,* and at least two other completely forgettable Technicolor features touring the drive-ins that summer, he revealed that the book consisted of a well-worn outline and a dozen pages of notes.

He was sure, however, that he could do a treatment for Mr. Borden in five weeks, perhaps even as fast as three weeks if he were flown out to Hollywood to get the proper creative stimulation.

Later that evening we discussed the possibility of Willi simply buying an option on the treatment, but Willi was short on cash at the time, and Nina was insistent. In the end the young writer opened his femoral artery with a Gillette blade and ran screaming into a narrow Greenwich Village side street to die. I don't believe that anyone ever bothered to sort through the clutter and debris of his remaining notes.

"It could be like that writer, *ja,* Melanie?" Willi patted my knee. I nodded. "He was mine," continued Willi, "and Nina tried to take credit. Remember?"

Again I nodded. Actually he had been neither Nina's nor Willi's. I had avoided the party so that I could make contact later without the young man noticing he was being followed. I did so easily. I remember sitting in an overheated little delicatessen across the street from the apartment building. It was over so quickly that there was almost no sense of Feeding. Then I was aware once again of the sputtering radiators and the smell of salami as people rushed to the door to see what the screaming was about. I remember finishing my tea slowly so that I did not have to leave before the ambulance was gone.

"Nonsense," said Nina. She busied herself with her little calculator. "How many points?" She looked at me. I looked at Willi.

"Six," he said with a shrug. Nina made a small show of totalling the numbers.

"Thirty-eight," she said and sighed theatrically. "You win again, Willi. Or rather, you beat *me* again. We must hear from Melanie. You've been so quiet, dear. You must have some surprise for us."

"Yes," said Willi, "it is your turn to win. It has been several years."

"None," I said. I had expected an explosion of questions, but the silence was broken only by the ticking of the clock on the mantelpiece. Nina was looking away from me, at something hidden by the shadows in the corner.

"None?" echoed Willi.

"There was . . . one," I said at last. "But it was by accident. I came across them robbing an old man behind . . . but it was completely by accident."

Willi was agitated. He stood up, walked to the window, turned an old straight-back chair around and straddled it, arms folded. "What does this mean?"

"You're quitting the Game?" Nina asked as she turned to look at me. I let the question serve as the answer.

"Why?" snapped Willi. In his excitement it came out with a hard *v*.

If I had been raised in an era when young ladies were allowed to shrug, I would have done so. As it was, I contented myself with running my fingers along an imaginary seam on my skirt. Willi had asked the question, but I stared straight into Nina's eyes when I finally answered. "I'm tired. It's been too long, I guess I'm getting old."

"You'll get a lot *older* if you do not Hunt," said Willi. His body, his voice, the red mask of his face, everything signaled great anger just kept in check. "My God, Melanie, you *already* look older! You look terrible. This is *why* we hunt, woman. Look at yourself in the mirror! Do you want to die an old woman just because you're tired of using *them*? Willi stood and turned his back.

"Nonsense!" Nina's voice was strong, confident, in command once more. "Melanie's *tired*, Willi. Be nice. We all have times like that. I remember how *you* were after the war. Like a whipped puppy. You wouldn't even go outside your miserable little flat in Baden. Even after we helped you get to New Jersey you just sulked around feeling sorry for yourself. Melanie *made up* the Game to help you feel better. So quiet! *Never* tell a lady who feels tired and depressed that she looks terrible. Honestly, Willi, you're such a *Schwachsinniger* sometimes. And a crashing boor to boot."

I had anticipated many reactions to my announcement, but this was the one I feared most. It meant that Nina had also tired of the Game. It meant that she was ready to move to another level of play.

It had to mean that.

"Thank you, Nina darling," I said. "I knew you would understand."

She reached across and touched my knee reassuringly. Even through my wool skirt, I could feel the cold of her fingers.

My guests would not stay the night. I implored. I remonstrated. I pointed out that their rooms were ready, that Mr. Thorne had already turned down the quilts.

"Next time," said Willi. "Next time, Melanie, my little love. We'll make a weekend of it as we used to. A week!" Willi was in a much better mood since he had been paid his thousand-dollar prize by each of us. He had sulked, but I had insisted. It soothed his ego when Mr. Thorne brought in a check already made out to WILLIAM D. BORDEN.

Again I asked him to stay, but he protested that he had a midnight flight to Chicago. He had to see a prizewinning author about a screenplay. Then he was hugging me good-bye, his companions were in the hall behind me, and I had a brief moment of terror.

But they left. The blond young man showed his white smile, and the Negro bobbed his head in what I took as a farewell. Then we were alone.

Nina and I were alone.

Not quite alone. Miss Kramer was standing next to Nina at the end of the hall. Mr. Thorne was out of sight behind the swinging door to the kitchen. I left him there.

Miss Kramer took three steps forward. I felt my breath stop for an instant. Mr. Thorne put his hand on the swinging door. Then the husky little brunette opened the door to the hall closet, removed Nina's coat, and stepped back to help her into it.

"Are you sure you won't stay?"

"No, thank you, darling. I've promised Barrett that we would drive to Hilton Head tonight."

"But it's late—"

"We have reservations. Thank you anyway, Melanie. I *will* be in touch."

"Yes."

"I mean it, dear. We must talk. I understand *exactly* how you feel, but you have to remember that the Game is still important to Willi. We'll have to find a way to end it without hurting his feelings. Perhaps we could visit him next spring in Karinhall or whatever he calls that gloomy old Bavarian place of his. A trip to the Continent would do wonders for you, dear."

"Yes."

"I *will* be in touch. After this deal with the new store is settled. We need to spend some time together, Melanie . . . just the two of us . . . like old times." Her lips kissed the air next to my cheek. She held my forearms tightly. "Good-bye, darling."

"Good-bye, Nina."

I carried the brandy glass to the kitchen. Mr. Thorne took it in silence.

"Make sure the house is secure," I said. He nodded and went to check the locks and alarm system. It was only nine forty-five, but I was very tired. *Age*, I thought. I went up the wide staircase, perhaps the finest feature of the house, and dressed for bed. It had begun to storm, and the sound of the cold raindrops on the window carried a sad rhythm to it.

Mr. Thorne looked in as I was brushing my hair and wishing it were longer. I turned to him. He reached into the pocket of his dark vest. When his hand emerged a slim blade flicked out. I nodded. He palmed the blade shut and closed the door behind him. I listened to his footsteps recede down the stairs to the chair in the front hall, where he would spend the night.

I believe I dreamed of vampires that night. Or perhaps I was thinking about them just prior to falling asleep, and a fragment had stayed with me until morning. Of all mankind's self-inflicted terrors, of all its pathetic little monsters, only the myth of the vampire had any vestige of dignity. Like the humans it feeds on, the vampire must respond to its own dark compulsions. But unlike its pretty human prey, the vampire carries out its sordid means to the only possible ends that could justify such actions—the goal of literal immortality. There is a nobility there. And a sadness.

Before sleeping I thought of that summer long ago in Vienna. I saw Willi young again — blond, flushed with youth, and filled with pride at escorting two such independent American ladies.

I remembered Willi's high, stiff collars and the short dresses that Nina helped to bring into style that summer. I remembered the friendly sounds of crowded *Biergartens* and the shadowy dance of leaves in front of gas lamps.

I remembered the footsteps on wet cobblestones, the shouts, the distant whistles, and the silences.

Willi was right; I had aged. The past year had taken a greater toll than the preceding decade. But I had not Fed. Despite the hunger, despite the aging reflection in the mirror. *I had not Fed.*

I fell asleep trying to think of that writer's last name. I fell asleep hungry.

Morning. Bright sunlight through bare branches. It was one of those crystalline, warming winter days that make living in the South so much less depressing than merely surviving a Yankee winter. I had Mr. Thorne open the window a crack when he brought in my breakfast tray. As I sipped my coffee I could hear children playing in the courtyard. Once Mr. Thorne would have brought the morning paper with the tray, but I had long since learned that to read about the follies and scandals of the world was to desecrate the morning. I was growing less and less interested in the affairs of men. I had done without a newspaper, telephone, or television for twelve years and had suffered no ill effects unless one were to count a growing self-contentment as an ill thing. I smiled as I remembered Willi's disappointment at not being able to play his video cassettes. He was such a child.

"It is Saturday, is it not, Mr. Thorne?" At his nod I gestured for the tray to be taken away. "We will go out today," I said. "A walk. Perhaps a trip to the fort. Then dinner at Henry's and home. I have arrangements to make."

Mr. Thorne hesitated and half-stumbled as he was leaving the room. I paused in the act of belting my robe. It was not like Mr. Thorne to commit an ungraceful movement. I realized that he too was getting old. He straightened the tray and dishes, nodded his head, and left for the kitchen.

I would not let thoughts of aging disturb me on such a beautiful morning. I felt charged with a new energy and resolve. The reunion the night before had not gone well but neither had it gone as badly as it might have. I had been honest with Nina and Willi about my intention of quitting the Game. In the weeks and months to come, they—or at least Nina—would begin to brood over the ramifications of that, but by the time they chose to react, separately or together, I would be long gone. Already I had new (and old) identities waiting for me in Florida, Michigan, London, southern France, and even in New Delhi. Michigan was out for the time being. I had grown unused to the harsh climate. New Delhi was no longer the hospitable place for foreigners it had been when I resided there briefly before the war.

Nina had been right about one thing—a return to Europe would be good for me. Already I longed for the rich light and cordial *savoir vivre* of the villagers near my old summer house outside of Toulon.

The air outside was bracing. I wore a simple print dress and my spring coat. The trace of arthritis in my right leg had bothered me coming down the stairs, but I used my father's old walking stick as a cane. A young Negro servant had cut it for father the summer we moved from Greenville to Charleston. I smiled as we emerged into the warm air of the courtyard.

Mrs. Hodges came out of her doorway into the light. It was her grandchildren and their friends who were playing around the dry fountain. For two centuries the courtyard had been shared by the three brick buildings. Only my home had not been parceled into expensive town houses or fancy apartments.

"Good morning, Miz Fuller."

"Good morning, Mrs. Hodges. A beautiful day, isn't it?"

"It is that. Are you off shopping?"

"Just for a walk, Mrs. Hodges. I'm surprised that Mr. Hodges isn't out today. He always seems to be working in the yard on Saturdays."

Mrs. Hodges frowned as one of the little girls ran between us. Her friend came squealing after her, sweater flying. "Oh, George is at the marina already."

"In the daytime?" I had often been amused by Mr. Hodges's departure for work in the evening: his security-guard uniform neatly pressed, gray hair jutting out from under his cap, black lunch pail gripped firmly under his arm.

Mr. Hodges was as leathery and bow-legged as an aged cowboy. He was one of those men who were always on the verge of retiring but who probably realized that to be suddenly inactive would be a form of death sentence.

"Oh, yes. One of those colored men on the day shift down at the storage building quit, and they asked George to fill in. I told him that he was too old to work four nights a week and then go back on the weekend, but you know George. He'll never retire.

"Well, give him my best," I said.

The girls running around the fountain made me nervous.

Mrs. Hodges followed me to the wrought-iron gate. "Will you be going away for the holidays, Miz Fuller?"

"Probably, Mrs. Hodges. Most probably." Then Mr.

Thorne and I were out on the sidewalk and strolling toward the Battery. A few cars drove slowly down the narrow streets, some tourists stared at the houses of our Old Section, but the day was serene and quiet.

I saw the masts of the yachts and sailboats before we came in sight of the water as we emerged onto Broad Street.

"Please acquire tickets for us, Mr. Thorne," I said. "I believe I would like to see the fort."

As is typical of most people who live in close proximity to a popular tourist attraction, I had not taken notice of it for many years. It was an act of sentimentality to visit the fort now. An act brought on by my increasing acceptance of the fact that I would have to leave these parts forever. It is one thing to plan a move; it is something altogether different to be faced with the imperative reality of it.

There were few tourists. The ferry moved away from the marina and into the placid waters of the harbor. The combinaion of warm sunlight and the steady throb of the diesel caused me to doze briefly. I awoke as we were putting in at the dark hulk of the island fort.

For a while I moved with the tour group, enjoying the catacomb silences of the lower levels and the mindless sing-song of the young woman from the Park Service. But as we came back to the museum, with its dusty dioramas and tawdry little trays of slides, I climbed the stairs back to the outer walls. I motioned for Mr. Thorne to stay at the top of the stairs and moved out onto the ramparts.

Only one other couple—a young pair with a cheap camera and a baby in an uncomfortable-looking papoose carrier—were in sight along the wall.

It was a pleasant moment. A midday storm was approaching from the west and it set a dark backdrop to the still-sunlit church spires, brick towers, and bare branches of the city.

Even from two miles away I could see the movement of people strolling along the Battery walkway. The wind was blowing in ahead of the dark clouds and tossing whitecaps against the rocking ferry and wooden dock. The air smelled of river and winter and rain by nightfall.

It was not hard to imagine that day long ago. The shells had dropped onto the fort until the upper layers were more than protective piles of rubble. People had cheered from the rooftops behind the Battery. The bright colors of dresses and silk parasols must have been maddening to the Yankee gunners. Finally one had fired a shot above the crowded rooftops. The ensuing confusion must have been amusing from this vantage point.

A movement down below caught my attention. Something dark was sliding through the gray water—something dark and shark silent. I was jolted out of thoughts of the past as I recognized it as a Polaris submarine, old but obviously still operational, slipping through the dark water without a sound. Waves curled and rippled over the porpoise-smooth hull, sliding to either side in a white wake. There were several men on the tower. They were muffled in heavy coats, their hats pulled low. An improbably large pair of binoculars hung from the neck of one man, whom I assumed to be the captain. He pointed at something beyond Sullivan's island. I stared. The periphery of my vision began to fade as I made contact. Sounds and sensations came to me as from a distance.

Tension. The pleasure of salt spray, breeze from the north, northwest. Anxiety of the sealed orders below. Awareness of the sandy shallows just coming into sight on the port side.

I was startled as someone came up behind me. The dots flickering at the edge of my vision fled as I turned.

Mr. Thorne was there. At my elbow. Unbidden. I had opened my mouth to command him back to the top of the stairs when I saw the cause of his approach. The youth who had been taking pictures of his pale wife was now walking toward me. Mr. Thorne moved to intercept him.

"Hey, excuse me, ma'am. Would you or your husband mind taking our picture?"

I nodded and Mr. Thorne took the proffered camera. It looked minuscule in his long-fingered hands. Two snaps and the couple were satisfied that their presence there was documented for posterity. The young man grinned idiotically and bobbed his head. Their baby began to cry as the cold wind blew in.

I looked back to the submarine, but already it had passed on, its gray tower a thin stripe connecting the sea and sky.

We were almost back to town, the ferry was swinging in toward the slip, when a stranger told me of Willi's death.

"It's awful, isn't it?" The garrulous old woman had followed me out onto the exposed section of deck. Even though the wind had grown chilly and I had moved twice to escape her mindless chatter, the woman had obviously chosen me as her conversational target for the final stages of the tour. Neither my reticence nor Mr. Thorne's glowering presence had discouraged her. "It must have been terrible," she continued. "In the dark and all."

"What was that?" A dark premonition prompted my question.

"Why, the airplane crash. Haven't you heard about it? It must have been awful, falling into the swamp and all. I told my daughter this morning—"

"What airplane crash? When?" The old woman cringed a bit at the sharpness of my tone, but the vacuous smile stayed on her face.

"Why, last night. This morning. I told my daughter—"

"*Where?* What aircraft are you talking about?" Mr. Thorne came closer as he heard the tone of my voice.

"The one last night," she quavered. "The one from Charleston. The paper in the lounge told all about it. Isn't it terrible? Eighty-five people. I told my daughter—"

I left her standing there by the railing. There was a crumpled newspaper near the snack bar, and under the four-word headline were the sparse details of Willi's death. Flight 417, bound for Chicago, had left Charleston International Airport at twelve-eight A.M. Twenty minutes later the aircraft had exploded in midair not far from the city of Columbia. Fragments of fuselage and parts of bodies had fallen into Congaree Swamp, where fishermen had found them. There had been no survivors. The FAA and FBI were investigating.

There was a loud rushing in my ears, and I had to sit down or faint. My hands were clammy against the green-vinyl upholstery. People moved past me on their way to the exits.

Willi was dead. Murdered. Nina had killed him. For a few dizzy seconds I considered the possibility of a conspiracy—an elaborate ploy by Nina and Willi to confuse me into thinking that only one threat remained. But no. There would be no reason. If Nina had included Willi in her plans, there would be no need for such absurd machinations.

Willi was dead. His remains were spread over a smelly, obscure marshland. I could imagine his last moments. He would have been leaning back in first-class comfort, a drink in his hand, perhaps whispering to one of his loutish companions.

Then the explosion. Screams. Sudden darkness. A brutal tilting and the final fall to oblivion. I shuddered and gripped the metal arm of the chair.

How had Nina done it? Almost certainly not one of Willi's entourage. It was not beyond Nina's powers to Use Willi's own cat's-paws, especially in light of his failing Ability, but there would have been no reason to do so. She could have Used anyone on that flight. It *would* have been difficult. The elaborate step of preparing the bomb, the supreme effort of blocking all memory of it, and the almost unbelievable feat of Using someone even as we sat together drinking coffee and brandy.

But Nina could have done it. Yes, she *could* have. And the timing. The timing could mean only one thing.

The last of the tourists had filed out of the cabin. I felt the slight bump that meant we had tied up to the dock. Mr. Thorne stood by the door.

Nina's timing meant that she was attempting to deal with both of us at once. She obviously had planned it long before the reunion and my timorous announcement of withdrawal. How amused Nina must have been. No wonder she had reacted so generously! Yet, she had made one great mistake. By dealing with Willi first, Nina had banked everything on my not hearing the news before she could turn on me. She knew that I had no access to daily news and only rarely left the house anymore. Still, it was unlike Nina to leave anything to chance. Was it possible that she thought I had lost the Ability completely and that Willi was the greater threat?

I shook my head as we emerged from the cabin into the gray afternoon light. The wind sliced at me through my thin coat. The view of the gangplank was blurry, and I realized that tears had filled my eyes. For Willi? He had been a pompous, weak old fool. For Nina's betrayal? Perhaps it was only the cold wind.

The streets of the Old Section were almost empty of pe

destrians. Bare branches clicked together in front of the windows of fine homes. Mr. Thorne stayed by my side. The cold air sent needles of arthritic pain up my right leg to my hip. I leaned more heavily upon father's walking stick.

What would her next move be? I stopped. A fragment of newspaper, caught by the wind, wrapped itself around my ankle and then blew on.

How would she come at me? Not from a distance. She was somewhere in town. I knew that. While it is possible to Use someone from a great distance, it would involve great rapport, an almost intimate knowledge of that person. And if contact were lost, it would be difficult if not impossible to reestablish at a distance. None of us had known why this was so. It did not matter now. But the thought of Nina still here, nearby, made my heart begin to race.

Not from a distance. I would see my assailant. If I knew Nina at all, I knew that. Certainly Willi's death had been the least personal Feeding imaginable, but that had been a mere technical operation. Nina obviously had decided to settle old scores with *me*, and Willi had become an obstacle to her, a minor but measurable threat that had to be eliminated before she could proceed. I could easily imagine that in Nina's own mind her choice of death for Willi would be interpreted as an act of compassion, almost a sign of affection. Not so with me. I felt that Nina would want me to know, however, briefly, that she was behind the attack. In a sense her own vanity would be my warning. Or so I hoped.

I was tempted to leave immediately. I could have Mr. Thorne get the Audi out of storage, and we could be beyond Nina's influence in an hour—away to a new life within a few more hours. There were important items in the house, of course, but the funds that I had stored elsewhere would replace most of them. It would be almost welcome to leave everything behind with the discarded identity that had accumulated them.

No. I could not leave. Not yet.

From across the street the house looked dark and malevolent. Had *I* closed those blinds on the second floor? There was a shadowy movement in the courtyard, and I saw Mrs. Hodge's granddaughter and a friend scamper from one doorway to another. I stood irresolutely on the curb and tapped father's stick against the black-barked tree. It was foolish to dither so — I knew it was — but it had been a long time since I had been forced to make a decision under stress.

"Mr. Thorne, please check the house. Look in each room. Return quickly."

A cold wind came up as I watched Mr. Thorne's black coat blend into the gloom of the courtyard. I felt terribly exposed standing there alone. I found myself glancing up and down the street, looking for Miss Kramer's dark hair, but the only sign of movement was a young woman pushing a perambulator far down the street.

The blinds on the second floor shot up, and Mr. Thorne's face stared out whitely for a minute. Then he turned away, and I remained staring at the dark rectangle of window. A shout from the courtyard startled me, but it was only the little girl — what was her name? — calling to her friend. Kathleen, that was it. The two sat on the edge of the fountain and opened a box of animal crackers. I stared intently at them and then relaxed. I even managed to smile a little at the extent of my paranoia. For a second I considered Using Mr. Thorne directly, but the thought of being helpless on the street dissuaded me. When one is in complete contact, the senses still function but are a distant thing at best.

Hurry. The thought was sent almost without volition. Two bearded men were walking down the sidewalk on my side of the street. I crossed to stand in front of my own gate. The men were laughing and gesturing at each other. One looked over at me. *Hurry.*

Mr. Thorne came out of the house, locked the door behind him, and crossed the courtyard toward me. One of the girls said something to him and held out the box of crackers, but he ignored her. Across the street the two men continued walking. Mr. Thorne handed me the large front-door key. I dropped it in my coat pocket and looked sharply at him. He nodded. His placid smile unconsciously mocked my consternation.

"You're sure?" I asked. Again the nod. "You checked all of the rooms?" Nod. "The alarms?" Nod. "You looked in the basement?" Nod. "No sign of disturbance?" Mr. Thorne shook his head.

My hand went to the metal of the gate, but I hesitated. Anxiety filled my throat like bile. I was a silly old woman, tired and aching from the chill, but I could not bring myself to open that gate.

"Come." I crossed the street and walked briskly away from the house. "We will have dinner at Henry's and return later." Only I was not walking toward the old restaurant; I was heading away from the house in what I knew was a blind, directionless panic. It was not until we reached the waterfront and were walking along the Battery wall that I began to calm down.

No one else was in sight. A few cars moved along the street, but to approach us someone would have to cross a wide, empty space. The gray clouds were quite low and blended with the choppy, white-crested waves in the bay.

The open air and fading evening light served to revive me, and I began to think more clearly. Whatever Nina's plans had been, they certainly had been thrown into disarray by my day-long absence. I doubted that Nina would stay if there were the slightest risk to herself. No, she would

be returning to New York by plane even as I stood shivering
on the Battery walk. In the morning I would receive a telegram. I could see it. MELANIE. ISN'T IT TERRIBLE ABOUT
WILL? TERRIBLY SAD. CAN YOU TRAVEL WITH ME TO THE FU-
NERAL? LOVE, NINA.

I began to realize that my reluctance to leave immediately
had come from a desire to return to the warmth and comfort of my home. I simply had been afraid to shuck off this
old cocoon. I could do so now. I would wait in a safe place
while Mr. Thorne returned to the house to pick up the one
thing I could not leave behind. Then he would get the car
out of storage, and by the time Nina's telegram arrived I
would be far away. It would be *Nina* who would be starting
at shadows in the months and years to come. I smiled and
began to frame the necessary commands.

"Melanie."

My head snapped around. Mr. Thorne had not spoken in
twenty-eight years. He spoke now.

"Melanie." His face was distorted in a rictus that showed
his back teeth. The knife was in his right hand. The blade
flicked out as I stared. I looked into his empty, gray eyes
and I knew.

"Melanie."

The long blade came around in a powerful arc. I could
do nothing to stop it. It cut through the fabric of my coat
sleeve and continued into my side. But in the act of turning
my purse had swung with me. The knife tore through the
leather, ripped through the jumbled contents, pierced my
coat, and drew blood above my lowest left rib. The purse
had saved my life.

I raised father's heavy walking stick and struck Mr.
Thorne squarely in his left eye. He reeled but did not make
a sound. Again he swept the air with the knife, but I had
taken two steps back and his vision was clouded. I took a

two-handed grip on the cane and swung sideways again, bringing the stick around in an awkward chop. Incredibly, it again found the eye socket. I took three more steps back.

Blood streamed down the left side of Mr. Thorne's face, and the damaged eye protruded onto his cheek. The rictal grin remained. His head came up, he raised his left hand slowly, plucked out the eye with a soft snapping of a gray cord, and threw it into the water of the bay. He came toward me. I turned and ran.

I *tried* to run. The ache in my right leg slowed me to a walk after twenty paces. Fifteen more hurried steps and my lungs were out of air, my heart threatening to burst. I could feel a wetness seeping down my left side and there was a tingling—like an ice cube held against the skin—where the knife blade had touched me. One glance back showed me that Mr. Thorne was striding toward me faster than I was moving. Normally he could have overtaken me in four strides. But it is hard to make someone run when you are Using him. Especially when that person's body is reacting to shock and trauma. I glanced back again, almost slipping on the slick pavement. Mr. Thorne was grinning widely. Blood poured from the empty socket and stained his teeth. No one else was in sight.

Down the stairs, clutching at the rail so as not to fall. Down the twisting walk and up the asphalt path to the street. Pole lamps flickered and went on as I passed. Behind me Mr. Thorne took the steps in two jumps. As I hurried up the path, I thanked God that I had worn low-heel shoes for the boat ride. What would an observer think seeing this bizarre, slow-motion chase between two old people? There were no observers.

I turned onto a side street. Closed shops, empty warehouses. Going left would take me to Broad Street, but to the right, half a block away, a lone figure had emerged from a dark storefront. I moved that way, no longer able to run, close to fainting. The arthritic cramps in my leg hurt more than I could ever have imagined and threatened to collapse me on the sidewalk. Mr. Thorne was twenty paces behind me and quickly closing the distance.

The man I was approaching was a tall, thin Negro wearing a brown nylon jacket. He was carrying a box of what looked like framed sepia photographs.

He glanced at me as I approached and then looked over my shoulder at the apparition ten steps behind.

"Hey!" The man had time to shout the single syllable and then I reached out with my mind and *shoved*. He twitched like a poorly handled marionette. His jaw dropped, and his eyes glazed over, and he lurched past me just as Mr. Thorne reached for the back of my coat.

The box flew into the air, and glass shattered on the brick sidewalk. Long, brown fingers reached for a white throat. Mr. Thorne backhanded him away, but the Negro clung tenaciously, and the two swung around like awkward dance partners. I reached the opening to an alley and leaned my face against the cold brick to revive myself. The effort of concentration while Using this stranger did not afford me the luxury of resting even for a second.

I watched the clumsy stumblings of the two tall men for a while and resisted an absurd impulse to laugh.

Mr. Thorne plunged the knife into the other's stomach, withdrew it, plunged it in again. The Negro's fingernails were clawing at Mr. Thorne's good eye now. Strong teeth were snapping in search of the blade for a third time, but the heart was still beating, and he was still usable. The man jumped, scissoring his legs around Mr. Thorne's middle while his jaws closed on the muscular throat. Fingernails raked bloody streaks across white skin. The two went down in a tumble.

Kill him. Fingers groped for an eye, but Mr. Thorne reached up with his left hand and snapped the thin wrist. Limp fingers continued to flail. With a tremendous exertion, Mr. Thorne lodged his forearm against the other's chest and lifted him bodily as a reclining father tosses a child above him. Teeth tore away a piece of flesh, but there was no vital damage. Mr. Thorne brought the knife between them, up, left, then right. He severed half the Negro's throat with the second swing, and blood fountained over both of them. The smaller man's legs spasmed twice, Mr. Thorne threw him to one side, and I turned and walked quickly down the alley.

Out into the light again, the fading evening light, and I realized that I had run myself into a dead end. Backs of warehouses and the windowless, metal side of the Battery Marina pushed right up against the waters of the bay. A street wound away to the left, but it was dark, deserted, and far too long to try.

I looked back in time to see the black silhouette enter the alley behind me.

I tried to make contact, but there was nothing there. Nothing. Mr. Thorne might as well have a hole in the air. I would worry later how Nina had done this thing.

The side door to the marina was locked. The main door was almost a hundred yards away and would also be locked. Mr. Thorne emerged from the alley and swung his head left and right in search of me. In the dim light his heavily streaked face looked almost black. He began lurching toward me.

I raised father's walking stick, broke the lower pane of the window, and reached in through the jagged shards. If there was a bottom or top bolt I was dead. There was a simple doorknob lock and crossbolt. My fingers slipped on the cold metal, but the bolt slid back as Mr. Thorne stepped up on the walk behind me. Then I was inside and throwing the bolt.

It was very dark. Cold seeped up from the concrete floor and there was a sound of many small boats rising and falling at their moorings. Fifty yards away light spilled out of the office windows. I had hoped there would be an alarm system, but the building was too old and the marina too cheap to have one. I walked toward the light as Mr. Thorne's forearm shattered the remaining glass in the door behind me. The arm withdrew. A great kick broke off the top hinge and splintered wood around the bolt. I glanced at the office, but only the sound of a radio talk show came out of the impossibly distant door. Another kick.

I turned to my right and stepped to the bow of a bobbing inboard cruiser. Five steps and I was in the small, covered space that passed for a forward cabin. I closed the flimsy access panel behind me and peered out through the Plexiglas.

Mr. Thorne's third kick sent the door flying inward, dangling from long strips of splintered wood. His dark form filled the doorway. Light from a distant streetlight glinted off the blade in his right hand.

Please. Please hear the noise. But there was no movement from the office, only the metallic voices from the radio. Mr. Thorne took four paces, paused, and stepped down onto the first boat in line. It was an open outboard, and he was back up on the concrete in six seconds. The second boat had a small cabin. There was a ripping sound as Mr. Thorne kicked open the tiny hatch door, and then he was back up on the walkway. My boat was the eighth in line. I wondered why he couldn't just hear the wild hammering of my heart.

I shifted position and looked through the starboard port. The murky Plexiglass threw the light into streaks and patterns. I caught a brief glimpse of white hair through the window, and the radio was switched to another station. Loud music echoed in the long room. I slid back to the other porthole. Mr. Thorne was stepping off the fourth boat.

I closed my eyes, forced my ragged breathing to slow, and tried to remember countless evenings watching a bow-legged old figure shuffle down the street. Mr. Thorne finished his inspection of the fifth boat, a longer cabin cruiser with several dark recesses, and pulled himself back onto the walkway.

Forget the coffee in the thermos. Forget the crossword puzzle. Go look!

The sixth boat was a small outboard. Mr. Thorne glanced at it but did not step onto it. The seventh was a low sail-boat, mast folded down, canvas stretched across the cockpit. Mr. Thorne's knife slashed through the thick material. Blood-streaked hands pulled back the canvas like a shroud being torn away. He jumped back to the walkway.

Forget the coffee. Go look! Now!

Mr. Thorne stepped onto the bow of my boat. I felt it rock to his weight. There was nowhere to hide, only a tiny storage locker under the seat, much too small to squeeze into. I untied the canvas strips that held the seat cushion to the bench. The sound of my ragged breathing seemed to echo in the little space. I curled into a fetal position behind the cushion as Mr. Thorne's leg moved past the starboard port. *Now.* Suddenly his face filled the Plexiglass strip not a foot from my head. His impossibly wide grimace grew even wider. *Now.* He stepped into the cockpit.

Now. Now. Now.

Mr. Thorne crouched at the cabin door. I tried to brace the tiny louvered door with my legs, but my right leg would not obey. Mr. Thorne's fist slammed through the thin wooden strips and grabbed my ankle.

"Hey there!"

It was Mr. Hodges's shaky voice. His flashlight bobbed in our direction.

Mr. Thorne shoved against the door. My left leg folded painfully. Mr. Thorne's left hand firmly held my ankle through the shattered slats while the hand with the knife blade came through the opening hatch.

"Hey—" My mind shoved. Very hard. The old man stopped. He dropped the flashlight and unstrapped the buckle over the grip of his revolver.

Mr. Thorne slashed the knife back and forth. The cushion was almost knocked out of my hands as shreds of foam filled the cabin. The blade caught the tip of my little finger as the knife swung back again.

Do it. Now. Do it. Mr. Hodges gripped the revolver in both hands and fired. The shot went wide in the dark as the sound echoed off concrete and water. *Closer, you fool. Move!* Mr. Thorne shoved again, and his body squeezed into the open hatch. He released my ankle to free his left arm, but almost instantly his hand was back in the cabin, grasping for me. I reached up and turned on the overhead light. Darkness stared at me from his empty eye socket. Light through the broken shutters spilled yellow strips across his ruined face. I slid to the left, but Mr. Thorne's hand, which had my coat, was pulling me off the bench. He was on his knees, freeing his right hand for the knife thrust.

Now! Mr. Hodges's second shot caught Mr. Thorne in the right hip. He grunted as the impact shoved him backward into a sitting position. My coat ripped, and buttons rattled on the deck.

The knife slashed the bulkhead near my ear before it pulled away.

Mr. Hodges stepped shakily onto the bow, almost fell,

and inched his way around the starboard side. I pushed the hatch against Mr. Thorne's arm, but he continued to grip my coat and drag me toward him. I fell to my knees. The blade swung back, ripped through foam, and slashed at my coat. What was left of the cushion flew out of my hands. I had Mr. Hodges stop four feet away and brace the gun on the roof of the cabin.

Mr. Thorne pulled the blade back and poised it like a matador's sword. I could sense the silent scream of triumph that poured out over the stained teeth like a noxious vapor. The light of Nina's madness burned behind the single, staring eye.

Mr. Hodges fired. The bullet severed Mr. Thorne's spine and continued on into the port scupper. Mr. Thorne arched backward, splayed out his arms, and flopped onto the deck like a great fish that had just been landed. The knife fell to the floor of the cabin, while stiff, white fingers continued to slap nervelessly against the deck. I had Mr. Hodges step forward, brace the muzzle against Mr. Thorne's temple just above the remaining eye, and fire again. The sound was muted and hollow.

There was a first-aid kit in the office bathroom. I had the old man stand by the door while I bandaged my little finger and took three aspirin.

My coat was ruined, and blood had stained my print dress. I had never cared very much for the dress—I thought it made me look dowdy—but the coat had been a favorite of mine. My hair was a mess. Small, moist bits of gray matter flecked it. I splashed water on my face and brushed my hair as best I could. Incredibly, my tattered purse had stayed with me, although many of the contents had spilled out. I transferred keys, billfold, reading glasses, and Kleenex to my large coat pocket and dropped the purse behind the toilet. I no longer had father's walking stick, but I could not remember where I had dropped it.

Gingerly I removed the heavy revolver from Mr. Hodges's grip. The old man's arm remained extended, fingers curled around air. After fumbling for a few seconds I managed to click open the cylinder. Two cartridges remained unfired. The old fool had been walking around with all six chambers loaded! *Always leave an empty chamber under the hammer.* That is what Charles had taught me that gay and distant summer so long ago, when such weapons were merely excuses for trips to the island for target practice punctuated by the shrill shrieks of our nervous laughter as Nina and I allowed ourselves to be held, arms supported, bodies shrinking back into the firm support of our so-serious tutors' arms. *One must always count the cartridges,* lectured Charles, as I half-swooned against him, smelling the sweet, masculine, shaving soap and tobacco smell rising from him on that warm, bright day.

Mr. Hodges stirred slightly as my attention wandered. His mouth gaped, and his dentures hung loosely. I glanced at the worn leather belt, but there were no extra bullets there, and I had no idea where he kept any. I probed, but there was little left in the old man's jumble of thoughts except for a swirling tape-loop replay of the muzzle being laid against Mr. Thorne's temple, the explosion, the—

"Come," I said. I adjusted the glasses on Mr. Hodges's vacant face, returned the revolver to the holster, and let him lead me out of the building.

It was very dark out. We had gone six blocks before the old man's violent shivering reminded me that I had forgotten to have him put on his coat. I tightened my mental vise, and he stopped shaking.

The house looked just as it had . . . my God . . . only forty-five minutes earlier. There were no lights. I let us into the courtyard and searched my overstuffed coat pocket for the key. My coat hung loose and the cold night air nipped at me. From behind lighted windows across the courtyard came the laughter of little girls, and I hurried so that Kathleen would not see her grandfather entering my house.

Mr. Hodges went in first, with the revolver extended. I had him switch on the light before I entered.

The parlor was empty, undisturbed. The light from the chandelier in the dining room reflected off polished surfaces. I sat down for a minute on the Williamsburg reproduction chair in the hall to let my heart rate return to normal. I did not have Mr. Hodges lower the hammer on the still-raised pistol. His arm began to shake from the strain of holding it. Finally I rose and we moved down the hall toward the conservatory.

Miss Kramer exploded out of the swinging door from the kitchen with the heavy iron poker already coming down in an arc. The gun fired harmlessly into the polished floor as the old man's arm snapped from the impact. The gun fell from limp fingers as Miss Kramer raised the poker for a second blow.

I turned and ran back down the hallway. Behind me I heard the crushed-melon sound of the poker contacting Mr. Hodges's skull. Rather than run into the courtyard I went up the stairway. A mistake. Miss Kramer bounded up the stairs and reached the bedroom door only a few seconds after I. I caught one glimpse of her widened, maddened eyes and of the upraised pocker before I slammed and locked the heavy door. The latch clicked just as the brunette on the other side began to throw herself against the wood. The thick oak did not budge. Then I heard the concussion of metal against the door and frame. Again.

Cursing my stupidity, I turned to the familiar room, but there was nothing there to help me. There was not so much as a closet to hide in, only the antique wardrobe. I moved quickly to the window and threw up the sash. My screams would attract attention but not before that monstrosity had gained access. She was prying at the edges of the door now. I looked out, saw the shadows in the window across the way, and did what I had to do.

Two minutes later I was barely conscious of the wood giving way around the latch. I heard the distant grating of the poker as it pried at the recalcitrant metal plate. The door swung inward.

Miss Kramer was covered with sweat. Her mouth hung slack, and drool slid from her chin. Her eyes were not human. Neither she nor I heard the soft tread of sneakers on the stairs behind her.

Keep moving. Lift it. Pull it back—all the way back. Use both hands. Aim it.

Something warned Miss Kramer. Warned Nina, I should say; there was no more Miss Kramer. The brunette turned to see little Kathleen standing on the top stair, her grandfather's heavy weapon aimed and cocked. The other girl was in the courtyard shouting for her friend.

This time Nina knew she had to deal with the threat. Miss Kramer hefted the poker and turned into the hall just as the pistol fired. The recoil tumbled Kathleen backward down the stairs as a red corsage blossomed above Miss Kramer's left breast. She spun but grasped the railing with her left hand and lurched down the stairs after the child. I released the ten-year-old just as the poker fell, rose, fell again. I moved to the head of the stairway. I had to see.

Miss Kramer looked up from her grim work. Only the whites of her eyes were visible in her spattered face. Her masculine shirt was soaked with her own blood, but still she moved, functioned. She picked up the gun in her left hand. Her mouth opened wider, and a sound emerged like steam eaking from an old radiator.

"Melanie . . ." I closed my eyes as the thing started up he stairs for me.

Kathleen's friend came in through the open door, her small legs pumping. She took the stairs in six jumps and wrapped her thin, white arms around Miss Kramer's neck in a tight embrace.

The two went over backward, across Kathleen, all the way down the wide stairs to the polished wood below.

The girl appeared to be little more than bruised. I went down and move her to one side. A blue stain was spreading along one cheekbone, and there were cuts on her arms and forehead. Her blue eyes blinked uncomprehendingly.

Miss Kramer's neck was broken. I picked up the pistol on the way to her and kicked the poker to one side. Her head was at an impossible angle, but she was still alive. Her body was paralyzed, urine already stained the wood, but her eyes still blinked and her teeth clicked together obscenely. I had to hurry. There were adult voices calling from the Hodgeses' town house. The door to the courtyard was wide open. I turned to the girl. "Get up." She blinked once and rose painfully to her feet.

I shut the door and lifted a tan raincoat from the coat-rack.

It took only a minute to transfer the contents of my pockets to the raincoat and to discard my ruined spring coat. Voices were calling in the courtyard now.

I kneeled down next to Miss Kramer and seized her face in my hands, exerting pressure to keep the jaws still. Her eyes had rolled upward again, but I shook her head until the irises were visible. I leaned forward until our cheeks were touching. My whisper was louder than a shout.

"I'm coming for you, Nina."

I dropped her head onto the wood and walked quickly to

the conservatory, my sewing room. I did not have time to get the key from upstairs; so I raised a Windsor side chair and smashed the glass of the cabinet. My coat pocket was barely large enough.

The girl remained standing in the hall. I handed her Mr. Hodges's pistol. Her left arm hung at a strange angle and I wondered if she had broken something after all. There was a knock at the door, and someone tried the knob.

"This way," I whispered, and led the girl into the dining room.

We stepped across Miss Kramer on the way, walked through the dark kitchen as the pounding grew louder, and then were out, into the alley, into the night.

There were three hotels in this part of the Old Section. One was a modern, expensive motor hotel some ten blocks away, comfortable but commercial. I rejected it immediately. The second was a small, homey lodging house only a block from my home. It was a pleasant but nonexclusive little place, exactly the type I would choose when visiting another town. I rejected it also. The third was two and a half blocks farther, an old Broad Street mansion done over into a small hotel, expensive antiques in every room, absurdly overpriced. I hurried there. The girl moved quickly at my side. The pistol was still in her hand, but I had her remove her sweater and carry it over the weapon. My leg ached, and I frequently leaned on the girl as we hurried down the street.

The manager of the Mansard House recognized me. His eyebrows went up a fraction of an inch as he noticed my disheveled appearance. The girl stood ten feet away in the foyer, half-hidden in the shadows.

"I'm looking for a friend of mine," I said brightly. "A Mrs. Drayton."

The manager started to speak, paused, frowned without being aware of it, and tried again. "I'm sorry. No one under that name is registered here."

"Perhaps she registered under her maiden name," I said. "Nina Hawkins. She's an older woman but very attractive. A few years younger than I. Long, gray hair. Her friend may have registered for her . . . an attractive, young, dark-haired lady named Barrett Kramer—"

"No, I'm sorry," said the manager in a strangely flat tone. "No one under that name has registered. Would you like to leave a message in case your party arrives later?"

"No," I said. "No message."

I brought the girl into the lobby, and we turned down a corridor leading to the restrooms and side stairs. "Excuse me, please," I said to a passing porter. "Perhaps you can help me."

"Yes, ma'am." He stopped, annoyed, and brushed back his long hair. It would be tricky. If I was not to lose the girl, I would have to act quickly.

"I'm looking for a friend," I said. "She's an older lady but quite attractive. Blue eyes. Long, gray hair. She travels with a young woman who has dark, curly hair."

"No, ma'am. No one like that is registered here."

I reached out and grabbed hold of his forearm tightly. I released the girl and focused on the boy. "Are you sure?"

"Mrs. Harrison," he said. His eyes looked past me. "Room 207. North front."

I smiled. *Mrs. Harrison.* Good God, what a fool Nina was. Suddenly the girl let out a small whimper and slumped against the wall. I made a quick decision. I like to think that it was compassion, but I sometimes remember that her left arm was useless.

"What's your name?" I asked the child, gently stroking her bangs. Her eyes moved left and right in confusion.

475

"Your *name!*"

"Alicia." It was only a whisper.

"All right, Alicia. I want you to go home now. Hurry but don't run."

"My *arm* hurts," she said. Her lips began to quiver. touched her forehead again and *pushed*.

"You're going home," I said. "Your arm does not hurt You won't remember anything. This is like a dream that you will forget. Go home. Hurry, but do not run." I took the pistol from her but left it wrapped in the sweater. "Bye-bye Alicia."

She blinked and crossed the lobby to the doors. I handed the gun to the bellhop. "Put it under your vest," I said.

"Who is it?" Nina's voice was light.

"Albert, ma'am. The porter. Your car's out front, and I'l take your bags down."

There was the sound of a lock clicking, and the doo opened the width of a still-secured chain. Albert blinked in the glare, smiled shyly, and brushed his hair back. I pressed against the wall.

"Very well." She undid the chain and moved back. She had already turned and was latching her suitcase when I stepped into the room.

"Hello, Nina," I said softly. Her back straightened, but even that move was graceful. I could see the imprint on the bedspread where she had been lying. She turned slowly. She was wearing a pink dress I had never seen before.

"Hello, Melanie." She smiled. Her eyes were the softest, purest blue I had ever seen. I had the porter take Mr. Hodges's gun out and aim it. His arm was steady. He pulled back the hammer and held it with his thumb. Nina folded her hands in front of her. Her eyes never left mine.

"Why?" I asked.

Nina shrugged ever so slightly. For a second I thought she was going to laugh. I could not have borne it if she had laughed — that husky, childlike laugh that had touched me so many times. Instead she closed her eyes. Her smile remained.

"Why Mrs. Harrison?" I asked.

"Why, darling, I felt I owed him *something*. I mean, poor Roger. Did I ever tell you how he died? No, of course I didn't. And you never asked." Her eyes opened. I glanced at the porter, but his aim was steady. It only remained for him to exert a little more pressure on the trigger.

"He *drowned*, darling," said Nina. "Poor Roger threw himself from that steamship — what was its name? — the one that was taking him back to England. So strange. And he had just written me a letter promising marriage. Isn't that a *terribly* sad story. Melanie? Why do you think he did a thing like that? I guess we'll never know, will we?"

"I guess we never will," I said. I silently ordered the porter to pull the trigger.

Nothing.

I looked quickly to my right. The young man's head was turning toward me. *I had not made him do that.* The stiffly extended arm began to swing in my direction. The pistol moved smoothly like the tip of a weather vane swinging in the wind.

No! I strained until the cords in my neck stood out. The turning slowed but did not stop until the muzzle was pointing at my face. Nina laughed now. The sound was very loud in the little room.

"Good-bye, Melanie *dear*," Nina said, and laughed again. She laughed and nodded at the porter. I stared into the black hole as the hammer fell. On an empty chamber. And another. And another.

"Goodbye, Nina," I said as I pulled Charles's long pistol

from the raincoat pocket. The explosion jarred my wrist and filled the room with blue smoke. A small hole, smaller than a dime but as perfectly round, appeared in the precise center of Nina's forehead. For the briefest second she remained standing as if nothing had happened. Then she fell backward, recoiled from the high bed, and dropped face forward onto the floor.

I turned to the porter and replaced his useless weapon with the ancient but well-maintained revolver. For the first time I noticed that the boy was not much younger than Charles had been. His hair was almost exactly the same color. I leaned forward and kissed him lightly on the lips.

"Albert," I whispered, "there are four cartridges left. One must always count the cartridges, mustn't one? Go to the lobby. Kill the manager. Shoot one other person, the nearest. Put the barrel in your mouth and pull the trigger. If it misfires, pull it again. Keep the gun concealed until you are in the lobby."

We emerged into general confusion in the hallway.

"Call for an ambulance!" I cried. "There's been an accident. Someone call for an ambulance!" Several people rushed to comply. I swooned and leaned against a white-haired gentleman. People milled around, some peering into the room and exclaiming. Suddenly there was the sound of three gunshots from the lobby. In the renewed confusion I slipped down the back stairs, out the fire door, into the night.

Time has passed. I am very happy here. I live in southern France now, between Cannes and Toulon, but not, I am happy to say, too near St. Tropez.

I rarely go out. Henri and Claude do my shopping in the village. I never go to the beach. Occasionally I go to the townhouse in Paris or to my pensione in Italy, south of Pes-